Proof by Seduction

Dear Reader,

I've always loved science. But as much as I love science, "love"—of the romantic variety—and "science" don't often go together.

Perhaps that's why, when I wrote a historical romance, I set myself the hardest task I could imagine. I chose as my hero a rigidly logical marquess, a scientist who retreated behind scientific proof, because he couldn't make a formula out of love.

Gareth Carhart was going to be a hard nut to crack. He needed to learn that some things—squishy, unscientific concepts like "love" and "friendship"—are not susceptible to scientific proof. But how to do this?

Then I imagined my heroine. I knew she was going to shake the foundation of his world. Jenny Keeble needed to teach Gareth how to have fun—and despite his best efforts, he wasn't going to be able to resist her.

I hope you'll have as much fun reading this book as I had writing it.

Courtney Milan

COURTNEY MILAN

Proof by Seduction

ISBN-13: 978-1-61523-857-6

PROOF BY SEDUCTION

For Tessa and Amy. You believed in me. You pushed me. You waved off every setback and squealed for joy when good things happened. And when I most needed you in a dark, dark time, you held my hand and kept me going.

Every book—especially a debut novel—
owes a debt to an enormous number of people.

This list is lengthy, but not exhaustive:
Tessa and Amy, for everything.

Franzeca Drouin saved me from innumerable
errors more times than I can count. David Berry,
Rupert Baker and Stephanie Clarke answered strange
and nitpicky questions.

Amy Atwell, Jackie Barbosa, Anna Campbell,
Lenora Bell, Darcy Burke, Diana Chung,
Amanda Collins, Lacey Kaye, Lindsey Faber,
Sara Lindsey, Terri Osborn, Elyssa Papa, Janice Rholetter,
Erica Ridley, Maggie Robinson and Sherry Thomas
all read pages at various points along the way and
encouraged me. Kristin Nelson, my extraordinary agent,
and Sara Megibow, her awesome assistant,
made all my dreams come true, even the ones
I was scared to dream.

Finally, thanks to the team at Harlequin Books,
particularly my editor, Ann Leslie Tuttle, and
Charles Griemsman, for believing in this book
and doing such a beautiful job in launching it.

Proof by Seduction

CHAPTER ONE

London, April, 1838

TWELVE YEARS SPENT PLYING HER TRADE had taught Jenny Keeble to leave no part of her carefully manufactured atmosphere to chance. The sandalwood smoke wafting from the brazier added a touch of the occult: not too cloying, yet unquestionably exotic. But it was by rote that she checked the cheap black cotton draped over her rickety table; routine alone compelled her to straighten her garishly colored wall hangings, purchased from Gypsies.

Every detail—the cobwebs she left undisturbed in the corner of the room, the gauze that draped her basement windows and filtered the sunlight into indirect haze— whispered that here magic worked and spirits conveyed sage advice.

It was precisely the effect Jenny should have desired.

So why did she wish she could abandon this costume? True, the virulently red-and-blue-striped skirt, paired with a green blouse, did nothing to flatter her looks. Layer upon heavy layer obscured her waist and puffed her out until she resembled nothing so much as a round, multihued melon. Her skin suffocated under a heavy covering of paint and kohl. But her disquiet ran deeper than the thick lacquers of cream and powder.

A sharp rat-tat-tat sounded at the door.

She'd worked twelve years for this. Twelve years of careful lies and half truths, spent cultivating clients. But there was no room for uncertainty in Jenny's profession. She took a deep breath, and pushed Jenny Keeble's doubts aside. In her place, she constructed the imperturbable edifice of Madame Esmerelda. A woman who could see anything. Who predicted everything. And who stopped at nothing.

With her lies firmly in place, Jenny opened the door.

Two men stood on her stoop. Ned, her favorite client, she'd expected. He was awkward and lanky, as only a youth just out of adolescence could be. A shock of light brown hair topped his young features. His lips curled in an open, welcoming smile. She would have greeted him easily, but today, another fellow stood behind Ned. The stranger was extraordinarily tall, even taller than Ned. He stood several feet back, his arms folded in stern disapproval.

"Madame Esmerelda," Ned said. "I'm sorry I didn't inform you I was bringing along a guest."

Jenny peered behind Ned. The man's coat was carelessly unbuttoned. Some tailor had poured hours into the exquisite fit of that garment. It was cut close enough to the body to show off the form, but loose enough to allow movement. His sandy-brown hair was tousled, his cravat tied in the simplest of knots. The details of his wardrobe bespoke an impatient arrogance, as if his appearance was little more than a bother, his attention reserved for weightier matters.

That attention shifted to Jenny now, and a shiver raced down her spine. With one predatorial sweep of his eyes, he took in Jenny's costume from head to toe. She swallowed.

"Madame Esmerelda," Ned said, "this is my cousin."

A cold glimmer of irritation escaped the other man, and Ned expelled a feeble sigh.

"Yes, Blakely. May I present to you Madame Esmerelda." The monotone introduction wasn't even a question. "Madame, this is Blakely. That would be Gareth Carhart, Marquess of Blakely. Et cetera."

A beat of apprehension pulsed through Jenny as she curtsied. Ned had spoken of his cousin before. Based on Ned's descriptions, she'd imagined the marquess to be old and perhaps a little decrepit, obsessed with facts and figures. Ned's cousin was supposed to be coldly distant, frighteningly uncivil, and so focused on his own scientific interests that he was unaware of the people around him.

But this man wasn't distant; even standing a full yard away, her skin prickled in response to his presence. He wasn't old; he was lean without being skinny, and his cheeks were shadowed by the stubble of a man in his prime. Most of all, there was nothing unfocused about him. She'd often thought Ned had the eyes of a terrier: warm, liquid and trusting. His cousin had those of a lion: tawny, ferocious and more than a little feral.

Jenny gave silent thanks she wasn't a gazelle.

She turned and swept her arm in regal welcome. "Come in. Be seated." The men trooped in, settling on chairs that creaked under their weight. Jenny remained standing.

"Ned, how can I assist you today?"

Ned beamed at her. "Well. Blakely and I have been arguing. He doesn't think you can predict the future."

Neither did Jenny. She resented sharing that belief.

"We've agreed—he's going to use science to demonstrate the accuracy of your predictions."

"Demonstrate? Scientifically?" The words whooshed out of her, as if she'd been prodded in the stomach. Jenny grasped the table in front of her for support. "Well. That would be..." *Unlikely? Unfortunate?* "That would be unobjectionable. How shall he proceed?"

Ned waved his hand at his cousin. "Well, go ahead, Blakely. Ask her something."

Lord Blakely leaned back in his chair. Up until this moment, he had not spoken a single word; his eyes had traveled about the room, though. "You want *me* to ask her something?" He spoke slowly, drawing out each syllable with precision. "I consult logic, not old charlatans."

Ned and Jenny spoke atop each other. "She's no charlatan!" protested Ned.

But Jenny's hands had flown to her hips for another reason entirely. "Thirty," she protested, "is not old!"

Ned turned to her, his eyebrow lifting. A devastating silence cloaked the room. It was a measure of her own agitation that she'd forsaken Madame Esmerelda's character already. Instead, she'd spoken as a woman.

And the marquess noticed. That tawny gaze flicked from her kerchiefed head down to the garish skirts obscuring her waist. His vision bored through every one of her layers. The appraisal was thoroughly masculine. A sudden tremulous awareness tickled Jenny's palms.

And then he looked away. A queer quirk of his lips; the smallest exhalation, and like that, he dismissed her.

Jenny was no lady, no social match for Lord Blakely. She was not the sort who would inspire him to tip his hat if he passed her on the street. She should have been accustomed to such cursory dismissals. But beneath her skirts, she felt suddenly brittle, like a pile of dried-up potato parings, ready to blow away with one strong gust of wind. Her fingernails bit crescent moons into her hands.

Madame Esmerelda wouldn't care about this man's interest. Madame Esmerelda never let herself get angry. And so Jenny swallowed the lump in her throat and smiled mysteriously. "I am also not a charlatan."

Lord Blakely raised an eyebrow. "That remains to be proven. As I have no desire to seek answers for myself, I believe Ned will question you."

"I already have!" Ned gestured widely. "About *everything*. About *life* and *death*."

Lord Blakely rolled his eyes. No doubt he'd taken Ned's dramatic protest as youthful exaggeration. But Jenny knew it for the simple truth it was. Two years earlier, Ned had wandered into this room and asked the question that had changed both their lives: "Is there any reason I shouldn't kill myself?"

At the time, Jenny had wanted to disclaim all responsibility. Her first impulse had been to distance herself from the boy, to say she wasn't really able to see the future. But the question was not one a nineteen-year-old posed to a stranger because he was considering his options rationally. She'd known, even then, that the young man had asked because he was at his wits' end.

So she'd lied. She told him she saw happiness in his future, that he had every reason to live. He'd believed her. And as time passed, he'd gradually moved past despair. Today, he stood in front of her almost confident.

It should have counted as a triumph of some kind, a good deed chalked up to Jenny's account. But on that first day, she hadn't just taken his despair. She'd taken his money, too. And since then, she and Ned had been bound together in this tangle of coin and deceit.

"Life and death?" Lord Blakely fingered the cheap fabric that loosely draped her chairs. "Then there should be no problem with my more prosaic proposal. I'm sure you are aware Ned must marry. Madame—Esmerelda, is it?—why don't you tell me the name of the woman he should choose."

Ned stiffened, and a chill went down Jenny's spine. Advice hidden behind spiritual maundering was one thing. But she knew that Ned had resisted wedlock, and for good reasons. She had no intention of trapping him.

"The spirits have not chosen to reveal such details," she responded smoothly.

The marquess pulled an end of lead pencil from his pocket and licked it. He bent over a notebook and scribbled a notation. "Can't predict future with particularity." He squinted at her. "This will be a damned short test of your abilities if you can do no better."

Jenny's fingers twitched in irritation. "I can say," she said slowly, "in the cosmic sense of things, he will meet her soon."

"There!" crowed Ned in triumph. "There's your specifics."

"Hmm." Lord Blakely frowned over the words he'd transcribed. "The 'cosmic sense' being something along the lines of, the cosmos is ageless? No matter which girl Ned meets, I suppose you would say he met her 'soon.' Come, Ned. Isn't she supposed to have arcane knowledge?"

Jenny pinched her lips together and turned away, her skirts swishing about her ankles. Blakely's eyes followed her; but when she cast a glance at him over her shoulder, he looked away. "Of course, it is possible to give more specifics. In ancient days, soothsayers predicted the future by studying the entrails of small animals, such as pigeons or squirrels. I have been trained in those methods."

A look of doubt crossed Lord Blakely's face. "You're going to slash open a bird?"

Jenny's heart flopped at the prospect. She could no more disembowel a dove than she could earn an honest living. But what she needed now was a good show to distract the marquess.

"I'll need to fetch the proper tools," she said.

Jenny turned and ducked through the gauzy black curtains that shielded the details of her mundane living quarters from her clients. A sack, fresh from this morning's shopping trip, sat on the tiny table in the back room. She picked it up and returned.

The two men watched her as she stepped back through a cloud of black cloth, her hands filled with burlap. She set the bag on the table before Ned.

"Ned," she said, "it is your future which is at stake. That means your hand must be the instrument of doom. The contents of that bag? You will eviscerate it."

Ned tilted his head and looked up. His liquid brown eyes pleaded with her.

Lord Blakely gaped. "You kept a small animal in a sack, just sitting about in the event it was needed? What kind of creature are you?"

Jenny raised one merciless eyebrow. "I was expecting the two of you." And when Ned still hesitated, she sighed. "Ned, have I ever led you astray?"

Jenny's admonition had the desired effect. Ned drew a deep breath and thrust his arm gingerly into the bag, his mouth puckered in distaste. The expression on his face flickered from queasy horror to confusion. From there, it flew headlong into outright bafflement. Shaking his head, he pulled his fist from the bag and turned his hand palm up.

For a long moment, the two men stared at the offending lump. It was brightly colored. It was round. It was—

"An orange?" Lord Blakely rubbed his forehead. "Not quite what I expected." He scribbled another notation.

"We live in enlightened times," Jenny murmured. "Now, you know what to do. Go ahead. Disembowel it."

Ned turned the fruit in his hand. "I didn't think oranges had bowels."

Jenny let that one pass without comment.

Lord Blakely fished in his coat pockets and came up with a polished silver penknife. It was embossed with laurel leaves. Naturally; even his pens were bedecked with proof of his nobility. His lordship had no doubt chosen the design to emphasize how far above mere commoners he stood. The marquess held the weapon out, as formally as if he were passing a sword.

Soberly, Ned accepted it. He placed the sacrificial citrus on the table in front of him, and then with one careful incision, eviscerated it. He speared deep into its heart, his hands steady, and then cut it to pieces. Jenny allotted herself one short moment of wistful sorrow for her after-dinner treat gone awry as the juice ran everywhere.

"Enough." She reached out and covered his hand mid-stab. "It's dead now," she explained gravely.

He pulled his hand away and nodded. Lord Blakely took back his knife and cleaned it with a handkerchief.

Jenny studied the corpse. It was orange. It was pulpy. It was going to be a mess to clean up. Most importantly, it gave her an excuse to sit and think of something mystical to say—the only reason for this exercise, really.

Lord Blakely demanded particulars. But in Jenny's profession, specifics were the enemy.

"What do you see?" asked Ned, his voice hushed.

"I see…I see…an elephant."

"Elephant," Lord Blakely repeated, as he transcribed her words. "I hope that isn't the extent of your prediction. Unless, Ned, you plan to marry into the genus Loxodonta."

Ned blinked. "Loxo-wha?"

"Comprised, among others, of pachyderms."

Jenny ignored the byplay. "Ned, I am having difficulties forming the image of the woman you should marry in my mind. Tell me, how do you imagine your ideal woman?"

"Oh," Ned said without the least hesitation, "she's exactly like you. Except younger."

Jenny swallowed uncomfortably. "Whatever do you mean? She's clever? Witty?"

Ned scratched his chin in puzzlement. "No. I mean she's dependable and honest."

The mysterious smile slipped from Jenny's lips for the barest instant, and she looked at him in appalled and flattered horror. If this was how Ned assessed character, he would end up married to a street thief in no time at all.

Lord Blakely's hand froze above his paper. No doubt his thoughts mirrored hers.

"What?" Ned demanded. "What are you two staring at?"

"I," said Lord Blakely, "am dependable. *She* is—"

"You," retorted Ned, "are cold and calculating. I've known Madame Esmerelda for two full years. And in that time, she's become more like family than anyone else. So don't you dare talk about her in that tone of voice."

Jenny's vision blurred and her head swam. She had no experience with family; all she remembered was the unforgiving school where an unknown benefactor had paid her tuition. She'd known since she was a very small child that she stood alone against the world. That had brought her to this career—the sure knowledge that nobody would help her, and everyone would lie to her. Lying to them instead had only seemed fair play.

But with Ned's words, a quiet wistfulness filled her. Family seemed the opposite of this lonely life, where even her friends had been won by falsehoods.

Ned wasn't finished with his cousin. "You see me as some kind of tool, to be used when convenient. Well, I'm tired of it. Find your own wife. Get your own heirs. I'm not doing anything for you any longer."

Jenny blinked back tears and looked at Ned again. His familiar, youthful features were granite. Beneath his bravado, she knew he feared his elder cousin. And yet he'd stood up to the man just now. For her.

She wasn't Ned's family. She wasn't really his friend. And no matter what had transpired between them, she was still the fraud who bilked him of a few pounds in exchange for false platitudes. Now he was asking her to repay him with more lies.

Well. Jenny swallowed the lump of regret in her throat. If deceit was all she had, she would use it. But she hadn't saved Ned's life for his cousin's convenience.

Lord Blakely straightened. His outraged glower—that cold and stubborn set of his lip—indicated he thought Ned *was* a mere utensil. That Lord Blakely was superior in intelligence and birth to everyone else in the room, and he would force their dim intellects to comprehend the fact.

He thought he was superior to his cousin? Well. She was going to make the marquess regret he'd ever asked for specifics.

"Ned, you recently received an invitation to a ball, did you not?"

He puckered his brow. "I did."

"What sort of a ball?"

"Some damned fool crush of a coming-out, I think. No intention of going."

The event sounded promising. There were sure to be many young women in attendance. Jenny could already taste her revenge on the tip of her tongue.

"You will go to this ball," she pronounced. And then she swept her arms wide, encompassing the two men. "You will both go to this ball."

Lord Blakely looked taken aback.

"I can see nothing of Ned's wife in the orange. But at precisely ten o'clock and thirty-nine minutes, Lord Blakely, *you* will see the woman you *will* marry. And you will marry her, if you approach her in the manner I prescribe."

The scrape of Lord Blakely's pencil echoed loudly in the reigning silence. When he finished, he set the utensil down carefully.

"You wanted a scientific test, my lord." Jenny placed her hands flat on the table in satisfaction. "You have one."

And if the ball was as crowded as such things usually were, he would see dozens of women in every glance. He'd never be able to track them all. She imagined him trying to scribble all the names in his notebook, being forced by his own scientific methods to visit every lady, in order to fairly eliminate each one. He would be incredibly annoyed. And he'd *never* be able to prove her wrong, because who could say he had recorded every woman?

Ned's mouth had fallen open. His hand slowly came up to hide a pleased smile. "There," he said. "Is that specific enough for you?"

The marquess pursed his lips. "By whose clock?"

One potential excuse slipped from Jenny's grasp. Not to worry; she had others.

"Your fob watch should do."

"I have two that I wear from time to time."

Jenny frowned. "But you inherited one from your father," she guessed.

Lord Blakely nodded. "I must say, that is incredibly specific. For scientific purposes, can you explain how you got all of this from an elephant?"

Jenny widened her eyes in false innocence. "Why, Lord Blakely. The same way I got an elephant from an orange. The spirits delivered the scene as an image into my mind."

He grimaced. She could not let her triumph show, and so she kept her expression as unchanging and mysterious as ever.

"So," Ned said, turning to his cousin, "you agree, then?"

Lord Blakely blinked. "Agree to what?"

"When you find the girl in question and fall in love, you'll agree Madame Esmerelda is not a charlatan."

The marquess blinked again. "I'm not going to fall in love." He spoke of that emotion in tones as wooden and unmoving as a dried-out horse trough.

"But if you did," Ned insisted.

"If I did," Lord Blakely said slowly, "I'd admit the question of her duplicity had not been scientifically proven."

Ned cackled. "For you, that's as good as an endorsement. That means, you'll consult Madame Esmerelda yourself and leave me be."

A longer pause. "Those are high stakes indeed. If this is to be a wager, what do you put up?"

"A thousand guineas," Ned said immediately.

Jenny nearly choked. She'd thought herself unspeakably wealthy for the four hundred pounds she'd managed to scrimp and save and stash away. A thousand pounds was more money than she could imagine, and Ned tossed it about as if it were an apple core.

Lord Blakely waved an annoyed hand. "Money," he said with a grimace. "What would either of us do with that paltry amount? No. You must risk something of real value. If you lose, you'll not consult Madame Esmerelda or any other fortune-teller again."

"Done," said Ned with a grin. "She's always right. I can't possibly lose."

Jenny couldn't bring herself to look at him. Because Ned could do nothing but lose. What if he began to doubt Jenny's long-ago assurances? What if he discovered that he owed his current happiness to the scant comfort of Jenny's invention? And Jenny could not help but add one last, desperately selfish caveat: What if Ned learned the truth and disavowed this curious relationship between them? He would leave her, and Jenny would be alone.

Again.

She inhaled slowly, hoping the cool air would help her calm down. The two men would go to the ball. Lord Blakely would look around. For all she knew, he might even decide to marry a girl he saw. And once he rejected all the women whose names he'd recorded, she'd tell him he'd seen a different woman at the appointed time out of the corner of his eye.

The wager would become a nullity, and she wouldn't have to see the fierce loyalty in Ned's eyes turn to contempt. Jenny's pulse slowed and her breath fell into an even rhythm.

Lord Blakely lounged back in his chair. "Something has just occurred to me."

The devilish gleam in his eye froze Jenny's blood. Whatever it was the dreadful man was about to say, she doubted he'd thought of it at that minute.

"What will stop her from claiming it was some other chit I was meant for? That I saw two girls at the designated time, and chose the wrong one?"

He'd seen through her. A chill prickled the ends of Jenny's fingers.

Ned frowned. "I don't know. I suppose if that happens, we'll have to call the bet off."

The marquess shook his head. "I have a better idea. Since Madame Esmerelda's seen everything in the orange, she'll be able to verify the girl's identity immediately."

He met her eyes and all Jenny's thoughts—her worries for Ned, the loneliness that clutched her gut—were laid bare in the intensity of his gaze.

His lip quirked sardonically. "We'll take her with us."

CHAPTER TWO

Gareth Carhart, Marquess of Blakely, had allocated one hour to this endeavor. Fifteen minutes to travel to the fortune-teller's lair, fifteen minutes to return home. Half an hour, he had supposed, would suffice to shred her lies like the insubstantial foolscap that they were.

"I can't go." Madame Esmerelda's voice was soft and uncertain.

"Why ever not?" Ned turned to her, a look of genuine befuddlement spreading across his face. Gareth's young cousin sat with his hands on his knees, his whole body canting toward the woman. And therein lay Gareth's problem.

When Gareth had left England years before, Ned had been a child, whining and hanging on at every opportunity. Now, he was barely twenty-one—but still damnably vulnerable. And Ned believed every word that this woman spoke.

With Ned's father dead, Gareth was the closest thing Ned had to a patriarch. Ned was his responsibility—and responsible marquesses did not let their young cousins fall into the clutches of fortune-tellers.

"I'm sure Madame Esmerelda had a perfectly legitimate reason not to come." Gareth raised an eyebrow at the woman and dangled his bait. "I suspect she had another appointment at the same time."

Let her agree. When she did, he would ask her to name the date of the ball. She wouldn't be able to, despite her vaunted powers and he would end this foolish charade before it even began.

But she did not take the easy way he offered. Her nostrils flared, and she pressed her lips together. "You're attempting to trick me, my lord."

Gareth barely transformed his jerk of surprise into an arrogant chin-lift. "I assure you," he said in his coldest tone, "I had no such intention."

She rolled her eyes. "You want this to be a scientific test? Let it be a scientific test. But don't set little verbal traps for me. And don't ever lie to me. You intended precisely such a thing."

Electricity prickled the hairs on his arms, and Gareth sat back, the silence pressing uncomfortably against his skin. Madame Esmerelda leaned toward him, her hands gripping her skirts. It had been a long while since anyone had spoken to him in that manner. He *had* lied to her. He had intended to trick her into playing her hand too soon. He just hadn't expected her to notice.

"You're trying to change the subject," he accused her. "Why can you not go to the ball?"

"Because I wasn't invited," she snapped. And then she looked down. "And besides, I have nothing to wear."

Ned gave a high crack of laughter.

And no wonder. It was such an absurdly ladylike thing to say. He glanced at her again. In that moment—a trick of the light, perhaps, or the way her lashes obscured her eyes—Gareth felt a jolt. Madame Esmerelda was not a lady, but she was most definitely a woman. A pretty one at that. She'd hidden her femininity beneath those unflattering layers of dark paint and the kerchief. Lies, those;

just ones composed of fabric and powder instead of words. He wondered idly how far down her back that mass of hair would reach if it were not bound up. She lifted her chin and met his eyes.

Gareth didn't believe in fortune-telling. He was a scientist; he'd devoted years to a naturalist's expedition in Brazil. He'd only returned to England when his grandfather died, and responsibility required he take on the demands of the title. He had come here because responsibility also demanded that he free his cousin from Madame Esmerelda's grasp. But he would take it as a matter of personal pride to strike a blow against the illogical superstition that this woman represented.

Her particular choice of lies, however, would take far longer than his allocated hour to disprove. He should have been annoyed. And yet he couldn't intimidate Madame Esmerelda.

In the year since he'd been back in England, he hadn't faced anything like a real challenge. Now he did. It was going to be extremely satisfying when he exposed her as the fraud that she was.

He relished the prospect of matching wits with her, of pulling the truth from her.

Gareth snapped his fingers. "The invitation," he said, "I can fix. The clothing I can fix. I'm willing to do much in the name of science."

"Oh, no. I couldn't." She looked away again. "Besides, I can't accept—"

Disparate details collided in Gareth's mind. The proper curtsy she had dropped. The educated precision of her intonation. Her reluctance to accept a gift of clothing from a man. These facts all added to one overwhelming conclusion: Madame Esmerelda had been educated as a gentlewoman. What on earth could have driven her to tell fortunes?

"Of course you can," he insisted. "Madame Esmerelda, if this is to be a scientific test, I don't believe you should lie to me, either."

Some emotion flickered in her eyes. She shook her head—not a denial, but a swift, short shake, as if she were putting everything to rights. And when she met his gaze again, her face was smooth.

She had thought of something, Gareth realized. She saw a way out of the mess he had created for her.

He should have been disappointed.

Instead, he couldn't wait to foil her plan.

IT DIDN'T TAKE LONG for Gareth to regret his eagerness. He hadn't realized finding Madame Esmerelda appropriate attire would turn into an ordeal. But Ned had thought it necessary to take the woman to the modiste himself. And Gareth knew if Ned had a moment alone with the charlatan, she would find a way to turn his head inside out. Again.

Which is how Gareth found himself in his closed carriage the next afternoon, accompanied by his chattering cousin, a fraud and a growing headache.

"So," Ned babbled, "we're going to the ball next Thursday, and then we'll meet Blakely's wife. I should like to see him fall in love. I'm rather looking forward to it."

Madame Esmerelda adjusted the kerchief on her head—red, this time—and slanted a careful look at Gareth. "Identify."

"Identify?" Ned repeated. "What do you mean, identify?"

"We are going to *identify* the woman in question. I

never said your cousin would meet her that day. In fact, the time for their meeting is not yet here."

Gareth inhaled in trepidation. "Not yet here? How long will this take?"

The smile touched her eyes, if not her lips. "Oh, I couldn't say. The time is not measured by years, but by tasks. Three of them."

"Tasks?" repeated Ned, incredulously.

"Tasks?" Gareth said sharply. "You said nothing of tasks."

"Oh? What did I say, I wonder?" She looked up at the roof of the carriage, innocently.

Gareth drew out his notebook and fumbled for the page. "At precisely ten o'clock and thirty-nine minutes, you will see the woman you are to marry if only you approach her in…" He faltered, and looked up.

That innocence had faded from her eyes. She'd known what she'd said. Baited him into this, no doubt, to make him look foolish.

"If only I approach her in the manner you prescribe," he finished dully.

"Ah, yes. The manner I prescribe." She smiled. "And I prescribe tasks."

He'd thought himself so clever, trapping her into making an easily disprovable statement. All he had to do, he'd thought, was *not* marry a girl. He'd succeeded at not marrying women all his life. He'd been too confident, too sure he'd backed her into a corner.

He'd underestimated her. He'd been so intent on winning, on *disproving* her statement, that he'd not seen the exit she planned for herself.

He could walk away at any moment. But if he did, he'd leave her influence over Ned unabated.

"*I* never got tasks," mumbled an aggrieved Ned.

"Of course not," Madame Esmerelda soothed. "But you must think how monumental an undertaking it will be for your cousin to convince a woman to care for him. If I didn't set him tasks, he'd use logic instead, and just think how that would work out. You don't need tasks. Everyone likes you already."

Gareth clenched his hand in suppressed fury and pushed his knuckles into the leather squabs. "And what," he snapped, "is the first task? Mucking out stables? Killing lions? Or must I chop down an entire orchard of citrus trees?"

She tapped a finger against her lips. "It is a trifle premature to tell you. But I suppose it can't hurt. You must carve an elephant out of a piece of ebony."

"An elephant?" Gareth looked up at the roof. "Why is it always elephants?"

The coach slowed to a halt. The footman opened the door, and dust motes danced in the rays of sunshine in front of Madame Esmerelda. They made her look…well, mystical. Drat her.

"I am," Madame Esmerelda said, "just a poor conduit for the spirits. As you will be a mere conduit for the elephant. You will give your future wife the elephant when first you meet."

Her eyes danced, and she exited the conveyance. Gareth bit back a pained yelp.

No doubt he could find a way to present such a gift in a dignified manner. If she thought to make a fool of Lord Blakely, she was vastly mistaken. But maybe she intended to fight him to an impasse. If she made those tasks onerous enough, she doubtless thought he would walk away. And with her conditions unfulfilled, he would have no proof she was a fraud—and that meant his cousin would continue to see her. Unacceptable.

By the triumphant spring in her steps as she approached the shop, she thought so, too.

Gareth's thoughts boiled as he entered the little shop. He paid little mind to Ned bothering Madame Esmerelda, whining about some irrelevant trifle. Bolts of colorful fabric decorated the front waiting room; they faded to dim gray in his mind. He didn't even notice he was pacing the floor, scarcely saw when Madame Esmerelda was whisked away to the back room. He wanted to rip the fashion plates off the walls and shred the sample cards laid demurely out on the tables.

Gareth did not like losing. He would not be outdone by some fraud. He'd looked forward to the challenge when he thought he would vanquish her. The situation became far less entrancing when her victory was possible.

Tasks. He couldn't let this continue.

He turned to Ned, who was fidgeting on the edge of his seat. "Ned," he said.

The boy looked up attentively.

"Do you think Madame Esmerelda will need a shawl?"

"I suppose—"

"Go buy her one." Gareth fumbled for a bank note and held it out.

Ned frowned, his fingers closing on the paper. "Why can't the modiste just choose one? What I know about ladies' shawls, I could fit—"

Gareth fixed Ned with his coldest look. "I think it would mean more to her if you chose it yourself. Don't you?"

Ned offered a few more halfhearted protests. Easy enough to dismantle those; soon his cousin scurried out the front door.

The workroom door swung open, and one of the seam-stresses popped out, her arms flowing with colored silks.

Gareth took a deep breath. This charade had gone on long enough. "Is Madame in a condition to receive me?"

She sniffed primly. "My lord. As you wish, my lord."

But as soon as he ducked through the doorway the servant indicated, he halted. A half-mirror stood on the otherwise empty wall, and Gareth's lungs contracted at the profile reflected in it. Rounded hip, and a swell of breast.

Madame Esmerelda wasn't wearing a fashionable dress. She wasn't wearing much of anything at all—nothing but a thin, worn chemise. The seamstress must have assumed he was the fortune-teller's lover, or she'd never have sent him back here. His body moved of its own accord, turning toward her, like a plant tracking the path of the sun.

Christ. Underneath the colorful skirts, now lying in a discarded heap, Madame Esmerelda had a waist. She had a bosom. She had a damned remarkable bosom. From five yards away, he could see the hazy outline of her legs through worn muslin. He could even make out the dark nubs of her nipples. The curling ends of her hair fell all the way to the small of her back.

She wasn't anything like the slender sylphs society favored. She was a Grecian fertility goddess, round and soft all over. And with her rosy lips frozen, half-open, she looked almost inviting.

Not that her invitation extended to him.

Gareth's brain tumbled to a halt. What remained in his

head was no rational thought, but simple greed. His mouth dried, and every muscle contracted in anticipation of the feast on display before him.

She stood, rooted in place, her eyes wide in horror. If she were a lady, he would have apologized profusely and left the room. Not that he could help his own reaction. It was more than just the sight of a beautiful, nearly naked woman that set his heart hammering. It was the way she'd challenged him, the way she'd undermined him. It had been years since anyone had out-thought him. And so what he felt was a sharp desire to possess her. To obtain her surrender in every way a woman could surrender to a man. It was lust, pure and simple.

But this woman was trying to make an idiot of Gareth and a dupe of his cousin. There was nothing pure or simple about her. And so he stuffed his physical response as best he could behind the safety of a cold, businesslike demeanor.

"Madame Esmerelda," Gareth said, "you win. There will be no tasks. No elephants."

Her eyes narrowed. "Get out."

"One hundred guineas, if you tell Ned you're a fraud and disappear from our lives."

She inhaled and her chest expanded. She pointed to the door. "Get out *now.*"

"Think it through. I doubt you'll be able to milk that much from him in your entire acquaintance. He'll outgrow your advice soon enough. And you could live for years on the money."

She took a deep breath, and those remarkable breasts shivered underneath the thin chemise. "I wouldn't do it for a hundred—" she began.

Gareth covered his rising lust with a nonchalant shrug. "Two hundred."

Her lip curled, and she shook her head in outrage. "Not for two *thousand*. Not for *ten*."

"Oh?" He flicked an insultingly familiar glance down her chemise. "You'd do it for ten. But you'll do it for two hundred."

She started toward him, her fingers curved like claws. He deserved to be slapped, and more, for the insult his look had implied. If he was right, and the woman was gently bred, she'd not appreciate the aspersions he'd just cast on her character. But he couldn't let her near him. He feared his own response if she came within arm's length.

"Really, Madame. Once you dispose of your fabricated outrage, you'll realize this is the best solution for everyone."

Gareth inclined his head, all sardonic politesse, and stepped back through the opening. He eased the door into place behind him, and let the insolent sneer slide off his face.

He leaned against the wall, his breath ragged. The challenge between them had become more than a territorial war over Ned's future. Now it was sensual.

Madame Esmerelda was extremely intelligent. She was devious. And if she had any idea how she affected him, she'd take advantage, unscrupulous creature that she was. And how idiotic that he wanted her to take that advantage. He wanted her to befuddle his wits until he lost all control and took *her.*

Gareth gripped his hands into fists. In his time in the jungles of Brazil, he'd cataloged close to a thousand insects. Now he let them march through his mind. Cockroaches. Poisonous, furry caterpillars. Maggots. He thought of every creeping thing ever to mar the face of the planet. He imagined them crawling about on his skin. And he didn't stop until his ardor subsided and the memory of her body dissolved from his mind.

It took a lot of millipedes.

JENNY HADN'T REGAINED HER COMPOSURE by the time she fastened, with shaking hands, the final layer of Madame Esmerelda's outrageous costume. Bad enough that this whole experiment had extended the lie of Madame Esmerelda far outside Jenny's usual sphere of business. Worse still, she'd been made to endure the pricks and pokes of the contemptuous seamstress who'd assumed the worst of Jenny's relationship with Lord Blakely.

But the crowning glory had been when the marquess had marched in on her as if he owned her body. He hadn't even bothered to avert his eyes. She wasn't sure which had been more insulting—the look he gave her, or his assumption that she'd be willing to abandon Ned if only he offered a high enough price.

Not since that first day, that first *hour,* had she been tempted by Ned's money. She wouldn't leave the poor boy to suffer under his cousin's unemotional auspices.

Jenny stormed out into the front room, her loose hair tangled around her shoulders.

Lord Blakely leaned against a wall next to an unclothed dress form. His eyes snapped open as she slammed the door behind her. But she didn't let him move. She jammed a finger into his chest and glared up at him.

"Just because you ignore everything around you except facts does not mean everyone else can be reduced to a number."

He looked down at her, astonishment in his eyes. "What the devil?"

She poked his chest again. "There are some things in life for which there are no figures. You don't comprehend what your cousin really needs or why he finds it necessary to speak with me. No matter what number you choose, you will never, ever be able to describe him. Not with a hundred guineas. Not with a thousand."

"Very well." He swallowed, focused on some spot on the ceiling. He didn't even bother to meet her gaze. "I shan't offer you bribes again."

"That's not enough. If it's not money you enumerate, you'll latch on to some other figure. The number of times I make an accurate prediction. The degree to which I specify what is to happen. Attach as many numbers as you like to my relationship with Ned, but they will not help you understand."

She was Ned's confidante. She'd be damned if she sold that role for mere money. She wouldn't let Lord Blakely reduce her to that level.

The man drew himself up. "You can disparage figures all day long, but that's what proof means. It means one has a factual basis for one's assertions."

"You call what you're doing proof," Jenny snapped. "But you prod and poke and pick. You have no interest in *proving* anything."

"What do you know of scientific proof?"

"Oh, you're the sort to pin insects to cards in order to study them. After several months spent perusing their desiccated carcasses, you'll announce your triumphant discovery: all insects are dead! And you'll delight in the ascendancy of scientific thought over human emotion."

Lord Blakely cocked his head and looked at her, as if searching for some hidden meaning in her face. "I study animal behavior. It's imperative I not kill the subjects of my inquiry. Dead macaws rarely flock."

"There's no need to murder the analogy by overextending it, atop your other crimes."

His gaze slid down her body. "The only question in my mind was whether you believed your own lies or were actively attempting to defraud Ned. I suppose it is a compliment to you that I have decided you are too clever for the former."

"Naturally. You don't believe anything you cannot taste or touch."

"I believe in Pythagoras's theorem, and I can't taste that. I believe there may be some truth to Lamarck's theories on inheritance of traits. But no, I do not believe in fate or fortune-tellers."

"Fate, fortune-telling—or feelings." Jenny snapped her fingers in his face. "The important things in life cannot be bound like so much paper to form a monograph."

The insouciant look on his face faded into cold steel. "A monograph?"

She inhaled, sharply. "Listen to yourself. You cite Lamarck instead of talking of your cousin's future. I have never seen you laugh. I've never even seen you smile. No wonder Ned would rather listen to me. You're a cold, unemotional automaton."

"An automaton?" His shoulders jerked and he stiffened.

Jenny wasn't done with him. "Just because you're as dispassionate as sawdust and as brittle as old bone doesn't mean everyone around you must ossify."

"Ossify." His nose flared and his chin lifted, as if parroting her syllables constituted some kind of brilliant argument. He looked down at his right hand, clenched into a fist in front of him. The muscles in his neck tensed. Jenny took a step back and wondered if she'd gone too far. Madame Esmerelda would never have let anger carry her away.

Then he looked up, and her doubts froze like so much lake water in winter. His eyes reflected some boreal wasteland, inhabited only by wind and a cold sweep of snow. Jenny felt the chill through every layer of Madame Esmerelda's costume, and she shivered.

When he spoke, there was no emotion in his voice at all. "You should have taken the two hundred guineas. After that outburst, I shall enjoy proving you a fraud."

BY THE TIME the carriage rumbled back to the Blakely home in the heart of Mayfair divested of all inhabitants but Gareth, it had begun to rain. It wasn't the warm tropical downpour he'd enjoyed in Brazil; instead, it was the frigid, anemic drizzle that typically plagued London. Drop after sullen drop sank to the earth.

So he was a cold, emotionless automaton? Strange, then, that he felt so damned furious. Gareth gritted his teeth as he stepped outside the carriage. Servants swarmed around him, attempting to rush him inside, out of the wet.

He brushed away their hands. "Leave me. I'm going for a walk," he snapped. They exchanged glances—his servants often exchanged glances—but they let him go.

Walking was an eccentricity he had developed in Brazil. It was, after all, the only way to make his daily rounds of observations. He'd brought the activity home with him. In London, the habit was inconvenient at best. The streets were all muck, and there was no overhead cover—neither wide-leafed jungle trees nor thick canopies—to speak of. But at a time like this—with his thoughts disordered, his mind awhirl and his body as ready to ignite as tinder—he needed this solitary exercise more than ever.

He set off into the dark. Cold rain ran down Gareth's spine in rivulets, but it did nothing to dampen the fury raging inside him. Dispassionate as sawdust?

Madame Esmerelda was wrong. It wasn't science that killed emotion. It was this place. These people. This *title*. He'd spent years in the rain forest, where life and color flourished anywhere it had the smallest chance of surviving. Here, geometric brick building followed geometric brick building, separated only by growing torrents of mud. Drawn shades clotted pallid windows; leaves like faded clay clung to half-dead grass. London was sterile. The rain had washed away all but the most persistent of the city's fabricated smells—the stink of coal and the scent of cold, wet stone.

If the city was desolate, its inhabitants were worse. He'd left London eleven years ago because polite society nearly suffocated him. It was the rigor of scientific thought, the clarity of observation, the control he gained over the universe as his understanding bloomed, that kept some vital part of himself in motion since his return. He had realized long ago that he would never really fit in. During these last months, the mornings he spent sorting through the naturalist's journal he'd kept in Brazil were all that helped him hold tight to some notion of who *Gareth* was. Without it, he would have drowned everything real about himself in Lord Blakely's unending responsibilities.

Gareth shook the rain from his shoulders and, sighing, looked up. He'd been trudging through muddy puddles for nearly half an hour. He was soaked to the bone; were it not for the furious whirl in his mind and the fast pace he'd been keeping, he'd have been chilled.

Unconsciously, his feet had traced the steps to the neighborhood where Madame Esmerelda lived. The streets were decidedly dingier than Gareth's own address, brown rivulets of running water skirting slushy horse dung strewn about the cobblestones. But the area was by no means dangerous. Families here hovered below respectability, but somewhat above poverty.

He found her windows. Tucked in the basement, down a flight of stairs. They glowed with an orange light that put him in mind of hot tea and a hearth. Anger, hot and irrational, welled up as he thought of her ensconced in a warm, comfortable room, while he prowled outside in the rain like some kind of bedraggled panther.

His whole response to her was as irrational as the idea of a fortune-teller consulting the spirits about the future. It was as stupid as the concept of wooing women with ebony elephants. It was, he admitted, as incomprehensible as a fraud refusing an offer of several hundred guineas in exchange for doing nothing. Perhaps that was why he drifted toward her door, his boots clomping heavily against the cold, wet stairs leading down.

He had a sudden image of confronting her, of explaining scientific thought and rigor. He wanted to knock the wind out of her with his words, as she had from him. He wanted her to feel as off balance as he did now. He wanted to *win,* to prove to her she was wrong and he was right. How idiotic of him. How unthinking. And yet—

He knocked.

And he waited.

Madame Esmerelda opened the door. She was carrying a tallow candle. It smoked and illuminated her face; he could see her pupils dilate in shock when she saw who stood on her doorstep. She didn't say a word—didn't invite him in, just blocked the opening and looked up at him in openmouthed surprise.

She hadn't donned that ridiculous costume again. Instead, a simple robe of thick, dark wool covered her. The thin white line of her chemise peeked over the neckline. That hint of muslin forcibly reminded Gareth of the afternoon. Of the expanse of soft flesh separated from his hands by two cloth layers and so much dampened air. A fist-size lump lodged itself in his throat and a dark mist formed in his mind, blanketing his carefully planned diatribe.

She curled one arm around herself, as if it were somehow *she* who needed protection from *him*.

"Do you know how I can tell you're a fraud?" he croaked.

She gazed up at him.

"Because you're wrong. You're completely wrong."

He fumbled in his mind for his prepared speech. *Science is about answers. It raises us above those who do not question.*

But before he could start, Gareth made a colossal mistake: He looked into Madame Esmerelda's eyes. He'd thought she was black-eyed as a Ggypsy. But from eighteen inches away, with the candle so close to her face, he realized her eyes were in fact a very dark blue.

With that simple observation, the blood drained from his brain. Gareth's structured defense of scientific thinking washed from his head. Instead, he took a step toward her. He let the veil drop from his eyes, let her see the inferno raging inside him.

She sucked in air. "Why do you say I'm wrong?" Her voice quavered on the last word.

"I'm not an automaton." The words came from some vital place deep inside him—his solar plexus, perhaps, rather than his uncooperative brain.

Gareth took another step closer. She continued to hold his gaze, as incapable of looking away as he. The white vapor of her breath swirled in the cold night air. Its cadence kept time with the rise and fall of her chest. He could taste every one of her exhalations, sweetness coalescing against his mouth.

It was an act of self-preservation to reach out and pinch the candle flame. To stop the flow of sensual images before they seared themselves permanently into his flesh. The wick sizzled and the light died between his wet fingers. Her eyes disappeared into the navy darkness of nighttime.

It didn't help. He could still smell her. He could taste the honey of her breath on the tip of his tongue. And the distant streetlamp cast enough illumination for him to see when she licked her lips. Heat seared him.

"I'm not made of wood." Gareth reached out again. This time, his hand grazed the warm flesh of her cheek. And still the silly woman didn't jerk away. She didn't even flinch when he tilted her chin up. Instead, her lips parted in soft, subtle invitation.

The thought of her mouth against his snuffed what little guttering intellect remained to him. Her flesh seemed to sizzle beneath his fingertips. He lowered his head until her lips were a tantalizing inch from his.

"Most of all," Gareth said, his voice husky, "I'll be damned if I let you call me dispassionate."

CHAPTER THREE

JENNY EXPERIENCED ONE SECOND of blinding clarity before Lord Blakely's lips touched hers. Madame Esmerelda would have stepped away the moment he extinguished her candle. Madame Esmerelda would never let herself be rooted in one spot with hunger.

With five minutes to think it through, she'd have pushed him away. Her disguise depended on it. But she had one second, and so her reasoning took on an entirely different cast. The heat of his breath against her lip. The spark that shot through her when his hand, ungloved and still wet from the rain, grazed her cheek.

Mostly, though, something vitally feminine deep inside her chest insisted she stay, a bud yearning to unfold after years of lies and denial. Madame Esmerelda wouldn't have cared. But the pretense of Madame Esmerelda had eroded every bit of real human contact from Jenny's life for years. Jenny was tired of not caring.

Jenny stayed.

She did more than stay. She stepped into Lord Blakely's rough embrace and lifted on tiptoes. He didn't evince the least surprise at her brazenness. Instead, his hands settled on her hips and he pulled her up into his kiss.

For all the carefully controlled power in the strong

arms holding her, his mouth descended on hers with surprising gentleness. His lips brushed hers, sweet and lingering. A soft, sensual nip, and then another. Beguiling. As if there were nothing he'd rather do than sample her breath, taste her lips.

He was slow but not hesitant. He coaxed her to give up her every secret, and Jenny was beyond artifice. Every sensation—the sweep of his tongue against her bottom lip, the light brush of her nipples against his chest, the clamp of his hands around her waist—reverberated through her aching body.

She opened her mouth. He entered, as confident as an advancing army. His tongue captured hers, and everything warm and womanly in Jenny welled up in response.

Without breaking the kiss, he pushed forward inside her rooms. Three steps, and her back met the rough surface of her entry wall, his lips and tongue teasing her. His hands tightened, each finger branding her hips through her dressing-gown.

Jenny wanted everything she had denied herself these last long years. She wanted every last scrap of femininity she had hidden behind the voluminous yards of her garish Gypsy costume. She wanted to touch him, experience flesh pressed against flesh. If only for this moment, she wanted to believe herself safe and secure. It was idiotic beyond all comprehension for her to indulge that fantasy with any person, let alone this man.

But she did.

Lord Blakely pulled away. He swiveled briefly, casually flicking her door shut with one hand. The sharp click of its closing awoke Jenny from her dream.

The marquess turned back to her.

One tentative glance at his face and Jenny understood exactly how foolish she'd allowed herself to be.

The set of his lips was no longer grim, but it was still devoid of warmth. He considered her, his eyes alert and observant, darting from her mouth to the hand she held up to halt his advance. For all the passion she'd imagined in his kiss, the look he gave her was considering. Intellectual. And he wasn't even breathing hard.

Jenny smiled tentatively at him, her heart slamming painfully against her chest.

His expression didn't lighten one iota.

She swallowed and looked at the floor. She'd just told him everything, and she hadn't even spoken a word. Life was brutally unfair, sometimes. But she'd had years to become accustomed.

"I think you've proven your point." She could taste her own bitter shame in every word. It had taken him seconds to breach her defenses. Moments to prove he could command her female response. Mere hours to expose her lies.

For a heartbeat, he didn't react.

Then he reached out an arm. "Not in the slightest. Give me your hand."

The nonchalance in his demand stiffened her spine. She took another step back. "You've touched me enough for one evening, I should think."

His gaze skittered down her robe. Her nipples were already peaked. He could not miss those tips poking against the fabric. Nor could he fail to note the pale rose heat that suffused her face and hands.

He shook his head slowly. "I suppose you should think so. But you don't. You're as ravenous for me as I am for you."

A gasp escaped Jenny's unwilling lungs. "I—I'm not—"

"Don't bother lying to me." His voice was dark and deep, scraping like gravel against her senses. "You've already told me what I need to know. You're no fortune-teller."

Lord Blakely lounged with his back against the door. She glanced down—but the damnable loose cut of his trousers gave no hint as to his physical state, and he exhibited frightening composure for a supposedly ravenous man. Jenny was the one who ached all over. And he was right. She wanted his touch again; she hungered for it.

He crooked one finger. "Now come. Give me your hand. I promise I shan't bite."

She swallowed. "Really? Then why ever do you want it?"

A flicker of appreciation flared in his eyes. "I am going to read your palm."

Confusion sparked in Jenny's mind. "But you don't believe in fortune-telling."

He pushed off from the door and wandered from the tiny entryway into her front room. He paused before her table and lifted the cheap black cotton off the wood with his thumb and forefinger.

"I don't believe in *this*."

He dropped the material to the floor. It landed in a whispering sigh.

He turned to the brass tray where she burned her incense. She'd cleaned it of ash and filled it with fresh sandalwood shavings in preparation for the next client. He picked up a handful of fat curls. "I don't believe in these, either."

He clenched his fist, and short stubs of sandalwood rained down on the black cloth.

Lord Blakely turned to face her. His features were still hard and unmoving and his gaze roved around the room, avoiding her. "Let me tell you what I do believe. I believe in intelligence. I believe in clever tricks. And I believe you have no shortage of the two."

Two steps forward, and he was once again within touching distance. He held out his hand once again. "Give me your hand, and I'll show you how your trick is performed."

Jenny shook her head.

He gave her no chance to move away. Instead, his fingers clamped about her wrist and he drew her toward him. Jenny's skin prickled with the heat wafting off him. But he didn't take advantage of her proximity. Instead, he flipped her hand palm up and examined it with logical detachment.

"There is no real difference between your palmistry and mine. Except I eschew cosmic references. I'll explain where I get my oranges and elephants, scientifically speaking." The pads of his fingers traced a molten line down her palm. "The first thing I see in your hand is that you have been well-educated, almost certainly at one of the small schools that trains gentlewomen in the outlying areas of the country."

Jenny inhaled. "I— What makes you say—"

He ticked items off on each of her fingers. "You are familiar with bugs pinned to cards. You know the precise degree of deference owed a marquess. When you become angry, you use words like *desiccate* and *ossify*. You sit as if you were trained with a book on your head. You speak like a young lady drilled in her aitches, which you enunciate quite precisely." He paused, tapping his thumb against her smallest finger. "I am out of fingers, and not yet out of observations."

Jenny pulled against his grip. He didn't loosen his hold.

Instead, he trailed his fingers along her palm. Years of doing her own cleaning had left her hands rough. She had no doubt that frightening brain of his was calculating the precise amount of laundering she had performed.

"I doubt there was much money in your family—perhaps it was charity that paid for the education?"

Jenny swallowed, and her fingers curled into a ball.

He straightened them out between the palms of his hands. "Or a bequest. A patron. You should have been a governess. I suppose that was the point of all that education?"

Jenny had felt less naked that afternoon, wearing nothing but a chemise.

"Either you chose not to, or you were ruined beyond any hope of governessing."

Don't, oh, don't let him see the truth. It would give him far too much power over her. If he knew she were ruined—if he knew that she'd once tried to be a mistress—he would no doubt think she was open to the possibility again.

He looked up from her hand and stared at the wall behind her. "Both, I should think. I have difficulty imagining your acceding to anyone's demands. If you had wanted to be a governess, you'd have found a way to be one. But you kiss like a temptress."

Heat flooded her. She'd kissed like a fool. Coldhearted demon that he was, he knew it.

"In any event, I wager you were not a favorite among the other girls at school."

Her breath hissed in, and she jerked away from him. Once again, he refused to relinquish her wrist, his grasp as tight as an iron manacle.

"If you had been," he said reasonably, as if his fingers weren't pressing against her hammering pulse, "you'd have options far more appealing than fraud. And more fundamentally, to even think of this profession, you must have discovered at a very young age that everyone lies. It's hard to learn that when you're a well-loved child. How old were you?"

"I was nine." The words escaped her lips, unbidden. It was the first time she'd verified his suspicions aloud. And now he knew. He knew everything. Jenny shut her eyes, unwilling to see the triumph of his response.

His fingers tightened about her wrist. His other hand trailed against her jawbone. Reluctantly, she let her lids flutter open. His eyes had focused on her lips again. He ought to have been crowing with delight. But there was no victory in his gaze.

"Precocious," he finally said, looking away. "I was twenty-one. Ned's age."

She could identify no hint of self-pity in his voice. He sounded as scientific as ever, reciting evidence to a lecture hall. And yet the tightness around his mouth suggested the memory was more substantial than mere data. Jenny had a sudden urge to kiss the fingers that encircled her wrist.

"I suppose I should read your future, as well as your past." He ducked his head, examining her palm again. "You will tell me your real name. It's not Esmerelda, that's for certain."

"It's not? Why not?"

He shrugged. "An impoverished English family would never name their daughter anything so fanciful. And then there's all that sandalwood and the ridiculous costume. 'Esmerelda' is too convenient. It is just another trapping in your particular subterfuge. Tell me your name."

Jenny pressed her lips together and shook her head.

"Margaret," he guessed. "Meg for short."

"Esmerelda," Jenny insisted.

That sardonic quirk of his lips again. "It won't do, Meg. You'll tell me your name eventually."

"If Esmerelda were not my name, why would I admit it to you?"

His thumb caressed hers. "Because I can't let you call me Gareth until you do."

He spoke so casually. "Why—" Jenny stopped, and squared her shoulders. "My lord, why would I want to call you by your Christian name?"

"I can see that future here—" he traced a line down her palm "—and here—" he touched her cheek near her eyes "—and here."

His thumb brushed her lips, and her mouth parted in anticipation. And still his expression lost not one whit of its scientific cast.

"I'm not going to marry whatever poor girl you pick out," he said softly. "I pit your prediction against mine. I predict you'll call me Gareth. When I bed you, Meg, I'll be damned if you scream anything else."

"If you're trying to prove you're not an automaton," Jenny said, "you really ought to consider varying your tone. You might as well be talking about the price of potatoes, for all the—"

He cut her off with a swift kiss. Heaven help her trembling body, she let him do it. And when he pulled back, it was her lips that clung to his.

"You see?" he murmured. "You'll scream."

"But we've already established that I am not dispassionate. I want to know—what will you do?"

For just one instant, he met her eyes. Those golden

orbs glimmered with a fierce light. It was the second hint of emotion she'd detected from him that evening. When he looked sharply away from her, she could almost believe she'd imagined it.

He let go of her wrist, breaking the connection between them. Then he shook his head, and Jenny realized they had been standing in the chilled entry for minutes. She hadn't even felt the cold.

She did now.

He set his hand on the handle of her door. "You want to know what I'll do when I bed you? I'll win." He turned away and opened her door. The rain had stopped and a light, swirling mist blanketed the street. Seconds later, he strode into the night. The fog muffled the sound of his steps and swallowed his disappearing figure.

Jenny shut the door and turned and sagged against it. Her hands covered her face. But no matter how tightly she closed her eyes, she couldn't erase the feel of his lips from her flesh or the taste of his mouth from her mind.

What a disaster. He had already won.

He'd seen everything, from the harsh order of the school where she'd been raised to the depths of her unfortunate attraction to him. She hadn't spoken what she felt in words, but his one kiss had teased out her admission of fraud.

In the scant space of a few hours, he'd unearthed her deepest secrets. Including, it seemed, a few she'd kept from herself. The desire to be touched. The desire to be *desired.*

One kiss, and she'd verified every dismissive thought Lord Blakely had ever had of his cousin. Because Lord Blakely's prediction was not just that he'd bed Jenny, but that he'd prove Ned's valiant defense false.

Once, her profession had seemed a game. It had made no difference what lies she told her clients. After all, few of them truly believed her. They saw her as nothing more than a distraction, an entertainment to be scheduled between boxing matches and the opera.

But Ned had been different. What had it hurt to foretell that he would become a strong and confident man, trustworthy and capable?

When Ned discovered she'd lied, Lord Blakely would never let him forget his foolishness. He'd store it in that brain of his, next to his theories of goose behavior, or whatever it was he studied. And he'd trot out the evidence any time Ned showed a hint of independence.

For all Lord Blakely's talk of ravenous hunger, he'd been the one to step away. Of course he would willingly take Jenny to his bed. After all, he was a man. That's what men did. And given the expertise he'd shown with his lips and tongue, she had no doubt he could make her scream if he got her there.

If? It had become a matter of when.

He'd held her close. He'd kissed her. He'd promised to make her scream in bed, and shamefully, she still longed for him to do it. But there was one thing Lord Blakely had not done—not once, in the hours she'd observed him.

He hadn't smiled.

Jenny took a deep breath. Silently, she made another prediction. Before he took her to bed, she'd break Lord Blakely. She'd make him realize Ned needed more than intellect and insult to sustain him. She'd make him respect Ned.

Damn it, she'd make him respect *her.*

Jenny had already lost. But that didn't mean the marquess had to win.

THERE WAS NO WAY TO WIN, Gareth thought helplessly, as he surveyed the tray that his sister, Laura Edmonton, had laid out in anticipation of this visit. Shortbread. Cucumber sandwiches with the crust removed. Once, many years ago, he'd enjoyed both. Now they lay, marshaled in grim rows, testament to an ongoing war. Gareth could at most hope to achieve a scrambling, ignominious retreat.

His sister—his much younger half sister, if Gareth was going to be precise about the matter—smiled at him. But the expression her eyes reflected wasn't hope or happiness; it was fear.

"Tea?"

The battle was always joined with tea. "Please," he answered.

He could direct the products of his estates without blinking. He had braved the rain forests of Brazil for months. But this quiet room, draped in pink silks, with the pleasant burbling of the fountain coming through the window… Well, it vanquished him every time.

Not so much the room as Laura. Her lips were compressed in concentration as she added a careful dollop of cream to Gareth's tea—precisely the quantity that Gareth preferred.

Every month, Laura tried desperately to please him. Today, she wore the finest morning dress she owned, made of some thin, pink flimsy cotton, the sleeves large and heavy and festooned with ribbons. Her sandy brown hair was pinned up with ruthless exactitude.

Laura handed over a delicate china cup and saucer, as if tea would magically heal the damage between them. It couldn't. After Laura had been born, Gareth had been too busy learning to be a marquess to become a brother.

Now that they were both adults, they'd frozen into this awkward pattern.

Awkward?

Every month, she invited him over for tea. Every month, he accepted. And every month… To call these unfortunate tête-à-têtes *awkward* would understate the matter by an order of magnitude.

Their afternoons always started this way. Gareth struggled for conversation, and Laura attempted to make up for his taciturn nature by speaking for them both.

"Do you like my reticule?" She set her saucer on the table with a clink and retrieved a puddle of pink silk that lay nearby. She held it out for inspection.

The object in question was embroidered with pink roses, which in turn sported pink leaves and pink thorns. It was of a size to fit a calling card—a *pink* calling card. Dyed pink feathers were sewed to the bottom. The handbag was not merely pink. It was fatally pink.

Gareth searched for an appropriately supportive response. "It seems…serviceable?"

She wrinkled her nose. "Oh. Because I took it with me when Alex took me driving, and he said it would spook the horses. He made me sit on it the whole way, and then he only took me in a single circuit around the park." Laura looked up at Gareth.

That look in her eyes—that damnable look that said that even after all his missteps, Gareth's opinion still mattered—made him hunch his shoulders. It made him wish he'd done one thing to deserve it. Madame Esmerelda had accused him of being an automaton. Around his sister, he felt like a clumsy marionette, poorly jointed, unable to manage even the simplest tasks. How she would laugh if she could see him now.

"Do you think," Laura asked in a small voice, "that my fiancé hates my reticule?"

Questions like these were more perilous than a company of marauding Turks. There were no right answers to give, not ever. Gareth tried anyway. "I rather suspect he likes your reticule. It's just that he's a man. He's not going to waste his time poring over needlepoint flowers, even if he is marrying you."

As soon as his sister winced, Gareth realized *waste* had been the wrong word. That his clipped delivery had struck the wrong tone. Because it had never been the tea or the cucumber sandwiches, with or without crusts, that rendered this endeavor futile. It was *Gareth.* He had no notion of pink silk and embroidery. And damn him, he had no notion of this woman before him. For all that she was his sister and the closest flesh and blood that he had on this planet, she was still a mystery to him.

They'd been playing out this scene ever since Laura was four and Gareth twenty, when in one of his short visits to his stepfather's estate, she'd invited him to a tea party with all her dolls. At the time, he'd thought that if only she were a bit older, if only the minute chairs in her chambers were a tad larger, perhaps he'd be able to converse with her.

But now she was nineteen. She was too much a lady to pelt him with shortbread and shriek that he was ruining her party.

Laura had turned her head, as if to contemplate the elms outside the wide windows. Her hands twisted the silk of her reticule round and round until the embroidered petals distorted into harsh lines. "And what do I do," she said quietly, "if he stops liking *me?*"

If that's what you fear, then you shouldn't marry him.

But saying that would be stupid and utterly selfish. Because Gareth couldn't shake the fear in his own mind that once she married, she would have no further need of her inept brother. She would figure out that these afternoons were a waste, and Gareth would be utterly displaced. Her invitations would slow from monthly to bimonthly events. They would eventually turn into salutations exchanged in passing at the opera. If Laura were at all rational, she'd have stopped inviting him years ago.

A real older brother would know precisely how to reassure his sister at a moment like this. He'd be able to alleviate the agitation that had her wringing the neck of her reticule. He would tell jokes and solve all her problems. But Laura had an ungainly lump of a brother, all marquess, and Gareth hadn't the faintest idea how to comfort anyone.

Just as she always invited him, Gareth always tried. "If you're really worried your fiancé won't like you, I'll double your settlement."

Her eyes widened, and her mouth crumpled.

"What?" he asked. "What did I say this time?"

"Is that what you think of me, Blakely?" Laura choked on the words. "You think you have to bribe Alex to care for me? That nobody will love me unless you pay him?"

No.

Gareth had hoped to buy Laura's love for himself. How could he make her see? He'd tried to bail himself out of these situations before, but all he ever managed was to reduce her to tears. Once a conversation started sinking, there was little choice but to abandon ship. Long experience had taught him that the way *not* to respond in situations like this was to enumerate the ways in which she was wrong. Somehow, every time he tried to explain that he hadn't meant what she heard, it came out sounding like "you are an irrational goose."

Instead of allaying her fears, he sat in his chair and gripped his plate until the delicate edge of the china cut into his hands.

Then he'd been silent too long, an entire species of error in its own right.

"Very well." Laura's voice trembled. "Double it. I don't care."

Nothing had changed since she was four except the chairs. He was still ruining everything.

Madness, a physician had once told Gareth, was repeating the same events over and over while hoping for a different result. That was why Gareth had no fear he would fall in love, no matter what Madame Esmerelda predicted for him. Love was watching his sister choke back tears. Love hoped that month after month, she would continue to issue invitations. And love believed, against all evidence, that one day, he would get it right, that he would learn to talk to her as a brother instead of the cold, unfeeling man she must have believed him to be.

In short, love was madness.

CHAPTER FOUR

HE'D EMBARKED on a new species of madness, Gareth thought as he shifted on the soft squabs of the closed carriage. It was the night of the coming-out ball that he and Ned were to attend. It had been almost a week since he left Madame Esmerelda's quarters, and the visceral pull she had on him should have waned. Tonight he would take the first step in breaking her power over Ned.

And yet...

He had thought he'd figured out Madame Esmerelda. Classified her, genus and species. One fraud, first class; motivated by greed. That ambition on her part was no doubt intensified by an early childhood where she'd not fit a predefined role. And, luckily for him, she was as susceptible as he to the powerful lust that burned between them.

Having identified the problem, the solution seemed obvious: Execute her tasks with maximum alacrity and minimum embarrassment, thus exposing her perfidy to Ned. Take her to bed, enjoy her thoroughly and dispel his unfortunate attraction to her in the most pleasurable manner possible.

He chanced a glance across the seat. She sat properly, her feet crossed and put to the side to avoid his own limbs. She had very carefully avoided his gaze all evening. Without saying a word to him, though, she'd destroyed the mental identification he'd made. She'd become an anomaly. Gareth's ordered mind abhorred anomalies.

Correction: Gareth loved anomalies. An anomaly meant there was a scientific mystery to explore. It meant some mysterious unknown cause had come into play, and if he could just examine the problem from the right angle, he could be the first person in the world to solve the puzzle. No; the scientist in Gareth adored conundrums. It was the marquess in him, the responsible Lord Blakely, who feared the consequences.

Because under the circumstances, it was dreadfully inconvenient to adore anything about her.

The first burning question in his mind was—why that gown? Oh, he'd sunk to new lows, contemplating a woman's wardrobe. Gareth was hardly an arbiter of fashion, but even he knew that these days the waist was fashionably pulled in by means of some corsetted contraption. Necklines skimmed the breasts. And sleeves were supposed to balloon like enraged puffer-fish.

He'd looked forward to seeing that remarkable bosom framed by a fashionably low neckline. He'd have engaged in some chance ogling or a brush of his hands against a creamy collarbone. In the dress he had envisioned, such accidents would have been delightfully inevitable.

But instead Madame Esmerelda's dress was brown—almost black, in the dimness of the carriage. The neck was unmodishly high, and the sleeves had only a hint of a puff to them. No lace, no ribbons and no fancy gold trim. No shaping of the figure.

Her choice of attire was as baffling as it was disappointing. After she'd raged at him the other day, he'd pulled out his notebook and disappeared into his scientific work. When the modiste had come to him in outrage, he'd brushed her away. He had assumed Madame Esmerelda would take advantage of his lack of focus. After all, she could have lived for a week on the price of a single gilt ribbon. Instead, she must have waged war with the modiste to obtain such an unflattering gown. And Gareth wanted to know why.

A first-class fraud, motivated by greed, would have ordered gold netting and badgered Gareth to provide sapphires to highlight the remarkable color of her eyes. It made no sense to do anything else.

He'd been staring openly at her since she'd entered his carriage. She'd gifted him with short glances that smoldered beneath his skin even after she turned her head. Kissing the woman should have given her the upper hand, should have revealed his weakness to her. A first-class fraud would have taken every seductive advantage. She would have kept his gaze and added burning promises with every lift of her brow. She would have taken advantage of the cover of darkness to rest her foot against his. After all, how better to reap the rewards, and potentially cloud Gareth's judgment?

He'd manfully prepared himself to resist her blandishments—for now.

But Madame Esmerelda was ignoring him as best she could from two feet away, and talking with Ned. And he didn't know which annoyed him more—that he wished she would try to cloud his judgment, or that it was clouding without any effort on her behalf at all.

Her behavior didn't fit. Nothing about her fit.

"Ned," she was saying, "don't lose sight of what you must do this evening."

Ned clasped his hands in front of him in barely contained excitement. "We're going to meet Blakely's future wife. How should I greet her?"

Gareth winced. From time to time, his cousin was prone to overexuberance. He could imagine the disruption the youth might cause.

Apparently, Madame Esmerelda could, too. She shook her head. "Oh, Ned. Be respectful and mannerly. And remember that Lord Blakely won't greet her until he's ready to present the elephant."

"Oh, very well." Ned slouched against the seat and folded his arms. "But only because you say so."

Gareth was not used to being ignored. Most especially not by women he kissed. He was already weary of it. "Madame Esmerelda."

She looked over, unwillingly.

"After I finish the third task, how soon do you predict I will fall in love and propose marriage?"

"Within a month." Her voice quavered uncertainly at the end of the sentence.

"And that's all I have to do—perform the three tasks, wait a month, and if I don't marry the girl, Ned will know you're a fraud?" He held his breath. If she agreed, this would give him precisely what he wanted. Verifiable performances. Measurable outcomes. And most importantly, a finite, achievable end that would justify whatever humiliation he felt because of her tasks.

"Another possibility is that you might follow the spirits' guidance and marry her."

Gareth snorted.

Ned kicked Gareth's leather half boot in the darkness. "Hurry up, then, and get carving."

There was a third anomaly to consider. Ned did everything Madame Esmerelda told him. If she had told him to hand over ten thousand pounds and leap off London Bridge wearing lead footgear, Ned would be fish food at the bottom of the Thames. For a first-class fraud, she was doing a miserable job extracting money.

"Never you mind about that, Ned," Gareth said. "There's no need for me to start carving."

"But the task—!" Ned almost choked on his indignation.

"There's no need to start, as I've already finished. I thought it best to get this over with as soon as possible." Gareth reached into his jacket pocket and pulled out an ebony lump. Light from a passing lamp glinted off the surface.

Madame Esmerelda motioned, and he handed it over. She took it in her hands, and then brought it close to her face, squinting, turning the misshapen chunk of wood over. The piece of ebony was as round as it was wide, scored and gouged with his pocketknife. Her mouth puckered as if she'd bitten a lemon.

Some explanation seemed necessary. Gareth pointed to the lump. "Elephant."

"Goodness." She rotated the figurine about its axis. "Could you perhaps have made it more…more elephantine?"

Gareth rather disliked being found wanting in any area. The fact that he couldn't carve should not have unnerved him. After all, he shouldn't care what she thought of his abilities on that score. It wasn't as if her opinion mattered. And it wasn't as if the skill was of any importance to a marquess. He folded his arms and mustered his coolest expression. "The assigned task did not precisely play to my strengths."

She sniffed. "What did you expect? To seduce a lady with a geometrical proof?"

"Seduction?" Gareth's gaze flitted down her bosom. "I had thought we were talking of marriage."

Madame Esmerelda colored and thrust the ebony back into his hands.

"Wait," protested Ned. "Let me see it."

Gareth handed over the lump. He made eye contact with his cousin, and silently promised dire retribution should Ned start laughing.

Ned saved his own life by merely frowning in puzzlement. "Where, ah, where is its trunk?"

Gareth fished about in his pocket and pulled out a thick splinter of wood. "It came off. During the carving."

Madame Esmerelda stared at it, and shook her head. "Well. This evening, I think you ought to engage in multiple activities that do not, as you say, play to your strengths."

"Yes," Gareth said with a noisy sigh. "I'll have to give away the elephant to whichever horrific debutante you point out."

Madame Esmerelda shook her head. "And."

"There's an and?"

"Lord Blakely, if there isn't an 'and' there's a 'but.' Give away the elephant. Please, try to do one other thing. Smile."

"Smile?" He glowered at her. "Is that the next task? To grin like a loon?"

"It's not a task," Madame Esmerelda said. "It's a suggestion."

"Why would I smile?"

Ned handed back Gareth's pitiful attempt at carving. "Smiling is that thing most people do with their lips to in-

dicate amusement or enjoyment." He turned to Madame Esmerelda. "You ask the impossible. You're a cruel woman."

The carriage came to a careful halt, and a footman
opened the door. Cool night air rushed in, and the conversation halted momentarily while the party exited the
carriage.

Gareth carefully placed the ebony in his pocket. "I'm
not going to feign amusement. Or enjoyment."

"Like I said," Ned replied airily. "Impossible."

Madame Esmerelda patted her skirts into place. "Have
you considered *actually* enjoying yourself?"

"In this venue? In this company?" Gareth glanced toward the brightly lit entry. "Ned's quite right. It's impossible." He stalked away, leaving Ned and Madame
Esmerelda in his wake.

"Whew." Behind him, Ned whistled between his teeth.
"Cold fish."

If only he knew.

"LORD BLAKELY. Mrs. Margaret Barnard. Mr. Edward
Carhart." The majordomo's announcement hardly cut
through the din of conversation that filled the glittering
room that opened up before Jenny.

She frowned at Lord Blakely—it was he, after all,
who'd directed the majordomo—just before he leaned in
and whispered to her.

"Congratulations, Meg. You have become a widow.
Also a very distant cousin of mine. Do try not to tell fortunes here." He tucked her gloved hand in the crook of
his elbow and led her forward.

He acted as if she were nothing but a liar, as if she'd
chosen her profession because she could not help but
speak mistruths every time she opened her mouth. It had

taken her years to perfect Madame Esmerelda's character, and almost a decade to bring her profession to this height, where word of mouth had replaced the need to advertise. She could not just adopt a persona on a whim.

But before she could think of a way to castigate him, she entered the ballroom, and all other thoughts were driven from her mind. The room seemed on fire, so bright was the illumination.

She had seen gas lamps on the street, dull globes of orange casting dim shadows about them. She'd even tangled with oil lamps herself on occasion—messy to fill, burning with a faint fishy odor. But she'd only walked outside houses illuminated as this one. The night fled from these bright chandeliers, shining with unspeakable wealth.

She'd never seen the like. The entire room was lit by what seemed a thousand golden suns. It was noon-bright, and twice as hot. No corner of the room stood in shadow. The only difference between this light and day was that the heavy yellow tinge of the lighting rendered the brown of her dress as mud.

Mud was what she felt like next to Lord Blakely.

His finery had been calculated to take advantage of the brilliance. The dark red embroidery in his black waistcoat subtly caught the light. Jet buttons, exquisitely cut, sparkled. In this light, she could make out the subtle, rich texture woven in the fabric of his dark jacket. All that black brought out the golden flecks in his eyes.

She had never felt so intensely shabby before. Her gown was plain and untrimmed. Simple lines; easy to put on and take off. The kind of dress that a woman, living alone, could don without assistance. And because only a woman living one step above genteel poverty would purchase a gown built on those lines, she'd chosen a sensible and serviceable brown. Anything else would have seemed out of place. But "out of place" was precisely where she stood now.

When she lifted her eyes to the scene in front of her, that feeling of unworthiness only intensified. She'd thought herself quite clever, putting up her hair in ribbons, with curls carefully crafted in papers the night before. Around her, she saw perfect, fat sausage curls dangling from exquisite coiffures, decorated with flowers real and silk, ribbons dyed with colors far richer and more exotic than the pink and faded beetroot she'd employed.

When the other ladies moved, their every step swayed with grace. They all seemed clean and crisp at the edges. Even from several feet away, she smelled ambergris and rich food.

And then there was the room itself. It fit as many people as the most crowded London street. She'd never seen so large a space indoors. Jenny followed the lines of the high Ionic columns ringing the room up, and up, and up, to a gilt-decorated ceiling towering five times her height in the air. It made her feet sweat. There was no reason for vertigo to afflict her when she was safely on the ground, looking up.

But it did.

Her fingers tightened on Lord Blakely's elbow.

"Don't fear, Mrs. Barnard," he said coldly. "We'll get you married off in no time."

It took Jenny a heartbeat to remember *she* was supposed to be Mrs. Barnard. *"What?"*

"Isn't that why we've brought you here? What think you, Ned? Are we bringing our distant cousin here in search of a new husband? We must agree on some fiction before we are set upon and introductions are demanded."

"Nonsense," Jenny said. "My husband died only a year ago. I'm uninterested in remarriage, but you've kindly decided to cheer me up."

"Kind?" said Ned. "Blakely? At least pick a tale the *ton* will believe."

Jenny smiled at Ned and transferred her hand to his elbow. "It must have been your idea, my dear."

Lord Blakely scrubbed at the crook of his arm, as if to erase her touch. "Notice, Ned, how easily she lies."

Jenny took a deep breath. Just because she felt like a cow wallowing among swans didn't mean she had to let Lord Blakely intimidate her.

"Oh, Lord Blakely," Jenny said. "You're not smiling. Whatever can we do to increase your enjoyment of this event?"

He opened his mouth, but Jenny cut off whatever he'd planned to say with a delighted clap of her hands. "I know!" she said. "Just the thing to lift your spirits. Shall we check the time?"

Lord Blakely glanced at the clock on the wall, but she shook her head.

"Your fob watch."

After a pause, he pulled a heavy gold watch from his pocket. He flicked it open and contemplated its face. "Well, Mrs. Barnard. Do your worst. It's thirty-eight minutes after ten."

HEADY ANTICIPATION WASHED THROUGH Ned as his cousin looked up from his watch. Only one minute left? Finally, Ned was going to watch his cousin fall in love. Then Blakely would get married and produce heirs. He'd have other people to treat as his inferiors, to inflict with his cold ways and perfect demeanor. Most importantly,

Madame Esmerelda—and Ned himself—would be vindicated.

Had a minute passed yet? Ned checked his impulse to reach for his own timepiece. Madame Esmerelda had said to go by Blakely's watch—and so Blakely's it must be.

But the blasted man had started to flick it back in his pocket. In one swift movement, Ned reached out and tugged the gold disc from Blakely's fingers. It resisted his pull.

Blakely grimaced in annoyance. "Ned, the chain is attached, as you may recall."

How could the man be so bloody *calm?*

Ned set his jaw. "Apologies," he muttered, giving the chain an unapologetic jerk. When Blakely made no move to relinquish control of his watch, Ned added, "Can you unhook that thing? We need it over here."

"My pleasure," Blakely said sarcastically. He made a tremendous fuss and bother of undoing the hook from his buttonhole and lifting the gold chain from his pocket. But all that dithering didn't matter, because the time was—

Still thirty-eight minutes after ten. Ned sighed. Well, little enough time had passed. It shouldn't have come as a surprise that it hadn't been a minute yet.

But just to be sure, Ned checked again.

Indeed. It was still thirty-eight minutes after. Ned sighed in frustration and looked up, scanning the crowd. He wondered which of the ladies he saw was intended for his cousin. None seemed particularly interesting.

"Ned," murmured Madame Esmerelda. "Do you recall what I told you about patience?"

"I *am* being patient," Ned muttered.

She cleared her throat. "Your foot."

Ned blinked, looking down. His damned foot was tapping in frustration. He willed it to stop, and then, because at least two seconds had elapsed, he allowed himself to look down again.

"*Still* thirty-eight after? Blakely, is the damned thing broken?"

Before his cousin could answer, it happened. The minute hand shivered, like a cat preparing to stretch. It trembled. And then… It ticked. A shiver shot through Ned's spine, and he glanced up at Madame Esmerelda.

"The thirty-ninth minute is upon us," Madame Esmerelda intoned.

"And woe betide us, every man." It was a mystery, how Blakely maintained that bored appearance with his future hanging in the balance.

But Madame Esmerelda would handle everything that mattered. Ned turned expectantly to her.

She was scanning the throng. "There," she finally said, pointing one long finger at an exceptionally thick portion of the crowd. "That's her. In the blue. By the wall."

Ned followed the line of her finger. He goggled. Then he gasped, choking on the impossibility of it all.

"Are you perhaps referring to the lady wearing the delightful feathers?" Blakely did not betray so much as a flicker of horror. "She's lovely. I think I'm falling in love already."

"She—I—that—" Ned turned to Madame Esmerelda, his hands aquiver. The incoherent stream of syllables from his mouth refused to resolve into anything so cogent as a complaint. He'd felt doubt before, looking into her wise and knowing face. But all those times, he'd doubted *himself*. He'd doubted he would escape the darkness that periodically captured him.

For one timeless second, though, the cold fingers of uncertainty touched the back of his neck, and Ned doubted *her*. If she'd pointed to a pig, he'd have believed it under an enchanted spell. One that could be broken with a kiss. But she'd picked the one woman who simply could not marry Blakely.

"Of course not her," Madame answered dismissively.

Ned's breath came back in a relieved gasp.

"I meant the *pale* blue. Moving. Right there."

Ned looked over to his left. He could see little more other than a beribboned hairpiece perched atop blond hair, and a blue-and-white gown. From behind, she looked young. She looked slender. When she turned, her gown glinted, and he realized that what he had taken for white fabric rosettes were actually pearls. Whoever she was, she was wealthy.

"Drat," said Blakely. "I had my heart set on Feathers."

Ned squinted across the room. Was Blakely's bride-to-be opening that door? She was. Ned's heart constricted. She was *leaving*.

"Well, Ned," Blakely said, without a care for the fact that his future wife was deserting him, "you queered the deal. Next time, let Madame Esmerelda pronounce without prompting."

Ned gave this inscrutable comment the moment's consideration it deserved, before deciding to ignore it. "What are we waiting for? Let's go."

Neither of his companions moved. Ned put one hand on his hip and gestured in the direction of the lady with Blakely's watch. "She's escaping. Don't you want to meet her?"

"Oh," said Blakely in a depressing tone. "Dear. What ever shall I do?"

Ned stamped his foot. "Nonsense. After her!"

Blakely smoothly plucked his watch from Ned's fingers and dropped it, chain and all, into his pocket. "Do calm yourself, Ned. We will attract more attention than this event warrants if the three of us pelt across the ballroom like dogs on a scent."

Ned scowled. "Madame Esmerelda," he protested, "tell Blakely he has to hurry. The way he's acting is just not *respectful.*"

Madame Esmerelda looked at him. "Ned, take a breath and calm down."

"I'm not—" Ned started, before he realized that he was, in fact, on edge with anticipation. He shut his mouth with a click.

"And, perhaps, Lord Blakely, you could consider putting one foot in front of the other. It would be the rational thing to do. If you must wait for her to come back, you'll have to present your elephant in front of the entire assemblage."

Blakely's lip curled in obvious distaste. "You make an excellent point."

Ned's cousin turned and strolled toward the exit where the blond lady had disappeared. Ned dashed in front of him, ducking between a surprised couple, and around one large man wearing a hideous waistcoat. It didn't take long to wrest open the unobtrusive door in the wall.

He stepped into a deserted servants' corridor, dim and hazy after the well-lit ballroom. The walls were a nondescript whitewash, and the narrow passage stretched before them. Why had she come here?

It didn't matter. Whatever she was doing, she hadn't gone far. She was a scant fifteen feet down the hall. She walked almost noiselessly. Despite the bare wood floors underfoot and the unadorned walls, the quiet tap of her steps faded, folding into the muted roar of the gathering behind them.

Behind him, Blakely's shoes clacked noisily. She heard the sound and paused.

Blakely took advantage of her hesitation. "Pardon me," he called.

The lady turned around slowly. Very slowly. Ned caught his breath. She was younger than he was. Her features seemed almost too sharp, too pronounced. But her eyes were wide and intelligent, and even though she'd been caught alone by three people she did not know, she held her head high and her shoulders straight. She did not speak; instead, she cocked her head, as if silently granting the rabble permission to approach. That aloof calm rendered those sharp features almost beautiful.

With that haughty demeanor, she would make Blakely an excellent marchioness. Ned darted a glance at his cousin. The man seemed unaffected by her elegance.

"I believe you dropped this back in the ballroom." Not an ounce of emotion touched Blakely's voice as he strode toward her, holding the gouged lump of ebony in his hand.

Ned wasn't sure which constituted the greater sacrilege: Blakely's cursory adherence to Madame Esmerelda's tasks, or his ability to remain unruffled when confronting his future wife. Annoyed, Ned scrambled after his cousin.

The lady frowned as Blakely came closer. "I dropped something? How clumsy of me."

Her voice sounded like bells, Ned decided, except not the harsh clanging kind. She put him in mind of clear, high chimes, ringing out in winter weather.

Her gaze fell on the indecipherable object in Blakely's

outstretched hand. That perfect brow furrowed in consternation. "I dropped that? I think *not*." A discordant note sounded in those bells.

Blakely shrugged. "As you wish." He swiveled from her.

The effrontery of the man! He wasn't even trying to give Madame Esmerelda's prediction a fair chance.

Ned clamped his hand about his cousin's wrist and turned him back around. "Oh, I think so. Where else could it have come from?"

Aside from Blakely's pocket. Or any of the fifteen other sources that sprang to mind.

"I assure you," she said with some asperity, "if that object had belonged to me, I shouldn't have waited until I attended a ball to dispose of it. Even if I had dropped it, I would never admit prior ownership when questioned."

"Well." Ned drew out the syllable and squared his shoulders. "If you didn't drop it, you must accept it."

Her lips thinned. "Why?"

Why? Damnation.

"I can't think of any reason," Blakely interjected. His gaze seemed subtly mocking. Ned's stomach sank. His cousin would continue to perform all his tasks in this halfhearted fashion. He had no intention of taking Madame Esmerelda's strictures seriously. He intended to do the bare minimum, and no more.

But Madame Esmerelda was right. She saw the future. She *had* to do so. Because if she were wrong about Blakely, then her prediction about Ned was suspect, too. And that he could not bear.

Ned plucked the ebony from his cousin's hand and held it out. There was only one thing for it. He was going to have to do all the work.

"Unfortunately—" Ned sighed "—there's no good reason. You're just going to have to take it anyway."

She peered at the unfortunate lump of wood. "What is that thing, anyway?"

"What do you think it is?"

The lady reached out one slim finger and tapped the dark surface. She pulled back the digit immediately, as if she'd tapped a hot stove. "It appears to be some sort of round, pockmarked, misbegotten, battle-blackened...citrus?"

"You see?" Triumph boiled up in Ned and he poked Blakely in the lapels. "She knew! She knew it was an elephant! You can't possibly deny Madame Esmerelda's power now!"

That, at least, finally got a response from Blakely. The man shut his eyes and covered his face with a hand.

The lady frowned. "An orange is an elephant?"

She was intimidating and elegant. Ned imagined the figure he must cut in her eyes. Boyishly skinny. Overshadowed by his taller cousin. Awkward, ungainly, and just a little too loud at all the wrong times. Most especially at this moment. He flushed from head to toe.

"Yes," Ned said. His voice still rang too loudly.

At precisely the same moment, Blakely said, "No."

She stared at the two men. "You," she said stabbing a finger at Ned, "are mad. You—" pointing at Blakely this time "—are tainted by association. And you—" here, she pointed at Madame Esmerelda standing behind them "—are very quiet. As for me, I am leaving."

If she left now, fate and all the angels in heaven couldn't bring her together with Blakely.

"Wait," Ned called. "We haven't been introduced! And you didn't take your elephant."

She turned around again. "No, we haven't been introduced. And I certainly couldn't accept a gift from a stranger."

Ned bit his cheeks and wondered if he could possibly—please?—disappear on the spot. "Oh, that stupid rule doesn't matter here. It's only applicable to nice things. Clothing or jewelry or the like. This is a piece of rubbish."

She stared at Ned and shook her head. "You really are mad."

"Yes," he agreed through gritted teeth. "Now humor the madman, and take the dam— I mean, take the dratted elephant."

She contemplated him for a long moment. Then, surprisingly, dimples formed on her cheeks. She did not smile, but her eyes sparkled. And she placed her gloved hand, palm out, in front of her.

He dropped the wood into her hand. "There," Ned said. "Now it's *your* misbegotten lump of citrus."

She looked up. Her eyes were gray, and Ned had the sudden impression that she saw right into his heart. That organ thumped heavily under her observation. Ned swallowed, and the world slowed.

Then she dropped a curtsy. "Thank you," she said prettily. She turned. Ned watched her leave. She strode as confidently as a queen. Ned felt humiliated and exposed. It was only when she turned the corner that he realized that they'd still not been introduced. Of course not. He'd just painted himself as the biggest fool in London. Who would want to make an acquaintance of him?

Not that it mattered. It was Blakely who was fated to have her. He could have her; he'd match her, his intimidating glares bouncing off her cold elegance. No doubt Blakely would fall in love with her.

He turned to his cousin. "Someday," Ned said bitterly, "you are going to thank me for what I just did for you."

Blakely gestured sardonically. "I wouldn't wager on that, were I you. For now, I'll thank you to head back to the ball."

CHAPTER FIVE

BEFORE JENNY SET FOOT back in the ballroom, bringing up the rear of their party, they were accosted. Lord Blakely swung the door open into the bright hall, and a voice called out.

"Blakely," said the woman, "why are you hiding in the servants' quarters? And why didn't you tell me you were attending tonight?"

Lord Blakely stopped so abruptly that Jenny nearly ran into him from behind. As she stumbled forward into the open hall, the lights dazzled her eyes. It took a moment to adjust from the dim illumination of the corridor, and when she was finally able to see who had confronted them—or, rather, who had confronted the marquess, she coughed.

It was Feathers. The woman in blue, the one she'd pointed to before Ned's choking reaction and Lord Blakely's own smooth acceptance convinced her to change her mind.

Feathers was not pretty. Despite her fresh-faced youth, her features were too angular to qualify for that label. But she gleamed with a sleek, polished air that would have made even the plainest lady pleasant to look at. She looked almost as imposing as Lord Blakely, dressed as she was in a fine light blue gown embroidered at the edges with flowers, and littered with silk rosettes. Luminescent pearls shone about her neck. Sandy brown hair was bound up in a tight mess of curls, from which her namesake—three waving peacock feathers—bobbed.

She was definitely not pretty, but she was striking in a way that struck Jenny as oddly familiar.

And yet Feathers showed not one iota of the confidence her dress and ramrod-straight posture should have imparted. Even younger than Ned, she ducked her shoulders and smiled, a universal signal that she was eager to please.

Here was a puzzle. For all her fine demeanor, Lord Blakely's earlier behavior suggested the lady was somehow unsuitable for marriage. But the lady had called him by the familiar "Blakely." And he hadn't corrected the importunity with typical frosty disdain.

Light dawned. No wonder she seemed so familiar. And no wonder the marquess had wanted Jenny to pick this woman.

"Lord Blakely," Jenny said. "You never told me you had a sister."

"See?" Ned flung his hands in the air. "How can you disbelieve her? I never said a word of it!"

Feathers eyed Jenny with open curiosity. "The rumor that swept the ballroom is that this lady is a distant cousin. I didn't know we had any Barnards in our family."

Lord Blakely grimaced. "Restrain yourself, Ned. Do recall we are at a very crowded ball. And, Laura, she is not your cousin."

The lady sighed. "Carhart side? Still, a cousin of yours is a cousin of mine." She looked at Jenny and smiled almost shyly. "Isn't that just like my brother, to ignore me when I'm so obviously angling for an introduction? What is Ned jabbering on about?"

Ned put his hands on his hips. "Well, don't ask the

great Marquess of Blakely for explanations. Or introductions. He can't even be bothered to deliver his own elephants. He doesn't believe anything unless it's right in front of his nose."

The blue feathers in the lady's coiffure bobbed earnestly. "Oh, don't I know." She glanced at Jenny again, and then imparted in confiding tones. "He doesn't even trust my fiancé to handle my funds in the future. He doesn't trust anything he can't see and smell and taste."

Lord Blakely didn't act either to scold or to assuage his sister's obvious worries as to how her teasing would be received.

"Actually," Jenny interjected earnestly, "he's even more discriminating than that."

Lord Blakely's shoulders stiffened. His lips pressed together and a furious warning lit his eyes. Jenny met his angry gaze and dropped one lid in a lazy half-wink.

"Believe me," she said. "He really *doesn't* believe everything he tastes."

Lord Blakely's mouth dropped open a fraction. His eyes dropped to her lips; he was undoubtedly remembering the hot openmouthed kiss they'd shared. He froze, almost as if he'd experienced a great stabbing pain. And then a miracle occurred.

He smiled.

The expression changed his whole face from serious and frozen to warm and tinged with the pink of embarrassment. The effect was immediate and electric. He looked almost ten years younger. Jenny's toes curled in her uncomfortable heeled slippers and she caught her breath.

No wonder the man never grinned. He would have posed a serious danger to womankind if he did so more than once a decade.

He blinked, horrified, as he suddenly realized what he was doing. The corners of his lips turned down sharply. He blew out his breath and turned abruptly to his sister.

"If I failed to greet you earlier, Laura, it was precisely to avoid this moment. I have no intention of introducing you to this woman."

Jenny felt as if she'd been smacked with an icicle. It was almost as if she'd been back at school. As if the girls were talking about *that Jenny Keeble* again, pretending Jenny was not standing right in front of them.

The feathers drooped as Laura bowed her head. "Surely, in the family—"

Lord Blakely interposed his body between Jenny and his sister. He dropped his voice, but pitched his words loud enough for Jenny to hear. She had no doubt he intended her to absorb every last hateful sentence. "She's not a Carhart cousin, either. She's not any sort of relation. She's a fraudulent fortune-teller who has sunk her claws into Ned, and she's not fit for you to know."

Not fit. Every word he said was undoubtedly true. It still hurt, scraping a wound that was raw even after a dozen years. Jenny had run away from school to escape the snide remarks about her family and her likely fate. Even after all these years, it stung to hear them repeated.

"Oh, dear." Laura peered around the marquess's lean form. "Do you really tell fortunes? Can you tell mine? Do you pay house calls, or shall I visit you?"

Jenny could imagine Lord Blakely's teeth grinding.

"She's fabulous at it," Ned answered. "Two years and she's never been wrong. And now she's predicted Blakely's marriage."

The marquess winced. "Hush," he remonstrated. "There's no need to shout—"

But his sister's eyes lit up like two candles. "You want Blakely to marry? Capital! I knew I liked you." She side-stepped her brother and linked her arm in Jenny's.

Jenny looked at the arm in hers. She was too shocked to do anything other than goggle. She hadn't expected a friendly face smiling into hers after the marquess's cold dismissal. A lump formed in her throat.

Naturally, Lord Blakely interrupted.

"Mrs. *Barnard*," he emphasized coldly, offering her his arm, "I do believe we have terms to discuss. Laura, I'll see you—I'll see you next month."

The smile slowly slipped off his sister's face as she re-alized she'd been dismissed. She unlocked her arm from Jenny's, pausing only to give Jenny's hand a squeeze. Her brother's visage darkened at the gesture.

He opened the servants' door they had just come through and led Jenny a few steps down the dim hall be-fore brushing her hand off his arm and turning to tower over her. He stood inches away, his features implacable.

"Ned is one matter," Lord Blakely said. "He is my re-sponsibility. Do not doubt that no matter what else may occur between you and me, I will eradicate your influ-ence over him. But my sister…"

"Your sister seems a pleasant enough young woman."

His lip curled. *"Miss Edmonton,"* he emphasized icily, "is no consideration of yours. She is my junior by sixteen years, and I don't mean to see her hurt. I tell you this as a warning, not an invitation. Interfere with my sister, and I will destroy you."

Jenny put her hands on her hips. "Is that what you think I see when I look at her? A potential dupe?"

"I saw the way you looked at her when she took your arm. As if she'd handed you a gift."

Jenny looked down to hide the sharp pain in her eyes. She felt like the twisting fibers in the carpet at her feet—threadbare and a bit frayed. In Lord Blakely's scintillating world, both it and she would have been traded to the ragman. "I bow to your perceptive talent, Lord Blakely. It takes a special sort of intellect to make out only the worst in those around you."

"Is that what you think I'm about?" He took her chin, turning Jenny's face toward his. She couldn't escape that searching gaze. "I can't risk your lies on this point."

Lies. Jenny swallowed shame. He dismissed her so easily. In a way, she shouldn't have been surprised. She knew how the upper classes saw her all too well.

She'd given up on being good because her behavior made no difference. No matter how kind or good or sincere she may have been, they would all condemn her just the same. No matter what she did, she would remain baseborn, her parents unknown to her. What had she to lose by becoming a fraud?

If a gentleman saw her as anything other than an extra panel on the wainscoting, he saw what Lord Blakely did—a potential vessel for his seed, worthy of his notice only for the space of time it took to use her for sexual release. She'd escaped their world, but the only thing that had changed was the face of the man making the offer.

A week ago, Lord Blakely had seen clear through to the truth of her lonely childhood. Now he deemed her unworthy. Looking up into his eyes, she felt the most awful desire to kiss him. It was like the urge to pick off a scab—painful, idiotic and sure to start the bleeding all over again. Had she really been stupid enough to think this man different?

Aside from the sheer physical heat that dwelt between them, he was exactly like everyone she'd ever known.

"Tell me," he growled at her. "Tell me truthfully you'll not interfere with her."

No. Not exactly alike.

There was one way he differed. He deemed her unworthy, but she was not alone in receiving his condemnation. Ned, his sister—he'd spoken harshly of them both. To him, *everyone* was wainscoting. He might as well have been alone in that crowded room out there.

His fingers dug into her chin. "Say the words," he ordered.

She wondered, suddenly, how he saw himself. Cold, undoubtedly. Different, and superior to everyone else. He saw himself as the kind of man who could make a woman scream while he experienced little more than inconvenient lust. Maybe Lord Blakely despised lesser mortals who let their control lapse into such gauche and unforgivable errors as the giving of trust, the acceptance of affection.

The poor man.

"I don't see your sister as a potential mark, my lord. My only surprise is that you do."

He searched her eyes in the dim light. He must have found the truth in them, because he released her chin.

Jenny rubbed the spots where his fingers had pressed. Five points were emblazoned into her jaw. It hadn't been painful, but she felt humiliated. After all these years, she should have been used to the feeling. At least, she thought bitterly, Lord Blakely had some real reason besides her birth to believe her dishonest.

He shook his head disdainfully. "I try to see the truth even in those I care for. I have no desire to fool myself. What else should I see?"

There were a million answers. Jenny hesitated, searching for the perfect response. Finally, she picked the cruelest possibility. She picked the truth.

"I thought you would see a younger sister who, despite everything you said to her, still adores you."

His lips whitened. His hands clenched.

Oh, he strove to hide it. But that miserable flinch showed that Lord Blakely *could* care about someone, much as he tried to deny it.

This tantrum, she realized, was her punishment, unjustly meted out for winning his smile. For breathing warmth into the ice of Lord Blakely. It was his rage, that he'd caused his sister pain, when he'd meant only to keep her safe. Jenny was not the object of his anger, just its recipient. It shouldn't have made her feel better, to play the scapegoat. And yet it did.

Jenny stretched up and placed her hand against his cheek. A moment of heat; a hint of stubbled roughness.

And then he recoiled as if a beetle crawled across his skin.

Yes. She was going to make him pay for this moment in the very currency he rejected. Heat. Smiles. And, oh—perhaps just a touch of humiliation. He must have seen the promise in her eyes because he backed away.

"Think whatever you like," he said, retreating toward the crowded, well-lit hall. "Just stay away from my sister."

JENNY'S HEAD ACHED from exhaustion. Only the sharp chill of the evening and the throb in her feet kept her from falling asleep while standing. Her little party waited for Lord Blakely's carriage on the stone path leading away from the ball. She'd come from a room crowded with oppressively bright fabrics, rich dyes, jewels and food that must have taken the poor servants days to prepare. But just outside those white stone walls, Mayfair shared the same night as all of England.

No amount of money could drive away the pervasive London fog that shrouded the street in dimness. In the darkness of night, lords and commoners looked much the same.

There were differences. Ned drooped next to Jenny. He yawned; his teeth reflected dim gaslight from the windows behind him. But Lord Blakely stood as straight and crisp as he had at the start of the evening. Jenny was willing to wager his feet didn't ache in the slightest. Unsurprising; if they were cut from the same stone as his features, they likely lacked nerves with which to feel pain.

"I looked for her," Ned mumbled through a yawn. "But I couldn't find her again. Now how do we track her down?"

Lord Blakely looked straight ahead into the gloom. "Simple. We ask for Lady Kathleen Dunning. She's the Duke of Ware's daughter, and it appears she's made her come-out this year."

"Good." Ned yawned again. "Your way is clear. Now where's the carriage?"

Lord Blakely clasped his gloved fingers together. "Coming 'round the corner. Right…now."

At Ned's startled glance, Lord Blakely sighed. "I heard it coming. I know the gait of my own cattle. And if you'd pay any attention to your surroundings, you'd know it, too. Just as you'd know your dear Madame Esmerelda nearly matched me with my own sister. Had you not called attention to the matter with your coughing and hacking, you'd have undeniable proof of her lack of skill at this moment."

That, at least, Jenny told herself, was unfair. She'd been warned off the lady in question the instant Lord Blakely pretended interest.

"Even then," Ned mused, "I was wondering—can you unmake sisters the same way you make them?"

A long exhalation from Lord Blakely. "*Make* sisters?"

"I read about it in a book of Norse mythology. Well, I read about brothers, really, and the making of a blood oath. You cut your palms until they bleed, and press them together so the blood mingles—"

"More claptrap. Must you believe everything you read? One cannot manufacture brotherhood. It arises out of biology and breeding. As you would surely know if you thought at all."

Ned tried not to react, but Jenny could read his hurt in the turn of his shoulders away from the approaching conveyance. And when it rumbled to a stop, Ned's fingers clenched hers in bitter shame as he handed her in. Lord Blakely arranged himself precisely on the opposite seat, unaware of the devastation he'd wrought.

Oh, yes. Jenny was going to make him pay.

She leaned forward. "Lord Blakely," she said, "for all your rational bent, I notice you're hard at work performing your own particular sort of alchemical magic."

The marquess's hand dropped slowly to his knee. "I beg your pardon? Did you accuse me of alchemy?"

"Yes, Master Paracelsus, I believe I did."

"Explain yourself." His words huffed out, colder than the clammy fog enveloping their carriage.

"The typical alchemist attempts to transmute lead into gold. But, being stubborn and perverse, you of course have insisted on reversing the process."

"You're talking nonsense."

When Jenny had said the words, she hadn't known what she intended. But there he was, attempting to distance himself from any hint of irrationality. A plan burst into her mind, brilliant as the midday sun.

"Oh, you'll figure it out," she said. She grinned so hard her cheeks hurt. "I'm speaking of the second task."

For several seconds, the only sound was the clatter of their passage over cobblestones.

"You want me to convert gold into lead?" A hint of bafflement; a touch of disappointment. "I suppose, I should be delighted you have been defeated so easily. After all, if something downright impossible is a precondition for your prediction, you admit your fortune-telling will never come to pass."

Jenny leaned forward and patted his cheek. "Oh," she said, "you silly naturalist. Are you always so literal-minded? I've watched you turn gold to lead ever since I met you."

As she'd hoped, he growled deep in his throat in response. The vibration rumbled through the hand she had rested on his cheek. It served him right; he subjected everyone around him to his constant arrogance. It was her turn to give him a taste of his own condescension, and see how well he liked it.

"I do hope you're planning to give more explanation than that. Those of us who are dangerously literal require something less ambiguous than an occult mumble."

"I've watched your interactions with your cousin all this time. Anyone can see Ned has a heart of pure gold."

Ned made an embarrassed motion with his hands—adolescent language Jenny deciphered as "I would rather be stabbed to death with a toasting-fork than receive an honest compliment."

"Given your constant criticism and bullying, I can only conclude that through some arcane alchemical process, you are intent on transforming your cousin into some baser metal."

"A diverting analogy, Madame Esmerelda." There was no amusement in Lord Blakely's harsh voice. "I assume you are getting to the part where you explain the task?"

"Change lead back into gold," Jenny said. "Simple, is it not?"

He tapped his lips, working through the implications. "You want me to find something good to say about Ned here?" His dubious tone implied the task she'd set was as impossible as alchemy.

That, above all, was why she'd assigned it. She'd learned early on that telling her clients what they wanted to hear produced more income. But when she said those nice things, she'd begun to believe them herself. The act of searching for good engaged her sympathies. If the same happened with this arrogant man, it would be a fine start on his payments.

Thinking of his debt sparked a second gleeful, wicked impulse inside Jenny. *Humiliation, too.* "Oh, the process should be more open than that, don't you think? The spirits demand that you sing his praises in public."

"Announce it? Well." He appeared to consider this. "I suppose I could manage a public compliment or two."

"My comments about transmutation were metaphorical. But when I told you to *sing* his praises, I meant that. Literally."

The stony silence was broken only by the muted clop of the horses' hooves. Even that sound seemed dampened, as if the animals knew better than to interrupt their master's fury.

Lord Blakely drew himself up, a frightening tower on the opposite seat of the carriage. "You want me to *sing?* In public?"

"An ode of your own composition, if you please." She smiled at him.

No answer. He sat in baffled outrage. A streetlamp they passed sent a rectangle of light over his hands, where they quivered on his knees. The horses clacked on, a serene counterpoint to the tension building in the close quarters.

"You're trying to humiliate me."

Absolutely. Among other things.

"It won't work," he told her. "Better men than you have tried and failed."

Jenny shook her head. This was an even better idea than the elephant. The horses drew up as they reached Jenny's home. As the footman opened the carriage door, Jenny delivered her deathblow.

"Oh, and, Lord Blakely?"

No acknowledgment. Not even a twitch of an eyelash in her direction.

Jenny grinned and wagged a finger. "You are required to mean every word."

CHAPTER SIX

GARETH STARED GLUMLY at the two sheets of paper laid in front of him. His desk was laden with hundreds of other papers, all demanding his attention. Both Lord Blakely's work for the estate and his personal scientific correspondence weighed heavily on his shoulders. But his mind was blank. Depressingly blank, like the sheets in front of him.

That was what he deserved, he supposed, for playing truant from the estate work that should have taken up the bulk of his afternoon. But Madame Esmerelda's task, assigned late the previous evening, had tied his mind in knots.

It had not taken him long to figure out how to sing without humiliation. But the subject matter…

"Good things about Ned," he'd labeled the mostly blank page. And then he'd numbered one through fifteen down the side of the page. It was precisely the method he'd employed earlier that day, when he'd labeled a page "Possible Explanations for Swallow Migration (Taking into Account Known Patterns)." Except he hadn't stared at that page for half an hour without the slightest inkling of how to proceed. He'd filled that sheet of paper in minutes.

Things that were good about Ned. Hmm. It would

have been much easier, and more satisfying, to sing a song about things that were wrong—*desperately* wrong—with Madame Esmerelda.

Across from Gareth, his man of business quietly and efficiently sorted through correspondence. William White was young for his position—scarcely older than Gareth—but intelligent and well-versed in modern innovations. His dark hair had been clipped close to his head. He bent over the desk industriously. No doubt he imagined Gareth was addressing matters of similar gravity. Gareth had no desire to disillusion the man.

Two tasks left. He didn't have to complete them; he could walk away at any time. But if he did, Ned would continue to consult the woman, and worse—if he gave up, she would win.

He couldn't let her do that. He just had to start writing.

Ned is not so bad to see.

There. A first line. It had a nice trochaic meter to it, if he did say so himself. It wasn't, perhaps, the greatest compliment one man had ever delivered to another, but he wasn't about to wax rhapsodic over Ned's curly brown locks. Gareth had a certain amount of dignity to maintain, after all.

Now all he needed was a rhyme.

Ned is not so bad to see.

That's because he looks like me.

It wasn't quite true, of course; Ned had a few years yet to grow into the breadth of Gareth's shoulders. But it rhymed and had meter. And it was a compliment.

The only problem Gareth saw—well, perhaps not the *only* problem, but at least one major one—was that when Madame Esmerelda said to write his cousin an ode, she hadn't intended Gareth to identify all the ways he and his cousin were similar. She demanded he turn Ned to gold. Transmuting Ned into Gareth would be unlikely to pass muster, and the thought of being forced to repeat the song horrified him.

Reluctantly, Gareth crumpled the sheet of paper in front of him.

"White."

His man of business looked up, his pen arrested mid-dip in the inkwell. "My lord?"

Tell me all the good things about my cousin.

No. That would be cheating. He'd carved his own elephant. By God, he'd write his own ode to Ned.

"What rhymes with 'trusting'?" he asked.

The ever-efficient White didn't even need a moment to think. "Lusting. Disgusting."

Gareth took another leaf of paper from his drawer and began to write.

My cousin Ned is not disgusting.

Even if he is too trusting.

Also not the most complimentary of couplets. Gareth gritted his teeth and crumpled this second piece of paper.

"My lord." White's tone was cautious, undoubtedly chosen to keep carefully within the bounds of his station. "Are you writing a *poem?*"

"No." Gareth scowled at the desk in front of him.

First, he wasn't writing it. He was failing to write it. Second, it was an ode rather than a poem. And third, even if he were writing a poem, he saw no point in letting the man know. Because if he shared one irrelevant detail with his staff, they would expect others. Pretty soon, Gareth would be nattering on about all sorts of things.

Like the fact that he was writing the ode to his ridiculous cousin. And soon he'd whine that he had been coerced into writing it by the most annoying woman ever to walk the face of the planet.

And the last thing he wanted to discuss with his man of business was Madame Esmerelda. Because after he'd raved about how impossible she was, he might add that when she'd left his carriage the previous night, he'd been too struck by that sudden mischievous grin on her face to do anything but imagine her in the gown she *should* have chosen, shoulders exposed to his touch, skirts puffed out by multiple layers that he could remove one by one to reveal petal-smooth skin...

White still watched him, interest sparkling in his eyes.

For one stupid second, Gareth thought about telling the man everything. The thought of confiding in him— a servant, a lesser man—sent shivers down his spine. He silently damned Madame Esmerelda again. "I am not writing a poem," Gareth said stiffly.

"As you say, my lord." White turned back to his work.

His oppressive tone had worked. It always did. The last thing he needed was to start seeing unasked-for good in those around him. He liked being solitary. He liked not confiding in anyone. And damn it, he had no desire to change.

THE LIVERIED FOOTMAN—or foot*boy,* Jenny supposed she should call him—delivered the message to Jenny's door just before ten in the morning. For a moment, she hoped it came from one of her regular clients, expecting to schedule an appointment to see her. There were several she hadn't seen in months, and she wondered how one client in particular, a shy, unassuming woman named Mrs. Sevin, had fared with her husband.

But the words were written in a precise hand that could only have belonged to Lord Blakely.

Have finished ode. Musicale tomorrow at 7 PM. You will attend. -B.

He assumed she was his to command. What if she had made an appointment for that time? Jenny wished she had, so that she'd be able to prove that she had a life separate from his, that she existed for a reason besides satisfying his whims.

The note was accompanied by a bulky brown package tied with heavy twine. The boy—really, he couldn't have been any older than seventeen—pushed the bundle at her. An errant hank of blond hair had escaped from under the boy's white wig. He tried to look composed. But no matter how stiff and straight he held his spine, he could not hide the fact that his red velvet uniform was much the worse from traversing the streets. Dots of muck— possibly manure—flecked the tails of his coat. He still cut a finer figure than Jenny.

She took the package. Harsh bits of twine cut her fingers as she pulled at the hard knots, and the paper crinkled, creased, and finally gave way. The package contained a gown. And some other things—silk stockings and heeled shoes and a proper corset. The dress was carefully folded, but Jenny could already see it would pose a problem. It was a complicated gown, with tapes and laces and gold-colored piping outlining seams between red-and-cream stripes.

She sighed. Lord Blakely was generally observant and reasonably intelligent. What had happened?

"Is there to be a reply? His lordship told me I was to bring any such back." The boy was too well-trained to fidget. Instead, he stood unusually still, his back held in a rigid posture of attention that would have suited a sergeant better than a seventeen-year-old.

Jenny flipped the note over and scrawled her response on the back.

Unfortunately, I cannot wear this dress. Enjoy your evening. Yrs, etc.

She handed the note—and the package—back to the servant.

He gave an undignified gulp and shook his head. "But that's for you."

Jenny shook her head. "Not anymore, it isn't. Now it's for Lord Blakely. Do you think he'll look well in it?"

Those well-trained eyes blanked in evasive consternation.

"No, you're right," Jenny said. "The gown's too short for him."

Boyishly puffy cheeks swelled in affront. The idea of *laughing* at Lord Blakely strained his mental abilities. Jenny sighed. Apparently, Lord Blakely's predisposition toward dour looks was not an inherited condition. He spread it like some unhealthy contagion.

"Return it," she said. "I'm not keeping it, and he'll want to know." She gave him a smile to soften the blow. Perhaps those could be contagious, too.

But the boy didn't respond with a similar expression. Instead, he gave her a brisk, businesslike nod and set off at a lope.

It was nearly an hour before the footboy returned. His livery had lost any hint of crispness in the streets. His boots were covered in mud, clear up to his calves, and the red-and-gold coat was damp and dripping from the pervasive fog. And he was still carrying that brown package, much worse for the journey. A second note was tucked on top.

He thrust his armload at Jenny. She took it and plucked the piece of paper from where it had been secured under the twine.

Irrational. Unethical. Really, Madame Esmerelda, there's no need to add "tedious" to your many sins. -B.

Tedious? Well. If there was anything more tedious than conducting this exchange via drooping delivery boy, Jenny couldn't think of it. She pushed the wrapped gown back at the boy, but he raised his hands and stepped back.

"No, ma'am. I'm not to take it back. His lordship said so. He also said I was to tell you there would be no further debate, and he'll accept your thanks along with your agreement."

Jenny tapped her foot. Clearly Lord Blakely thought she was engaging in recalcitrance for the sake of recalcitrance. It wasn't a poor guess on his part; it just wasn't true in this particular instance. Well. She was not expecting clients to come by until the next morning.

If his servant wouldn't tote the dress back, Jenny had little choice. Lord Blakely had no one to blame but himself.

"Will you wait for my reply?" Jenny asked.

He nodded, and Jenny dashed into action. She donned half boots and grabbed a heavy shawl and a bonnet. The footman bit his lip in growing trepidation.

"Right," Jenny said, hefting the package into her arms. "I'm ready."

"Um." The boy scuffed his boots against her floor.

"Well? Lead on."

"But—"

"None of that, now. He told you to bring the reply. The reply is me. He'll fume if he doesn't hear what I have to say."

His gaze flicked up and down, from her head to toe. Even

in his soiled state, he still looked grander than Jenny in her faded clothing. "He'll fume if he does," he finally said.

"Yes, but he'll fume at me."

That argument apparently carried the day. He shook his head, straightened his wig, and set off down the street at a brisk pace. Jenny followed. As the journey went on, the streets became cleaner and the houses larger. By the time they reached Mayfair, the rows of stolid houses rose over her head like a military encampment, heavy stone walls stretching up past the tops of the trees. Flowers bloomed. The squares were carefully curried: bushes trimmed to exacting geometric shapes, bits of lawn clipped to perfect smoothness.

The people they passed on the streets no doubt took Jenny for some kind of a delivery girl. Their eyes slipped right past her, as if she didn't exist. After all, she carried a heavy package, and the washed-out pattern of her unfashionable skirts proclaimed her a member of the servant class.

Jenny felt increasingly out of place. The hem of her skirt was muddied, and her sturdy blouse was cut from heavy material designed to last for years. Its color had dulled to a nondescript gray.

That feeling of bone-deep dinginess only intensified as the footboy darted alongside a tall mausoleum of gray-streaked stone. She ducked after him, down a set of stairs and through the servants' entrance. They entered an unaccountably clean pantry, its shelves stocked with dry goods. Two maids in the doorway took one look at Jenny and fell to squawking. They waved their arms and directed her to a corner of the kitchen where she was instructed to remove her muddy boots. As she undid the laces, a heated conference developed in the corner. A dour-faced butler appeared. He was gesticulating at a matronly housekeeper. Neither smiled. There was talk from the butler of his high-and-mighty lordship, who must not be disturbed at any cost. The poor master was working, agreed the housekeeper, and if he didn't take time to eat—

They weren't debating whether to let her upstairs to face Lord Blakely's wrath. They were wondering whether to throw her out now, or let her clean up and warm by the fire first.

Jenny set her muddy boots in the corner. Thankfully, it hadn't been so wet that her stockings were damp. They were still clean and serviceable. She had nothing to be ashamed of. She drew herself up, channeling Madame Esmerelda's outward poise. There was no reason to be intimidated by this household, caught as it was in the contagious grip of a bad case of Lord Blakely's grims.

Well, no reason other than the crisp starch of the scullery maids' uniforms. And the gleam of scrubbed copper pots. And the wide, warm kitchen, larger than her rooms put together and trebled, smelling of the sort of savory things Jenny had only read about in books.

The poor footboy had been pulled into the argument. He did not hunch; that would have been poor posture. But he did bend enough to look unhappy.

Jenny glanced across the room and spotted a narrow servants' staircase. Somewhere above her, Lord Blakely prowled. Her skin pricked at the thought of him pacing in some room above her head, unaware how near she was. How would he react? Badly, she supposed. How far away was he? If she knew him at all, she'd wager he had a study tucked at the back of the house, away from all the noise and bother of the street. Undoubtedly, he'd also receive men of business there. The first floor would be most convenient for that.

Jenny sauntered carefully across the room, hugging the bulky package to her chest. If anyone asked, she would say she planned to set it on one of those wide counters. She stopped, pretending to ogle her distorted reflection in the side of one of the copper pots. Nobody paid her any mind. She was as invisible now as she'd been on the streets of Mayfair.

Good.

She very carefully didn't look at the stairs until she stood at the bottom. Then, before anyone could stop her, she pounded up them and out the scullery door.

Shouts erupted behind her.

She threw open another door across the way before anyone could follow her.

The hallway she entered was part of the family quarters. Landscapes hung in polished, pristine wood frames, showing idyllic scenes of a countryside Jenny had never known. Her stockinged feet sank into a rich, thick carpet. To the right lay the entry, where two additional liveried footmen turned to face her. Jenny turned left and dashed to the back of the house. She opened one door. There was a large rectangular dining table, the sort that could seat an entire legion of soldiers. She swiveled and faced one last door. Her heart pounded from exertion, and her breath burned in her lungs. It was this, or nothing.

The handle turned smoothly.

Jenny's vision swam. In front of her were books. Books. Books. Books—and Blakely. Light from the fire glinted off his tawny hair. Here in his study he seemed relaxed, almost boyish. He looked very different from the cold man who'd last confronted her. The lines of his face were freed from some subtle tension and his lips were parted. Something inside her chest froze painfully at the sight. She had a sudden vision of the marquess hiding behind a solid facade of arrogance every time he went in society.

She could not shake the feeling that this man, stripped of the cold shell that surrounded him, was the true Lord Blakely.

He was seated at a heavy desk, paper piled in front of him. Paper on the table; on the chairs. Even stacked neatly on the floor. He scratched intently away with a dip pen. He didn't look up at her entrance. Instead his hand moved protectively over the documents before him as they rustled in the draft of the door's opening. She slipped inside and shut the door.

"Well," came that precise drawl, "did she send a reply? And what had she to say for herself?" Still he did not look up.

Jenny stepped forward, clutching the paper package.

"She says, I *can't* wear this dress."

That brought his head up, his eyes widening in shock. For one instant, his mouth opened in a near welcome. Then that protective armor slammed into place. His spine stiffened.

If she had any sense, she would have been intimidated. But he wasn't looking through her. He didn't see a delivery girl, no matter how faded the color of Jenny's blouse. His lips parted, almost in welcome; his gaze took her in from muddied skirts on up. He focused on her with almost savage intensity. Intensity, Jenny could handle. It was indifference that would have sunk her. She tossed the parcel on his desk. Papers scattered.

He grabbed for them. "You! You can't come in here."

"Why not? After all, *you* invaded my rooms without invitation the other night."

"That was different. I—"

"Oh, yes. It was different. It was different because you are six inches taller than me, three stone heavier and twice as strong. And *I* was all alone, whereas you are surrounded by staff who will no doubt pour through that door in a matter of seconds, ready to send me away."

He set his pen down.

Jenny took off her shawl and looped it over a stack of books. His eyes dropped to her damp blouse. The garment clung to her breasts. His gaze rested there, an almost palpable touch against her hardening nipples.

"No, my lord, when you say it is different, you mean that *you* are Lord Blakely and I am nobody."

"Quite." Ice and steel in his tone, belied by that gaze, still fixed on her bosom. There was a hint of his former vulnerability in that look, a youthfulness that he had not managed to dispel.

She wanted to crack the solid casing that surrounded him. And now, he'd shown her how to do it.

Jenny lifted one foot and set her toes on the edge of a chair. The motion pulled her skirt just above her ankle, and his gaze traveled to her foot and arrested on that hint of stocking-clad limb. His mouth opened and he leaned forward.

"And yet," Jenny said softly, "it was not Lord Blakely who offered to seduce me, was it? It was *Gareth*."

On this cue, the door burst open and the butler burst into the room. He grabbed Jenny's arm in a bruising grip and jerked her. Jenny's ankle twisted against the chair's upholstery, and she barely managed to keep her balance.

"My lord," the man panted, "my apologies. We'll take her out directly."

Lord Blakely tore his eyes from Jenny's stockinged ankle. What flickered in those golden-brown depths was no emotion she could identify.

"Ah," Lord Blakely said softly. "Will you?"

The butler wrenched her shoulder in its socket, but Jenny pulled back, holding her ground.

"Let go of her."

The man's eyes widened. His Adam's apple bobbed in his throat, and he slowly released his tourniquet clasp on Jenny's arm.

"Leave us."

Another bow, and the butler left before he could be admonished again. Lord Blakely turned to face Jenny—and her damp clothing and her disarrayed skirt. He leaned back in his chair, his expression still. He put her in mind of some great beast, crouching. Whether to pounce on her or dash away, Jenny could not say. But she had started this game. Now it was time to continue it.

"Well? I should like to know what you'll try next. Scientific interest, of course."

She slowly brought her skirt up to her knee, exposing the rest of her limb. He did not move. All was stillness—his gaze, and the room itself, which was oddly bereft of the London street noises that Jenny could not escape anywhere in her own rooms. Back here, in Lord Blakely's private haven, the silence grew to an almost overwhelming roar.

She leaned over and untied her garter. She made sure he caught a glimpse of the swell of her breasts as she did so.

One of the reasons it was so quiet was that she could

not hear him breathe, so intent was he. She had not, technically, shown him an inch of skin—only so much knit stocking.

She remedied that now. She eased the fabric down her leg, her skin prickling with the awareness of his gaze. He watched, heat simmering in his eyes. When she pulled the garment over her toes, he exhaled. The sound split the silence.

"You have my complete attention. More of this, and less fortune-telling, and I…"

Jenny straightened and let her skirt fall. She set the stocking on her shoulder and rounded the desk toward him. As she came closer, he leaned back in his chair. He was in his shirtsleeves. Good; that would make her task all the easier. She walked forward slowly, until she stood within inches of him. His head tilted up so he could look into her eyes. He sprawled in the chair, his legs out to either side.

Jenny set her bare foot on his chair between his legs. "Are you going to stop me?"

"I wouldn't dream of it. You're a damnable siren, you know."

"Not so tedious now, am I?"

His eyes met hers, a current of amusement running through them. No smile, unfortunately. She touched her finger to his chin. His lips tilted up toward hers. Asking. Promising. A current of heat swept through her and she shivered at the thought of kissing him. But Jenny didn't take his mouth. Instead, she picked up his hand and placed it on her bare calf. His eyes shivered shut, and his fingers floated down her leg. They brushed the bones of her ankle and then up the backside until he tickled her knee. Excitement sparked where he touched.

She pulled away from him. He opened his eyes, his hand left outstretched in bare air. He looked as dazed as she felt.

"Give me your hand, Lord Blakely."

When he didn't move, she reached out and touched his linen shirt at the elbow. Her finger traced down his arm to where his wrist bloomed from the cuff. Then she clasped his hot palm against hers and flattened his hand against the smooth surface of her neck. His hand convulsed around her skin, and he exhaled again, looking in her eyes. She dragged his hand down, slowly. Past collarbone. Up the top of her breast, to the sensitive summit and then down the other side. Heat trailed down her body, rib by rib. Down she pulled his hand, to her waist.

She was dizzy with lust when she stepped away from his grasp again.

And he was rampant, his erection a thick bulge in his trousers. He didn't chase after her, though; he was enjoying the sensual exercise as much as she. She circled him and knelt behind his chair. One tap on his elbow. "Give me your hand," she breathed.

This time, he complied, letting his arm swing behind the chair.

She kissed it, taking his thumb into her mouth. He groaned, his hand tensing in her grip. Her other hand grasped the discarded stocking she'd set over her shoulder and worked stealthily. When she was ready, she looped the noose over his wrist.

Like that, his hand was secured to the back of the chair.

Before he realized what she'd done, she scrambled to her feet and came round the chair. She sat on his lap, so he couldn't stand.

He tugged on his bound arm. The lust in his eyes gave way to puzzlement before settling on anger.

"Untie me," he hissed.

He was still hard underneath her, despite the ire in his voice. His member, hot and rigid, twitched against her bottom. Jenny leaned against his chest and looked soulfully into his eyes. "Untie yourself," she sang sweetly.

"As well you know, in this position it's—"

"Impossible?" Jenny purred. "Now you know what I meant when I said I *can't* wear that gown. It's not tediousness or fractious foot-dragging. It's a physical impossibility. I can't reach behind my back, either."

He closed his mouth and stared at her in stunned silence.

"I can't lace the corset I need to wear this gown," Jenny said. "I can't untangle all those ribbons and tapes to do them up properly. I don't have a servant to help me dress, Lord Blakely."

"Christ." Lord Blakely's free hand slipped around her waist. He looked up, the tawny gold of his eyes flickering. "And it would have been too difficult to send a note explaining yourself like a *rational* person? Pah. You didn't need to come here and tie me up."

His palm was warm against her side. Jenny smiled, and his fingers cinched around her.

"I didn't need to. But where would be the fun in a note?"

"Fun?" He raised one eyebrow. His tone disparaged the preposterous. *Magic? Killer unicorns? Fun?!*

"Fun," Jenny repeated adamantly. "*Very* fun. Just think, Lord Blakely. How often does anyone tie you up and force you to do anything?"

"What would you know? Look behind you."

She turned around and took in the paper scattered over the surface of his desk.

Rough ink sketches—astonishingly lifelike—detailed

wings, claws. Birds, the likes of which she'd never seen before. Vines. Seeds. Further notations in his careful hand filled the pages. A title page off to one side labeled this *A Study of Brazilian Macaws.*

"Underneath that thin layer of drawings," he said, "is a stack of economic accounts. I hate them. But three counties over, a harvest failed. I am all that stands between my dependents and the various famines that have swept this country over the last years. So, yes. I do know something of being tied up. Though it's usually with sums rather than stockings."

Reluctantly, Jenny turned back to face him.

There was no anger in his eyes now. Instead they seemed clear. Young, in a way that tugged at her heart.

"I grant myself these morning hours, so that I have the fortitude to face the finances in the afternoon. This is the only time I have to spend as I desire."

Jenny swallowed an uncomfortable lump in her throat. "And here I am, interrupting you and tying you up. No wonder you're always angry." She'd meant to tease him out of his solemnity.

But he raised his free hand to her cheek. "You'll make up the difference."

He turned her face down toward his.

Her palms rested against his chest. One shove—one good push—and she'd be free. But she couldn't untangle herself from that look in his eyes, or the smell of bay rum on his collar.

She swallowed.

And he kissed her. His lips were light on hers, but he seared her nonetheless. Her hands drifted up to cup his face, still morning-smooth beneath her fingers. His body pressed against hers, hard planes of muscle and sinew.

His tongue darted out like a lick of flame. He was going to burn her up.

She'd been burnt before. She scrambled off his lap while she still could and beat a hasty retreat across the room. He watched her go and then stood, somewhat awkwardly, shuffling round the chair until he could reach the knot she'd made of her stocking.

Jenny backed to the door, preparing to run.

He looked up. There was a lightness about his expression. "Tell me, which did you enjoy more? Outwitting me, or allowing me to run my hands over you?"

"Both, I should think." She put her hands on the door handle. "Which did you enjoy more? Kissing me, or tricking me into running away so you could untie yourself?"

He didn't answer. Instead, he jerked his hand free and straightened. "You were right about one thing."

"Pardon?"

"Lord Blakely—his responsibilities do not extend to seducing you. I reserve that pleasure for myself."

And on that incomprehensible note, Jenny fled.

GARETH HELD HIS BREATH until the door shut behind Madame Esmerelda. He should have followed her out and made sure his servants did not harass her. But he was too confounded by what had just transpired to move from his seat.

She'd seduced him. She'd seduced *Gareth*. Oh, not all the way, unfortunately. But those clear eyes of hers had seen right past Lord Blakely. Past the title that bound him. One word—his Christian name—and he'd let her tie him in knots, of both the literal and figurative varieties.

Where would be the fun in that? she'd asked. Lord Blakely had no room in his life for fun. Even when he made time for the sexual act, he kept the transactions as cold and business-like as possible. Impersonal exchanges, money for temporary physical satisfaction. It had never been about fun; it had been about relief from his body's demands.

Gareth clenched his hand. The specter of his title had robbed everything good and convivial from his life. His mother. His sister. His own chance at a family. But Gareth would allow himself this one thing: this woman, in his bed. Until he no longer risked forgetting that there was a man beneath the mask of Lord Blakely.

And if, in addition to the physical longing that racked him, she awoke some deeper wistfulness... He looked down at his fist. He was still clutching her stocking in his hand. Fun. Wistfulness. *Loneliness.*

Physical pleasure would purge these longings from his system. It *had* to. And if it didn't work the first time, he'd do it over and over, until finally her hold over him dissipated like smoke.

In the meanwhile, he'd send back the dress.

But this time, he'd send along a maid.

CHAPTER SEVEN

NED WAS VERY FIRM in his notion of what constituted an enjoyable time. It started with a few good friends and a tankard of ale. Add in a horse race or some kind of boxing match, and a girl who wouldn't mind showing her ankles. There followed jokes and laughter. More liquor. More ankles. In the two years since Madame Esmerelda had helped him banish his black despair, he'd learned to enjoy the finer things in life.

And so this musicale, attended in his dour cousin's company, was hardly his idea of fun.

As a general rule, a good time did not include starched ladies whose voluminous gowns rejected the notion that women existed below the waist. Especially if one of those ladies was the cold and lovely Lady Kathleen.

Lady Kathleen sat as far from Ned as she could get in the ordered rows, and behind him, so that he had to turn his head to even get a glance at her.

Ned had neither the need nor the desire to look at her regularly. She was destined for Blakely.

Still, Lady Kathleen drew his eyes. Perhaps it was the confidence in her carriage, the assurance in her every movement. Perhaps it was the way her eyes snapped to his when he turned in her direction.

Perhaps it was just that there were not so many other

people worth ogling. For instance, there was the stiff baroness who served as the hostess for this horrible event, standing to announce the next performance. She looked as if she'd turned into fossil before ankles were even invented. Ned suspected if he lifted her skirts, he'd find nothing but layers of lace and petticoats.

Ned sighed. At least looking was better than listening. Ned had no ear for music. He shifted impatiently in his chair.

"Next," warbled the hostess, "we are in for a special treat."

Yes, yes. The opera singer. Hired to give a professional performance, and somehow convince all these people to sit through the amateurs. Why Blakely had insisted Ned come to this event was a mystery. Perhaps, Ned thought longingly, Blakely had heard that Lady Kathleen would attend. That had to be it. After all, Blakely had come with Madame Esmerelda in tow—and she'd come dressed in London finery, making her a surprisingly pretty lady. Why else had Blakely come here, if not to impress his future wife?

Perhaps his interest in her had sparked. He would marry her, and Madame Esmerelda would be proven right.

"Lord Blakely," continued the baroness, her Chinese-screened fan fluttering in her hand, "will honor us with a performance."

Shocked, Ned remembered that Blakely had promised to deliver an ode to a crowd. Surely he didn't intend to sing in *this* crowded venue? But Blakely stood up, calmly as ever, and made his way to the front.

The baroness's fan fluttered at an increased rate. And no wonder. What a coup this must be for her. The reclusive Marquess of Blakely had not only come to her musical evening, but—for the first time ever—he'd also offered a public performance.

The hostess was not the only one beaming in obvious interest. Around him, he saw women lean forward. A hush fell, and so when Blakely paused by the baroness, everyone in the room heard their exchange.

"My lord," she twittered, "will you need any accompaniment?"

Blakely cocked his head to the side, as if considering. It was one of his affectations, Ned knew—meant to make him look intelligent. Not that it didn't work; just that he hardly needed to pretend.

"The work I intend to perform," he eventually said, "is of my own composition. And it is in a style that, were it performed in Brazil, where I have visited, would likely be called *terrivel*."

"Oh, my!" The baroness almost dropped her fan in excitement. "Brazil! How exotic!"

Blakely could not have looked more bored with her enthusiastic response. He looked away, across the room. "Which is to say, it could not possibly be improved by accompaniment."

She looked shocked. "The style of—uh—ta heevil? No. Of course not. I understand completely."

Blakely nodded, high-handed dismissal writ across his face, and continued to the front of the room. He faced the crowd. His gaze swept over the gathered throng as if it were a mass of lepers. Then he clasped his hands behind his back, and sang.

A frog croaking a tuneless, off-key baritone would have handily beaten Blakely in a singing competition. Ned's expectations had risen as high as the soles of his shoes. They'd been too high.

This wasn't an ode. It was carnage.

Ned put his hand in his mouth and bit down. It didn't do much good. His shoulders still shook with laughter.

And then there were the words. Dear God. How long had it taken him to come up with them?

"One thing about Ned that will never spoil," Blakely sang, "Is that he is indefatigably loyal/No matter the troubles in which they're embroiled/He will not from his friends recoil."

Ned bit harder. Teeth pierced glove and ground into flesh. He chanced a look around him. The faces nearest his were very guarded in response. Everyone's, that is, except Madame Esmerelda's. Her eyes were lit by a mischievous joy.

Happily, Blakely was not yet finished. "Ever jolly is Ned's disposition/For this much, at least, he deserves recognition/He would make a fine politician/If ever he stood for a good proposition."

Ned wasn't sure whether that worked out to a compliment. "Ever jolly" certainly bore no resemblance to the truth. He chanced a look behind him. Unlike the rest of the crowd, Lady Kathleen was not watching with pretended interest. She looked carefully from side to side, her fingers cinched around the arm of her chair. As if the details of the room were of greater interest than the spectacle Blakely presented.

Blakely continued. "Ned is worthy of great esteem/For he is precisely as he seems/He has no plots or deceitful schemes/Unlike the one I intend to make—"

Blakely drew out that last note—if you could call that low, cracking tone by so innocent a name. He was looking directly at Madame Esmerelda, and Ned tried to fill in the rhyme to come. *Make dream? Steam? Scream?*

Madame Esmerelda blushed pink, one hand on her throat. How strange.

"—wince as I finish the last line without any sense of meter or rhyme," Blakely concluded.

There was a moment of silence. *Blessed* silence. The glances around Ned all said the same thing—*Dear God, please tell us it's over.* Blakely eyed the gathering with his typical lofty indifference, daring them to boo.

They did not dare. Ned could see the thoughts skim through their minds. He was a marquess, after all. Perhaps things were different in Brazil. The performance was exotic. It was short. And it wasn't much more dreadful than the Chinese opera that had been performed last year.

"Bravo!" Ned called. He applauded madly. Thankfully, everyone joined in.

Blakely bowed, rather stiffly, and picked his way through the rows toward his seat. He didn't even make eye contact with Ned, didn't acknowledge that Ned had just saved him.

Ha. Just because Blakely had no humility didn't mean Ned couldn't try to humiliate him further.

"Encore!" Ned shouted.

Blakely fixed Ned with a look that promised eventual dismemberment. Luckily for the future attachment of Ned's limbs, nobody else took up the cry. Blakely made his way through the seats amidst very polite, and not particularly encouraging, applause.

He brushed by Ned and had reached his seat on the other side of Madame Esmerelda, when the annoying woman on Ned's right leaned over.

"Lord Blakely," she said. "What an *unusual* style. I just want to know—who is Ned?"

Ned suppressed a grin. That, perhaps, was the best part. Almost everyone thought of him as Mr. Carhart. Just Carhart, to the friends he'd made at school. Only near family—he included Madame Esmerelda in that number, of course—called him "Ned."

Blakely arranged the tails of his coat and sat down, straight-backed, before answering. "A person." No further encouragement passed his lips.

"Oh." A pause. "Is the style *intended* to be sung like that?"

Ned felt perfectly free to twit his own cousin, but he'd be damned if he let anyone else do it. "Dissonance," Ned said airily, "is all the rage abroad this year. It's such a shame London is behind the times."

Blakely's brows drew down and he shot Ned an unreadable look.

Ned decided to feel encouraged. An unreadable response was heaps better than an unprintable one.

Two tasks completed; one more to go. Now Ned only had to sit through the remainder of tonight's entertainment— which had suddenly become much more entertaining. Was Lady Kathleen watching Blakely? Had she been won over by that awful performance? For the fourth time that evening, he swiveled in his seat and glanced toward Lady Kathleen's position. Four, he told himself, was a commendably low number. He might have glanced at anyone four times. Perhaps five would not be—

Except she wasn't in her seat. Ned looked up, to see her brushing her way past the last seats in the row. Nobody looked at her; all eyes were riveted on the opera singer who had just begun an aria far more melodic than the previous song. Lady Kathleen glanced around the room and Ned quickly turned away.

When he looked back, she was ducking through a door. How odd. It was the second time Ned had seen her leave some entertainment through a servants' entrance.

Without thinking, he stood. And he followed.

As soon as he'd closed the tiny door, muting the music behind him, he dashed after her. "Lady Kathleen!"

She turned around. "Oh. It's Madman Carhart. And you're alone."

Ned halted. She'd discovered his name—good. But she doubted his sanity. Bad. Very bad.

She shook her finger at him. "We haven't been introduced. I don't think you should speak to me. And you definitely should not be with me unaccompanied."

"Nonsense," Ned said. "You know my name. I know yours." He put out his hand. "Let's just shake like gentlemen and be friends."

Her gaze arrested on his outstretched fingers.

"Right." Ned balled his hand into a fist and pulled it back slowly. "Ladies don't shake hands. Never mind, then."

Her gaze had followed his hand. "Do you realize there are *toothmarks* on your glove?"

Ned whipped his hand behind his back. His ears burned. "I bit myself," he explained. "I was trying not to laugh at Blakely. You would have done it, too."

"Bit you?" She raised one eyebrow. And then, as if she'd realized what she had said, she flushed. It was the first hint of unease Ned had seen her exhibit. But she didn't turn away in embarrassment. She didn't even glance away demurely. She met his gaze steadily. "Your entire family is mad, you know."

"Oh, no," Ned said. "Just Blakely. He's been like that for ages. I, on the other hand, am completely sane. Just—just a little—nervous, you know."

"You should be, following me like that." She shook her head. The motion was almost severe, but the tone of her voice had softened. "You really ought to leave, I suppose, before someone spies us alone like this and assumes the worst."

Ned was not yet willing to be dismissed. "Well, if you didn't go charging off alone into the servants' corridors, you wouldn't have that problem."

Her eyes widened. Something like real surprise flashed in them. "I'm not—that is to say, I don't—"

"Yes," Ned corrected, "you do, too. Every time I've met you, you've been off, invading dimly lit corridors. It's a mystery. I shall have to get to the bottom of it. I shall consult Madame Esmerelda."

She frowned at him, as if to deny the charge. But what she said was, "Madame Esmerelda?"

"Yes," Ned said soothingly, "She's the one who predicted the match between you and Blakely."

Her eyes widened even more, and she stepped back. "Match? Predicted? *Blakely?* What match?"

"Ah." Ned winced. "Hmm. *What* match?"

"You're trying to match me with a man you just told me is mad? That's why you're following me?" Her eyes had widened, and she drew herself up. She still stood inches shorter than him. "You're following me for your cousin? I thought—"

Ned raised his palms soothingly. "I can explain. What I said just now about Blakely—the madness and all? Not true. He's not—well, he's not so bad. In fact, he has several good qualities."

"Well. I suppose. There is his singing, after all."

"Um," Ned said. "Maybe not that particular quality, so much. But he *is* a marquess."

She gave a brusque shake of her head. "Well, he can't exactly take credit for that, can he? He was born that way."

"He's tall. Women like tall men, don't they?"

"He was born that way, too."

"No." Ned's confidence returned. "He wasn't. He was born a baby, just like everyone else. He only grew taller later on."

She blinked at him for a second, and then lifted a glove to her mouth. "Yes," she said, "but he doesn't make me laugh." She looked at him, her gaze direct. "This is another one of your jokes, I assume. You don't really mean to give me to him, do you? He's so old, after all."

She looked up at him, and Ned felt an uncomfortable spot of warmth in his stomach. He shouldn't have felt encouraged, that she was rejecting his cousin. Still, in comparison with Blakely, Ned felt ungainly, all clumsy elbows.

"Blakely is very responsible," Ned said dutifully. "Heaps more responsible than me."

She frowned dubiously. "Which is why he's sending his younger cousin to arrange a match for him? That won't wash."

"Look at him." Ned leaned against the wall easily. "Can you imagine him falling in love without a little prodding from someone like me? He's so scientific and cold and rational. He needs me. Why would any woman want him?"

In the silent seconds that followed, Ned realized precisely why these moments of too-bright clarity seemed so familiar. He'd reached the apogee again. Twice before, he'd experienced this crystalline sense of over-reaching. It heralded an inevitable loss of control, and a descent into darkness.

Ned knew. He'd fallen before.

But Madame Esmerelda had broken that cycle of dark following light. She'd promised he could live without fear of that downward spiral. She'd told him he was not mad, and for two perfect, brilliant years, she'd been right.

And here he was, fouling everything up again.

"Why *would* any woman want your cousin?" Lady Kathleen echoed Ned's last words with a shake of her head. She glanced again down the hallway, and sighed. "Don't match me for his sake. But if you want to talk with me…" Her voice trailed off and she looked up at him, a hint of inexplicable wistfulness washing over her features.

He shook his head in confusion, and she pointed a finger behind him, directing him back toward the music room. Faint strains of applause drifted down the hall.

"Just go," she said.

Ned went.

GARETH ESCAPED out the open doors of the music hall onto the veranda. After the thirteenth polite inquiry into the singing styles of countries of South America— excessively larded with exuberant compliments that could not possibly have been sincere—he needed fresh air. He gulped it in.

Of course, the air was only London-fresh. At least it wasn't perfumed with the bouquet of packed bodies. But the word that came to mind instead of fresh was *heavy.* Night brought thick fogs, barely pierced by dim blurs of gas lighting. Every lungful of air he took in was moist enough that he might well have been some kind of amphibious salamander. That extra moisture carried all the fragrances of London. Wet soil from the small back garden he'd escaped to. The scent of unfurling buds and mulching leaves. Green smells; nature smells. They didn't mask the underlying stink of London: particles of coal suspended in vapor and—even in this fine neighborhood—the distant smell of sewage.

As his eyes adjusted to the darkness, he realized he was not alone. Madame Esmerelda sat on the edge of a cold granite bench, her back straight and her arms, stiff as ramrods, supporting her. She looked up into the night sky. The dense mist rendered it as impenetrable as a slab of slate. There were neither stars nor moon. She hadn't seen him yet.

He took the opportunity to look her over, in a more leisurely fashion than he'd dared earlier. She looked respectable in the cream-and-red-striped dress he'd chosen. And with her hair dressed by the maid he'd had sent over from the agency, she fit in this crowd seamlessly. The cut of the gown accentuated her bosom and waist. A shame that it hid all hint of her hips. And her ankles.

He'd dreamed of touching those delicately boned ankles last night, of sliding his hand up those limbs again. In his dream, she hadn't pulled away.

Through the French windows behind him, light leaked out. Long shadows crisscrossed the terrace. He followed those dark lines, treading as silently as he could. But he could not muffle the sound of leather striking the paving stones. Her head turned toward him in startled surprise.

"Hiding?" he asked.

She met his gaze, then looked away. "Now we are equal."

"Equal?" Thoughts of revolutionary Frenchmen danced through Gareth's head. *Liberté, egalité,* and all that tripe. "Nonsense."

"I tied you up," she explained. "Now you've had your revenge on me by trussing me into this bloody corset. I can't even take a proper deep breath."

Gareth let out a covert exhalation. She was keeping track in their curious little competition. Of course. She'd not meant anything else by the comment.

"You'll get used to it."

"Why would I want to? I do not believe I wish to play Mrs. Margaret Barnard any longer."

"Not even for this scintillating company?"

She smiled at his dry words. "I was asked if I wished to be invited to a meeting of the Ladies' Beneficial Tea Society. Apparently, the attendees embroider handkerchiefs for future dissemination. The aim is to increase hygienic practices among the deserving poor."

"You are not fond of charitable causes? Or do you disapprove of hygiene?"

"I think that those embroidered handkerchiefs are likely hawked by their recipients within minutes of their distribution. What a colossal waste of time. Do any of these ladies enjoy their roles?"

"No. Nor the men."

Gareth spoke absently, but she tilted her head.

"Surely you like playing Lord Blakely. Ordering them around. One look at your steely countenance, and society is set a-wondering whether they, too, should learn to sing in that absurd style. Do you not feel the slightest sympathy for your fellow man?"

"No." Gareth spoke without hesitation. Sympathy? The vicissitudes of society had condemned his mother when she remarried a commoner a bare year after the passing of her lordly husband. His grandfather had curled his lip, and she'd acquiesced to his demands, leaving

Gareth with the old man. To learn how to become a marquess. What had remained of his childhood had shriveled into an unending stream of duties and requirements. Society and his grandfather had never had sympathy for *him.*

Gareth shook his head to dislodge the memories. "I may have fooled them with regards to the quality of Brazilian singing, but it was no more than they deserved."

"We may be more equal than I thought. What if I said the same thing about my role as Madame Esmerelda?"

"Is that why you've engaged in this fraud? To condemn polite society? To laugh at us? Do you snicker up your sleeve knowing you can make Ned dance at your beck and call?"

She was silent. "Maybe when I first started. Back then, it seemed like such a lark. But Madame Esmerelda grew once I put on her skirts. And then Ned... Well, it's impossible to condemn him. It's a dangerous business, pretending to be a person you're not. Before you know it, you're locked in a role, unable to change what you do. Some days, I almost think I hate Madame Esmerelda."

Some dim corner of Gareth's mind noted she'd as good as admitted she was a fraud. There was no triumph in the thought, though. She'd only said what they both knew. Until she said those words to Ned, her admission did no good.

And what she said was too much an echo of his own thoughts. Some days, he hated Lord Blakely.

She turned her head and peered up at him. Her eyes were dark pools in the night. The light from the windows danced across the expanse of her chest; her bosom swelled, up and down, in time with her breath. Shorter breaths indeed than she might once have taken. Shorter breaths; faster movement. How shallow would her breaths become if he licked that creamy curve just above her nipple?

He desired her. Not just those smooth swells that would fit so perfectly in his palm. He desired the woman who tied him up.

"You must know you cannot win. I have only one more task. I shall undoubtedly complete it with alacrity. In a short space of time, I will have followed your every directive. And I have no desire to marry the Lady Kathleen. Ned will discover you for the fraud that you are. Slavish adherence to your plan gains you nothing."

"It is not what I stand to gain, my lord. It is what you stand to lose."

Gareth shook his head in bafflement. "My reputation? If I could stave off the gossip tonight with arrogant superiority and a freezing look, surely you must realize my good name is impervious to any task you can dream up. I have commanded society far longer than you have been attempting to embarrass me. You shan't succeed on that score."

"No." She looked off into the distance. "But then, that is not what I expected to win."

Anyone watching from the main room would see their silhouettes. At this distance, their conversation would appear to be idle words. An exchange of compliments. A discussion of mutual acquaintances. Nothing more, so long as he didn't do anything so foolish as touch her.

He longed to breathe foolish words against the skin of her neck.

"You could win my patronage instead. Give up this quest." His tongue felt thick in his mouth. "Become my mistress. Forget whatever idiotic goal you'd hoped to achieve."

"If I wanted to be a mistress, I'd never have gone to all the trouble of creating Madame Esmerelda. I'm not interested."

"You wouldn't be just any man's mistress. You'd be *mine.*"

She shook her head. "I told you long ago why I wouldn't back down. You prod. You poke. You proposition me with a logical weighing of costs and benefits. Do you know, I believe the only emotions you allow yourself to show are pride, anger and disdain? Not a hint of amusement or enjoyment. No sadness. No despair."

"Just because I don't choose to show my every thought—"

"You don't choose to show particular types of feelings," Madame Esmerelda said. "Why *not* smile?"

"Why not hang my head in abject humiliation? Why not tear my hair out in sorrow? Why not slobber like an affectionate dog over everyone who takes my fancy? I have my pride, Meg."

"Most people do. But they don't hold on to it at the expense of their humanity. Or that of those around them."

She thought him inhuman? "I see," he said. He pushed all the coldness that clenched his heart into his voice. "You dislike me."

She tipped her head back and looked Gareth in the eyes. Once again, lust struck him—a deep, piercing blow to his groin. She'd whetted his appetite over and over. Kisses. Touches. God, he wanted her, skin against skin. He wanted to feel her hair, now pinned up, spilling over his bare chest.

"No. I rather dislike Lord Blakely. I wonder why you play the marquess so often."

"*Play* the marquess? I *am* the marquess."

"And I am Madame Esmerelda. And Mrs. Margaret Barnard. Do you think I don't recognize a facade when I see it?"

Gareth swallowed. "A facade? What do you suppose I am hiding?"

She put her head to one side and studied him. "You have all the marks of a man who was once an extremely awkward child. A boy who lived on the edge of his parents' life. Quiet. Studious. Too quiet, perhaps, and a little too interested in natural science, and inexplicably bored by sport. When you met other children your age, you no doubt found them baffling. And when they massed in groups, as children are wont to do, you feared, deep down, that they were all laughing at you."

"An interesting theory. A shame you lack evidence for it." Gareth struggled to maintain the coldness in his voice. His hands were trembling. He had not thought of those first horrible years at Harrow in an age. He'd buried them in his mind. But her words brought them all back, right down to that nauseous feel in the pit of his stomach.

Let lust remain ascendant. Let him think of sliding inside her, of her gasp of sweet surrender. He held on to those heated thoughts to dispel the other images she conjured.

But she would not let him hide. "You were right. They *were* all laughing at you."

They had been. His hands clenched in remembered helplessness.

"Then you discovered you could make them stop. They couldn't laugh at a man made of stone. And they were all afraid of your position in society."

"None of this is relevant to my offer. You tell Ned you are a fraud. I take you to bed."

"But that is not what either of us wants, your lordship.

You don't want Lord Blakely to take me to bed, either. And yet I think you've forgotten how to be Gareth—just Gareth—altogether. And everyone suffers. I suffer. Ned suffers." She paused. "Even your staff suffers. How ever did you train them all not to laugh?"

"I don't take responsibility for the expressions on their faces."

"Really? Name one you've seen smiling."

Name? To the best of Gareth's knowledge, the vast majority of his servants were nameless. To the extent that they came to his attention at all, it had better be hiding behind a feather duster. Servants were *supposed* to blend into the background. Gareth was aware that his servants were real people. They undoubtedly had real emotions to go along with that status. That didn't mean he needed to familiarize himself with those details.

Madame Esmerelda frowned at him.

"There's White," he finally offered.

"White is…"

"My man of business."

"Excellent," Madame Esmerelda said. "Make friends with him."

"What? *Friends?*"

"Friends," she affirmed.

"Insupportable. I'd rather take you to bed."

It was the most terrible task she had set to date. The worst part was that some treasonous organ deep within him—perhaps his liver—wanted to comply. He *wanted* to talk to the man, as if it were perfectly normal.

"I can't make friends with him."

"Why ever not?"

"He's in service," Gareth protested. "Think what his origins must be. Madame Esmerelda, I am a marquess."

He folded his arms and nodded. "Surely you must see I cannot go about making friends of all and sundry." He was arguing with himself as much as her.

"One man," Madame Esmerelda said, "hardly constitutes 'all.' Nor is the man you yourself hired properly cast as 'sundry.'"

It wasn't the prospect of having friends that bothered him; it was the process of making them. Gareth remembered those first years at Harrow. He hadn't been able to do it then. He'd tried, those first, tentative efforts so painstakingly slow. But the others his age formed their little groups so quickly, he'd been left on the margin. He wasn't bullied, like some—his lineage had made sure of that—but he had been isolated. Two years of hesitant advances, gently rebuffed; two years standing silently, only thinking how to add to the conversation long after the moment passed.

"Oh, do stop looking so sullen," she admonished.

What had started as awkwardness and isolation had soon become superiority and a fierce reclusiveness. He'd stopped desiring others' good opinion. And that, of course, was when they'd granted him theirs. It was a terrible thing she did to him, rousing these old memories. As if she *were* his equal, free to disturb his past. As if he were the sort of man who could make friends with his man of business. Who could have *fun* with a woman.

"Friends. Bah."

She tsked quietly.

Gareth looked down at her. It was not so dark that he missed the rounding of her eyes, the subtle relaxation in her cheeks. He knew exactly what she felt right then.

Pity.

He almost hated her for the emotion. He almost hated himself.

But she shook her head. "My poor Lord Blakely. It must be very lonely being superior to everyone else in the world."

And that, more than anything else, froze the lust right out of his body.

She was a fraud and a charlatan and a veritable succubus of a ruined woman. But she'd seen right into his desolate heart. And without once touching him, she'd tied him up.

Again.

CHAPTER EIGHT

THE TASK MADAME ESMERELDA had laid Gareth had
seemed monumental on the dark of the previous evening.
In the bright light of the next afternoon, it became clear
the task was not just monumental. It was insurmountable.

The scritch of White's pen reverberated throughout
Gareth's study. The sound should have been dampened
by the thick, red-and-gold carpet that lay over the wooden
floors. But even the dark velvet curtains covering the
windows didn't swallow the incessant scratch of writing.

Scientifically, Gareth knew that the apparent volume of
noise must be the product of his own fevered mind. Logi-
cally, he knew noise could not echo in the room; there were
no hard surfaces present for the sound to bounce around.

Knowing this did nothing to lessen the irritation he felt
at the continuing scrape of nib against paper. It did nothing to ease the sullen ire that lodged deep in his breast.

Madame Esmerelda had the matter completely backward. Gareth had no desire for friendship. He wasn't
lonely. He'd spent weeks at a stretch without human contact in Brazil, and he'd never hungered for conversation.

Well, maybe once. Or twice. A day. But it had been
the same sort of longing he'd had for a warm bath or a
swallow of brandy—a temporary thirst, one that could be
eventually slaked and then forgotten.

Whatever point Madame Esmerelda hoped to make with this latest task was assuredly based on faulty logic. Gareth didn't need anyone. And even if he did, a friendship with his man of business was not the balm that would assuage the temporary itch in his breast.

Scratch, scratch. Rustle.

Gareth looked up in irritation. White turned over a leaf in the account book, spreading a new sheet of paper on the desk in front of him. No doubt penning a quick suggestion on how best to modernize some mill on one of Gareth's far-flung estates. Later in the afternoon, they would discuss those ideas. Rationally. Businesslike. At an impersonal arm's length, as Gareth preferred.

He wasn't going to befriend the man. The idea was ludicrous. He'd tell her as much. He didn't give a snap for Madame Esmerelda's foolish tasks, and he would tell Ned—he would tell him—

But this third task wasn't about Ned any longer. It wasn't even about the triumph of science over illogic. No; it was about Gareth. The year his father died and Gareth had been shipped off to Harrow, he had openly hungered for the sort of easy camaraderie the other boys enjoyed. He'd thought that desire had left him. Instead, it had only lurked like some subterranean beast, waiting to be drawn to the surface by Madame Esmerelda.

Gareth damned her.

"White." The word tasted chilly and forbidding in his mouth. The delivery was just as his grandfather had taught him.

White looked up. "My lord?"

Gareth stared at the man's pen, the source of his annoyance, in veiled frustration. What was he to say? He couldn't order the man to leave off doing the work he was hired to do. Gareth made an impatient motion with his hand. The excessively competent White correctly deciphered the gesture as *put down that damned pen and listen to what I have to say.*

No doubt he expected some discussion of Gareth's estate. Unfortunate that he was getting small talk. Friendly talk.

"Are you married?"

The attentive look in White's eyes faded into puzzlement. "Yes, my lord."

"Have you any children?"

"Four."

Silence stretched. Gareth bit his cheek and shut the estate book on the desk in front of him with a slam. Befriend his man of business? The very notion was impossible. Their situations were entirely dissimilar. Gareth paid the man's salary. White was a family man, with children and a wife. Surely, Gareth had nothing to say to him. It was absolutely ludicrous to suppose friendship possible.

Ludicrous seemed to be Madame Esmerelda's style.

Gareth performed a mental inventory of his library. Volumes on agriculture. Texts in Latin and Greek. Taxonomy; biology; natural philosophy. Mathematics. He'd read them all. Many, more than once.

He could think of no fewer than six ways to prove Pythagoras's theorem off the top of his head. He had at least twelve ideas for new industries to stimulate employment in his East Midlands holdings.

The ways he could think to continue this conversation totaled zero.

He tried anyway. "What think you of the weather?"

He could hear the cold formality in his own voice. It clanged, unpleasant even to his own ears. He sounded as if he were embarking on his own personal branch of the Spanish Inquisition—perhaps the heretical meteorology division.

"My lord?" Unsurprisingly, White looked uneasy. "Are you feeling well?"

Gareth flung the ledger on his desk open. Numbers— cold, yet comforting—sprang to life in front of him. The sums detailed debits and credits, purchases and sales. Feed for livestock; investments in a new pottery-works on one of his properties that had been recently connected to a rail line. Money flew forth and trickled back, adding up after months and months into substantial sums. Every last penny was accounted for between these pages.

All those books in his damned library. Every shilling in his accounts.

And after thirty-four years, Gareth still had no idea how to make friends.

"Never mind," he muttered, and stared furiously at the page.

After a pause, White's pen started up again. Scritch, scratch. Rustle, rustle. It was only in Gareth's imagination that the sound magnified to a roar.

THAT EVENING, Lord Blakely slammed open the unlocked door to Jenny's rooms with a bang. Jenny jumped, her heart racing.

He strode inside without so much as a by-your-leave. He was accompanied by a breeze pregnant with all the youthful possibilities of spring rain. None of those possibilities entered the room with him. Instead, he seemed to suck them from the air, until Jenny's world constricted to the glower on his face.

He didn't say anything. Instead, he advanced on her,

like a general accosting his lowliest foot-soldier. But the heat in his eyes was hardly military. And even the cruelest officer bent on discipline wouldn't have trapped his subordinate against the wall, his arms forming a cage around her. Lord Blakely's lips pressed together into one thin, white line.

Jenny felt a touch of irritation. She drew herself up straight and glared at him. "Lord Blakely, you can't just stroll into my home as if you had permission."

He snorted. "And who will stop me, do you suppose? Do think the matter through. I am a marquess. And you…" His hands bracketed her face. "You," he scoffed again, disdainfully.

"Me?" The word squeaked out.

"If I see the worst in people," he said, each word snapping out in carefully controlled fury, "it is because they won't see it in themselves. Take you, for instance. There is no excuse for what you are doing to my cousin. You can couch it in whatever pretty terms you like, but ultimately, you are lying to him. You are deceiving him. And you are taking his money."

Jenny put her hands against his chest. "That doesn't justify your behavior here." She pushed, hard.

He didn't budge. "So you don't deny it."

"It's not like that," she said. "You don't understand Ned. You've never bothered to understand him. He's never had one scrap of encouragement in his life. You weren't around when he was sent down from Cambridge, and you don't understand—"

"You play on his worst fears. You cannot deceive me. I doubt you can even deceive yourself. You aren't helping him. The world is not an encouraging or an understanding place. When Ned one day stands in my shoes as marquess, do you think anyone will care if he's had friends? He doesn't need to be happy. He needs to be *ready.* Look at him once through my eyes, Madame Esmerelda."

Jenny pressed back into the cold wall. "If you had any notion of friendship, you'd never ask me to abandon him."

"If you can't think of Ned, then think of yourself. I admit, you present a very pretty package when you haven't gaudied yourself up to play the part of fortune-teller. And I cannot help but admire your intelligence. But look at yourself once through my eyes. What do you think I see?"

Jenny screwed her eyes shut. She couldn't stop up her ears, though, couldn't shut off the prickle of nerves up and down her arms as he leaned closer.

He trailed one finger down her cheek, searing an unforgiving line into her skin. "You're a fraud and a liar and a cheat. What notion of friendship do you entertain? You've bilked Ned of how much money? And you can't even tell him your name."

The truth burned the breath from her lungs. He tipped her chin up. When she opened her eyes, her vision swam. She willed the tear not to drop.

It didn't.

But he did not miss the liquid sheen in her eyes. His thumb touched the corner of her eye and traced a damp track down her cheek. "You can't tell Ned your name." His voice dropped. It was so low, she could feel the vibration through his hand on her jaw. "But you can tell me."

"If you think so little of me, then why are you touching me?"

His hand froze on her jaw. His nostrils flared.

"Because," he said roughly.

"You see more than you've said." She wanted to believe it. Had to. "When you look at me, you see—"

"I see nothing," he said in clipped tones, "except a bloody good shag."

And then he bent his head and kissed her. There was nothing tender or gentle about the embrace. His lips came down on hers with a controlled fury. And heaven help her, Jenny wanted to melt into his arms, wanted to sigh up into his kiss. She wanted him to put his hands on her and ferret out all her womanly secrets. She wanted, Jenny thought bitterly, to pretend that he cared for her.

She couldn't. He didn't kiss her as a lover. He kissed her as if she were a falsehood, and this rough embrace the proof of her perfidy. She wanted him, but not like this. Never like this.

Jenny clamped her lips together and turned away from his mouth. "Stop." She was begging, her breath ragged.

His hand found her chin. "No." He jerked her face back and leaned in again.

Jenny slapped him. She put her whole body into the blow. His head whipped to the side with the force of her strike.

Slowly his hands dropped to his sides. Disbelief echoed in his raging eyes.

Jenny shook out her stinging palm. "I don't care who I lied to. I don't care what your title is. When I see myself, *I* see a woman worth more than a modicum of your respect. And don't you dare touch me if you disagree."

Lord Blakely rubbed his cheek and scowled at her. "Damnation."

"Do you know what I see when I look at you?"

"I don't care." He folded his arms. "I don't care about you. I don't care about my man of business. Or friendship. You can all go hang. I'm done trying. It never does any good."

Pieces fell into place. The inchoate rage storming in his eyes. His unhappiness. His fury. Unwillingly, Jenny saw what had brought on this spectacular tantrum. He had made an effort to make friends with his man of business. And he'd failed. It should not have been surprising. Friendship could not be commanded, and Lord Blakely had little experience with any other sort of interaction.

"Lord Blakely," Jenny said slowly, "I don't care how spectacularly you fail at friendship. I will not be made a scapegoat for your frustration."

"That's not what I'm doing," he said sulkily. "I'm acting this way because I *enjoy* it."

Jenny sighed. "You're an intelligent man. On occasion, you even act like one. Don't make excuses for yourself."

His hands clenched at his sides. "I just don't make friends. It's easy for you to—"

"Friendship is easy, my lord. Even commoners like me manage it. All you have to do is find what you have in common with an individual and talk about it. The rest will follow. Try conversing instead of commanding. Try seeing something good in a person, instead of seeing the worst."

Lord Blakely pulled at his cuffs, adjusting them with minute precision. He turned his hands over and examined his palms. His jaw worked. And when he raised his head, she saw in his gaze a bleak and unrelenting wilderness, harsh and devoid of inhabitants.

She'd said it once to wound the man. But now, the

sentiment escaped her before she had a chance to think it over. "My God, Lord Blakely. You really are lonely."

The silence stretched. Finally, he turned away. "I had better leave."

Jenny had nothing to do but shut the door behind him.

THE AFTERNOON AFTER Lord Blakely's intrusion, Jenny checked the dark cloth covering her furniture for the third time. It was symmetrically arranged, as it had been when she'd checked it two minutes before. Tiny brass bells blew in the light breeze flowing from the open window. She'd chosen them because their tinkling tones sounded Eastern and exotic. Rationally, Jenny knew she'd perfected the right atmosphere.

And yet as she ushered Ned in, the familiar scent of sandalwood cloying her senses, she sensed something was missing. It was nothing that could be fixed with incense or any quantity of black cloth. No; it was something more vital. She hadn't the heart for this any longer.

"Madame Esmerelda," Ned intoned, "I come seeking advice."

That old formula. Again.

Jenny held out her palm. "Cross my palm with silver."

The shillings he piled into her hand were as cold as ice, heavier than lead. Ten shillings. Money that would pay the quarterly rents due in the next week. But the reminder only pricked her conscience further.

Nothing had changed on the outside. On the inside, however, Jenny watched herself through Lord Blakely's critical eyes. What she saw left her nauseated. She was weak. Greedy. She wasn't lying to Ned for money. No, she was lying to him for friendship, and that was by far the more devastating fraud.

Jenny swallowed bitter bile and pulled a weak smile into place. "How can I help you, Ned?"

Ned leaned forward, gripping his knees. His eyes shone with a ferocious intensity.

"It's not *working.*" He must have read the puzzlement in her eyes, because he explained. "The tasks. They're not working. Blakely's not falling in love with Lady Kathleen, and she's not falling in love with him."

Jenny met Ned's gaze. Two weeks ago, she'd have sighed and told him to trust her. She'd have counseled patience and fortitude, and perhaps added occult platitudes. *With Jupiter nearing, good things will come to those who wait.* But two weeks ago, Lord Blakely had been nothing other than a mythological cousin mentioned by Ned in awestruck tones.

If I see the worst in everyone, he'd told her, *it is because they refuse to see it in themselves.*

Well. Jenny was seeing the worst of herself now. It was reflected in the hopeful glint in Ned's eyes. It was mirrored in his clear, unwrinkled forehead, as he awaited her response. Waited for her to solve a problem she'd created.

She'd hoped to help Ned by softening Lord Blakely. She'd wanted the marquess to see the good in his cousin. She'd believed he'd eventually see the good in others beside himself. But even Ned could tell the tasks weren't working.

Lord Blakely hadn't softened one bit. And no matter how harsh or unwelcome his delivery had been, he'd had the right of Jenny's interactions with Ned.

Through his eyes, Jenny could now see her own selfishness. She recognized a deep hunger inside her, a wistful desire to be treated as someone worthy of respect. But what sort of honor did she deserve? She'd never been esteemed when she was Jenny Keeble, so she'd created Madame Esmerelda. Madame Esmerelda hadn't cared, and she'd found clientele who hung on her every word as the truth. That superficial honor, however, hid nothing but a swindler beneath a thin veneer of mumbo jumbo. The light in Ned's eyes was directed at a woman who didn't exist.

She hadn't earned Ned's praise. Even seeing Ned's obvious distress, she could not bring herself to tell him the tasks were her own invention, that there were no spirits and she was a fraud. She couldn't bear to see that light grow dim.

Now that Jenny was seeing the worst in people, she could see the worst of what she'd done to Ned. He was dependent on her to advise him in the smallest ways. And still she was too selfish to say the words that would make him turn away in disgust.

"Ned." There was a quaver in her voice. There shouldn't have been. Madame Esmerelda didn't quaver. But it wasn't Madame Esmerelda who spoke now. It was Jenny.

Ned frowned at her distressed tone.

Maybe she could make things…well, not right. Two years of lies made it too late for right. But less wrong.

"Remember what I told you, years ago? That one day you would become a man?"

He nodded.

"It's time. Not time to *start* becoming a man. It's time to *finish.*"

He stared blankly at her. "I don't understand. What are you saying I should do?"

"Ned, in this matter, you want to trust me. You want me to tell you what to do."

He nodded vigorously.

"That's a laudable sentiment, but it's not right. Don't wait for my advice. Don't—" she choked on the words "—don't trust me."

He shook his head, baffled. As if his world were turning upside down. "How can it be wrong to trust you?"

Oh, God. Seeing herself through Lord Blakely's rational eyes was torture. It was maddening. The guilelessness of Ned's query, the foolishness of his response stung her heart. How Lord Blakely would scorn the two of them if he could hear this conversation. And he would be right, damn the man.

"Ned," Jenny said, "you have to learn to trust yourself. You have to learn to make your own decisions. You cannot rely on me for every last answer."

He shrunk from her.

"You want to be a man, Ned?"

He nodded, his arms folding around his torso protectively.

"It's a terrible burden, being a man. It entails responsibility, choices. It requires hard work and intelligence. And this time—right now—it requires that you stand on your own two feet without anyone to help you."

"Alone?" His voice was soft and scared. His lips trembled.

Lord Blakely's jaded world disappeared from Jenny's mind in a puff of smoke, and she saw Ned with her heart again. A strong young man, hoping to be the best he could.

She reached out and took his hand. And then she opened his fingers and smiled. Slowly, she put the coins back into his hands, one by one. Each one felt like a heavy weight coming off her heart. With the last shilling, she felt almost buoyant. She didn't let go of his hand. Instead she gripped it tight. And deep inside her, she said farewell.

"No, Ned," she whispered. "You don't have to be alone. Just—just be wiser in your choice of companions."

Her eyes threatened to water. Her voice was hoarse.

Ned looked up into her face and he swallowed. Then he pulled his hand from hers and looked away into the corner of the room. "I think I understand," he said. He, too, was hoarse.

"Do you?"

He nodded, refusing to meet her eyes. Maybe he did understand. Maybe he'd finally comprehended the words Jenny could not bring herself to say. *I am a fraud. You have been duped.*

And maybe this response—this not-looking, this not-speaking—was his way of saying he'd finally seen through her, and he would not rely on her any longer.

He left silently.

For long minutes after he'd gone, Jenny stared at the room around her. She had acquired a number of occult trappings over the years. The artful cobwebs she'd allowed to build up in the corner. The depressing black, eating up the light that shone through the window. The only illumination in her room was the fitful glow of coal behind the grate of her fireplace.

All the savor had gone from her work. Playing fortune-teller had once been exciting. It had been enthralling. She'd watched, oh-so-carefully, for those tiny hints of reaction in her clients' faces. She'd told them what they wanted to hear. They'd listened.

Secretly, she'd laughed. It had been Jenny Keeble's revenge on her childhood.

She'd been no better than Lord Blakely, thinking herself above her clients that way. But there was no way to laugh at the way she'd betrayed Ned's sweet loyalty.

As she looked into the dim flames, Jenny acknowledged another truth. "I cannot go on like this."

She spoke the words aloud—to whom, she could not say. Perhaps to the fire. Perhaps to the spirits she had for so long pretended to call upon. There was no answer except a small, burning center deep in her chest. A resonance, agreeing that this portion of her life had come to an end.

And yet what was she to do with herself now? As a woman, most professions were closed to her. She could sew piecework—and ruin her eyes while eking out a living. Perhaps, after all these years, she could attempt to find work teaching. Although with no character references to speak of—she could hardly ask Lord Blakely, after all—the opportunities that presented themselves were likely to be unsavory.

The employment offered to the girl of unknown family hadn't been savory even before she'd run away to London.

She could retire to the country, where the coins she'd saved would stretch further. She could make a pension of the money, and hope that twelve pounds per annum would keep her for the remainder of her life. It would, so long as she was hale and hearty and capable of cooking and cleaning for herself. A gamble; and a life that sounded frighteningly blank and devoid of purpose.

None of that sounded right. All those possibilities echoed emptily in the hollow of her lungs. Jenny breathed out and thought of what she wanted.

What would she do if she were to start her life over again, from the very beginning? What would she change? That old, deep aching overtook her.

She wanted a mother.

God, she wanted a *child.*

She wanted to make someone of herself that even the fastidious Lord Blakely would have to respect.

Three impossibilities. She shook her head.

Jenny had no idea where she would end, but she did have some idea where to start. Slowly, ceremonially, she pulled the black fustian from her tables and chairs. She gathered the heaped cotton in her arms and hauled it to the fireplace.

It landed in the hearth in a swirl of ash and coal dust. Jenny coughed the particles from her lungs and waited. For a few seconds, the dark material cut off all light and heat. Then it glowed red, and finally caught in a crackling blaze. Jenny pulled off her multicolored skirts, one by one, and tossed them atop the fire. Her kerchief flew next, and then her shawl. Finally, she stripped down to her shift. The conflagration lasted only minutes, but it scorched the front of her thighs with its heat.

When the flames died down, the last of Madame Esmerelda had burned away.

CHAPTER NINE

AS NOTES WENT, the one Gareth received from his cousin two days after his disastrous encounter with Madame Esmerelda struck him as particularly opaque.

Meet me, it said. *Musicale at Arbuthnots'. Eight o'clock. In the blue dining room. Very important. Don't bring Madame Esmerelda. You were right about her. Ned.*

Gareth couldn't bear to think of Madame Esmerelda. Every time he thought of that evening, a hot stab of shame lanced through him, like a burning poker stabbed in his side. Sitting in his study, pretending to industriously pore over a stack of bills and reports, it should have been easy to put the woman from his mind.

It wasn't. After all, he *was* in his study with his man of business.

There was no place for nervousness in Gareth's relationship with his servants. Until these last few days, his interactions with White had been simple. The man dealt with the estate correspondence; Gareth paid his salary. Gareth liked simplicity. He liked not having to worry about what the man thought. He liked not wondering whether his latest ham-handed attempt at conversation would result in humiliation and unease.

He didn't like feeling like an ass. And Madame Esmerelda's dreadfully clear eyes—the ones that had seen Ned as something other than a childish irritant—had dismissed him. He'd told her to look at herself through his eyes, but if she had really done so, she would not have been ashamed. If she'd understood how bravado and bluster had transformed in his breast to hunger, she'd have laughed outright.

Who was he fooling? She had known it. She had spoken the truth that he'd hidden for so long behind a scowl and a cutting phrase. He had no way of conversing with others. He didn't know how to make friends. He cringed, feeling awkward and ungainly every time he made the effort. And so long ago—more than twenty years before—he'd given up the task entirely.

But there came a time in a man's life when he no longer wanted to cut down everyone around him. Gareth didn't need to read tea leaves to see the future that lay ahead of him if he continued on this solitary path.

He was going to be lonely. And not just the little loneliness that he experienced now, the soft wistfulness for someone to talk with and touch, but a fierce longing, one that whispered that it could all have been different if only—if only—

If only he what?

Because of all the things she had said that night, the one that had cut the deepest—the one that had slashed through layers of muscle and subcutaneous fat, to score the artery—was that it was his choice to be who he was. For years he had told himself that he had no choice about the way he was. That coldness and calculation were natural to his personality. That he responded to threats by eviscerating them with his mind.

He'd believed he could not be the warm, loving brother his sister longed for; that he could not bring Ned under his wing as a friend instead of a subject, to be ordered about.

She had stripped his illusions away. He'd chosen this life, and what seemed bearable when it resulted from implacable fate became untenable as a matter of option. If he did not change in the years to come, the thought that he had chosen this path would nibble away at him, like a mouse at a sack of grain, until nothing was left.

If only he had the courage to make different choices.

If he was going to have that courage, he could not put the matter off. He could not wait for some far-off time or place in dreams and fairy tales. It was now she demanded. This moment. In his study.

He said the dreaded word. "White."

At the sound of his name, his man of business looked up obligingly. "My lord?"

There was a cool draft in the room. It didn't stop Gareth's palms from moistening with a hint of cowardice. He fixed his gaze on the velvet curtains behind White. Conversation was easier if he didn't have to look into the man's eyes. The fabric rippled in the breeze, and Gareth found courage as best he could.

"It occurs to me that we have—" Gareth took a deep breath, and the rest of the words spilled out all in rush "—a number of things in common."

"We do?"

From the corner of his eye, Gareth saw faint puzzled lines furrow White's forehead.

Gareth clenched his hand and resisted the urge to punch his leg in frustration.

"Yes," Gareth said. "We do." And damn it, there he was again, using that quelling tone. One couldn't have a conversation if one quelled the person one was attempting to converse with.

"Perhaps my lord would care to enumerate?"

Gareth didn't care to enumerate, damn it. But he was going to have to try if he ever expected to get anywhere. Gareth shuffled through the dismally tiny selection of facts that he knew about the man.

"Well," he suggested, "we are both men."

White put his head to one side. The motion drew Gareth's eyes from the drapes and forced him to look his employee in the face. Gareth swallowed.

"Yes," said White. "We are."

"And," Gareth plunged forward, "we are of a similar age."

"Indeed, my lord."

Gareth tapped his closed fist against his hip. There the known similarities ended. Gareth felt like ten kinds of an idiot—as Madame Esmerelda had no doubt intended. White waited, that curious expression on his face. He reminded Gareth of a pigeon considering a crust of bread held in the hands of a small child. Apparently, he expected something additional. But what could Gareth say?

We are both literate.

We both have fewer than five children.

"And we both enjoy the company of women."

Stupid, stupid, stupid. He knew it was stupid as soon as the words left his mouth. There was an extremely befuddled pause from White's side of the room. As if the child had lobbed the entire loaf of bread at the pigeon, and White didn't know whether to fly away or tear at the bounty.

"Shocking similarities, my lord," said White. That straight, unblinking gaze seemed subtly mocking in Gareth's mind.

The tips of Gareth's ears heated. He grabbed the edge of the desk and squeezed, as if to throttle that damned fortune-teller by proxy. There was a good reason Gareth didn't attempt to make friends. He wasn't any good at it. And he *hated* not being good at things.

He was making a scapegoat of her again.

If she ever found out about this, she'd mock him, and she would be right. He knew he used his social status as a shield to prevent this awkwardness. It had worked. It had worked ever since he was twelve.

It was only now that it failed. The import of that failure hit him directly in the chest. If he couldn't even talk to a man who depended upon him for his livelihood, who would he ever connect with? He would be isolated all his life. Gareth fumbled for a topic of conversation.

"What's it like, then? Marriage."

White leaned back. Puzzled lines crinkled the corners of his eyes. "It's a marvelous state."

"But doesn't Mrs. White ever lie to you?"

White was no fool. Those lines relaxed and smoothed away, as if he'd finally understood the reason for the inquiry. "All the time. The benefit of marriage is that it becomes so easy to recognize when one's spouse lies."

Gareth frowned. That state of hypocrisy seemed unbearable. It reinforced all his reasons for avoiding lengthy relationships. "What sort of lies does Mrs. White tell?"

White put his hands to the side of his head and batted his eyes in a manner Gareth supposed was intended to be femininely flirtatious. On the man's sharp, masculine features, the expression was closer to frightening. "Oh, no, William. The shawl was quite inexpensive."

The high falsetto proceeding from his normally baritone man of business made Gareth sit back in surprise.

"Of course," White added in his normal voice, "I lie
to her, too."

"Oh?"

"Just this morning, I told her, 'Nonsense, my dear, you
haven't aged a day.'"

Gareth shoved at the papers on his desk morosely. He
had no experience with this sort of interaction. It sounded
mundane and comforting. How could it seem both foolish
and enviable at the same time?

White laid a piece of blotting paper over the letter he
had been working on. "This may be an impertinent question, my lord—but hypothetically speaking, is there a
particular woman that you are thinking about?"

"Hypothetically speaking?" Gareth sighed. It was not
as if he could possibly lower himself any further in
White's estimation at this point. "Yes."

"And has this, uh, hypothetical woman perhaps told
you lies?"

"Hypothetically, everything out of her mouth has been
a lie," Gareth complained, much aggrieved. "Everything
except her kisses. She meant them."

White nodded, as if he regularly dispensed advice on
women to lovelorn lords. "Are you wondering if you can
trust her? Hypothetically, of course."

"Oh, I know I can't do that. What I really want to know
is…" Gareth's thoughts slowed like sap. He really wanted
to know if his near-obsession with a woman whose name
he didn't even know would end if he took her to bed. He
wanted to know if he'd ever eradicate that cold, lonely
emptiness in his heart, the one that still longed to have
people about him he could not intimidate.

He wanted to know when his mind had split on the subject of Madame Esmerelda. One half demanded he take her in simple, sexual conquest. The other wanted to…to make her his friend. He swallowed.

That wouldn't happen anytime soon. Not after the way he'd behaved.

He doubted he'd ever see her eyes cloud with lust again. Not when he'd shown her what an ass he really was. He glanced up at White, who watched him attentively. Envy at the man's calm complacence flickered in Gareth's breast. He'd wager White knew what to do in situations like this one.

"White," he said uncomfortably, "what I really want to know is—do you know how to apologize to a woman?"

THE CLOCK SHOWED ten minutes before eight. Ned's gut clenched and beads of sweat dampened his forehead. The Arbuthnots' annual gathering should have been no cause for consternation. But Ned had a plan and it stewed, like an indigestible lump of gristle, deep in his stomach. His every instinct told him he should stop the madness he'd set in motion before it sprouted heads like a mythical hydra. His infernal sense of honor had been twinging all day. Everything he had ever been taught counseled him that what he schemed was wrong. Really, really wrong, in a life-changing, reputation-destroying way.

This would not have been much of a test if the work had been easy. He knew what needed to be done. Madame Esmerelda had told him the matter was entirely in his hands. Her words tumbled through his mind, over and over.

Don't trust me, she'd said.

But how could Ned not trust her? Long ago, she'd predicted he would win free of the deep malaise that gripped him. He had. She'd predicted Ned would make something worthwhile of himself, something worth living for. He hoped that he would. But now, he sensed that awful darkness lurking, a vile monster hiding just beyond the periphery of his vision.

Not trust Madame Esmerelda?

If he couldn't trust her, he couldn't trust that she had been right that day so long ago, when she'd told him to live. He couldn't believe she'd seen a future for him, free of that stultifying despair. If she hadn't seen the future then all Ned's hopes for his future were lies.

She couldn't be wrong. He wouldn't let her be.

This, Ned concluded, was a test.

He couldn't rely on anyone else. He couldn't rely on Madame Esmerelda's tasks. He couldn't even assume Lady Kathleen's icy elegance would bring Blakely to his knees. No. Ned would make sure Blakely married her, even if he had to trap them into it.

But Blakely had not yet arrived.

In the half hour since Ned had arrived at the Arbuthnots' soiree, he'd been watching Lady Kathleen from the corner of his eye. He would have been aware of her even without his plan. His chest constricted every time she drew breath. It was a perfectly natural response, he told himself, after what he'd planned.

Even now, across the wide expanse of the great room, he sensed her. She was dressed in a white gown that would have been simple, were it not for the hundreds of brilliants sewn into it, in patterns that dazzled his eye every time she moved. They made her blond hair look almost white, as if it were made of platinum.

She, on the other hand, had spent her evening looking everywhere else—at the other men who danced attendance on her, strutting ravens all, at the orchestra performing in the corner, even up at the ceiling, patterned in red paint and gold leaf. She'd looked at him once—a long, searching glance—and then colored and looked away.

Directly opposite his quarry stood his second group of players. To wit: There was Laura, Blakely's sister. She stood by Ned's mother, a stick-thin matron, graying hair twisted and curled and adorned with flowers that reminded him of spring. And close by these two ladies was Lady Bettony, an inveterate gossip, whose talent for spreading rumors was surpassed only by the keenness of her observation.

Ned met Laura's gaze across the ballroom. She gave him a terse nod. She was ready; she understood the task Ned had appointed for her. Laura had been curious, and therefore easily bribed. He'd given her Madame Esmerelda's address, in exchange for her services tonight.

It was five minutes before eight now, and Blakely still had not appeared.

Lady Kathleen had betrayed tiny signs of nervousness all evening, which Ned detected even from this distance. Her manners were more formal; her light laugh perhaps a touch heavier than usual.

Hardly surprising, given the circumstances.

After all, Ned had sent her a note.

Correspondence with an unmarried lady was a breach of etiquette. Correspondence suggesting that she meet him to explore the unmarked servants' quarters at the Arbuthnots' was downright barbaric. But he hadn't suggested anything truly indelicate. Instead, he'd thought of that look on her face. For all her haughty airs, she'd almost seemed to enjoy talking to Ned. Strange; inexplicable, even. But then, of course fate would serve Madame Esmerelda's purposes.

He'd turned Madame Esmerelda's advice over and over in his head. Briefly, he'd considered the horrifying possibility that Madame Esmerelda was admitting she was wrong. That her predictions would not come true. But he couldn't accept it—wouldn't accept it, no matter how the possibility ate away at his heart. He had to believe she'd been right that night long ago when she'd told him to live. He had to believe she'd seen his future, free of darkness.

You must stand on your own two feet, without anyone to help you. No; there was only one conclusion. Given Blakely's stubbornness, Madame Esmerelda's tasks could only do so much to bring the fated couple together. The rest was up to Ned and the next four minutes.

Assuming Blakely made an appearance. Ned suppressed the touch of fear that accompanied that thought. Blakely would appear punctually. He was always cutting when Ned missed an appointed meeting by even a paltry minute.

But speaking of time, the first player swished into action. Lady Kathleen didn't look at Ned. She didn't even glance in his direction. But she waved her hands prettily, as if making her apologies, and slipped from the room.

Ned shut his eyes and envisioned her walking quietly down the gold-papered hall toward the ladies' retiring room. The blue dining room was only steps beyond the parlor set aside for that purpose, and from the reports of the servants, it was the perfect venue for this little tableau.

There was only one exit, and nowhere to hide. A couple alone in the room would be seen the instant the door opened.

A hint of desperate nausea turned Ned's stomach. He was openly sweating now, and his nerves fluttered. One word to Laura, and he could still avert the coming storm. A few phrases of his own to Lady Kathleen—if he hurried, he could catch her still—and the scene would not play out as he'd envisioned. He'd asked her to meet him there, and despite the impropriety of it all, she was going. It had to be fate.

Everything Ned hated about his own life—his powerlessness, the respect he never seemed to command—he was doing to her. He had wanted to control his own life; now he was wresting control from her, trapping her into matrimony. Even in the heated press of bodies in the open room, covered as he was by layers of linen, wool, and waistcoat, Ned shivered.

A last, desperate chivalrous corner of his mind shouted it was not too late. But Ned thought of Madame Esmerelda's face, so obviously distraught. He thought of the depths to which he could yet fall. And he steeled himself to let events go forward as planned.

As they would, if only Blakely were present. Lady Kathleen undoubtedly thought—as the note Ned sent her implied—she would be meeting *Ned* to discuss the reasons why she slipped from the crowds and wandered in servants' quarters. He didn't want to think what it meant, that she'd left to meet him under such improper circumstances.

Because Ned wouldn't meet her. Instead, Blakely would arrive prepared to gloat over Ned's claimed surrender. A conversation between the two of them would ensue. Fate and the spirits might bring bodies together where recalcitrant minds had previously resisted. And then shortly after Blakely and Lady Kathleen closeted themselves alone, Laura would lead that tight knot of women to their discovery. Scandal, the blow to Lady Kathleen's reputation and Blakely's own sense of responsibility would take care of the remainder.

And Ned had no doubt—no real doubt, that is, as he didn't count that roiling pit of denial in his stomach—that what started as responsibility would grow into real affection. With Madame Esmerelda's imprimatur, it could do little else. The only reason Ned saw not to order the wedding punch directly was that Blakely had not yet appeared that evening.

Unless his cousin hadn't been announced, and had instead proceeded directly to the dining room.

Horrifying thought. Lady Kathleen could be meeting his cousin now. Asking, perhaps what he was doing there. Blakely was no fool; if he figured out what Ned had done, he would leave before their fates were sealed. If Blakely was there, Laura needed to make her appearance now.

Ned glanced across the room. Laura hadn't moved.

Suppose on the other hand Blakely had been delayed. Then Lady Kathleen would be cooling her heels in the blue dining room. Lady Bettony could hardly burst in on a solitary girl—or at least, if she did, there would be no gossip in it.

A lady's reputation was supposed to be a fragile thing. Why, then, did it take so much effort for Ned to crack this one? Cold sweat trickled from his armpits.

Madame Esmerelda had never said Ned's task would be easy. She'd told him to rely on himself. And maybe, just maybe, that's what he needed to do right now. Taking a deep breath, Ned set off toward the dining room.

He'd intended to listen at the door and ascertain if both parties were inside. But Lady Kathleen stood just outside the room, angrily tapping her foot. One hand rested on her hip. The other beat an impatient tattoo against her skirts. The rhythm made that net of brilliants send coruscating flashes of light all about her, as if she were Zeus, sending out little sparks of lightning. When she saw him, she pressed her lips together.

"And you've just chosen to appear, then?" A hint of anger slipped in her voice and transformed the tinkling melody into something harsher. "I shouldn't have come. I should have ignored your letter. I should have insisted on obtaining the proper introduction, because this is most improper. I didn't imagine you would make me *wait*. If you're trying to talk to me alone, you're doing an awful job of it."

She cast a look at him, as if waiting for an apology.

"You haven't seen anyone else?"

Instead of answering, she glanced down the hall and turned on her heel, disappearing into the room behind her.

Ned perforce followed.

The blue dining room was cold, unheated either by fire or the press of closely packed bodies. Two things were missing. First, and most oddly, the walls were cream and gold without a speck of the expected blue in evidence. Second, Blakely was nowhere to be found. A clock on the wall showed two minutes past eight. His cousin was late.

Once inside, Lady Kathleen whirled around and pulled the note he'd sent her from the sash of her gown. Her hands shook and the crisp white ribbon tore away. With it came the seam of her dress. It gaped, white cloth at her waist falling to reveal inches of tantalizing ivory petticoats. She looked down and her fists bit into the paper.

"This," she said, waving his note in his face, "is the most horrific breach of etiquette I have encountered. You should know better than to ask to speak with me alone. I should know better than to do so." She turned her head away, slightly. "So why am I here?"

"Lady Kathleen." Ned raised his hand against the rising tide of her ire. "My cousin—"

"Your cousin." Her words were flat. "Stop hiding behind your cousin." Her eyes glinted, gray ice against the furious flush of her cheeks. "You can't really expect me to believe this is about him."

Ned waved his hands in placation. "Look. I can explain. I needed to talk with you privately, because I just wanted to—to—"

To separate you from everyone else so I could trap you into marrying Blakely. Ned winced. There was no way to honestly complete his sentence. Talk about tossing fuel on the fire.

"You wanted to *what?*" Her hand rose slowly to touch her lips.

"You won't believe this," Ned said slowly, "but I wasn't attempting any impropriety between us."

Her brow clouded at that.

"I just—I just wanted to—to—" Ned gave up trying to come up with a favorable explanation for his behavior. It wasn't possible. "I'm sorry." He took a handkerchief from his pocket and wiped his forehead. "I know I haven't acted well. It's just—you see, I'm in a bit of a bind. And—and—things are not going well for me right now."

That was a bit of an understatement. As he spoke the

words, Ned suddenly realized how Not Well things were going for him. He'd muddled everything up again. Black horror filled his mind at the thought. He really wasn't good for anything.

Ned stuffed his handkerchief in his pocket. "Just forget it all. Understand?"

She looked at him in bafflement. "You know," she said, "I was not serious earlier when I suggested you were mad. But—are you?"

Matters went from Not Well to Very Unwell.

"In fact, you look exceedingly ill." She pulled off her glove and put one cool hand on Ned's forehead.

At the touch of her bare fingers, Ned's body responded. He was twenty-one, and only too human. And she was close enough that he could see down her neckline. He could trace the valley between her breasts with his eyes. He was humiliatingly, uncontrollably erect. He prayed she didn't look down.

She didn't. Instead, she frowned and moved her hand along his forehead. "You feel a little warm."

Very Unwell slid into Please Let Me Die in the Next Minute. Ned was alone with a woman. He was aroused and embarrassed, and she was stripping off her clothing— well, her glove—and touching him. He was trying to compromise her into marrying another man. She feared he might be sick. Or mad. Probably both.

Ned knew all too well that her fears had some basis. On his darkest days, he worried he carried some species of madness. And to have this confident woman look at him in that pitying way… Matters couldn't possibly sink any lower than they were now.

And then, of course, they did.

Ned heard the well-tuned snick of a door easing open.

He didn't even have time to give voice to the terrible, wordless scream that roared through his mind. In that bare instant, he only had time to grab her wrist; no time at all to push her away.

As he'd so carefully planned, there was no place for a trysting couple to hide.

Time froze. The door opened at what seemed a leisurely pace, swinging inward inch by deliberate inch. Ned couldn't react; his nerves were made of wood, and his limbs of jelly. He could only watch, and wince at the cozy tableau they presented.

There was Lady Kathleen, her face warm and solicitous. Her glove had fallen to the floor. Her gown gaped, disordered, at the waist, where her untied sash dangled. Her bare hand rested against Ned's face.

Ned had his hand atop hers, almost as if he were pulling her into an embrace.

And it was five minutes after eight. Please, he begged. Please let that be Blakely opening the door. Because if it were not, Ned would have succeeded in compromising Lady Kathleen.

The only problem was, she would have been compromised with the wrong man.

CHAPTER TEN

THE CHURCH BELLS HAD JUST SOUNDED half past seven when someone knocked. Jenny paused before the door, wondering whether she should open it. Her next appointment was tomorrow morning, and she had not yet decided how to handle her clients. With her room stripped of its lies and returned to boring functionality, what could she say?

She would have to find out sometime.

Jenny inched the door open. But no client of hers waited on the stoop.

"Look here," Lord Blakely said, "I know you are about to slam this door on my nose. But please don't."

Jenny inhaled crisp evening air. Lord Blakely was disheveled in the most casually devastating way. He carried his cravat in his hand and had left his waistcoat unbuttoned. His hair was wind-tousled. The last light of the sun imparted a wild gleam to his eyes. Seductiveness wafted off him, and Jenny was reminded of the rough feel of his mouth against hers.

That memory burned through her. Even the air around him was charged with electric anticipation. From two feet away, she could smell his subtle, masculine musk, feel a hint of the heat from his body. An illusion, most likely, composed of lust and wistful thinking on her part.

But she also remembered the cold disrespect he'd shown her the last time she faced him.

"You have one sentence to explain why I should hear you out."

He accepted this with far better grace than Jenny expected. "Fair enough." Lord Blakely glanced up into the air, his lips compressing. His eyes narrowed as he no doubt searched for the argument that would change her mind.

A kiss—a real one, a gentle one, unlike that travesty he'd forced on her two nights ago—might have done the trick. But eventually he shook his head.

"I can only think of lies," he admitted with a sigh. "Really, you should slam the door. I would, if I were you."

Jenny fiddled with the handle. "I'm feeling magnanimous tonight, my lord."

He took a deep breath and stepped forward.

"You can have *three* sentences."

At first, she thought that frozen look in his eyes was a warning not to make inappropriate jokes. But then miraculously, he smiled. It was a small smile, a bit rusty, as if his face was still unused to such expressions. But it was genuine. And this time, he didn't stuff the expression behind stony arrogance. He didn't turn away. He looked a bit less like an unkempt, untouchable Greek god, and a bit more like an extremely handsome and very touchable mortal.

Jenny's breath caught.

It was just like him. Lord Blakely hadn't needed any sentences after all.

He used them anyway.

He looked down and fingered the edge of his coat uncomfortably. "I am," he said in a rush of words, "desperately sorry for my behavior the other night. What I did was unacceptable. You didn't slap me nearly hard enough."

Whatever Jenny had expected, it wasn't that. Her mouth dropped open. "Why would you bother to apologize to *me?* I should have thought my feelings beneath your notice."

"I'm not apologizing to you to assuage your *feelings.*" That icy outrage was more like the Lord Blakely Jenny remembered. "I'm apologizing to you because I damn well owe you an apology." He nodded, as if that explained everything.

"Lord Blakely," Jenny asked, "do you have any idea what an apology *is?*"

He raised one haughty eyebrow at her. "I have some small acquaintance with the concept," he said in his most freezing tone. And then, he rather ruined the proud expression by adding, "I asked White."

Jenny's head spun. "Who?"

"My man of business." He crossed his arms in front of his chest, guarding against her laugh. "I'm not expecting anything in response."

But his gaze arrested on her lips and gave the lie to his statement. "Besides, I'm supposed to meet Ned at eight sharp, and so I can't stay. I just wanted to tell you." He looked away. "And now I have."

That look, Jenny thought, would be her undoing. "Do you have five minutes?" she heard herself ask. "I've just put on the teakettle." Jenny nearly bit her tongue. Tea was normal. Mundane. Mortal. One didn't ask the Marquess of Blakely in for a cup of tea.

He looked at her with guarded wariness. And then, wonder of wonders, he nodded.

A minute later, Lord Blakely was seated at the table in her back room with a clay mug in front of him. He'd looked speculatively around her stripped-down front room, her rickety wood tables freed from their heavy black shrouds. But he hadn't asked any questions. And when she'd led him down the short hall into her living space in the back room, he hadn't so much as wrinkled his nose at the close quarters. He'd sat in a squeaking chair at the table where Jenny ate her meals. He'd waited quietly while she readied the leaves. After she poured, he picked up the cup and turned it around in his hands. Jenny imagined him cataloging every imperfection in its surface, every chip at its edge.

"I don't have any sugar to offer you," she eventually essayed.

"Sugar." Lord Blakely's nostrils flared. "I do not take sugar," he said in a voice of disdain.

It was the same tone of loathing Jenny imagined a bloodthirsty pirate would have employed to say, "I do not take prisoners."

Lord Blakely did not, in fact, take prisoners. What he took instead was a cautious sip of tea.

"White," he said rather stiffly, "says that an apology given to a woman needs to be accompanied by at a minimum, flowers. He also told me you would ask what I was sorry for. And that I would not have a good answer to the question." He glanced up at her, swiftly, and then returned to contemplation of his cup. "White is very competent. It is disconcerting to discover that he is not correct in every particular."

"So you talked to White?"

He took another sip of tea. "Yes. I talked to White. I had a very long conversation with White." He flashed another glance at her.

"And did you enjoy it?"

"I—well." He looked down into his mug and swirled

the liquid around. "I think so. Probably. Yes." Miracles doubled, and another smile played across his lips.

"Three," said Jenny in pleasure.

"Three?" He set the cup down. Tea sloshed over the edge and seeped into the wood of the table. "Three *what?*"

"Three points."

He shook his head in befuddlement. "Points? What points?"

"I get a point every time you smile," she explained. "I've decided to award myself five if I can ever make you laugh."

He drew himself up in that manner he employed just before he said something cruel. He looked offended. But he bit his lip. He paused, almost as if counting. What finally came out of his mouth was: "How do I get points?"

Jenny tried to mask her shock. He wasn't trying to cut her down with arrogant drivel. Maybe the tea had turned his mind. She was going to have to make a note of the leaves: bohea, good for taming arrogant lords. But his temporary lapse was no reason to give up her advantage. She pursed her lips and put her head to one side. "You don't."

"Why not?"

"*You* like numbers. I need points. *Lots* of points. It's protection, you see."

He glowered at her. "If you collect points, I have to get something. It's inequitable otherwise."

She shrugged. "Well, I don't like numbers. So you can't have points."

His fingers drummed against the table. The liquid in his cup sloshed. "That makes an odd sort of sense, in a world devoid of all logic. White warned me about that, too." He sighed. "What *do* you like?"

"And I thought you didn't care." The bitter words spilled from her before she could call them back.

"Ah." Lord Blakely's voice was all steel blade again, like a cold knife against Jenny's throat. "Madame Esmerelda—Meg—whatever your name is." He swallowed and placed his hands flat on the table.

"I have a confession to make," he said, in that voice forged from hard, cold metal. "It will come as no surprise. But it seems that every time I *do* care, I find myself saying something harsh in response. As if I could sever any emotion that attaches me to anyone else."

That flat, unemotional tone took her aback. She'd heard it from him so many times before. She was learning not to trust his tone. His eyes glimmered, and he stared at the wall behind her. He was not a dispassionate man, Jenny was beginning to realize. He was just very, very uncomfortable letting his emotions show.

"I care," he said flatly. "And I am trying to stop responding the way I do. I told you I was sorry. I meant it."

Jenny's heart trembled. It did more than tremble. It flipped over, exposing its tender underbelly. She had no idea how to take this side of Lord Blakely. He apologized in the same arrogant tone of voice he'd used to cut her to shreds the other night. And yet she suspected the tone he used was as ingrained in him as his intellect.

"Now," he continued in a businesslike tone. "About those points of yours. What do you like?"

If she were a lady, Jenny would own that violets were her favorite flower. If she were a courtesan, she would confess a desire for emeralds. But she was Jenny Keeble, and she didn't want gifts from this man.

Her brow furrowed in mock concentration. "Would you know," she said softly. "I find that I am partial to..."

He leaned forward, intent on her answer.

"Elephants," Jenny finished.

Lord Blakely raised his chin. "You're trying to make me laugh," he accused. "It shan't work. Citation to a mere mammal is not worth five points."

He was every bit as arrogant as he had been before. But there was something warmer about the cast of his features. Something that hadn't been there before tonight. And so Jenny laughed. She couldn't help herself, and she wouldn't have, even if she wanted to. When she did, he smiled along with her, his face lighting up. Their eyes met. Locked.

He shoved his mug of tea across the table and stood up.

"Damnation," he said.

"What's the matter?" she asked, before she remembered he was supposed to meet Ned, and he would undoubtedly have to take his leave.

"I'm going to have to apologize to you again."

Jenny brushed her skirts into place and looked away. "I understand. You have to go—"

He stepped toward her. "That," he said brusquely, "is not what I have to do." He was so close she could smell his soap and the earthy, masculine scent of bay rum.

"You see," he whispered, "when you laugh, it's as if this light spreads all around you. I can't figure out how to respond. I'm not sure if I should scurry from it, like a cockroach, or fly closer, like a moth. I've tried scurrying. It didn't work. So I have a control in the experiment. Shall I modify a variable?"

It took Jenny a second to realize he was talking about kissing again. By that time, he had raised his hand to her cheek. Two warm fingers slid against her jawbone.

"Tell me to stop," he said, "and I'll stop. Tell me to leave, and I'll leave. But I would prefer you didn't tell me to leave."

"Kiss me." The words were from her mouth before she had a chance to think them over.

His finger rubbed her lips, as if to capture her acquiescence. His hand stroked down the side of her face. Then his lips came down on hers.

His kiss drove all thought of elephants and points, arrogance and loneliness, from Jenny's mind. The world receded until there was nobody present but the two of them. Until only the liquid sounds of the mating of their mouths filled her ears. His taste—tea mixed with sweet mint—enveloped her. His hands whispered down the simple muslin of her dress.

She brought her palm up against his chest, ran it down fine linen. He exhaled and his chest pressed against her fingers. And then he, too, explored her, his hands tracing her shoulder blades, down each vertebra to the small of her back. His fingers traveled up again, gilding her spine with their heat. Then her shoulders. The nape of her neck. And his mouth, always his mouth, hot on hers. She gasped, and he drank in the sound of her desire.

He pulled away from her, and she blinked dizzily. But he only moved to sit. Wood creaked as he distributed his weight. And then he pulled her atop him to straddle his thighs. Her skirt rucked up to her knees, and she let herself sink against his hard muscles. His body's arousal pressed, hot and rigid, between her thighs. Her own excitement pooled in response.

He kissed her again, tongue and lips hot against hers.

His hands slid up her waist, sliding over her chest. Jenny gasped as he thumbed her breasts. His fingers circled the tips, coaxing them into hardness. And then he pulled away from her mouth, and placed his lips around her nipple through the material of her dress.

A white blaze of light seared through the layers of cloth, and Jenny threw back her head. His practiced hands adjusted the bodice of her dress and pulled down her loose chemise and the thicker stays. He lifted a firm globe free. The cool air touched it for only a second before he closed his mouth around the tip. He licked it and a wave of pleasure crashed against her. He sucked it, and the wave became an ocean rising up eagerly to meet her.

Another kiss, this time on her mouth again. She drank him in, as tipsy on his taste as he appeared to be on hers. His hands came around her fiercely, and he fumbled behind her. Thank God for simple gowns. Her dress loosened. He pulled it down around her shoulders and it fell to her waist. Stays followed, and then her chemise.

"God," he whispered, tracing the contours of her breast with one long finger. "You have no idea how many times I have fantasized about this."

Before she could come up with an answer, he took her other breast in his mouth, and all possibility of words washed away in a hot surge of desire. Jenny clutched his shoulders, pressed herself against the hard ridge between his legs.

"You're even more passionate than I dreamed," he said. "The smallest touches. The way you move against me. Oh, God, Meg. Tell me your name."

His mouth came down on her nipple again. This time he bit it lightly, and Jenny made a sound in her throat. She was drowning against him. But he showed no signs of letting her catch her breath to answer.

He lifted his head. "Tell me your name."

Jenny, she thought. *It's Jenny Keeble.* Her thoughts moved at a snail's pace; her nails dug into his back.

"Can't you feel it?" he whispered. "We're going to explode together. Tell me your name. And I can be inside of you."

Her inner muscles clenched at the thought.

He slipped his hand under her skirt and found her wet slickness waiting for him. He touched her between the legs, rubbed her where she was hot and slippery. Where she was sensitive, and those featherlight touches sent pulses of pleasure from head to toe.

"Yes," he whispered. "God, I know you want me. Let me—"

Jenny shook her head to remind herself. "I won't be your mistress."

He kissed her throat. "At present, I'm not interviewing for the position. I'm here because of what you said."

"What I said?"

"I *am* lonely. Damned lonely."

She closed her hands on his shoulders, his words scalding into her.

He nodded. "You don't like numbers. I'm trying to think what we have in common. That was what you said, right? Find what we have in common?"

It wasn't supposed to happen like this. He was supposed to stay cold and distant. Instead, he tempted her with her deepest desires.

"Right," he said, setting his jaw. "I can think of one thing we both enjoy." He put his lips back around her nipple. He teased the sensitive bud back and forth. And then his hand circled down below, rubbing the sensitive flesh between her legs.

"Oh, my God," she moaned. "Lord Blakely—"

He lifted his head, his eyes hooded. "Gareth," he said. "What?"

"My name is Gareth. Don't call me Lord Blakely. Not now."

He leaned his head against hers, nose to nose. Their breath mingled into sweet perfume. His hand, still trapped between her thighs, stroked gently. Jenny thrilled, half pleasure, half shame, that he touched her in that intimate way.

His eyes glowed. "Tell me your name," he insisted.

"Nobody's called me by my name in twelve years."

"Nobody's called me Gareth in twenty-four. I'll not go another day without hearing it."

Church bells struck the hour. It was the first event outside the two of them Jenny noticed. The heavy vibration from those deep tones echoed through her, a reverberation of the pleasure he sent through her with his touch. She counted the strokes. One, two…

His thumb stroked across her bare nipple again. "God almighty," he whispered against her neck. "Please tell me your name."

Three, four, five. Jenny rang like that bell. She tried to remember all the reasons why she couldn't tell him her name. Six. Why she couldn't allow him, naked and virile, into bed with her. Seven. Why he couldn't sink into her right now, stretching her wide. Eight, and the bells stopped.

Eight o'clock.

Another echo, this one in her own mind. His words, at the beginning, before he'd even entered her rooms.

It was now eight o'clock in the evening.

Jenny straightened, her hands flying to her cheeks in horror. "Ned!"

"Ned?" She felt his thighs contract. He drew back, a

scowl on his face. His tone was formal, with just a hint of offended sanctimony. "My name is Gareth."

Jenny shook her head in exasperation. "Your cousin Ned."

He sat, still and wary as a crouching leopard. He didn't even blink. But she felt understanding come to him in the gradual contraction of his muscles. First the thighs that supported her. The tension traveled up his shoulders, through his hands. Finally, she saw fine, dark lines spread like a net across his face.

He let out a breath. "Ned. Ah, yes. Ned. I had completely forgotten. Do I have to go to him?"

The last question made him sound like a plaintive child. But he made the decision without Jenny saying a word. She could see his choice in the squaring of his shoulders. As if he were hefting a great weight in donning the mantle of Lord Blakely. He'd said he would meet his cousin at eight, and so meet the boy he would. His implacable honor and responsibility allowed no other option.

She stumbled to her feet, freeing him of her weight. He adjusted his clothing—fastening buttons, brushing his coat into some semblance of order. He didn't look at her.

"I will return." He fastened his cravat around his neck with the air of one tying a hangman's noose. "As soon as is practicable. It's only fifteen minutes there and back. This shouldn't take long."

He paused, his hand resting on her naked shoulder. And then he walked away.

CHAPTER ELEVEN

A BLAST OF HEAT from the massed, milling bodies struck Gareth in the face as he entered the crowded room at the Arbuthnots'. He was already overheated from hurrying, and tense with thwarted desire.

Under the best of circumstances, he despised crowds. They made any room feel a bit too small. They stank, scents of human sweat layering atop rosewater and jasmine in nauseating fashion. And even though he knew rationally it was not so, he always felt as if everyone were looking at him.

This crowd was no more appealing than usual. He scanned male faces, attached to somber black suits, looking for his cousin. Next to him, a majordomo announced him in a carrying tone.

So intent was he in his search for Ned that at first Gareth didn't notice the preternatural hush that fell. But it was unmistakable. For several moments, there was neither a clink of glass nor one single out-of-place whisper. At first, he attributed the odd sensation to temporary mental disorder brought on by unfulfilled lusts. Then he thought it a simple lull in conversation. A statistical anomaly, to be sure, but the anomalous occurred all the time.

But the sea of surrounding wide-eyed faces aligned toward Gareth like iron filings in a magnetic field. In a single gut-clenching moment, he realized the silence was not happenstance. Everyone really was looking at him. And—a quick check—he'd buttoned his jacket properly and his cravat was not askew.

Three seconds after the hush fell, conversation swelled about him in renewed fervor. He snatched pieces of conversation. "Carhart" he heard from an elderly lady. He strained his ears listening for others. But they were indistinct in the hubbub. "Embrace," he heard quite clearly. And "compromise."

Not three words he wanted to hear in close connection. Perhaps there was a perfectly reasonable explanation. There was no need to panic just yet. For instance, what the matron had whispered could very well have been something like, "It's a good thing Mr. Edward *Carhart* has finally decided to *embrace* reality and come to a reasoned *compromise* with his cousin."

It could have been.

And the hostess could have suspended the law of gravity for this fête.

Slowly, Gareth made his way through the densely packed crowds. They opened around him. Nobody spoke to him. Nobody even looked at him.

As he walked, those he neared shut their mouths and kept quiet. It was incredibly annoying. The first time he actually wanted to overhear a conversation, and nobody dared oblige him. Gareth did manage to grasp a few pieces here and there. Every phrase he heard was like picking up a sharp shard of glass, painted in a distinct color. Individually, the pieces meant nothing; a blur of color, a few lines. But by the time he reached the other end of the hall, he'd obtained enough bits to construct a damning—and damnable—mosaic.

Ned had been caught sharing an indiscreet embrace with Lady Kathleen, who was now considered thoroughly compromised. In the intervening minutes since this had happened, Ned had been punched in the nose, and he'd bled through somewhere between two and five handkerchiefs. Whether the punch had been thrown by the lady herself or by her father, the Duke of Ware, was unknown.

Bad enough on its own. But matters grew worse.

Even if the duke hadn't thrown the punch, it was clear the man had not stood idly by. There was a challenge. A duel, in this day and age. Pistols or swords, Ware had offered, and Ned had little experience with either weapon. Not that it mattered, because Ned couldn't fight a man well in his sixties, and a peer of the realm.

The hostess's attempts to calm the man had been to no avail; the point, Ware had apparently announced to the titillated hordes, was not to satisfy honor but to slay the bastard who'd touched his daughter.

"Oh, Blakely. Thank heavens."

Gareth halted at the gasping words. They were the first anyone had dared speak to him all evening. Even through the stress and strain and tears that threatened to choke the speaker, he recognized her voice.

He turned to greet his sister.

Laura skidded to a halt in front of him. For one horrendously awkward moment, he thought she might actually throw herself into his arms. In public. With everyone watching. The flowers in her hair dangled on broken stems and her eyes were red-rimmed and puffy.

Unfortunately, she checked her impulse toward affection. Gareth drew himself up, straight and tall. It was just as well. He wouldn't have wanted to comfort her in front of all these people, anyway.

"Where—" He didn't even have time to start.

"Come with me. You have to come with me." She was hoarse. Little pockets of interested silence formed around the two of them. Everyone managed to look not quite in their direction, heads cocked and ears open.

The spectacle clearly had not yet finished. Gareth had no desire to play out this scene for public consumption, knowing it would be repeated ad nauseam in every last London drawing room for the next weeks. He'd go to the devil before he heard his sister's name on everyone's lips.

As Laura turned to lead him away, Gareth realized his options were extremely limited. He was already on the devil's doorstep.

Gareth followed his sister. The crowds parted for them, and the murmurs grew to a roar. They walked sedately, not touching. Not that it would have mattered if they'd linked arms and skipped the length of the hall, because all eyes were on them nonetheless. Once they entered a hallway, Gareth felt relief from the pressure of that attention almost immediately. No suffocating crowds. No watching eyes.

He need only deal with whatever madness Ned had managed to create. Laura paused before a door, squared her shoulders and opened it.

Inside, all the parties had congregated. This, then, was the room where the incident had taken place. A long table stretched end to end. The chairs were strewn about the room in a chaotic whirl, arranged for a madman's tea party. Lady Kathleen huddled in one corner, her mother fluttering over her like a protective warbler. Ned's own mother sat in the corner, watching Ned with dark, sad eyes. And there in the middle, straddling an upholstered chair, sat Ned. He slumped miserably, his arms folded against the back of his seat.

Next to him, the Duke of Ware towered. The man's bald pate shone in the orange gaslight. He, too, was gesturing. And talking at—definitely *at* rather than *to*—Ned. At Gareth's entrance, he curtailed his tirade.

"Blakely." The older duke had clearly been waiting for this moment.

Gareth returned his nod. "Ware."

Gareth walked closer. Ware stepped carefully around Ned to make room for them both. The careful dance reminded Gareth of two predators circling the same carcass, each uncertain whether to share the kill or fight for solitary rights.

"Your boy here—" Ware jerked his head in angry indication "—can't explain himself worth a damn."

"That's hardly news to me. Nonetheless," Gareth said, "I can't allow you to kill him. His death would be a terrible inconvenience for me."

Ware snorted. "If this is a sample of his behavior, his death couldn't be so inconvenient as his life."

Ned didn't even wince at that blow. Undoubtedly he'd been showered with compliments in a similar vein ever since this scene had collapsed in on him.

And collapse it had. A man with half Gareth's intelligence could easily make sense of everything that had taken place. Ned believed that Gareth was supposed to marry Lady Kathleen. And Gareth had been supposed to arrive half an hour earlier.

If it hadn't been for Madame Esmerelda and her tea, Gareth, rather than Ned, might have been caught in this scrape.

"Ah," Gareth said.

Ned buried his forehead deep into his arms.

The damned thing was Gareth couldn't even work up

a proper temper. He should have been angry. He should have been fuming at Ned's machinations.

What he felt instead was a terrible sympathy for the boy folded into that chair. What Ned had done was wrong. But Gareth understood what drove that impulse. It had been pride, a desire to be right at all costs, and that damned, trusting loyalty.

It was the same impulse that had driven Ned to offer Lady Kathleen the elephant, that had pushed the boy to his feet, clapping and shouting, after Gareth finished that terrible song. Ned had somehow convinced himself this was the right thing to do.

"Blakely." Ned's voice was obscured by so much superfine sleeve. "It wasn't supposed to be me here. It was supposed to be you."

"What?" Ware purpled, and grabbed the back of Ned's coat. "You compromised my daughter, and you didn't even want her for yourself?" He hissed the words. "If you ever tell her that, I'll—"

Gareth held up his hand. There were not many men who would have the effrontery to silence a duke. There were fewer still who could do so successfully. By some small miracle, Gareth discovered he was one of the lucky few. Ware relaxed his hold on Ned's jacket.

"Ware. We *will* talk to you. First, however, I must ascertain what has transpired here, and why."

"I've been trying to ascertain the whys all evening," Ware growled, "and your boy here hasn't made a lick of sense."

"I need to talk with him alone. At this point of the proceedings, I doubt we could settle anything in an intelligent fashion. Take your daughter and your wife home, and we can discuss this later."

"But I want to kill him *now.*"

Gareth met the man's eyes. "You want to kill him. But you'll take your daughter home instead."

The duke's square jaw snapped shut. For a long while, he met Gareth's gaze, clearly longing to lay waste to marquess and hapless cousin alike. Then he turned on his heel. "Come, poppet. No sense staying where tongues will wag. Let's get you home."

Gareth escorted the remaining players from the room. But even as he shut the door on the last one, Ned remained slumped in his seat on the chair. He hadn't even lifted his head from his sleeve.

"I shall make your confession easy." Gareth tried to gentle his voice. It didn't work. Instead, his words came out a fierce rumble. "I have already determined it was I who should have been trapped in whatever elaborate and idiotic tableau you had planned."

Ned didn't lift his head. Instead, he mumbled into his sleeve. "I did it for your benefit. It was supposed to be for the best. Someone has to be able to fix this."

That someone, Gareth thought, was going to be him. Responsibility again. Responsibility and, he realized, fault. He'd been a cold, unfeeling brute to Ned. Now, perhaps, he had a chance to patch matters up.

"I'm sorry," Ned said. "I knew it was up to me. And I—I just couldn't do it. She told me to rely on myself," Ned continued. "I did. And so it *has* to come out right. Doesn't it?"

"She?" A cold chill collected in Gareth's lungs. "Ned," he said slowly, "I need you to do something for me. I need you to tell me as best you can *exactly* what Madame Esmerelda told you to do."

IT HAD BEEN MORE THAN AN HOUR, and Lord Blakely had not yet returned.

Unable to sleep, unable even to rest, Jenny paced up and down the front room. At first, every noise she heard set her heart fluttering in anticipation. The leisurely beat of shoe leather against cobblestones started her pulse racing. She rushed to the windows—and then turned away in disappointment as an elderly ragman tramped by in the gloom. The warm spring night brought many such disappointments—noises that could have heralded his return. The passage of high-stepping horses. The slap of reins against hindquarters the next street over. London streets teemed with activity, even at this late hour. If one expected company, every last sound brought hope.

None of the activity she heard signified the return of Lord Blakely.

Jenny gradually let go of her arousal. Eventually, she slumped into the disheartening territory of outright discouragement. It was foolish, she chided herself, to engage in preposterous mental games, to come up with reasons without knowing what kept him away. But she could not help but play with possibilities.

Jenny was well aware she was hardly a diamond of the first water. She wasn't a diamond of any sort of water. When Lord Blakely had left her, he'd been physically excited. But he could easily have found a willing widow, one closer to his class and station, to tempt him. Why, then, would he bother to return?

And now that Ned agreed Jenny was a fraud, perhaps Lord Blakely had no reason to continue his campaign of seduction. Perhaps this was his revenge—this half state of desperate physical desire he'd left her in. Perhaps he was, at this very moment, imagining her shaking her fists in frustration. No doubt he was chuckling evilly, wherever he was.

Now she really knew she was letting her imagination run away with her. It was not in Lord Blakely's character to behave in such a fashion. He didn't chuckle.

Once unleashed, though, her imagination veered wildly afield. He could have been struck by a stampeding horse. Or perhaps he'd been abducted by rival ornithologists, intent on torturing him in order to steal his data on macaws.

All lies. Lies and ridiculous stories Jenny invented to avoid thinking about the one possibility that lurked kraken-like beneath the spinning maelstrom of her thoughts.

Lord Blakely had gone to meet Ned. When she'd last seen the boy, she'd told him not to trust her. With Ned cut loose, what reason would Lord Blakely have to return?

She'd been abandoned. Again.

She didn't even remember the first time it had happened. After all, she'd lived the entirety of her life in its aftermath.

Jenny assumed she had parents. Not only was it a matter of biological necessity, but someone had paid the bills at the Elland School in Bristol. They'd paid for fourteen years, from the time of Jenny's arrival through to her departure at eighteen. Even before then, Jenny dimly remembered a stocky farmwife employed to look after her.

That unknown someone had paid for her upkeep and arranged for her education, the transactions run anonymously through purchased annuities and a string of whey-faced solicitors. Nobody answered the letters Jenny sent, and she'd penned them from the first moment she'd been able to scratch tentative words.

Jenny's parents had been nothing more than a set of bank bills, perfunctorily issued at quarterly intervals. At the age of eighteen, she'd been told the annuity providing for her care would be extinguished soon and so she'd best think about finding employment. Whatever emotional connection she'd had with those bank drafts had been severed.

Jenny sighed and smiled wryly. After thirty years, she ought to have been reconciled to that feeling of abandonment. She'd never known anything else in her life. If Lord Blakely had disappeared from her life, he would only be leaving just like everyone else before him.

And yet, stupidly, this latest in her long string of abandonments felt just as devastating as the first. She feared he'd walked out, leaving her mired in a fog of emotion. Just like her desire to make phantom parents out of the solicitors' payments, she'd be plagued by thoughts of what might have been. What it would have felt like when Lord Blakely entered her body, inch by desperate inch. Whether his bare skin would have been warmer than hers. She would have wanted to see if the expression on his face warmed when he entered her in that most intimate way.

Jenny took a deep breath and allotted herself one minute longer of this ridiculous self-pity. There was little enough room for it. After tonight, she had a new life to claim.

When her minute passed, she brushed her hands and stood up.

"Well," she remarked to the empty room.

It listened, walls heavy.

"I didn't want him. Not really."

The night swallowed her lies.

IT WAS ONLY HALF AN HOUR LATER when something roused Jenny. Disoriented, she jumped out of bed, her heart pounding. The night was quiet, but the tiny back room in which she'd been asleep seemed to crouch, empty but waiting.

A knock sounded. This time Jenny identified the sound she'd heard in her sleep. It was him. She slid trembling hands down her chemise. She couldn't meet him like this. What was he doing here, at this time of the night? And what was she to do about it?

She fumbled for a wrapper. A third impatient rap sounded. As Jenny raced down the short hall between her rooms, she tried to think of words to hide the fluttering in her stomach. Words to prove that the delay had meant as little to her as it obviously had to him.

You're late.

You? I had forgotten about you.

She wiped damp palms on the wool of her wrapper and threw open the door. "I suppose you think—"

Lord Blakely's expression, shrouded in shadows, was as cold as if he'd never sat at her table. As if they hadn't kissed earlier that evening. As if the last time he saw her, he hadn't begged for her name with longing on his face. But he was not just cold. He looked wearier than the toll of the passing hours could explain.

It was not his expression that stole the words from her mouth. It was his companion. Ned slumped next to him. He contemplated the threshold of her door. His shoulders sagged and his features wilted.

"Ned," Jenny said, "what are you doing here?"

No answer. Ned turned his head away, biting his lip.

"Tell her," Lord Blakely rumbled. "Start from the beginning and go through the end. But tell her what you've done."

Ned heaved a great sigh. Then he pushed past Jenny and flung himself into a chair. Something was dreadfully amiss here—more than the usual bickering that took place between the cousins.

Lord Blakely motioned with a hand, and Jenny preceded him into the room. The door clicked shut behind them, and Jenny felt her way through the darkness until she'd found the candles on her table and the spills on the mantel.

A touch of illumination and everyone's faces became clear. But the flickering flame shed no light on what had brought the two of them here.

Jenny had no words to break the silence, and Lord Blakely seemed disinclined to prompt Ned further. Finally Ned put his head in his hands and spoke into his fingers. "The tasks weren't working. So that meant it was up to me to bring Blakely and Lady Kathleen together."

Jenny let out a little gasp, but Ned continued, oblivious to her horrified response.

"Both seemed recalcitrant, so I arranged for the two to meet each other secretly. And to be caught by—by various people, who would gossip about the arrangement. But Blakely did not come, and when I went to investigate, it was I who was caught."

"Oh, God, Ned. Why?"

"You *said*." Ned's accusation couldn't have been more petulant. "You said I had to rely on myself."

"I was speaking in generalities. I didn't mean you should force two people into a marriage neither wanted!"

"But they would have wanted it. Eventually. You said so." Ned raised red-rimmed eyes. "And now it will never happen, and it's all my fault. I'm not good enough—I'm not strong enough. Madame Esmerelda, you thought I was ready to make do without your advice, but I'm not. I've fouled up everything beyond all comprehension, and you have to help me fix it."

Jenny didn't need to meet Lord Blakely's gaze to know he hadn't brought Ned here to listen to more of her predictions. She should have made herself admit her fraud when last Ned was here. Selfishly, she'd wanted to spare herself the pain of uttering those words. What her selfishness had cost Ned, she was just starting to fathom. His freedom. His cousin's respect. His own sense of self-worth. He'd lost everything she'd told herself she was helping him achieve with her selfish lies.

Lord Blakely examined his fingernails in the candle-light. "Lady Kathleen's father finally agreed not to shoot Ned outright." Lord Blakely's even voice was a smooth contrast to Ned's ragged words. "What else may transpire as the result of this evening is still a matter of ongoing negotiation. Much depends upon what Ned believes he should do."

Jenny didn't know where to look. Not at Ned—she couldn't bear to see that despondent fear writ on his face. Nor could she look at Lord Blakely. She didn't know if she'd see disinterest, displeasure or disappointment. But she didn't dare lose the courage to do what must be done.

"Ned." There was a quaver in Jenny's voice. "When I told you to rely on yourself, I didn't mean for you to take the matter of your cousin's marriage into your own hands. I meant—"

She took a deep breath. There was no shying away

from the consequence she feared most. She looked one last time into those trusting eyes. She would never see them look at her with devotion again.

And then she made herself do it.

"I meant," she continued, "that your cousin is right. I can't tell the future. I don't speak to spirits. I don't have any occult powers. You need to rely on yourself because you cannot trust me."

Ned flinched with every phrase. But what she saw was not disillusionment, but disbelief. "No!" He looked around the room wildly. "This is some kind of test. To— to punish me for my failure this evening. I know I can show my loyalty."

Jenny's heart cracked. "Ned, it's not a test. It's the truth."

"But all your predictions! Your arcane powers. How did you always know what to say?"

"I only told you what you wanted to hear, Ned."

And still his eyes met hers in denial. His hands trembled. "They can't be lies," he said thickly. "What you told me. I need it to be true. I won't *let* it be otherwise."

"I have been lying to you for two years. I just—I didn't intend *this*."

Ned stared at her. "This is some kind of nightmare. Madame Esmerelda—Blakely—someone tell me I'm dreaming." He bit his thumb and then stared at the digit, as if somehow it had betrayed him instead of Jenny.

Jenny shook her head sadly.

"But—if you have no powers, why is it that this chamber—"

He stopped, registering the austerity of the room in the dim candlelight for the first time. No black cloth. No crystals. No chimes. Nothing but cheap and rickety wood furniture. No hint of the arcane any longer.

"Your name," he said next. "With a name like Madame Esmerelda, surely…"

Jenny didn't have to say anything. The realization hit him. His shoulders stiffened. His nostrils flared. He spread his hands on the table in front of him as if to steady himself. Finally, he had accepted that she was a fraud.

Jenny knew his reactions well. And what she saw in the curl of his lip and the hunch of his shoulders wasn't the disdain she'd feared. It was even worse.

Because what Ned was feeling was self-loathing.

"Ned—"

"Don't call me that. Don't call me by my Christian name as if you know me." He was trying to snuffle his tears away.

Lord Blakely watched Ned in appalled horror.

"Mr. Carhart." Jenny choked on the unwieldy name. "I owe you a great debt. One that I don't suppose I will ever repay." She could not even look away. There was one final sentence she needed to speak.

She owed it to Ned.

And then there was Lord Blakely. She had few illusions about him. Right now, he knew precisely what her selfishness had wrought. She wouldn't blame him if he never spoke with her again. Whatever he might once have thought of her, surely she'd now lost his good opinion.

And with reason.

If she told him her name, she might never see him again. At best, he'd stay for that one night. He would abandon her, and she couldn't blame him for it. It was only what she deserved.

But she'd spent all her adult life masquerading as another woman. She'd become Madame Esmerelda to run away from the options she hadn't wanted. Until she met Lord Blakely, she'd never asked herself what she wanted to run *toward*. It had taken him two weeks to convince Jenny to claim herself.

On his own merits—ridiculous, excessively rational, and undeniably attractive though they were—she owed Lord Blakely, too. Giving him her name would be the ultimate surrender. In a strange way, he'd given Jenny herself. The least she could do was give herself back to him.

Her mouth was dry, the unformed words tasting like chalk. She forced herself to speak anyway.

"Should you ever need me, my name—" Her voice caught.

Lord Blakely leaned forward. There was no heat in his expression, no hint of longing. Only that blank weariness.

"My name," she whispered, "is Jenny Keeble."

Let them do with that as they willed.

CHAPTER TWELVE

JENNY KEEBLE.

Gareth held on to the promise of her name all through the oppressing drive back to the more fashionable Mayfair. Ned sat sullenly on the seat across from him, arms folded.

Gareth repeated her name in his mind when his cousin left the carriage with a wordless nod. And when he sent his driver home, alone, to warm stables, he whispered the syllables in staccato counterpoint to the rhythm of his stride.

Jenny. Jenny.

In these dark hours after midnight, the streets lapsed into a silvery silence. The coppery light of gas trickled through London's dense fog. As he approached her door for the third time that evening, the swirling mist roiled down the steps that led to basement rooms. The dense vapor stifled the sound of his shoes into muffled clops as he descended the stairs.

He knocked.

The mist swallowed the sullen squeak of hinges. Flat orange illumination from the streetlamps dribbled through the crack of the door as it opened. The edges of the light gilded her features into an unforgiving mask. She appeared to be a goddess cast from bronze, a statue

draped in white muslin and black shadow. Gareth sucked
in a lungful of cold fog.

She swallowed and looked up into his eyes. "You're
here."

Gareth's tongue seemed dry in his mouth. "Well,
Jenny." His voice creaked out, thick and husky. It was the
first time he'd spoken her real name aloud.

For moments neither moved. Then she curled her fingers about his elbow and drew him into the dark cavern
of her room. Her fingertips rested on his arm as the door
swung shut behind him. Slowly, he brought his hand up
to her face. He could feel the tension in the solid set of
her jawbone. He traced the line of her chin, found her
mouth with his thumb.

He'd wanted once to conquer her. Now he had. He'd
won everything. Her admission of fraud; Ned's surrender.
She'd even given him her respect. This should have been
his moment. Rationality had triumphed over illogic.

But his fingers found the secret, sad downward curve
of her lips in the darkness. No wet tracks down her
cheeks. Just a stubborn, sorrowful desperation as she
yielded to his touch.

Gareth hadn't wanted vindication after all. He'd
wanted *her.*

"Don't stop." Her hand covered his. She pressed his
palm into the warmth of her face. Her fingers trembled.

Gareth would shake his head over this inconvenient
decision the next morning, but— "You're not under any
obligation because I won our little wager." He couldn't
resist tracing her lips again.

She stilled under his caress. "You *won?*" His palm
swayed gently side to side as she shook her head. "No. You
lost. Ned lost. You were correct, but that isn't winning."

Her other hand came between them to rest against his coat. But instead of pushing him away, she leaned into him.

Unbidden, his hand found the dark silk of her hair. "Why, then, if not obligation?"

"I lost, too."

The truth seared into him. In the darkness of the night, they could pretend they had not stolen victory from each other. Her lips trembled against his touch.

"And so what is this?"

"Comfort," she replied. Her breath heated the tips of his fingers. "That, and farewell."

Farewell. Gareth froze. He hadn't wanted to admit it, but there was no other possibility. Not between a fraudulent fortune-teller who didn't want to become a mistress and the Marquess of Blakely. For tonight, Lord Blakely would be set to one side. Tonight was just for Gareth and Jenny…and farewell.

Jenny took his hand in the moonlight. She led him in the dark, into the back room, her steps sure. Just this evening, he'd taken tea at the tiny table he felt brush by his legs. Just this evening, he'd seen that bed, and had thought of her lying naked upon it.

That contact—the feel of her warm fingers closing around his, the illusion of the whorls of her fingerprints burning into his hand and branding him—was all the greeting his body needed to leap up in recognition. *You.* It was not so much a word that her touch sparked, but a resonance. Like a glass goblet shivering under a soprano's song, his soul thrilled at her touch. *Yes. You.*

In Gareth's time with this woman, he'd developed quite a vocabulary for her. Fraud. Charlatan. Madame Esmerelda. Liar.

The quiet night swallowed all those words before he could voice them. They didn't resonate inside him.

Confidante. Friend. *Lover.* He didn't speak these, either, but they settled into his flesh nonetheless. A mere touch on her cheek could not suffice. He pulled her into his arms, felt her breasts press and flatten against his chest. Her breath warmed his jaw. Those unspoken syllables surrounded them both.

After all these weeks, he had expected this kiss—the one that preceded intimacy—to shake him with lust. It would burn high and hot, like kindling. After that bright flare had burnt itself out, there would be nothing left but ash.

Ash, and victory.

But from the first moment his lips touched hers, he realized how wrong he had been. Her soft lips did not feel like the temporary slaking of lust, nor did they taste like a stopgap cure for the loneliness that lodged deep in his breast. Her mouth met his, sweet and trusting, even after all these weeks, after everything they'd said to each other. Her hands touched his elbows, slid up his shoulders. Her body molded against his, settling around him as close and welcome as hot bathwater.

Their mouths melded into one. He lost himself in her taste, in the sweet scent of the breath sighing from her. The kiss was apology for deception and every harsh word. It was acceptance and understanding. It said what words could not. *You. You. I want you.*

In the silent darkness, he let his body spell the truth. He wanted her. He wanted the courage of the woman who had told Ned about her deception. He wanted the intelligence that had thrown him off balance for the last few weeks.

"Jenny," he murmured against her lips. Her name. An incantation, a prayer.

The kiss changed from recognition to need and hope. He hoped she might remember Gareth rather than Lord Blakely. Just as she'd divested herself of Madame Esmerelda, and had, with her kiss, become only Jenny. It was that hope that drove him to run his hands down the inviting curves of her body. He hungered for human connection. For contact, skin against skin. Soul against soul. And with Jenny, his most private name on her lips.

Skin, flesh and soul—all three conspired, and Gareth drank in the swell of hips covered only by the thin material of her chemise. His palms molded the curves of her body, masked only by that inconsequential layer of warm muslin. The swell of her breast, the hard nub of her nipple. Up over her shoulders. He leaned his head and inhaled the scent of her neck.

She sighed against him and ran her hands through his hair.

His scalp tingled and fire raced through his veins.

The last twenty-four years of Gareth's life formed one long, lonely chain of days—strong, cold, iron links forged by the title his grandfather had held. An unbroken line of responsibility handed from father to son. It was not Lord Blakely, bound by the shackles of his title, who would join this woman.

It was Gareth. And Jenny's lips found his. Her mouth opened to him. Not his title. Not his money. But a man.

Her hands, cool in the dark of the night, fumbled against his neck and untied his cravat. He restrained himself, letting her slide the cloth off his neck. It swished to the ground. It took all his willpower not to rip his own clothing off in unseemly haste. Instead, he traced a pattern against her flesh—hip to breast, pausing to outline the circle of her nipple. Then back down to hip.

"Jenny," he whispered into her ear.

She shivered. She didn't give him his name back. Instead, her hands slid down his chest, unbuttoning his jacket and then attacking his waistcoat. Gareth shrugged out of them and pulled his shirt over his head. Cool night air pebbled his skin.

Her hands pressed against his bare chest. Each finger splayed across his torso, imprinting him with her warmth. Her scent. Desire rocked through him, and he could wait no longer.

He picked her up, his muscles straining, and walked to her bed. There he laid her. The light was poor—a few strains of starlight, filtered through uneven panes of yellowing glass and who knew how much airborne haze. He could see the lines of her limbs illuminated beneath him, but the details—the precise color of her skin, the swell of her hips—were obscured by shadow.

He found the soft skin of her bare knees just the same. He slid his hands up the curves of her thighs. The warmth of her limbs turned to heat as he neared the juncture between her legs. He caught the material of her chemise around his arms as his fingers skimmed higher. Breasts, soft hills topped by hard nubs, met his hands. The material gathered up around her collarbone as she adjusted her arms. And then it was over her head and she was bare, completely bare.

Bare to his hands and his mouth. This time, instead of circling the peak of her nipple with his thumb, he caught it in his mouth, tasting the sweet pleasure of her skin. He swirled his tongue around the tightening bud. She arced off the bed, belly pressing against his abdomen. Her thighs lay a scant inch from his member.

"Oh, God," she moaned.

He'd have preferred *Oh, Gareth.*

He set about drawing out that precious word.

Her hands fluttered against his bare shoulders. Her touch was as tentative as a butterfly, unsure if it should stay. Gareth tasted the light salt of her breast again, and her fingernails drove into the blades of his shoulders. She pulled him down to her. Now he sucked; he teased the end of her hard nipple with his tongue, and then with his teeth. Her hands ran slowly down his ribs, trailing fire as they did so. They found the fall of his trousers. She fumbled in the dark. He felt the fabric loosen. A few kicks, and the inconvenient material fell down his legs.

Her hands slipped against his skin. Gareth's heart beat wildly in anticipation. Her fingers slid around his erect member. Heat and pleasure filled him and he shut his eyes. A rising sea of lust besieged him with sensation. The warm clasp of her hand. The slide of her palm down his shaft. Here in the dark, her body pressed against his. Eager. Waiting.

Thank God for ruined women.

He was ruined, too. Ruined, and waiting for her to remove that last layer of pretense between them. To lift that cloak of anonymity and speak his name.

But she did not. And so instead of spreading Jenny's legs, he kissed his way down her body. He trailed his tongue in her navel, and she shuddered against him. He kissed her pubic bone.

And by God, though she moaned, still his name didn't cross her lips. He could feel her uncertain query by the tense quiver in her thighs. Her hands clutched the coverlet, bunching it into wrinkles underneath her grip. He answered the question her body asked with action. He pushed her legs apart and kissed her hot, sweet cleft. He dipped his tongue between her legs, tasting the salty sweetness of woman. She was wet and ready, but he wanted more from her than mere readiness.

His hand crept between her legs; he slid a finger into her passage. It was tight and hot, slippery and welcoming. Her muscles clamped around him, and he added a second finger, listening to her gasp. Learning the ways of her body. He found the spot right *there*—the one that made her moan and arch against him when he curled his finger up in a come-hither. He leaned forward and tweaked her nipple with his spare hand, and her passage contracted around his hand, harder. Heat mounted. He bent his head and ran his tongue against the sensitive spot between her legs.

Her body stiffened. Her passage clamped down on the fingers inside her. "Oh." The word was wrung out of her. *"Oh."* Again, and louder. Then—*"Gareth."*

His name swept through him, a sensation as primitively powerful as the strongest release. Wave after wave pulsed through them. He tasted her pleasure, felt it throb around his fingers. "Gareth," she screamed again, and his name on her lips seemed more intimate than the physical connection he shared with her.

She gasped so hard she could have been sobbing. Gareth was hard and erect. He levered himself over her. The erect tips of her nipples brushed his chest. She struggled up onto her elbows and kissed him. His tongue found hers. He wanted her desperately.

You.

The full length of his erection pressed against her belly. She spread her legs, angling her hips up toward his. As soon as her slick softness touched his member, he was lost.

He was lost, but he was coming home.

Her hips shifted, and the crown of his cock pushed against her body's opening. And then she rose to meet him—he pushed against her—and he was sinking inch by inch into her soft, waiting flesh. She was tight, so tight, around him. Hot satisfaction gripped him. She *fit*. Not just her slick female passage, but her body, her hips, her breasts. His hands were of a size to cradle her head. She molded against him as if he'd been made for her. She engulfed him. He filled her.

"Gareth," she said again.

"Jenny. Oh, God. Jenny."

The names came simultaneously. Gareth could restrain himself no longer. He took from her. He gave to her. It was an age-old dance, one more powerful and more riveting than logic. She was hot friction clasping him; sparking electricity tracing his veins.

She was his.

Her fingernails cut into his back. She pulled his mouth down to hers in the dark. She kissed him, and he tasted his name on her lips again. As he plunged into her, his mind filled with a coruscating fire. Heat rose around him. Beneath him, she stiffened. Her womb clamped around him in the beginning of a second release. And Gareth let himself go, let everything he had held back flood from him.

He pulled her against him in those final moments, shielding her from the chaotic storm that raged through his body. It passed, leaving him wrung out and sated, his limbs intertwined with hers.

He gulped for air and sanity. It was slow in coming.

What would she say now? Even though it was his body covering hers, his chest pressing her soft curves into the mattress, it seemed that Gareth was the one who was trapped. His lungs burned with exertion. Or emotion. No matter which, he could not find his breath again. It was buried somewhere inside her, deeper even than his still-throbbing cock, clasped in her womb.

What had he just experienced? It had been pleasure. Communion. Connection. It had been the end of a long, dark loneliness. Gareth could not bring himself to pull away from her. Because it had been *everything*.

Everything, that is, except the one thing she had asked it to be.

It hadn't been goodbye.

Her chest rose and fell beneath his. Her heart beat steadily against his sweaty skin. He couldn't see a damned thing through the dark night, but he could feel the heavy pulse in her throat thumping into the hollow cavern of his lungs.

A layer of London grime coated her windows, letting in only the barest hint of light from the street. He pressed his forehead to hers. *Say my name again.*

Instead, her muscles tensed in rejection. First her thighs grew taut underneath his own, then her stomach. The tension traveled up her shoulders. She put her hands against his chest. Infinitesimal pressure; unmistakable message. *Get off me.*

With a sigh, he withdrew from her body and rolled beside her. The mattress sagged as he moved, compressing under his weight. It was some kind of an uncomfortable straw tick. He could feel every hint of unevenness against his bare back. The ropes supporting them swayed with the movement.

On this small a bed, it was difficult to lie beside her without touching. Somehow, she arranged herself to manage precisely that. Gareth shut his eyes. He imagined a nimbus of heat and light surrounding her. Touching him, like a tentative kiss. When she rolled on her side, away from him, cool air washed over his bare skin.

"Well." His voice sounded foreign, clipped and shorn of emotion. "Maybe we should have said goodbye with a handshake."

"Where would be the fun in that?"

And just like that, she trussed him up. Because what Gareth wanted was *this*—this naked intimacy, from this woman. From the one woman who had seen that the isolating role of Lord Blakely was as much a facade as the colorful costume she'd once worn. He wanted her.

"Fun." The word tasted oddly in his mouth. *Fun* didn't encompass this.

"Fun," she repeated firmly, turning slightly toward him. "That's when people enjoy themselves. I hear it's even possible for lords with a serious, scientific bent."

When he didn't say anything, she sighed. "You can't tell me you didn't enjoy yourself just now."

"I believe," Gareth said quietly, "I was too busy enjoying you."

Damning silence. He'd said too much.

If he expected to maintain any dignity in this, Gareth knew precisely what to do—stand up, find his clothing in the darkness and walk out her door. Give her the farewell she'd asked for. But while the ferocity of lust had burnt through him, something far more primitive called to him. His skin ached for hers; his arms clamored to hold her. He wanted to feel the rise and fall of her chest as she nestled against him, wanted to run his hands down her skin slick with sweat, until the moisture evaporated.

Caught between hubris and hunger, his body responded in geological time, as if he were embedded in a

thick slurry of igneous debris. Cliffs could have crumbled
to nothingness in the silence that followed. Instants bled
into aeons.

"You needn't feel any responsibility," she whispered,
her words uncertain. "And you need have no fear I shall
kick up a fuss over you."

"I fear only that I am too exhausted to move any further." He let the muscles in his back slacken.

"Lord— Gareth?"

He still had no words for her. He feigned a sleepy murmur and turned, his arm sliding over her hip as if he were
tossing in his sleep. She stilled beneath him, tense as a
frightened cat. Then she sat up with a sigh and pulled the
blanket around him. Weight distributed on the bed as she
stood. The sound of splashing water followed. Minutes
later, she nestled against him, her skin cool. She relaxed
and gradually her breath slowed.

He was safe. She was close. Decisions would wait
until morning.

With the lust burnt out of him, he realized his final
words had been truer than he realized. Days of insufficient sleep and the worry of the passing night deadened
his limbs. And Gareth slipped into the dark haven of
sleep.

CHAPTER THIRTEEN

JENNY WOKE to the raucous sounds of midmorning. The market a few squares over was in full swing, and the street outside was busy. She was warm.

Lord Blakely's limbs were entwined with hers. He hadn't slipped out in the middle of the night as she'd expected. He was still here. She sent up a fervent prayer that their final farewells would not prove too awkward.

Then she opened her eyes. He lay on his side, watching her with those intent, contemplative eyes. His hand lay negligently on her naked hip and his sleep-rumpled hair gave him an air of lazy self-satisfaction. How long had he been watching her?

She'd seen little of his features in the dark last night. Perhaps it had been a good thing. Even disheveled as he was, he made her heart stutter. Those eyes. She could not have dared make love to him with those eyes boring into her, stealing her anonymity.

Before she could think of a greeting, he leaned forward and captured her lips.

There was no hesitation in his kiss, nor shyness in the way he moved against her. His hands slipped behind her neck, and the light fuzz of hair on his chest brushed her bare breasts. Her mouth opened under his. His hands trailed down her shoulders, touched the sides of her body confidently. She shivered in response, her body coming to life. He kissed her neck.

Jenny wished she could be so sure. But this was the last time he would touch her. The last time she would touch him. Lord Blakely. Gareth. Whatever he could have become had her life started differently, now was all she had of him: this one last time as a lover.

There were risks.

Jenny shut her eyes and her lips and thought about them. Risks? She might become pregnant. But she had four hundred pounds in the bank, an almost unshakable bulwark against such a future. The money, if carefully shepherded, would see her through any such eventuality.

And she'd have a child. Someone to care for, to raise. A child that she would never abandon, no matter what the world thought.

Risks? She would have Gareth again.

It was for precisely those risks that she wanted him now. She might never experience this kind of intimacy again. And she wanted this heated connection quite desperately.

Jenny shut her eyes and gave herself up to sensation. His touch burned her skin. He found a breast and licked the tip. Her nipple pebbled under his touch and a hot thrill washed over her.

She wished there were some way to capture these feelings, as if they could be reduced to scented oil. Attar of lovemaking. That way, she could dole it out, spoonful by precious spoonful, in the years to come. If she could bottle this moment—the feel of his body covering hers, the sweet taste of his lips, the growing heat that threatened to devour warm comfort and replace it with fierce desire—she would never be discontent again.

He pulled away. Jenny opened her eyes. He had hefted himself up on his forearms. His eyes were narrowed. With the golden light of the sun shining on him, she could see his naked body. A fuzz of tawny hair, a shade lighter than the hair on his head, covered his chest. His muscles were lean and corded, strong. Farther down, she caught a glimpse of his erect member, nestled in a cloud of darker hair. Vision rounded out the sensations he'd imprinted on her last night.

"Jenny," he said quietly. "Be so good as to stay with me when I kiss you."

The sound of his voice, dark and rumbling, startled her.

"I'm here." But she wasn't. She was pouring this moment into that bottle.

"Then touch me back. Don't lie there with your eyes squeezed shut. If I had wanted a quiescent china doll, I would have found some obedient lord's daughter years ago."

Jenny put her hands on his shoulders.

There were graver risks than the possibility of pregnancy. Risks that no amount of money could guard against. A quiescent china doll did not put her heart on the table. The way he held her, the way he traced her limbs, made her feel as if she were precious. The most dangerous feeling of them all.

Whatever had transpired between the two of them over the last weeks, it had been powerful. At times, it had hurt. It had taken one night, starting with his heartfelt apology, and ending with heartrending lovemaking, to transmute the power of those weeks into a soft golden glow.

But whatever Jenny's spirit felt, her mind knew precisely how foolish the idea was. Love with Lord Blakely? He would crush her heart. There was nothing for her here but abandonment.

Her fingers clenched against his shoulder blades. "You don't know what you're asking."

"Do I not?" He threaded his hands gently around her neck. "I'm asking you to make love with me."

That word again. She opened her eyes. "Gareth," she whispered. "Please. Don't. This is hard enough—"

She stopped speaking as his gaze pierced her. Incredible. Last night had seemed so intimate. And yet it had been so dark that she had not been able to see anything other than flashes of light, reflecting off the surface of his skin. Now she could look into his eyes. They were golden-brown. They were not cutting or dismissive. And even though she could see the desire smolder inside them, there was something else in them that turned her belly to liquid.

And like that, the answer came to her. If this was all she could have—this brief slice of time with him—she didn't want any regrets. Years from now, she wanted to remember that she'd stolen every scrap of pleasure she could from this moment. She wanted to fill the biggest bottle with as much of him as she could.

She smiled at him now. And wonder of wonder, he responded, his eyes glowing with satisfaction, an answering smile on his lips.

"Better," he said. "When you do that, I feel almost human."

He spread her legs with his own. She had one moment to feel the blunt head of his member against her before he slid inside her. Sore places stretched. Jenny exhaled. Their bodies fit together. He twitched, hard and thick inside her.

"Even better." His voice was hoarse.

And then he rocked into her wetness, sending shivers of ecstasy shooting up her body. Jenny gasped. She pushed against him, and together they found a rhythm. His hips met hers relentlessly.

A bubble of light formed around them. In a frenzy, she moved under him, reaching for something—she wasn't sure what. Until the bubble burst, and illumination cascaded around her. Above her, Gareth grasped her hips and pulled her against him, again and again. He, too, shuddered, and made a sound something like a groan.

He pulsed inside her one final time. Jenny opened her eyes. His were shut. His hair was plastered to his forehead, stringy and damp with the sweat of hard exertion. He breathed hard. And then he opened his eyes and looked down at her.

The experience had been amazing.

That glow slowly faded from his eyes. No doubt he was remembering all the reasons this could not be. Call it sex, call it a shag. Call it lovemaking. But he'd never suggested anything other than this act, and she didn't want him to see how deep her hunger for more burned.

"Well." She looked away from him. "And that's that."

He pulled away from her and said nothing. Jenny sat up and swung her legs over the edge of the bed. Behind her, she could hear the even rhythm of his breath and the soft scrunch of fabric. The bed shifted underneath them as he moved. He carefully lifted himself to his feet. As he shook out his trousers and stepped into them, he didn't look at her. Then he donned the wrinkled shirt that even Jenny could tell was too formal for morning wear.

Jenny clenched the ragged edge of her coverlet in her hands.

He straightened his cuffs and looked up. "Your bed. It's lumpy."

Jenny gasped in stung outrage. Lies or excuses would have been better than invective.

Lord Blakely—and he was now every inch Lord Blakely again, even though the waistcoat he was shrugging into was in dire need of pressing—did not seem to notice. "And your coverlet is far too thin."

"Is that all you can see? At a time like this? All you can do is criticize me?"

He paused, snapping his black cravat out, and cocked his head. "Was that a criticism of you? I don't believe I mentioned you at all." His voice was even, punishing.

"You—you—"

"Last I observed—and my observation was very thorough indeed—you were neither a mattress nor a blanket. If you wish to take every aspersion I cast on your furniture as a personal slur, I can hardly stop you."

"Lord Blakely—"

That imperturbable manner slipped and his eyes narrowed. "It's Gareth," he emphasized. "Damn well call me Gareth."

"You're leaving."

He reached for his jacket. "Indeed. I have a great deal to do today."

"So this is farewell."

His features froze. "What I am trying to say," he finally snapped in an accusatory manner, "is that despite the imperfections in the surroundings, I cannot—in all my recollection—remember passing a more enjoyable night."

Jenny's lips parted in confusion and he swooped down and gave her another kiss. His mouth took hers imperiously, but she could taste something desperate on his lips. As swiftly as he'd leaned in, he pulled back.

That little speech had been intended as an expression of admiration? It had felt like cold, spiked things gouging into her skin. No other man would strew compliments underfoot as if they were hard iron caltrops, designed to trip up the unwary horse or human who had the misfortune to tread upon them.

His gaze challenged her. *Care,* he shouted silently. *I dare you.*

Jenny couldn't afford to do so. She had a new life to find. Instead she raised one hand to touch his fingers tentatively.

"Goodbye, Gareth," she said.

He turned and accepted her farewell with grace. Or at least it seemed so, until he turned around at the last minute. "No," he said. "Goodbye for now."

And that was how she knew he was coming back. Jenny didn't know whether to weep or rejoice.

SOME HOURS LATER, after Jenny sent away a former client, she was forced to face one dire fact of reality. With Madame Esmerelda firmly out of the picture, she needed money. And soon.

So she donned the finest dress she'd owned before Gareth's gifts—a faded blue muslin—and left the house. The noon sun shone in the distance, unhindered by gathering storm clouds. The air was light, and a breeze blew toward the river, bringing with it the smell of fresh-baked bread. It seemed incongruous that mere hours after making love, Jenny should be setting off on a quest to break one of her long-standing rules.

She was headed for her banker on Lombard Street in

order to withdraw money rather than deposit it. For eight years, she'd scrimped and saved carefully. Every month, her balance grew and her sense of stability and independence increased. The knowledge that she need never depend on anyone or anything calmed her even now.

She'd returned Ned's shillings. And a mere hour earlier, Mrs. Sevin had arrived for her usual appointment. Jenny had looked in the woman's eyes and confessed her fraud. Another half guinea forgone, but despite Mrs. Sevin's pallor, the confession had felt cathartic.

Catharsis, however, paid no quarterly rents. And as the sum was coming due in a few days, Jenny had a journey to make.

The day was pleasant and muscles she had long forgotten were sore from last night's exertion. The walk was long enough to leave her invigorated, but not so long that by the time she turned onto Lombard Street her apparel had wilted from humidity.

She ducked inside the doors of the joint-stock bank that kept her funds. It was halfway through the noon hour. At this time, only a few lowly cashiers were present. Luckily, their number included the man who had helped her arrange this account.

Unluckily, Jenny recalled with a sinking in her stomach, that man was one Mr. Sevin, who had ostensibly arranged the account as a favor to his wife.

Most unluckily of all, the woman appeared to have come here to consult with her husband immediately after her interaction with Jenny. Man and wife stood in close proximity to each other. They did not touch—that would have been uncouth—but from the way they leaned toward each other when Jenny walked through the door, there was little doubt as to the topic of their conversation.

Mrs. Sevin gripped her reticule and glanced away. But it was her husband who minced forward, curtly motioning his wife to follow. She trailed behind him, her eyes down.

"Madame...Esmerelda."

Mr. Sevin turned his head, his gaze darting up and down as he took in her demure dress. The skin around his eyes crinkled. But he did not remark on the change in her attire from tawdry to tasteful. Instead, his lip curled in the pretense of a smile.

Jenny had long suspected that he disliked her. That he feared her supernatural powers. It was only now, seeing the smug satisfaction that lit his face, that she wondered if his cloying willingness to help had been motivated by fear. He'd thought she had seen his darkest secrets. It wasn't hard to guess at them; the scraps of information that his wife disclosed about their married life had been troubling.

"And how are you?" His voice boomed in the small room, a bit too jocular, a bit too loud. The polished wood of the empty desks reflected the sound back at him, and a few of the other employees looked up, idly. He puffed out his chest, a boy announcing while walking through a forest at night that he was not afraid of bears. "My wife, she reports an interesting conversation with you."

His chin lifted in infuriating bravado. Mrs. Sevin shrank back, crouching behind her husband.

Jenny gave the man her best pretense at a smile. He flattened his ink-stained hands against the top of his desk in response, a flash of triumph in his gaze.

"As it happens, Mr. Sevin, I am withdrawing from the business of fortune-telling."

Officious delight lit his face. "Yes. And that is because...?"

He knew, the terrible man. But he had to draw it out

of her, a cat playing with a mouse. Confessing her sins to the quiet, calm Mrs. Sevin had seemed only right. But her domineering husband seemed another matter entirely.

If she lied to this man now, would he lift his hand against his wife? He'd done it before as punishment for embarrassment and perceived disloyalty. There was no longer room for lies or half-truths. No mysterious statements could hide Jenny's perfidy. She just had to tell the truth, and quick, like drawing out an infected tooth. Eventually, she would find a way to win respect without lies.

Jenny took a deep breath. "I am quitting because I cannot tell the future."

He reached up one hand and pulled at his ear. "You mean, that the spirits no longer talk to you." He glanced at his wife. "Your powers might return?"

One nod of her head, and Jenny might be an object of pity instead of the target of scorn. But she couldn't do that to Mrs. Sevin.

"No," Jenny whispered, "I mean, that I never had any powers. It was all a—a—fabrication."

Her stomach dropped as she spoke. Everything she'd worked for—a position where some people gave her at least a modicum of respect, however ill she deserved it— was vanishing. Even this stomach-turning toad looked down on her now.

Mr. Sevin nodded slowly. "My wife, of course, never questioned your ability. I should have known better than to trust a woman's judgment of character."

"Oh," Jenny said, "don't blame her—"

"Blame? My dear, I only blame myself." He steepled his fingers and looked into the distance. "So you are capable of no arcane tricks."

She shook her head.

"You have no unnatural ability to see a man's deepest secrets?"

She shook her head again.

Something like a smile stretched his lips. It was a ghastly expression, containing neither amusement nor satisfaction. Instead, the grimace expanded ghoulishly, until it conquered the last hint of hesitance in his eyes. He licked his lips, and Jenny wondered how deep—and how dark—this man's secrets ran.

"Ten years, I've stuck my neck out for you at my wife's request. You know a bank as reputable as ours will not do business with those at *your* level of wealth. And what if someone had asked me why I allowed you to open an account? What of me, then?"

"I didn't think—"

"It would have meant my position, it would," Mr. Sevin said. "I have a wife. A *child*."

"But—"

"It seemed wise not to anger you. My wife said your skills were unnatural—but those fears, like so many female frailties, were chimerical." His voice was low and clipped. Mr. Sevin glanced furtively across the bank hall to see if anyone else was listening.

Unfortunately, nobody was. The halls were mostly empty, and the two remaining cashiers on the far side of the room leaned together in conversation. Mrs. Sevin, always quiet, had grown completely still. She studied the floor in contemplation. Jenny reminded herself that she was in the wrong here, and that his response, while cutting, was deserved.

"I apologize for the inconvenience," Jenny said. "I do appreciate your efforts on my behalf. And I understand your ire. You have every right—"

"*Every* right! You admit it." He licked his lips and leaned forward. There was a bit of an unholy rabid look about him. Jenny was beginning to understand why crowds burnt witches at the stake. It wasn't because people feared their power; an actual witch with power worth fearing could evade the fire. It was because once the mobs figured out they had nothing to fear, they needed to punish someone—anyone—for their irrational panic.

Mr. Sevin had just become a crowd of one.

"Look here," Jenny said. "Why don't I just withdraw my balance? I'll close the account. We'll not have to see each other again."

Mr. Sevin's lip curled. He contemplated her and then showed teeth in a distorted smile.

"What is your balance?" he asked.

Jenny pulled her passbook from her reticule and handed it over. The clerk took the bound pages. He licked his finger and flipped to the last entry, smearing an inky print on the paper as he scanned the years of careful deposits on Jenny's part.

He tore a draft from her book and handed it to her. "I'll need you to fill this out. Sign here. And here."

As she did, he stood up and crossed the room. When he returned, he cradled a thick, brown volume in his hands. Jenny recognized the signature registry from the day she'd opened the account. He set it on the desk and turned pages idly.

"Tell me," he said, "is your name really Madame Esmerelda?"

She was getting tired of answering that question. "No. It's Jenny Keeble."

"Hmm." He stopped on a page. "Good." Then he grabbed her passbook and the signed draft, opened a drawer in his desk, and dropped her records inside. Before Jenny could snatch the papers back, he slammed it shut and turned a key.

"Wait! You can't do that! Give those back to me!"

"Give *what* back to you?" His tone was innocent, but his lip curled with devilish intent.

"My records! The ones I just gave you!"

Mr. Sevin shook his head in puzzlement. "You gave me no records. Now, it happens that I have a record in my drawer at this moment. But that doesn't belong to a *Jenny Keeble*." He tapped the page in front of him where her signature—a fraudulent scrawl—lay black and malignant. "It's connected with *Madame Esmerelda's* account. And you are not she."

"You! You'd better, or I'll—I'll—"

"You'll what? You'll curse me? You've admitted you can't. You'll call the law on my head? How, when you yourself are attainted with fraud?"

"I—" She bit her lip in frustration.

If she kicked up a fuss now, the other cashiers would come to investigate. The evidence of Mr. Sevin's wrongdoing might not stand up in court, but it would certainly win Jenny the funds she now needed. But Mrs. Sevin still stood behind them both, a silent reminder of Jenny's own lies. Jenny knew all too well the woman fielded the bulk of her husband's dissatisfaction with his life. Some of it was physical; most of it sharp, verbal discouragement. Mrs. Sevin's first question to Jenny had been, "How can I be a better wife?"

Jenny took a deep breath. She had to pay her landlord soon, but she could come back at a time when Mr. Sevin was not present, on one of his half-days. That way, his wife would not take the brunt of his anger. She could explain the situation—somewhat—to one of the other cashiers who knew her on sight, but didn't know Madame Esmerelda's sordid history. It was a short delay, a temporary setback.

When put that way, Jenny had no choice at all. She owed Mrs. Sevin for her lies, just as she owed Ned.

Jenny stood up, and Mr. Sevin's mouth squished in satisfaction, like the smile of some bloated swine.

She looked past the man to his wife. "I'm sorry," Jenny said. "Truly. For everything."

As Jenny strode to the door, Mrs. Sevin's pig of a husband waved in farewell. "A pleasure, Miss Keeble," Mr. Sevin called after her.

Outside, it had begun to storm. It had wanted only that.

GARETH ENTERED HIS STUDY, stripping off his gloves as he did so. It was just after noon, and it had already been a long day. Not so long as the night that had culminated in Jenny's name and her body, but given the stack of papers accumulated at White's elbow, it promised to be longer yet, without any promise of enjoyment until much later. White glanced up, illuminated by the light of the fire. He nodded, once. It was a friendly nod.

Tentatively, Gareth returned the gesture. For once, he didn't feel awkward. Instead, he felt…well, he felt wonderful, to tell the truth.

He settled in a chair across from his man of business.

"Before we get started," White said, "there's a note from the Duke of Ware that simply cannot be ignored. I took the liberty of inquiring into the matter, and—"

White halted, his mouth open midsentence.

Gareth set his gloves on the desk. "Is something wrong?"

"Well, you must have resolved the matter already."

"Must I have? Why do you say that?"

"My lord," White blurted out, "you're *smiling.*" He winced and turned pink, as if he'd realized what he'd implied.

Gareth touched his own cheek. How unaccountably odd. He hadn't even noticed. He was smiling. And he didn't even feel like stopping. He shook his head.

"Well," Gareth said. "What's Ware got to say for himself?"

"He wants to arrange a meeting—you and he and the young Mr. Carhart. There is a list of points to address." White rummaged about on his desk and brandished a sheet of paper. Even from across the room, Gareth could see the angry, jagged penmanship, the underscored lines. "First, he's unwilling to marry his daughter to a man as—ahem, these are his own words—'as feckless and idiotic' as your cousin. Then it seems the Lady Kathleen is distraught, as Mr. Edward Carhart has not been to see her yet. A further point…"

Gareth stood and wandered to the window and looked out. It was raining, and London should have appeared muddy brown and drab gray as it always did in inclement weather. It did not. A spill of oil painted a silvery rainbow across a growing puddle on the street. Orange flowers, festooned with raindrops, bloomed in a box across the way. Despite the mud and clouds, there was more color in London than Gareth had expected.

"Finally, my lord, he thinks the three of you should dance naked together amongst the daisies as proof of your good intentions."

Gareth realized with a start that White had been speaking for some time. He turned around.

The man was tapping Ware's note against his lips, considering him. "You aren't listening."

"I'm afraid not."

White set the note down and glanced briefly at the stack of correspondence. "Are you going to listen to anything I say this afternoon?"

Gareth sighed. It was his responsibility to listen to all the complaints in White's tremendous stack, however minor they were, and resolve them. And the matter of Ned and the duke's daughter was no minor complaint.

It was his responsibility to take care of Ned. At the moment, however, it was not his *inclination*.

It had never been his inclination. If he'd cared one whit about Ned, he'd never have dealt with him in such a high-handed manner. No; Gareth hadn't wanted to help Ned.

He'd wanted to *win*.

Jenny had been right. Just because Ned needed to hear a thing, did not mean he needed to have his nose shoved in it.

Jenny. And what had she meant, saying *goodbye* this morning? Not *farewell and never see thee again,* surely. He wasn't done with her. And he'd bungled his way through his leave-taking. God knows what she thought of him now.

This was getting rather ridiculous. After sexual relations with her, he was supposed to have been able to put her out of his mind. Instead, thoughts of her tangled him up more than ever.

Gareth sighed. "Make the appointment with Ware. You have my schedule. And save the note. I'll go over the details before the meeting."

White made a notation.

"As for the rest of the business…"

White cleared his throat. "If I may be so bold?"

A nod.

"I take it she accepted your apology."

Gareth felt that smile creep over his face again. "She? Which she?"

"The hypothetical she, sir."

Gareth steepled his fingers. One night with the very unhypothetical Jenny was obviously insufficient to extinguish her from his mind. It had been enough to tantalize him, no more. After all, she still remained an enigma. Aside from her name, she'd told him almost nothing else. He didn't know where she was from, how she'd chosen the profession of fortune-teller.

Maybe if he learned more, he would care less. It didn't sound rational, and Gareth rather suspected he didn't want to let go of her. He just wanted to know more about her.

"White," he said. "I want you to make some inquiries for me."

His man was unperturbed by the meandering nature of the conversation. "Yes, my lord. About Ware?"

Gareth shook his head guiltily. "No. It's about a woman. Her name is Jenny Keeble. More than that, I do not know. Find out what you can. Discreetly. As for me…" His gaze fell on the stack of papers. "Make an appointment with Ware. Convey the time to my cousin. I'm going out. I need to make other arrangements."

CHAPTER FOURTEEN

NED ADJUSTED the screw on the barrel of the gas lamp, and the room in his mother's household fell into velvet dimness. Red streaks of afternoon painted dizzying figures through the elms outdoors, as leaves dipped up and down against the wall. The rain had stopped. Not that it mattered.

He could smell his own unwashed stink, collected against day-old sheets in desperate need of airing. Grime and sticky sweat had accumulated on his body after a full day spent feigning illness.

Not entirely feigning. Even spread out flat atop his coverlet, the world spun out of his control. He felt dizzy just lying still. And he didn't need to fib about that nauseated pit in the center of his stomach. He hadn't felt quite this way—dark and flattened, like some dried-out bladder—since two years before.

Two years ago, Madame Esmerelda had tricked him into thinking his life was worth living. She'd lied.

And he had been so desperate to believe her—so rashly convinced there was something of value about himself—that he'd destroyed Lady Kathleen's reputation just to prove Madame Esmerelda's predictions were right. If that didn't demonstrate what a useless blight Ned was, nothing else would.

He shut his eyes and imagined the view from his second-floor window. A square, a streetlamp. High dormer windows loomed across the way, carved into sloping slate roofs. Lower windows bricked to guard against taxes. A straight road disappeared between the white-walled town houses. If one followed it long enough, it led straight out of London. Straight out of this embarrassment.

Had Ned bothered to stand up and go to the window, he would have seen the sight for himself. Perhaps he would even have slid the pane of glass aside and rid the room of the subtle stench that had gathered in the close confines of the room over the last day.

That, however, would have required effort. And Ned's muscles were as responsive to his commands as water to whips.

It had been two years since he'd last fought this malaise. If one called "lying in bed and staring at the ceiling" fighting. One afternoon, two years ago, he'd remembered that fortune-teller he'd visited with friends on a lark. He'd struggled out of bed long enough to pay Madame Esmerelda a visit. She had promised him he would one day be a man. She'd told him to live on, that life would improve. It had. He'd begun to believe the drugging debility that curled around his heart like a dragon had disappeared for good.

But it hadn't been vanquished. Instead, the beast had only bided its time, waiting to wrest him off balance and out of control.

He'd known it. His desperation to marry off his cousin had been fueled by the feel of black claws sinking into his soul.

And Madame Esmerelda's long-ago promise had been worth less than the air it took her to utter the words.

Sometime during the hours of the afternoon, between Ned's brooding fit just at the noon hour and an attack of the sullens at tea-time, his cousin had sent over a note. At seven the next evening, the pleasure of Ned's company was required—required, not requested—so that the two of them could meet the Duke of Ware and Lady Kathleen. Some solution was to be found to this mess.

Ned had no doubt what the solution would be. He was going to have to marry her.

Even if she had been the sort of woman he would have chosen as a wife, the thought of marriage left him cold. Marriage was for men who could be *trusted,* men who did not collapse every two years in debilitating darkness. Marriage was for men who wanted children, not fools who feared they carried madness in their blood. He'd always believed he would never marry. But it would have been too much to say his spirit quailed at the thought. Quailing took effort; Ned had only the energy to feel an unwelcome pressure against his lungs.

Ned turned over and thought of that London street leading through the square just outside his window. If he were to get up now and put on clothing, he could set foot on that road.

He might walk on it, put one foot in front of the other, and then the other. He would disappear into the gloom of the night, never to be seen again.

Perhaps, he thought with a hint of interest, he would be set upon by thieves and robbers. Maybe he would fight them.

Maybe he would lose. Such sure and sudden defeat would certainly make his life easier.

Still, even if he expended all that effort, there was no guarantee he'd be waylaid, and the thought of walking far enough to escape Blakely's reach made Ned feel very tired indeed.

Besides, he'd never escape his own clutches, no matter how many miles he put between himself and London. And that was the biggest problem of them all.

So instead of setting off in search of thieves, he turned over on his side and fell back into a restive sleep.

"HERE THEN. Where'll you be wanting this?"

Jenny, still bedraggled from her walk home through the rain, stared blankly at the man in her doorway. He spoke around a piece of hay in his mouth. He smelled of unwashed laborer and his hair looked as if it had not been combed in upward of a month. Puddles lay around them, but the sun peeked out from behind dismal clouds. A shame; a wash might have done the man good.

Jenny stared in blank incomprehension out her door. Outside, a cart, pulled by a drooping nag, blocked half the street. Two men were dragging heavy slabs of oak out of the conveyance.

"Wanting what?"

The laborer looked at her as if she were daft. "The delivery. What else would we be discussing?"

"What delivery?"

"We're to be bringing in the new and carting away the old."

"But I'm not expecting any deliveries. New or old. Especially not a delivery of—of—what is that thing?"

"It's a bed, ma'am. And I was told the delivery was urgent by the gent." He grimaced then, and turned away.

The man was undoubtedly realizing what sort of women received beds as unexpected gifts. And this gift could have only one possible source. Lord Blakely. Jenny colored. If he intended to pay for services rendered with unwanted bedroom furniture, she'd tell him what to do with the bed. Stupid man.

She would have been extremely angry if the gesture wasn't so disarmingly sweet.

So much of Lord Blakely's cold manner was awkwardness, real uncertainty about how to talk to people as if they were...well, *people.* Some, of course—a goodly portion—was real arrogance. She couldn't begin to guess which predominated in this gift. Both? Neither?

Jenny let the men in, unease pricking the hairs on the backs of her arms.

The carpenter—for carpenter that sour-smelling man was—fitted the bed together, setting the precise wooden joins into place. He was careful not to look Jenny in the eyes. Not to look anywhere, for that matter, but on his work. Scarcely half a day since she'd ruined herself again, and this, apparently, was the attitude she would experience for the rest of her life: an honest man's contempt. She'd already experienced a dishonest man's connivance.

But the disdain the carpenter showed as he slowly hammered the final slats into place was not what curdled her stomach. It was the thought that mere days ago, she too had turned up her nose at *mistresses.* At those unfortunate women who had no choice but to sell their bodies, and to bow to a man's whim in order to maintain their livelihood. A mistress was all dependence without any of the benefits of respect. She'd tasted it once, then run as far as she could from the profession.

Had she become one without intending it?

The men carted away the old, rickety frame and her tick. Which really wasn't all that lumpy. Not if you knew where to sleep. Minutes later, another cart rumbled by—

this time with a mattress, the covering so thick and fine, and the fibers so tightly woven, Jenny had never seen its equal.

Of course, it was not lumpy anywhere.

Thick swansdown blankets and fine cotton sheets followed.

The bed was substantially larger than her previous furniture. In fact, it was almost *too* large, intruding into the small space she had in that back room.

Much as Lord Blakely had intruded in her life. He'd marched into her rooms with his pencil and notebook and turned her life upside down. He'd looked at her with that silent sneer. There'd been no room for his judgmental morality in her life. And yet here she was—stripped of income, stripped of clients, and now stripped of access to her bank balance.

She'd be damned if she let him take her independence. She wouldn't be turned into a pitiful creature, unable to act for fear of losing a protector.

She kicked the trunk she was unsuccessfully trying to shove into the last corner remaining after the new bed had been put in. "Idiotic Lord Blakely," she groused.

"And how many times have I said it?" said a voice. "It's 'idiotic Gareth' to you."

Jenny whirled around. He didn't look one bit tired, which was extremely unfair. And he looked well put together—pressed trousers and jacket, and a cravat tied with his usual careless air. His eyes flashed almost golden in the evening sun.

"Gareth!" She shook her head. "About that bed. I don't want your gifts. It makes me think—"

He examined his fingernails. "That," he said, "was not a gift."

"And I surely don't want to accept *payments.* If you feel—"

"It is a scientific experiment."

Jenny sat heavily on the edge of the new bed. It didn't so much as creak under her weight. "Pardon?"

"It occurred to me there were two possibilities. Perhaps I enjoyed last night because of your presence. Or perhaps it was the lumpy mattress. Scientifically speaking, if I am to distinguish between these two hypotheses, I must experience one without the other."

That dismissive toss of his chin dared Jenny to disagree. Dared her to suggest an alternate explanation for his behavior.

"Oh," said Jenny. "Now I understand. You took my old bedframe to your own home, and you'll sleep on that mattress alone tonight."

He was visibly taken aback.

"Scientifically speaking," Jenny said, "it would help you distinguish between the two." She gave him her most saccharine smile.

Wonder of wonders, he returned the expression. That ridiculously stuffed posture left him. No more Lord Blakely, freezing lesser mortals with his rationality. Instead, he was just Gareth.

"Five," said Jenny automatically.

He shook his head. "You've earned at least nine or ten points by now. I've been smiling all day. At odd intervals. My staff finds it exceedingly disruptive. I shall have to explain that I am engaged in a…a scientific exercise."

He walked toward her, his feet as sure as a leopard's stalking its prey.

Jenny raised an eyebrow. "I should have thought that

science and questions of the bedchamber were far removed from each other."

"That," said Gareth, holding out a hand to her, "is where you're wrong. Very, very wrong. Shall I show you?"

"That depends," Jenny said. "Will you need pen and paper? I had always imagined a man's skill had more to do with practiced technique and less to do with theory."

He took her hand. Instead of pulling her toward him, though, he knelt before her where she sat on the bed. "Never underestimate the power of theory. A certain amount of practice is, of course required. But a woman is not a boat race on a millpond, where repeated application of the proper techniques in the proper order assures victory. She is a science, and thus victory depends upon observation and induction."

Jenny swung her legs back and forth. "Induction?"

"Repeated testing. Scientific evidence is nothing more than proof by induction—by inductive reasoning, rather."

He captured her foot midswing. "Like this." He cupped the ball of her foot in one warm hand. The other he ran up her calf, his blunt nail tracing a sinuous line.

Jenny sucked in air as her skin prickled in response. "That's proof?"

"That's theory." His voice was as husky as her own. "I theorize that this part of your foot—" he caressed her arch near the ball of her foot "—is quite sensitive. And so I repeat the experiment."

He did. Jenny exhaled.

"Ah, see? I also theorize you'll enjoy being touched right here—right on the ankle bone." His forefinger seared against her skin.

Jenny shut her eyes. "How can you tell if you're right?"

"Little things. Your nostrils flare. Your hands contract. And your breathing becomes ragged." His hand walked up her calf, fingers tapping. "You see? Just like that."

His hands were warm and close; his words cold and distant. But when she let her lids flutter open, she could see the truth. For all that he'd spoken of *observation* and *induction,* what she saw in the intense press of his lips was simple.

Need.

And he was obscuring it behind scientific jargon— implying, somehow, that the desire and want were all hers, that her response was drawn from her as mechanically as a compass pointing north. All her lonely childhood, she'd poured her heart into companions who never returned her affection. Jenny's hands contracted—this time, not in lust.

"You may not be aware of this," Jenny said quietly, "but you are allowed to take an interest in me outside of science."

His hand contracted around the muscle of her calf. He swallowed hard. "Proof..." The word came out on a choking sigh.

Jenny stood up. "Proof can go hang. As can logic." They were all pallid excuses, and Jenny had enough of those to paper a drawing room. "If you want something from me, you'd better start admitting it. Stop hiding."

He stared at her from his stooped position on the floor, his mouth open.

Jenny reached behind her and undid the simple laces of her dress. They'd knotted hard in the rain, but a few good tugs loosened the strings. She let the material fall to the floor in a quiet rustle.

Gareth had not moved. His eyes were transfixed on the column of her throat—no. Lower. Her breasts peaked under his gaze.

"Let us not misunderstand one another," she said. Her stays followed her dress, and then she shrugged out of her chemise. The air was cool against her bare skin.

He watched her, openmouthed.

"There. You can have anything—everything—you want. But you have to ask for it first. And you have to want it for yourself. Not for science. Not for proof. For yourself."

Slowly he stood. He did not touch her. Instead, his gaze swept from the dark triangle between her legs up the line of her navel, past her breasts. Finally he met her eyes. "You. I want you." He licked his lips.

"If you want me, then take me, you fool."

Gareth was no fool. He pulled her into his arms, his crisp linen meeting her naked flesh, and then compressing as he pulled her against the hard muscle of his chest. His mouth bruised hers; his lips stole her breath. And by some magic, he doffed his own clothing while kissing her. It seemed mere seconds until his skin was warm and naked against hers.

"I want you to call me Gareth," he growled, his hands cupping her backside. "Gareth, and nothing else."

His erection brushed against her belly. That firm ridge leapt at the contact. He sat on the bed and pulled her so she covered his body with hers. The mattress sighed smoothly under their combined weight. The rough pads of his fingers were on her, sighing down her skin. He pulled her closer still.

"God," he breathed in her ear. "I want you to ride me."

Jenny stilled in confusion.

He looked up; her bafflement must have been written on her face.

His hands grasped her hips and he showed her his meaning. He angled her body with his hands and gently brought her to his hot, thick member. His hands took hers, and he pulled her down. She stretched around him as he guided her down the rounded head of his penis, down further, filling her with heat.

"Jenny. Say my name."

"Gareth." She squeezed him, deep inside her, as she spoke.

His hands moved again to her hips and he exhaled, his eyes fluttering shut.

And then he showed her his meaning again, guiding her up and down. His hands on her hips set the rhythm. They found a beat together. Warmth coalesced where their bodies joined, and then slick heat.

He surged into her, his hips slapping against her thighs. When she came apart in a flood of light, he groaned. Then he, too, shouted, thrusting into her.

When she finally slumped against his chest, Jenny ran her hand through his sweaty hair. Her body glowed like some kind of incandescent star. She pulled herself off him; his hand caught hers, and brought it to his mouth. He placed the gentlest of kisses against the blue veins of her wrist.

"You see, Gareth? No science necessary."

"Science." He turned to face her. "Observation is good for one thing. Really, Jenny. I thought you were ruined."

"What ever do you mean by that? I was. I *am*."

He snorted. "Then how is it you've never ridden a man before?"

She shook her head in confusion.

"And how, exactly," he asked, "did you become Madame Esmerelda?"

GARETH FELT Jenny's hand stiffen where it had been stroking his chest.

"Why do you want to know?" Her words crept out, wary and low.

Why? He wanted to uncover every unknown thing about her. Every secret of hers pulled at him like hidden string.

He shrugged. "I am naturally inquisitive."

"The story doesn't paint me in the best light."

"Jenny, I met you when you'd garbed and painted yourself as a Gypsy. You couldn't say anything that would *worsen* my opinion of you."

She blew out her breath, and Gareth winced as he realized what he'd said.

"I mean—"

She put her hand over his lips. "I know what you meant." There was a current of amusement in her voice. The light was fading fast. Her hips cast lengthy shadows down the bed.

"When I was eighteen," she said, "the older brother of one of my schoolmates fell in love with me. Or so he claimed."

"A lord?"

She shook her head against his shoulder. "You do me too much credit. A mill owner's younger son. He said he could never marry me, but that his love would never die. Et cetera et cetera and so forth." Her hand trailed the et ceteras down Gareth's abdomen. "So I ran away with him."

"You loved him?"

"No. But I wanted to be loved, you see. I should have known better. You said it once. Everyone lies. Even then, I knew that. Immortal love? Of course he was lying."

"Then why run off?"

"My future had been much on my mind. I felt trapped. I knew I'd need to make my own living. I could have tried for a position as a governess, but my references were not precisely stellar." A sniff, to indicate the statement drastically understated the truth. "And I had no family. So the best positions—even the middling ones—would have been closed to me. As for the worst ones… Well, if I had to sell my body, I didn't want to care for children alongside everything."

"You could have married. Most women do."

She snorted incredulously. "You recall I have no family to speak of. No dowry."

"Farmers. Clerks. Surely there are men willing to overlook a few defects of your birth in exchange for a good wife."

"A good wife? *Me?* To a farmer or a clerk or the like?"

Gareth considered this. On the one hand, he couldn't imagine Jenny marrying a straightforward fellow like White. She'd have tied him in knots within seconds. On the other hand, in Gareth's experience, Jenny's knots had proved to be…fun. "Well, aside from your recalcitrance. And a few other, um, minor character defects."

She rolled her eyes. "Gareth, you really have no notion what this world is like. The school I attended was in the business of turning out *ladies*. I learned how to curtsy properly. I learned the correct way to pour tea. I was drilled in my accent and taught just enough conversational French to start a good argument, but not so much that I would be able to do anything so gauche as to win it. I learned watercolors and a few rudimentary piano pieces. I did not learn how to milk a cow, or how best to promote laying among broody hens. What use would I have been to a farmer?"

There was the use Gareth had just made of her. There was the sense of playfulness that made him want to tug her close and hold her tight. There was her sharp intellect and her unflinching insistence that Gareth treat her with respect.

"I lacked the birth to match my education and the skills to match my birth. No, marriage was not an option for me. I ran away with the man because he seemed a pleasant enough fellow. And besides, he swore his undying love. I'd never experienced love of even the short-lived variety before. It seemed a rare treat."

Gareth knew how this story was going to end. It would end with Gareth wanting to punch the man. Even though he knew—not in his gut, but in one uncomfortable corner of his rational mind—that one day, he too would have to leave her.

"He brought me to London and set me up in a dull, unfashionable part of town. And two months later, he cheerfully handed me a silver bracelet and wished me well. I was…furious. You see, I knew his love would die. I just expected that its life span would be closer to that of a dog than a—a—"

"A dung beetle?" Gareth suggested.

She smiled at him and, thank God, snuggled closer.

"What did you do?"

She shrugged. "I had no desire to continue along the path he'd set me. Being a mistress is quite boring— there's no challenge, nothing new to discover. And at that point, any position I could obtain as a governess given my preceding conduct would have been unsavory indeed. I figured—everyone lies. Why shouldn't I?"

"You could have—" Gareth paused. What could she really have done? As a man with a solid education, she could have become a clerk. As a woman, though… "You could have made hats?"

"I'd have ruined my eyesight in short order, while starving myself on too little coin. Lodgings and food are dear in London. I had nobody to vouch for my character. And besides, I wanted more than that. I wanted independence. I wanted people to look at me with honor, as they'd never done—" Her voice trembled. "Do not lecture me for trying to have a tiny portion of what you've always known."

Gareth shut his eyes. He'd thought more knowledge would reduce her power over him. But it wasn't working that way. What he felt…

He didn't have a word for the images she'd conjured up in his head. Some unnameable emotion accompanied them. The thought of Jenny, betrayed at eighteen and deciding to show them all up, made him ache down to his bones. Whatever this nameless feeling was, it seeped into his soul like dirty black water, biting as the Thames in winter.

She hadn't curled up like a pill-bug, or hidden herself away like some fragile creature. She'd rejected the usual options and found a choice that afforded her everything she wanted.

"The best part of being Madame Esmerelda," she said, "was that I had to learn everything—gossip, of course, but finance, industry, even science. It's much easier to foretell the future if you're aware of the present. Before then, nobody had ever expected me to know anything."

He'd expected familiarity to breed, if not contempt, at least indifference. It didn't. It bred respect.

"Tell me," he whispered against her shoulder. "You

told me you learned everyone lied when you were nine. How did that come to pass?"

Twilight had passed. He could feel her breath in the expansion of her chest against the palms of his hands, hear it soft and sighing in his ears. But the visible line of her shoulders had faded to an indistinct silhouette, rising and falling with each exhalation.

"When I was very young," she said, her voice quiet as the sound of still water running, "I was brought to school. I was distraught and confused as only a four-year-old child can be. The instructor tasked with my care told me if I stopped sniveling and was good, my mother would come for me soon."

Maybe it was because his hands over her shoulders gave the illusion of closeness. Maybe it was because he hadn't expected a revelation of that magnitude from her. But he shook with the cruelty of telling a small child a lie of that nature. His hands tightened.

"So I was good." Her matter-of-fact delivery only drove the ice deeper into his bones.

"It may be hard to believe, but I was quiet and polite and…and honest. At that age, at least. I never wept, not even—well, you can imagine how cruel young girls can be."

Gareth had seen how the boys at Harrow tormented those not from the oldest of families. How they'd singled out the awkward and the quiet. He could extrapolate.

"I was uncommonly good until I turned nine. Then one of the other girls pushed me down and I skinned my knee and got mud on my dress. Nothing unusual, you understand. And while I was telling myself it would all come right when my mother came for me, I realized it had been years. She wasn't coming for me. Nobody ever would, no matter how good I was. Mrs. Davenport had lied to me, and I was all alone."

Gareth swallowed the lump in his throat. "So what did you do?"

Her shoulder blades leapt under his hand in what Gareth supposed was a fatalistic shrug. "I stopped being good. And here I am."

Here they weren't. She shifted and smiled at him. Pretending it didn't matter.

"But all this talk of me is boring. What of you? Twenty-one, was it, when you discovered everyone lied?"

Gareth paused, reluctant. In part, he held his tongue because he wanted to learn more of her than she did of him. But he also didn't want to air his petty complaints to her. Not now, in the barren aftermath of her revelation.

"The usual," he eventually said. "Delusions of love."

"A woman?" He must have made some sign of acknowledgment, because she covered his cold hand with hers. "And another man, I would imagine."

"And more than one man," he corrected. "One of whom was my grandfather."

Her breath hissed in. "Good Lord. How did that—I mean—why?"

"It was a wager. I'd planned to ask her to marry me. My grandfather—he had the training of me after my father died—thought she wasn't good enough to be the future Marchioness of Blakely. I said she was. He wagered he could prove otherwise."

"What do you mean, *wagered she wasn't good enough?* That sounds horrific."

No more horrific than sending Gareth's mother away from her son just because she remarried. Gareth waved his hand. "It was part of his lessons. Learn about the estates. Accept responsibility. Noblesse oblige. He said I had plebeian instincts, and he needed to drive them from me."

"So he—he—"

"So he shagged the woman I intended to marry, yes."

"And he called that a lesson? It sounds more like a travesty. How did he dare tell you what he'd done?"

"There was no need. He made sure I overheard them. She called his name, you see."

Long silence. "At the time," she finally said, "he would have been Lord Blakely, yes?"

Thank God for intelligent women, who understood the import of his little speech without him having to bare himself any more than he'd already done. Gareth traced his hand down the curve of her spine.

"So since you inherited—" she started.

"It's been years. And no. Since I became Blakely myself, I haven't been able to hear that name on a woman's lips. Not like that."

At twenty-one, he'd had as much perspective on life as an ant had of the horizon. He felt rather like that ant now—as if he were utterly trivial. A pimple on the face of an enormous mountain situated in a massive range.

She'd had nothing. By all rights, Jenny should have followed the path of doomed women everywhere. Increasing desperation. Sexual immorality. It should have culminated in her dramatic death in some snow-filled alley, as if she were some desperate female in one of those gothic serializations. But Jenny had not made a serial of herself.

Instead, it was her arm that fell comfortingly over his chest, her head that rested against his shoulder. She gave succor to him, and he, selfish creature that he was, sucked in all her heat, hoarding it as selfishly as he'd taken her body.

Years ago, he'd traded the uncertain comfort of companionship for the surety of superiority. It had been his grandfather's last gift—or perhaps his curse. If this was what he'd given up all those years ago, could he justify those years of loneliness?

Gareth shook his head and sent the dark thoughts back from whence they came.

Twilight had passed, and now he could make out nothing of her features in the thick darkness. He pulled her against him. She was limp and no doubt weary. She hadn't slept much the previous evening. Neither, for that matter, had he.

The last of the light faded as he held her close.

CHAPTER FIFTEEN

WHEN JENNY AWOKE the next morning, the side of the bed next to her felt cold. He must have left sometime in the night. She opened her eyes. Pale light touched the walls. Outside, she could hear the sounds of early morning in London. A cart rumbled by, and the market a few streets down was coming to life. A butter-maid's shout punctuated the dawn. "Freshly churned, freshly churned!"

Jenny sat up and looked around the room, stricken. Every scrap of clothing he'd set on the chair the previous night had vanished. After the conversation the previous evening, she had begun to believe she meant something more to him than a mere sexual relationship. She had thought that they had formed a deeper attachment.

The secrets they'd shared on the previous night had left her feeling vulnerable. Apparently, it had passed him by completely. It would be foolish for Jenny to harbor illusions about Lord Blakely. He wouldn't care for her. For him, this was a temporary circumstance. It was physical pleasure. And no matter how close he held her, he would one day leave. When he did, she would not let her life be as empty as this room.

She swung her feet to the side of the bed and stood up. She'd slept in nothing but his arms. She reached for her clothing, heaped in an uncertain pile on the floor.

Drawers first, and then her shift. The working woman's stays that provided support rather than shaping.

As she dressed herself, she realized one last thing: Her desire to be loved hadn't lessened during the decade since she'd embarked on that first disastrous affair.

Her feelings for Gareth had passed the point of danger. She was desperate to take everything he said as an indication that he cared for her. But aside from a few comments made in the heat of the moment, he treated Jenny as if she were nothing more than a mistress. And that she'd vowed never to become. Not again.

There was no good way to take his departure in the morning without so much as an explanation. No doubt he'd come back some other evening—and no doubt, he'd try to buy her participation in the sexual act with another piece of furniture. Perhaps he'd give her a silver bracelet when he was done with her.

Perhaps by that time she would be desperate enough to take it, to accept the bare monetary value he placed on her heart.

Jenny vowed not to let him fool her again. She'd let her own desperate loneliness overwhelm her. She had more important things to think about. Such as how she was to rescue her four hundred pounds from Mr. Sevin's clutches. And what she was to do with the funds once she had them in hand.

She hugged her knees.

Had she not foolishly told Gareth about her childhood last night, she could have withstood this. But she had felt naked and exposed—and afterward he'd held her so gently. She'd felt as if she'd come home. She'd never had a *home* before.

Damn him. The facts were simple. He was a lord. She

was a ruined woman he had taken on as a mistress. She accepted as payment the casual kindnesses he offered.

It had been many years since Jenny had allowed herself to cry.

She did, now. She cried hot tears for her own stupidity. For that raging desire that still burned inside her, her determination to be strong and respected. She buried her face in her blanket and sobbed. It felt strangely exhilarating to let her tears loose.

She'd always thought it weak to indulge in tears, but nothing else seemed to answer for the situation. Crying didn't solve any problems, but not crying hadn't proven particularly effective, either. She let herself weep.

The creak of hinges interrupted her. Heavy footsteps sounded in her front room, and a metallic scrape. Jenny looked up through tear-blurred eyes in time to see Gareth come down the short hall between her rooms. His hands were full; he held a bundle under one arm, and the kettle from the other room in his hand. He set the kettle on the hob-grate over the fire.

Then he glanced over at Jenny and froze in shock. The cloth he'd used to hold the kettle fell from his hand and fluttered to the floor. It landed with an ignominious plop.

"I'll be damned," Gareth said slowly, "if I ever have any idea what to say at times like this."

Jenny sniffled. "You didn't leave?"

He looked at her as if she belonged in Bedlam. "Of course I left. I was hungry, and I couldn't find anything to eat. I bought a loaf and some cheese. And oranges." He set his paper-wrapped package on the table. "Wait. You mean, you thought I had left. Without saying a word to you. Would I do that?"

He drew himself up, cold and affronted.

Jenny nodded.

His jaw clenched. "Damn it. You know better than most I'm no good at these things but even I am not *that* bad. Really, Jenny. Why would you believe such a thing of me?"

"I don't know," she said, mulishly. "Maybe because you once told me all you wanted from me was a good shag?"

"*I* said that?" He looked surprised, then contemplative. Then, apparently, he remembered, and winced. "God. I said *that*? Why did you even touch me?"

She glanced away so he could not see her heart in her eyes.

Steam was billowing from the kettle. Gareth stooped and plucked the cloth from the floor and grasped the handle. Jenny watched in fascination as he poured water into her teapot.

"What kind of a lord are you? You make your own tea?"

He set the kettle down with a faint sniff. "I'm not *completely* helpless. I lived with only a small entourage in a Brazilian rain forest for months. I can make perfectly respectable tea. And coffee. And porridge, for that matter." He gestured with the cloth. "You like oranges. Here. Let me peel one for you."

Jenny hiccuped through her tears. "How do you know I like oranges?"

"Why else would you have had one in that sack the day I met you? Now, come over here and eat. You'll feel better."

Jenny wrinkled her nose at him, but he was undoubtedly right. She sat and he handed her a section of orange.

"Tears," he said as she popped the tangy fruit into her mouth, "are irrational. You needn't fear I'll leave you with nothing but a silver bracelet. I'll take care of my responsibilities." He handed her a piece of cheese.

Jenny held up her hands in protest.

"No," she said in a low voice. "You won't."

"What do you mean, I won't? Of course I will. You can't imagine the money would mean anything to me, and so why wouldn't I—"

She jabbed a finger into his chest. "You won't," she said, "because I won't let you. I have…I have enough money. Saved. In a manner of speaking." Where that manner of speaking was exaggeration. She licked her lips. "And I don't want to be your responsibility." That she was more certain about. "I'm never going to be your responsibility. Do you think I *want* a periodic payment from you?"

"Why ever not? Most people would."

She shook her head mutely. Then she burst into tears again.

Gareth stared at her in horror. "What? What did I say *this* time?"

She kept crying.

"This doesn't make any sense," he cried. "It's inexplicable. You're an intelligent woman, Jenny. There's no need to cry because a man offers to provide a little financial assistance."

The admonition had no effect.

She had harbored girlish dreams about her mother. She'd never wondered, though, what her mother had experienced. Had she, too, been shunted off when some man she cared for coldly offered her a stream of dreary coins?

Jenny wouldn't accept it for herself. She'd lived on that sort of payment all her young life. Someone had employed a stream of uncaring women to raise her. She hadn't run away from a life as a governess to lapse into another man's *responsibility*. Because what a woman felt as cold obligation, a man saw as salve for his conscience. Financial absolution, as it were, in lieu of emotional ties.

She would not do this again. She'd become Madame Esmerelda because she didn't want a master. She'd felt pushed into one box or another. She didn't want to be another bloody line in his ledgers, and she'd be damned if she depended on another person again.

"Look," Gareth said a bit desperately, "I'll—I'll send financial assistance. *And* an occasional fruit basket."

Jenny couldn't help it. She laughed at him through her sniffles. "Oh, listen to you. 'A woman is not a millpond. She is a science.' Good God, if the Linnean Society could hear you now, they'd drum you out of their ranks."

"Well," Gareth huffed, "I don't know what to do. I was serious about the fruit basket. Or at least I would be, if it would make a difference."

"I know. Why do you suppose I started laughing? Honestly, Gareth. Could you be any more helpless?"

"Helpless?" Gareth frowned. "I'm not *helpless*. I just can't think of anything to say. And since you won't tell me what the matter is, I can't solve the problem."

"If you could solve the problem, I wouldn't be crying, would I?"

"What the devil am I supposed to do about a problem I can't solve?"

Oh, if only Jenny knew the answer to that one. But her future loomed ahead of her with frightening blankness. There was no home for her to return to; no *back* to go back to.

"It would help," Jenny said, her voice thick with tears, "if you would come over here."

He pulled his chair next to hers and sat, somewhat awkwardly. "Like this?"

She nodded. "And you could put your arms around me." "Like this?"

She relaxed into his hold. "Almost like that," she said, "but tighter. Right. Like that."

It was an illusion, and one she'd browbeaten him into displaying. But for a moment, she could imagine that he cared.

The mirage lasted only a moment. "This isn't a rational way to address a problem," he complained.

"Hush. Listen. Sometimes answers flow without words, through touch."

"Like completing an electric circuit?"

Jenny had heard only bits and pieces about the new theories of electric flow, and couldn't answer that. After a space, she spoke again.

"As much as I may find to deplore in my past conduct, I can't see what I would change. The life I rejected seemed very dreary to me, without possibility of reward or thanks. I know any God-fearing woman would not quail at such a thought, but God had never shown me particular favor. I felt as if I were being forced into a coffin, and told that if only I would lie rigidly enough, the screams of the damned would soon fade into gentle murmurs. I saw the teachers around me—cold, humorless women. They had no friends, no family. I couldn't join their ranks. I was eighteen, Gareth. It was too young to die. But now here I am. I'm not sure how to go on."

He ran his hand down her hair. "For now," he said, and then stopped. He leaned down, his nose brushing against her forehead. "For now, I'd like you to go on with me."

"See?" Jenny said. "That was good. A comforting gesture, and completely unprompted on my part. You're a quick study. Even you will have to admit that, despite your appeal to logic, touch works. All the cold in me flows to you."

"Cold can't flow," he said, pulling her closer. "Only heat. Thermodynamically speaking—"

"Gareth?"

He looked down.

"Don't ruin this."

He didn't.

HOURS LATER, Jenny ducked her head inside the bank. There were three cashiers about. None of them, Jenny saw with some relief, was Mr. Sevin. She approached another man, one with whom she had made deposits before. He regarded her with attentive politeness. Thank God; Mr. Sevin had not spread tales about her.

"Perhaps you can help me," Jenny said. "I seem to have, um, misplaced my passbook. And I had hoped to make a withdrawal."

"Of course," said the man. "I recognize you. Have you your account information?"

Jenny handed over a slip of paper. He scanned it and then disappeared into a back room. When he returned, he carried a sheaf of papers. His mouth contorted into a puzzled frown.

"Madame—Esmerelda, is it?"

Jenny thought about explaining further. But no. She'd learned last time not to admit to identifying herself under a false name until *after* she had her money in hand.

"Yes."

"Well, this is very strange. Typically, we do not maintain accounts when the balance sinks so low."

Jenny sighed. She'd heard this before. "I know. When I opened the account…" Well. She didn't want to alert him to Mr. Sevin's involvement. If he decided to talk to the man, goodness knows when she'd see her money.

"Exceptions were made," she said carefully. "The account was opened."

The man made a dismissive motion. "Yes, of course. We all make exceptions from time to time. Technically, we are not authorized to do so, but, well." He shrugged sympathetically. "It is just that nobody ever *wants* to maintain an account with a balance this low. There are no benefits to storing such a small sum, as the fees will eat any paltry interest."

Trepidation fluttered through Jenny. Bank cashiers were not usually wealthy fellows. They would not call the twelve or thirteen pounds she earned every year "paltry," no matter how flush the pockets of their clients.

"What amount is it that you see?"

"A little over one pound," the man said. "There was a withdrawal a few days ago. Would you like to see the entry?"

Jenny's mind filled with white-hot brilliant light. It washed out all thought, all emotion. She heard the sound of rushing water, as if she were the center of a deluge. She swayed dizzily and grabbed the counter in front of her to keep her balance. Her mind was empty. Completely empty.

Not so coincidentally, so was her bank account.

She'd been staving off panic by telling herself that her money was inaccessible. Unavailable, but there. An ineradicable bulwark against starvation. Twelve years of savings, insulating her from the depredation of time. She'd felt so brave sloughing off the trappings of

Madame Esmerelda without the prospect of future income. She'd forgotten the panic penury could induce.

"There is something rather strange about this final entry," the cashier was saying.

One possible oddity: All her money was missing.

"Usually, the person that records the totals breaks the numbers down by coins. You know—£1-3-4 in pounds, shillings, pence. But whoever made this last entry recorded it as thirty shillings straight. I wonder why."

That *Judas*. Mr. Sevin had emptied her account and left her a message in the total. Less than subtle—but then, he didn't need to be particularly sophisticated about his communication when he was stealing four hundred pounds. Although who Mr. Sevin believed to be the betrayed and who the betrayer, Jenny couldn't say.

The bank clerk eyed her with a quizzical expression.

"Would it be easier," Jenny said, "if I just closed the account now?"

He nodded and began counting coins. Jenny shut her eyes and did the same. Her total funds available hadn't increased much. She now had three pounds and change. Not enough to pay her quarterly rent. Not nearly enough to do something about this robbery. If she had more, she could raise a protest. Maybe bring the matter before a magistrate. But she'd be on the defensive if she did so. Her story would convince no rational man to award her the money. After all, the only proof she had of his perfidy was in the account sheets in front of her—made out to Madame Esmerelda, with the fraud signed in Jenny's own hand.

There was no need to panic. She had possessions she could sell. She'd have enough for months. And after that—well, surely she'd think of something. She always did. Her future was not imperiled. It was just…restricted.

"Sign here," the cashier said, pushing over a sheet of paper. Jenny signed in a daze.

The coins he handed her weighed nothing in her hand. They were no shield against the future, which had just become significantly more frightening.

SOMEHOW, NED HAD MANAGED not to slump as his servants washed and dressed him. He'd sat still as his valet applied soapy suds to his face and neck. And he'd looked straight ahead as the man plied the straight razor, shearing Ned of stubble, and rendering him fit company for a duke and his daughter.

It should have been a simple matter to wait in the parlor with his mother and all the stone statues. Her advice had as much effect on him as coins bouncing off a wall. She had talked to him in heartfelt terms about his duty, his future. He wanted to listen to her; she meant well. But none of her words made the least impression on the impenetrable numbness of his mind.

All Ned had to do was sit and wait, and Blakely would arrive and escort him to the imposing stone edifice where Ware lived. Blakely would arrange everything. Ned's life. If Ware pleased, Ned's death.

And yet Ned had not waited. Instead, he'd stood up, interrupting his mother midstream. She'd reached for him, but he'd walked right out the front door and down the steps, before she'd had time to understand what was happening. He'd not been able to bear the weight of her careful solicitousness.

He'd crossed the street in one straight line, not bothering to step out of the way of the pungent horse dung in the gutters. That smell—redolent of hay and stables— clung to him now.

It was seven o'clock, and he hadn't told anyone where he was going. Not Blakely, who would be apologizing to Lady Kathleen at this moment. Not the butler, who had opened the door for Ned in silence. Not even his mother, who had stared after him in pained confusion as he'd taken his leave.

The only person who knew where Ned was at this moment was Ned, and even he didn't know why he'd returned to this particular street corner after all these years.

From the outside, the dim lights of the gaming hell did not distinguish it from its neighbors. Both the brothel to its right and the opium den on the corner were composed of the same coal-streaked stone, their windows equally dingy. It had been two years since Ned had come to this neighborhood.

It felt like forever. That time two years ago—when he'd been in grave danger of being sent down from Cambridge, and in graver danger of failing his life altogether—seemed as misty and insubstantial as his consciousness felt now.

A different man had slunk to this quarter those twenty-five months before. And yet what separated the Ned of today from that boisterous lad?

Responsibility? Not a bit of it. Ned had entrusted two years of his life to a charlatan, a lying cheat of a woman his cousin had seen through in the blink of an eye. And yet what Ned had done to Lady Kathleen had exceeded even Madame Esmerelda's flexible sense of honor.

Experience? The experience of an idiot.

"Carhart?"

A hand clapped on Ned's back and he spun around, as much from surprise as a desire to distance himself from whoever touched him so familiarly.

The features he made out were only vaguely familiar

in the gloom. Ned had to add twenty pounds to the image in his memory. The ruddy glow of ale lighting those fat cheeks, however, was nothing new.

"Ellison," Ned said dully.

Ned's erstwhile friend, already slightly bosky, grinned. The sour smell of gin rose from him. Ellison had always been a man best known for using strong spirits to subjugate his weak will.

"It's been years," said the man. He landed another smack on Ned's shoulder.

Ned winced and twitched his shoulders out of slapping distance.

Ellison settled for a chest jab instead. "Thought you'd turned respectable."

"No chance of that." Ned's voice sounded as sour to his ears as the smell of wine and the underlying stink of vomit in these unwashed gutters. "I spent some time pretending, but I'm not cut out for respectability."

Any chance he had, he'd pissed away with this latest disappearance. Ned had a sudden image of Lady Kathleen and her bald-headed father. He wondered if she would be secretly pleased when Ned failed to appear. After all, her options were ruination or marriage to the likes of him. She seemed intelligent. After what she'd learned of him, she had to be hoping for ruination.

Ellison interrupted this grim little reverie by laughing. The sound was far louder than the occasion warranted. Ellison was the last man whose company Ned would have sought out at a time like this.

Perhaps that's why, when the man clouted him on the back once again, Ned forced himself to smile.

"What say you and I go inside?" Ellison gestured at the hell. "You're buying, eh? There's good brandy."

Ned had learned long ago that brandy was no salve for this condition that overtook him. Drunkenness acted only as a magnifier, and if he started drinking while in this listless state, his ennui grew to dangerous proportions.

But he could not bring himself to care.

CHAPTER SIXTEEN

IT TOOK GARETH AN HOUR to postpone—not avert—the
Duke of Ware's wrath at being summarily dismissed
without so much as a scrap of foolscap in explanation
from Ned. He spent another hour guiltily rousting White
from his family dinner, and directing a stream of minions
into London's underbelly. All told, it was eleven in the
evening before Gareth received word of his cousin.

Midnight had chimed when Gareth entered a heated
room where cloying cigar smoke wafted, and the rattle
of ivory markers rose. He had hoped the message was in
error, but there, in the corner, sat Ned. Drunk and gambling in this godforsaken gaming hell, when he should
have been negotiating with Ware over his future.

Gareth was too baffled to be angry.

He walked up to the table. Gareth had never needed
an excuse to feel uncomfortably stiff around others. But
now he felt ramrod straight. Ned's companions lounged,
their limbs contorted at odd, unnatural angles. Cravats
were, at best, untied; one dark-haired, red-faced fellow
had looped his in a disreputable bow around the neck of
the large-bosomed woman who sat next to him. Sticky,
cracked cups were stacked along the edge of the table.

"What's the pool again?" The ruddy-faced fellow finished the deal, six piles of three cards each.

Ned stared at the spray of cards dealt on the table without interest. "Damned if I know. Does it matter?"

"Two thousand," chimed in someone else, and Gareth winced.

A man with a loosened black cravat peered at his cards. "I have something better." He fumbled in his jacket pocket and pulled out a paper. "It's a private menagerie. Won it last night. A few lions, apparently. And a herd of striped horses called zebras. And all the way from Africa, an elephant."

Gareth winced again. Loo was a nasty game, with escalating stakes that ruined many a careless gambler. The odds were even more forbidding when one party was wagering money and the other, elephants.

"Ned," said Gareth.

No response. Ned's companions lifted heads and exchanged glances.

"Ned." Repeated a little louder this time. Ned heard, obviously, because he laid his head to one side. But instead of responding, he reached for his cards and aligned them edge-to-edge in his hand.

Play passed to him, and he let the two of diamonds drop from his hand.

"Ned," said Gareth, "you'll have to come with me when you've finished the play here. There's still some chance to patch matters up, even now."

Ned yawned loudly, covering his mouth with his hand. His friends giggled behind their cards, nervous that Ned defied his powerful cousin. But Ned didn't glance up. Instead, he played the three of clubs.

"Look here," Gareth said wildly. "This is madness. You don't get out of bed for two days straight. And then, on the evening when I need you to stay put, you wander off. I'm not talking to Ware for my own health, you know. The man's talking murder. And I don't blame him."

Ned played his last card. It was his highest card yet—a nine of diamonds. As spades had been trump, he lost once more.

"Looed again, Carhart." Red-face jabbed Ned in the shoulder.

Ned shut his eyes and—of all strange things—he smiled. It was a strange grimace, not quite one of pain. Gareth didn't understand. None of Ned's behaviors made sense. He reached out one hand to touch Ned's shoulder.

Ned didn't so much shrug—that would have taken real effort on the boy's part—as slump. Gareth's fingers slid off, and he curled his fingers in impotent agony.

You prod and poke and pick. The important things in life cannot be bound like so much paper to form a monograph.

He hadn't understood what Jenny meant. He hadn't cared. But he did now.

It was frightening how much he cared, how the sight of this gray and listless Ned squeezed his heart into a frozen fist. She'd made Gareth feel this sympathy. But she'd given him no way to help. And Gareth had nothing to offer of his own—nothing but papers and proof.

Ned listed away from Gareth. Then he rolled his neck until their eyes met. "Oh. You still here, then?"

"Ned," Gareth tried sternly, "if you don't leave now like a rational man, I'll—I'll—"

"You'll what? I'm not afraid of you. What are you going to do? Ruin my life more than I've already done? Go on then. You see, if I don't care, you can't touch me."

Gareth felt as if his nerves had been disconnected—temporarily—from his spinal cord, as if his brain had been utilized in some horrendous experiment in Dr.

Frankenstein's laboratory. His wants and desires simply ceased to exist. And for one brief second, he saw the world through the Stygian darkness of Ned's eyes.

At twenty-one, he too had once felt the same way. His life in ruins, or so he'd thought. Gareth had pushed off from London society altogether. He'd told himself then he didn't care. But he'd lied.

And now he cared for Ned. He cared so much his hands tingled and his chest constricted. He cared with a powerful, helpless fury, because there was nobody to attack, nothing to cut down. He had no words to say, no enemies to threaten. In that one second, he would have vanquished the world for his cousin.

Gareth was still in that disconnected state, mind not quite aligned with his body, when he tripped from the room. Maybe Ned would be rational if Gareth gave him a chance to recover. Maybe a breath of cool, fresh air—away from the smoke and all that volatilized brandy—would clear the muddle that inhabited Gareth's head.

And maybe Gareth was just running away from a problem he could not comprehend. Because when he stumbled down the stairs into the dark night, the muddle remained. He walked, because his feet were all he could bring into some semblance of order.

It took him some time to realize the close air inside hadn't muddled him. Rationally, he knew precisely how to handle this situation. Wash his hands of his cousin. Look for some other way to protect his estate from its eventual devastation. No; his head was clear on the matter. It was his heart that was all confused.

His collar was damp from rain. London—as much of it as ventured out at night—hunkered down in the determined drizzle. Had it only been weeks ago that he'd first kissed Jenny?

If only he'd never accosted her. If only he'd let that sham relationship between Ned and Jenny continue.

But no. He'd forced his way in, sure that he knew best. And he'd won. He'd beaten Ned and proven Madame Esmerelda a fraud.

Damn. Jenny had been right, that day she pounced on him in the modiste. He *hadn't* understood what was happening. He'd picked Ned to pieces, just as she'd said he would.

Gareth clenched his hands in denial. *No.* He would make this right. He was the Marquess of Blakely. All that superiority had to be good for something.

He thought of Jenny, then. But how could he face her and admit what he'd done? Besides, he rationalized, it was late, and she'd not want to see him. All he could hope was that her morning would prove more auspicious than his evening.

COMING ATOP Gareth's absence the previous night, the first encounter of Jenny's morning was decidedly inauspicious.

"I don't have the money." She squeezed her hands together in consternation as she said the dreaded words.

Broad lines of impatient unhappiness furrowed into her landlord's forehead. "What d'you mean, you don't have it? You always have the rents, and right on time, too. Tomorrow, then?"

Of course she always had the rents. She'd always been Madame Esmerelda, with attendant generous clientele and burgeoning bank balance. Madame Esmerelda had been the rock of stability upon which she'd built her world. But now Madame Esmerelda was gone, and come tomorrow, she would still just be Jenny Keeble.

And Jenny Keeble had barely three pounds, when the quarterly rent was six. Even if she were to come up with the money to pay this man, how would she survive? A place to stay was all well and good, but she had to eat. Jenny needed to be frugal until she came up with another plan. She'd needed spacious quarters as Madame Esmerelda; a safe room, separate from her own living arrangements. Business necessity—and the lies she'd communicated to her clients with that carefully controlled atmosphere—had demanded it.

But she didn't need the space any longer, and she could no longer afford the price.

If she stayed in London, she would have to move to more reasonably priced lodgings. Jenny swallowed at the thought. *If* she stayed in London?

"What if I paid you for a week?" she asked, desperate to put off the decision.

"I don't let by the week. There's no profit in it— weekly renters come in and tear up my good walls, they do."

"I'm not a weekly renter. I've been here twelve years!"

"And I'd always be coming round, too. That's no way for a man to spend his life, hounding tenants for the money what's owed him."

"I'll pay you a pound for the week," she said with a sigh.

A spark of interest flared in his eyes. "Pound," he mused. His lips moved as he calculated precisely how much she'd offered to overpay him. "And you'll pay the full quarterly amount next week. I'll make an exception this once, because we've known each other this long a time. But no more."

He shook her hand and took her money.

If I stay here. Frugality demanded she find another place to live. That she find some sort of work. So why was she balking at the thought? Jenny sighed and shut the door and walked to the back room. She opened the chest of drawers there.

That cream-and-red-striped gown Gareth had forced on her lay in place, wrapped in paper. She ran her finger down the smooth satin. It was finer than anything she'd ever owned. How much could she get for it? Ten pounds? Fifteen? She had no notion of the market for such things, having never purchased such a dress for herself.

Fifteen pounds. She could eke out an existence on that amount for over a year, if she found a bed in a rooming-house. But aside from the fact that it wouldn't be fun or comfortable to do so, she couldn't let herself admit the bare truth. If she stayed in London, it was for one reason only. For Gareth.

And there would be no Gareth if she took herself off to one of the places where she could survive on fifteen pounds a year. She might as well move to Morocco as far as he was concerned. His fastidious nature barely tolerated these rooms, clean and cozy as they were. A lodging-house, inhabited by cockroaches and lice, would have even less appeal for him than it did for her. As for finding one that allowed her gentlemen callers… Well, she could give up any hope of living at a decent address.

No. The fifteen pounds she collected from the sale of this dress would be a temporary solution only. Quarterly rent on these rooms. Fifteen pounds would give her time to investigate her loss at the bank more closely, to see if anything could be done to recover her savings. She would be able to think through her options carefully, rationally.

Find some position, somewhere, without need for panic. It would see her through the three coming months of summer. Three months of his touch… She could honestly expect no more. Dung beetles, not dogs.

At the end, there would be enough left to take her away from London, if that's what she decided.

It wasn't what she'd hoped for in her most secret dreams. But there was, after all, a reason she kept those foolish desires secret.

FOUR DAYS of Jenny's precious week elapsed. Three nights of Gareth's touch. Four days spent walking the city. Reading advertisements. Trying to find some possibility for her future.

She'd spent four days hoping without reason, and she still had no answer to the question that burned inside her: how could she stay Gareth's lover without becoming his mistress?

Her question was finally answered on the fourth evening. Gareth came to her rooms as he always did, at the point when the sun tinged the streets with red. He was dressed formally: black trousers and jacket, crisp white shirt and a yellow striped waistcoat with a silk cravat.

"Are you going somewhere tonight?" she asked.

He shrugged, more somber than usual. "Here. That's all."

"And do you plan to attend the opera in these rooms?"

"See here," he said. "Just shut your eyes."

She did, and lifted her face, expecting a kiss. Instead, his hands brushed wisps of hair off her shoulders. He reached behind her. And then heavy, cold orbs tumbled against her collarbones.

Her eyes snapped open as he hooked the clasp around

her neck. She couldn't see what he'd given her until she pulled the heavy stones away from her chest. Big sapphires, as thick as her thumb, linked together with intricately worked gold. The largest stone at the bottom twinkled a dark, clear blue where it hung in the valley between her breasts. The necklace dragged around her shoulders.

The piece must have cost thousands of pounds.

It felt like it *weighed* thousands of pounds.

She fumbled at the clasp behind her neck. The hook eluded her.

"Take it off me," she said. She was trembling, unable to think.

"You don't like it." He enunciated each word carefully, tasting them as if ascertaining that the wine had truly gone to vinegar.

"Of course I like it. It's beautiful."

But the neckline of her blouse was fraying. Against those gray threads, the sparkle of the stones seemed incongruous. She finally managed to unhook the necklace from about her neck. She dropped the messy tangle of jewels into his coat pocket. "I like it. But. Don't."

"Don't what?"

How could she explain? *Don't cheapen this. Don't turn this into money.*

"Don't pay me," she finally whispered.

Perhaps what she meant was *don't tempt me.* Because she never again wanted to be the kept mistress of any man, let alone this one. The stones choked her, silently screaming that she was his purchased thing, to be discarded at the very moment she became inconvenient.

He looked away. "It's not money," he finally said. "It's jewels. Isn't that what I'm supposed to do in a circumstance like this? Buy you jewels?" His voice rumbled through her, dark and forbidding.

"What kind of a circumstance do you think this is? I don't want *things*."

A corner of his mouth turned down. "Damn. It's all wrong again. I knew I should have asked White." He looked at her. "Very well. I can't give you furniture. I can't give you jewels. Tell me, what am I allowed to give you?"

If things were simple between them, she would take his coin and his necklace. But what then? It was a trap. As soon as she took them, he would begin to despise her. It would put him in a superior position. And what could she hope for then?

Only that he continued to desire her even after he'd conquered. And that she could respect herself, when she'd let him reduce her to a pocketful of polished minerals.

He tipped her chin up. "What do you want, Jenny?"

She wanted him, arrogant, awkward creature that he was. But that wasn't all.

His eyes seared hers and Jenny thought of all the things she yearned for. Respect won for her own achievements. Independence. His love, free of entanglements. None of the answers seemed right as she tried them on the tip of her tongue.

The word Jenny was looking for, she realized, was *marriage*. Oh, she didn't mean the ecclesiastical joining of man and wife in Anglican ceremony; that would have been too much to hope for. But she wanted a union. The kind that ebbed and flowed with the ups and downs of life. One where gifts were intended as kindness, not as financial shackles, forcing one party to her knees in stultifying dependence.

"Gareth." Jenny choked on his name. "I'm not sure what I want. But I don't want the kind of partnership where you buy my participation with cold stones."

"Is there another sort?" he asked quietly.

"The sort where…" she started slowly, and then stopped.

She wanted his respect. She wanted him to never look down on her again. She wanted him to cast those cold stones away, and she wanted this gulf between them— his title, her penury—to vanish like so much smoke into windy air. But the thought of depending on him shook her. She couldn't depend on him, because he would leave.

And that was how Jenny discovered the answer to her question. How could she remain Gareth's lover without becoming his mistress?

She couldn't.

The only question was whether this affair would end in three months or three days.

ONE MORE DAY was half over before it was interrupted.

"Madame Esmerelda?"

Jenny looked up. Spring sunshine streamed in through the door she'd left open to air out her quarters. The light tangled with dust motes, spangling the air before her. It lit the sandy-brown hair of the woman before her into a glorious mass, almost white with energy. Jenny jumped, and her pulse raced in recognition.

"Feathers!" Jenny exclaimed. "I mean…it's Miss Edmonton, isn't it? Whatever are you doing here?"

Gareth's sister was attired in a smart walking dress, all black-and-white stripes, wide starched cuffs and collar framing her face and wrists. She clutched a beaded reticule in white-gloved fists.

"I have a question for you."

Jenny winced, and imagined Gareth's reaction if he found his sister conversing with the woman he was bedding.

"Miss Edmonton," Jenny said, "I should tell you I am not a fortune-teller, no matter what Ned says. It was all invention."

Miss Edmonton raised her hand to her mouth in polite dismay.

"My name," Jenny said, "is Jenny Keeble." *And your brother once promised if I interfered with you, he would destroy me.*

Miss Edmonton's shoulders sagged. "I don't—that is to say, I have nobody else to talk with. And I desperately need advice."

"Nobody else?" Jenny ran through everything she knew of Gareth's family in her mind. It was surprisingly little. Mother—dead. Grandparents—dead. Miss Edmonton's father was not dead, but according to Gareth, he was not particularly intelligent. Then again, that was according to Gareth. A similarly scathing indictment would likely have been forthcoming no matter who he'd discussed.

"Surely your brother, your father… Either seems a more appropriate choice than I would be."

Gareth's sister shook her head. "Madame—I mean, Mrs. Keeble, it's a woman's problem." She wrung her hands around the tiny reticule in her hands. "I can't talk to my brother about it. You see, I have no mother. I am to be married in a few months, at the end of the Season. And I just had this talk with—well, with my aunt Edmonton."

"*That* talk?"

"Yes, Mrs. Keeble. *That* talk."

Jenny shut her eyes. "I really must tell you. It's Miss Keeble."

Miss Edmonton grimaced. "Really? Drat. I was hoping the part about your being a widow was true. So you don't know what happens on the night of—"

"Actually," Jenny interrupted, "I do. And that is precisely why you should find somebody else to talk with. It's not proper for you to talk with me."

A bright blush splotched Miss Edmonton's cheeks. She lifted a dainty hand to cover her mouth. Jenny waited for the woman to turn away in a swish of starched skirts.

But what the lady said instead was: "Excellent. I need improper. Will you answer my questions?"

Jenny thought about what Gareth would say if he found his sister in her rooms, asking improper questions. He'd be furious. And she could hardly blame him. A gently bred young lady should never spend time alone with a woman like her. Voices from her past surrounded her, mocking. *That Jenny Keeble,* they whispered. *You never can trust her.*

Jenny was weary of reacting to those memories. Whatever she achieved for herself in this life, those harsh words would never help. She touched the pouch at her waistband, briefly. Her three pounds had blossomed into sixteen and change with the sale of the dress. She had not yet chosen whether it was three days or three months she had left. If Gareth found out, his reaction would make her decision simple indeed.

"That depends," Jenny said. "Will you take tea with me?"

Ten minutes later, they sat ensconced around Jenny's kitchen table. Miss Edmonton watched solemnly as Jenny poured the tea into cups. Then the lady picked up her tea and took a delicate sip. "I don't even know where to start. It's too horrifying to even speak of."

"Nonsense," said Jenny. "Let's start with the basics. What did your aunt tell you?"

Miss Edmonton blushed again. "My aunt said that my husband will come into my room and pull my skirt up. And then he'll put himself inside of me. She said it hurts. She suggested I hold my tongue and pretend I am somewhere else until he is done."

Jenny stared at her. "Yes. I should think it would hurt if you did it that way. Good heavens."

"Whatever do you mean? Are there less painful ways to do it?"

"Suppose you are on the second floor of a house. How would you rather descend? By leaping over a railing? Or by walking down a staircase?"

Miss Edmonton looked at her. "The staircase. Are you trying to say my husband won't *have* to put himself inside?"

Jenny blushed. "That part's necessary. But if he does it slowly, and if he cares about whether you're ready for it, it won't hurt after the first time. And maybe not even then."

Jenny could hear voices and footsteps from the street. Even back here, in the room farthest from the street, a draft filtered through. She'd left her front door ajar, and a good thing, too. Both she and Miss Edmonton could use the breeze.

There was a light sheen of sweat on the other woman's forehead, one that could not be absorbed by any quantity of delicate rice powder. "But—that thing he puts in me— is it big?"

"If you're lucky," Jenny promised.

"And he'll make me do it every night? Sometimes more than once?"

Jenny tried not to think of Miss Edmonton's older brother. "If you're lucky."

"And he'll want me to do all sorts of wicked things with my mouth?"

If you're lucky, he'll do them back.

Jenny squeezed her eyes shut. "Miss Edmonton," she said, "these things are all so individual. They will depend on your husband and on your own predilections. Almost anything your husband wants you to do can be enjoyable, if you like and respect him. You just have to let yourself relax. If he's kind to you, and if you are kind to him, you'll find that most marital relations are quite enjoyable."

There was a long pause. Jenny wondered what the other woman could possibly be thinking.

"Is it true," Miss Edmonton finally said in a whisper, "that if I don't do as he says, he'll beat me?"

"No," said a dark, raspy voice. "Because if he does, you'll tell me straight away, and I'll kill him."

Miss Edmonton gave a little shriek, and Jenny opened her eyes. Gareth stood back, shrouded in the shadows cast by the short hall between her two rooms. When he stepped toward them, Jenny saw a grimace on his face. She wanted to shut her eyes again, to obliterate that fierce expression from her mind. Could she have done anything worse than tell his virgin sister about the sexual act?

He avoided her gaze, and her heart pounded.

"Come, Laura," Gareth said. "Enough of these questions. I had better take you home."

If he was going to hate her, Jenny decided, she'd give him real reason to do so. "No, Laura," she said. Her own voice sounded a little deeper to her own ears, perhaps a bit more mysterious. It was almost as if she were Madame Esmerelda again. But she was not. This time, Jenny Keeble did all the talking.

"Listen to me." She dropped her voice, and Laura leaned close. "And ignore him for now. Do not ever make the mistake of believing that as a woman, you must submit to men's rules—that if your husband beats you, your choice is either to submit, or to find a man to intervene on your behalf. Because when the moment comes, and he raises his hand to strike, there will be no man there to save you. Not in that moment, maybe not for days. Men leave. It's in their nature. If that time ever comes, you will save yourself."

"Legally, though—"

"A pox on legalities. If you know what you want, you'll find a way to get it. Men, or no men. And no husband or brother or—" she chanced a look at Gareth, who watched stonily "—lover will ever stop you. And that's the truth."

"You told me you couldn't see the future."

"I can't. But I can see the present." Jenny laid her hand on the other woman's shoulder. "What you did—coming to me, today, and asking these questions—was deeply courageous. Courage is stronger than physical strength. Remember that. Today, I see a powerful woman."

Laura blushed, deep red. "I don't know—"

"Maybe your brother could save you. But if you ever have need, you will save yourself."

Laura's hands clenched at her sides.

"Enough," Gareth said. His teeth gritted together. He didn't look at Jenny—he didn't even look at his sister. "More than enough. Come, Laura."

"Blakely," Miss Edmonton said, "I only wanted to—"

He inhaled. "You can argue your onlys on the way home."

He walked from the room without a backward glance.

CHAPTER SEVENTEEN

THE BEST Gareth could manage for his sister was a hired hack. The seats were sticky—with what, he dared not guess. The interior smelled like mold and vinegar. He spread his handkerchief on the seat, a flimsy barrier between Laura and the rest of the world.

The thin white cloth seemed so inadequate. She was vibrant and unsullied. She was scared of marriage. The weight of her fears settled in his chest.

"Blakely," she said. "Are you angry at me?"

Angry at her? He didn't know how to answer. He was angry at himself. He'd negotiated the settlements and had her fiancé investigated. He'd gruffly told her the man would do, but in his heart of hearts he had harbored doubts.

He would have harbored doubts no matter who the man was, so he'd swallowed his complaints. No man was good enough for Laura.

He regarded her. "I remember when you were born. I was at Harrow, of course, and living with Grandfather in the meantime. I didn't see you until you were six months old. And you grabbed my hair and smiled at me."

"I'm not six months old any longer."

"No," Gareth said. "You're not pulling my hair, either."

He sounded cold even to himself. He slouched against the cushions.

"It wasn't her fault," Laura was saying. "Miss Keeble's. She said you wouldn't be happy if I talked to her. But I insisted. I was just so scared, and I had nobody to talk with, and—"

"Laura," Gareth heard himself say. His voice sounded like icicles. Steel bands encircled his chest. But he didn't know how to change. When it came to Laura, he'd never been able to warm up. "You have me."

She was silent. Too silent. When he looked up at her, her lashes were wet. Gareth swore inside.

"Have I?" she said, shakily. "How? Every time I try, you brush me off. You make one of those horrible cutting comments. You make me feel so stupid."

God. He had no idea what to do. None at all. She was frightened. She was actually shaking. And the hell of it was, she was scared of *him.*

When his mother had remarried, Gareth's time with her had dwindled to a few days snatched between school terms. Learning to become Lord Blakely at his grandfather's estate had taken up his summers. Laura had worshipped him, almost painfully, on the days when he appeared. But she'd treated him as an Old Testament God—and one who would smite her at the first sign of perfidy.

"And now," Laura said, angrily swiping at a tear, "you're going to call off the wedding."

"How could I? I've signed the settlements, and I have no legal hold over you."

"You could convince Papa."

A fiercely protective part of him growled in agreement. If she feared this marriage so much, she'd be best off not marrying the man. He tested the waters tentatively. "And is it so important to marry him, then?"

"Not important at all." She turned her head. "I j-just love him, that's all."

"Oh." It was all Gareth could think to say. He'd expected her to list silly, inconsequential reasons for going forward with the ceremony. But he was too shocked to do anything but repeat himself. "Oh."

"And that's the problem." Tears were openly streaming down her face. "I love you, and that's never done me one bit of good. I'm *never* going to be good enough."

He had only thought he was tongue-tied before. Now words deserted him utterly. The rational thing to do would be to keep silent, to dump her back at her home, in hopes that she would cry herself out in her own room. But she was here now, and weeping quietly into her skirts. And he had run away too many times, leaving her to believe she wasn't good enough.

Touch is a circuit.

Gareth swallowed fear and awkwardness. He compressed them into a solid lump in his chest. And then he did something he'd never done before. He crossed the hired coach to sit beside his sister. And he put his arms around her.

She stiffened in shock. In those first delicate seconds, he almost pulled away. Then she folded into his embrace. To his surprise, he found that the cold really *did* flow out of him. And it didn't go into Laura. Instead, her sobs quieted to soft hiccups. They thawed each other.

Newton would have been flabbergasted. This kind of energy was not conserved.

By the time her sobs quieted, he'd found the right words. "I learned how to balance accounts," he said, "instead of how to be a brother. I'm not any good at it, although I'm trying to learn. But, Laura, I loved you from the first moment you pulled my hair. I always have."

She inhaled sharply. She tilted her face up to his, her eyes wet and round.

"Now come," he said. "Does your Alex love you back, or is he a hopeless idiot?"

"He loves me," she said quietly. "But I'm afraid he'll stop after we marry. He'll change his mind. He'll—"

"He'll love you more. Trust me."

"Really?" She was far too somber.

"Really." He had no words to make her smile, and so Gareth tweaked her nose.

And she giggled.

It had been a long time since he'd laughed. But despite all those years, he still remembered how. What he'd forgotten was the lightness of his soul when he did so. The moment was perfect.

Almost perfect. One small corner of blackness coiled beneath his good humor. He recognized it for the unworthy creature that it was, but still it poked its head out, whispering darkness.

Men leave. Why should Jenny's last comment sting so? It was no more than he deserved. And Laura, of all people, knew the truth of what she said. After all, he'd been leaving his sister since she was born, returning to his grandfather's estate after every short visit.

He'd lost years of Laura's life to the responsibilities of the marquessate. He'd likely lose Jenny, too. His title eventually devoured everything that mattered. But as he held his sister, he could not identify the purpose of it all. And that frightened him more than anything.

ONE HOUR PASSED as Jenny waited in trepidation. Then two. She could imagine all too well the cold castigation

Gareth might heap on her head. He'd told her not to interfere. And what had she done? Interfered, and in the worst way possible.

Her own fear gradually gave way to anger. Jenny's choices were dwindling with her remaining stock of coins.

The money Mr. Sevin had stolen would no doubt seem paltry to Gareth. But to her, that money had not been mere coin. It had been *independence*. Without it, she'd lost her ability to pretend Gareth was a lover, an equal, instead of the superior Lord Blakely. If she took his coins now, he would turn into another client, a person she'd have to please at the expense of her own feelings.

During the twelve years of Jenny's career, the weight of Madame Esmerelda had closed around her, suffocating. She'd tailored every word she said. She'd listened to every fear that her clients brought to her, and under the guise of a false persona, had given the reassurances they wanted to hear in return. There'd been no room for Jenny Keeble.

A week of freedom from those stultifying confines had convinced her never to crawl back into that small space. And so she refused to beg Gareth for his good opinion. She'd lived that way once. She'd never do it again.

Gradually, her feelings came to a roiling boil. How dare he, after all? How dare he look down his nose at her for telling his sister she was strong? How dare he make Jenny feel smaller than an ant? She was his equal—or, at least, she wanted to be.

Even if she didn't take his coins, she could not lie to herself any longer. His equal? She wasn't acting as if she were his equal. She sat here, awaiting his return so that he could pass judgment on her behavior. And so had it been ever since he'd visited her on that fateful night. He

PROOF BY SEDUCTION

decided whether to come to her or not. He waited on no invitation, and of course extended no reciprocal visiting privileges.

Something snapped inside her. She could do nothing about Mr. Sevin. She had no power to stay in London, once her coins ran out.

But she'd be damned before she let this dreadful imbalance continue.

She donned half boots and trundled out the door. The wind tossed her hair on the way and mussed her skirts. She looked a fright. But her anger had not lapsed by the time she reached the great stone edifice Gareth called home. She cast one look at the servants' entrance and then raised her nose in the air.

Right. His equal.

Jenny marched up to the solid black double doors that fronted the street, raising her chin in borrowed bravado. She rapped the brass knocker sharply.

The door swung open. The butler took one look at her and his face tightened in recognition. He drew himself up, and glanced down his nose at her faded blue dress.

"Tell Lord Blakely Miss Keeble is here to see him."

He pushed a silver salver at her. "Have you a card?"

"No. But you have a voice. Tell him."

"I'm sorry, Miss Keeble. He's not home." His tone was depressing.

"Oh, dear. But his lordship specifically said he would be here at this hour."

"He is about to leave."

"Excellent. I'll just sit here on the stoop and wait, then."

The man's eyes narrowed. "Although he may be delayed in his departure. Perhaps for as much as two hours."

Jenny smiled angelically. "Then won't he be angry when he finds you've made me wait all that time? Maybe you ought to consult him."

The butler grimaced and shut the door. Perhaps fetching reinforcements to oust her? Maybe asking his almighty Lordship what to do about the annoying woman encamped upon his doorstep. Jenny waited.

It was a bare minute before the door opened again. "His Lordship will see you, Miss Keeble." To his credit, the butler did not let a hint of his former contempt show.

Jenny let out the breath she'd been holding. Gareth allowed her entry into his home. She didn't know what to make of it. The butler led her down the familiar hallway.

Gareth's back was to her as she entered his study. He was seated, talking to another man. As the butler opened the door, both gentlemen stood. Gareth turned.

Any lingering anger on Jenny's part evaporated. He *smiled.* Not in polite welcoming greeting; in unpracticed pleasure. The expression was like a sunburst over her heart. And those golden eyes lit at her arrival. Her fingers curled of their own accord.

"Ah," said the other man before Jenny could be announced. "The hypothetical Miss Keeble."

"White?"

The other gentleman nodded at Gareth's terse command. "Out. Now."

As short and rude as Gareth sounded, Mr. White grinned and raised his fingers to tip an imaginary hat. And then he disappeared. The door shut on him and the butler, and silence fell.

Jenny ought to start the conversation. But her righteous anger had evaporated with his smile, and it seemed silly to declare war on a man who looked at her with that much pleasure.

He spoke for her. "Do you know what it's like to know your sister is afraid of you?"

His tone was calm, conversational. And like that, he sucked all the air from her lungs. Jenny shook her head, mutely.

"My grandfather had my guardianship after my mother remarried. He kept me on the estate with him, or here in London. To teach me, he said. But what I learned was not to show any emotion. Most particularly not tears, laughter or enjoyment. Those things, Grandfather said, were softness, inherited from my mother. She remarried as quickly as she dared after my father died. And she did so, knowing it would mean leaving me alone with my grandfather."

Jenny looked up into Gareth's eyes.

"Eventually, I just stopped showing what I felt. It was easier. And Grandfather was right. Because when you're a marquess, and you don't laugh when you should, people jump to make things right. When you're a marquess and you send a man a cold, cutting glance, he shivers. He taught me to be a scalpel."

"Well," Jenny said slowly, "given your skills at carving, that was foolish of him."

A smile fluttered on his lips. "Indeed."

"Would you know," Jenny remarked, "I don't believe I would have liked your grandfather."

"He was a complicated man."

Another pause. This one, Jenny felt, she must fill. She walked round Gareth's desk and glanced at the papers stacked on top. Columns of figures filled them.

"No drawings of birds this time?" she asked.

"It's after noon. I bundle up all the things I care about after noon. Now, it's only estate business."

"Hmm." Jenny poked under a stack of hot-pressed paper and found more figures. "Where did they go?"

He crossed to her side and slid out a drawer. A thick sheaf of papers, bound with green cotton tape, lay inside. Gareth removed it almost reverently and untied the ribbon.

"Here." He ducked his head as he spoke, as if he were embarrassed. "I'm working on this monograph." He shuffled pages—charts, drawings, and a great deal of text. When he looked up, there was a sparkle in his eye.

"You see, I've been thinking about Lamarck's theory—" He cut himself off and suddenly straightened, flattening the paper under flat palms. "That is to say—I fit everything I care for in the mornings. I have another appointment this evening in any event. And you don't care about Lamarck, anyway."

Jenny laid her hand over his. "But you do."

He glanced at the door, as wary as a child sneaking sweets from the pantry. "Well…"

Jenny plucked the pages from beneath his hands. "So this is everything you care for."

She flipped through his work before finding the ink sketches at the end.

"Here," Gareth said. "That's a male macaw. I wish I could show you the bright red of those wing feathers. There's no color here in England to match it. And there's the female, less splashy—"

He turned the page and froze.

Because the sketch on the next page was no impatient ink drawing of a macaw. It was her. He'd even labeled it: *Jenny.*

He'd drawn her in the same rough style he employed with the birds, strong, dark lines that hinted at movement and luminosity. Jenny could not have pointed to any one feature that was drawn incorrectly. And yet—

"I don't look like that," she protested.

Because the woman in Gareth's sketches seemed ethereal, light bouncing off dark eyes and coiled hair.

He compressed his lips together.

"You do to me," he finally said. He reached for the papers and stacked them together, binding them up again.

"Gareth."

He didn't look at her but wound the tape savagely around his work and cinched a knot. "I told you those pages held everything I cared about."

"Gareth."

He hefted his drawings from hand to hand.

"Some people," he said, looking down as if addressing the desk, "think that being a marquess means you sit in the House of Lords and collect myriad rents from dreary little tenants. They think it means you enter the dining hall before the earls and after the dukes. They think it means ceremonial robes, and plenty to eat even in times of hunger. They think you can sample a bevy of eager, beautiful women."

"And do you not?"

His hand danced idly down his drawings. "Maybe one beautiful woman. But that is not what it *means* to be a marquess here in England. You see, somewhere in my distant past there was a first lord, lifted above the common folk as reward for a great service to his king."

"What was it, with your ancestors?"

"Drubbing the Welsh, actually. But you see, the title is a reward with a sting—it is not a onetime payment for services rendered. It is a promise that condemns your firstborn son, and his, and his thereafter. It binds them, through the title, in service to the land. My grandfather was harsh, but there was a reason for it."

He set his bound drawings in the drawer and then slowly, firmly, slid it closed.

"When a marquess takes a man's pound in rents, he does not just make a profit. He makes a pledge. I cannot sleep at night, sometimes, thinking about those pledges. Should I establish a cotton mill, like the ones in Manchester? On the one hand, they provide employment, and if my dependents are starving, I am responsible. On the other, the accidents that inevitably result… Well, I am responsible for those, too. It did not take me long to realize why my grandfather deprecated laughter. There's little room for it in the marquessate. There's too much human suffering, and too little a marquess can do about it."

"You don't have to do this to yourself," Jenny said. "Hundreds of other lords don't—" She couldn't make herself tell him to become like everyone else. "There's no warmth in your life. How can you stand it?"

He made a little gesture. "Spare me your pity. Do listen to yourself. Poor Gareth—forced to be a marquess. I imagine the human suffering between me and my tenants is distributed in a relatively inequitable fashion."

"Hire an estate manager. Let others share the responsibility."

He spread his hands. "And who would I trust? I was born to do this. Nobody else has gone through the training my grandfather required. And it is *my* responsibility. How could I ask another to shoulder it?"

It sat between them, that crystalline thing. He'd been taught that he was bound ruthlessly into service, obligated to break his spirit against his iron-hard will. She wished she could despise him for it.

She could not. In fact, she was very afraid that the emotion that caused her hands to tremble was something close to the opposite. The man who hollowed himself out for the sake of a burden undertaken by his many-times-great-grandfather did not falter from responsibility, nor try to evade it.

Whatever it was she felt now, she knew it could not be love. Love would not feel like this. She would not feel his own hurt, as if she were clutching shards of glass to her chest.

"You understand—" He stopped, and took her hand. His fingers seemed cool against her own. His words sounded slow and metallic. "You understand," he finally continued, "why I am telling you this. It is not so you will pity me. It is because you need to know I will never risk legitimate sons."

Jenny's heart thumped. The corner of his lip curled. Not a smile, but an expression of ineffable sadness.

"You see," he explained, "I could never inflict the marquessate on anyone I cared about."

All the best of Gareth, Jenny thought, had been bound over to serve Lord Blakely. She turned his hand over in her palm and squeezed.

"So it won't bother you to inflict it on Ned?"

She intended to tease him, to make him forget his own pain. But he merely shook his head—not in answer, she thought, but frustration. "Now," he said softly, "you understand why I tried not to care for the boy."

Jenny looked away. Her chin trembled. He captured it with his fingers and turned her face to his. "And that," he said gently, "is why I will buy you anything you want."

He kissed her as if she were the sole source of sunlight. It felt as if he were spearing her with giant wooden splinters.

He wanted her to stay. He would give her anything she wanted. But what she wanted was to be able to respect herself. And the more he offered to buy her, the less likely the prospect seemed.

AFTER JENNY LEFT, grim responsibility once again beckoned to Gareth. He finished dressing. The journey to Ned's home was short, but weighed heavily on his heart.

But when he stepped onto the walk outside the stone stairs that led up to his cousin's door, he stopped in his tracks, unable to believe what he saw.

He'd pleaded with Ware and finally cajoled the man to agree to a second appointment. He'd informed Ned of the time most specifically. He'd underscored the importance of these discussions: As the days passed, gossip grew. Another tense week, and Ned could be ostracized, perhaps for good. Lady Kathleen was already the object of both pity and scorn.

But the situation could still be saved for the two of them.

Rather, it might have been saved, were it not for the scene unfolding before Gareth's eyes.

The good news was that Ned was dressed. And washed and shaved. The bad news was, he was not waiting for Gareth in the parlor as instructed. Ned was stepping into a closed carriage. Without Gareth. Too-loud laughter rang from the conveyance as his cousin reached for the door.

The out-of-kilter sound of that laugh was all too familiar. Gareth remembered that lopsided tempo. At Cambridge, it had always been mixed with loud conversation and the heady smell of cheap spirits. It had heralded annoying interruptions to Gareth's valuable study time. And complaints, of course, never had any effect on drunken men. Gareth's skin prickled in visceral reminder. It was still light out, and the men were already drunk. And Gareth had *specifically* told Ned to wait for him.

Gareth jumped from his own carriage and strode toward his cousin. "Wait one moment!" he called.

Ned's head turned. Gareth couldn't make out his expression from this distance, but he didn't need to be able to see his cousin's face to translate the sharp jerk of his head back toward the carriage. It was no surprise when Ned pulled himself in. Another fellow—hatless, cravatless, unbuttoned coat flapping untidily in the wind—looked around the street with a secretive air and then ducked inside the carriage, as well.

The door shut.

"Damn it." Gareth considered his options. Run, and flag down the vehicle. Or let Ned disappear, and miss a second meeting with Ware. Incongruously, he noticed the silhouette of a hat atop the carriage. The driver flicked his whip, and the carriage started off.

Gareth grabbed hold of his own hat and ran. "Wait! You there!"

He caught up with the vehicle before the horses had picked up speed, and he beat on the side of the moving carriage. "You in there! Stop!"

The carriage slowed, and then halted. A burst of laughter rose inside, and Gareth's spine prickled. He hated being laughed at. A voice inside broke through the cackles. "This will be excellent."

The door swung open. Hanging on the side was that red-faced fellow Gareth had seen with Ned in the gaming hell the other night.

"How may I be of sher—of service?" The fellow bowed and lost his balance, grabbing the handle of the door for support. The hinges torqued under his weight, but held. For a moment, the fellow swung suspended against the door.

Gareth peered inside. Ned was squashed, like a piece of cake in a hamper, between two men who were as round and red as apples. One of them was tippling from a silver flask. He handed the container to Ned, and Ned took a defiant swig.

Every face but Ned's stared at Gareth in drunken hope.

The fellow at the door scrambled to regain his footing. "Did you," he said in suggestive tones, "stop us because of the hat atop the carriage?"

For some baffling reason, this query sent the two apples flanking Ned into a raucous cheer. "Hat on top! Hat on top!"

Ned joined in with a halfhearted raise of his fist. "Huzzah. Hat on top."

Gareth reached up and placed his hand on the brim of the hat atop the carriage. "No. I'm here for Mr. Carhart."

He tugged, intending to toss the offending head-covering into the carriage at his cousin. But the hat didn't budge; instead, his fingers slipped and he lost his balance himself.

The maneuver was not missed by the onlooking drunkards. "Yah!" they screamed. "Hat on top!"

Gareth sighed heavily. "What is going on here?"

Ned didn't meet his eyes, but the door-hanger laughed and poked Gareth in the chest in an unbecomingly familiar fashion. Gareth stared at the offending finger.

"Hat on top—" the man enunciated his words very carefully, punctuating each one with a jab "—is a game. An *excellent* game. The most excellent game available to gentlemen in Britain. It requires only a carriage and a hat."

"And penny nails," shouted out one of the other men. "Don't forget the nails."

Gareth grabbed the man's hand before he could jab again. The palm was slick with sweat.

The door-hanger beamed with all the solicitude of the extremely drunk. "You *nail* the hat to the top of the carriage. Then you drive about, and take wagers about how long it will be until some officious do-gooder stops you, shouting you've left your hat atop the carriage."

The man's hand fluttered in Gareth's grip. He looked down and frowned, as if only just realizing his wrist was trapped.

Gareth let go. The only thing more appalling than the man's clammy hand was the fact that Ned planned to spend his evening playing Hat on Top instead of making things right with Ware and Lady Kathleen. Life wasn't a game. There was no time for childish drunken bouts. Gareth would have to straighten out Ned's priorities.

"That," said Gareth, "is the most puerile game I have ever heard of. It has absolutely no point and I cannot condone it. Come along, Ned. We're leaving. We don't want to be late."

Ned's friends turned in shock and broke into a babble.

"But we've only just started!"

"Come on, Carhart, you know Hat on Top is no fun with only *three*."

"You're not even *bosky* yet. And we promised to meet Branning at Gaither's. He'll be at the hell any minute, now."

Ned swiveled his head. He didn't quite meet Gareth's eyes. Instead, he stared at a point just past Gareth's shoulder.

"If you want to speak with me," he said coolly, "you'll

have to come along. There's always room for more in Hat on Top. And I'm not leaving."

Backslaps all around. Ned's lip curled in distaste.

Door-hanger seemed to think Gareth's participation was an actual possibility. He grabbed Gareth's arm.

Gareth shook off the officious grip. "Do you know who I am? I am the Marquess of Blakely. I don't play ridiculous games. And, Ned, you are coming with me *this instant.*"

His icy tone cut through the drunken merriment with satisfactory efficiency. The youths—they were none of them any older than Ned, if that—exchanged worried glances. Then door-hanger gave Gareth a negligent push in the chest. His sweaty palm left a dark print on Gareth's silk waistcoat.

"A marquess who was fooled by Hat on Top," he jeered. Laughter, this time with a nasty, dark edge, rang out. And then the door swung shut.

What logical arguments could one marshal against a fellow who preferred to tool around of an evening with a hat nailed to the top of his carriage, instead of setting the remainder of his life in order? Gareth had never felt so completely and utterly dumbstruck.

The carriage jerked and rolled forward, swaying from side to side as the twin bays pulled in their traces.

For the first time in his life, Gareth acknowledged there were things he couldn't do. And not stupid, inconsequential things like singing or carving. Important things. What Ned needed was completely outside Gareth's ken.

And he could turn to nobody now that he'd failed.

Really?

No. He had to admit it, even to himself. There was one person he could turn to. And he needed her now more than ever.

"COME WITH ME," Gareth said without preamble as her door opened. "We haven't a moment to spare."

He held his hand out to Jenny. She stared at him in confusion, her hair falling in wisps around her face. One strand was caught between her lips. She looked up at him, those eyes piercing straight through him.

The words he needed to say stuck in his throat, but he choked them out.

"I need you." There. He'd said it. There was no use hiding it any longer. He needed her for everything, and she… Well, she didn't need him for anything. He looked away. "*Ned* needs you. You were right." His hands clenched with the effort of his admission. "I can't do this. I need you to—to—"

To what? To work a miracle? To intervene?

"I need you to put things back the way they were."

She said nothing, but turned to find a cloak and bonnet. She had to succeed; Gareth had no other plans for his cousin. And if she couldn't help, then Ned was doomed—doomed to spiral downward without any hope of redemption.

It wasn't only Ned who needed redemption.

"Just come," he said. "Be Madame Esmerelda again. Conjure spirits. Tell fortunes. I don't care what you tell him, so long as you make this stop."

CHAPTER EIGHTEEN

DESPITE THE FACT that Gareth had referred to the gaming establishment as a hell, the room Jenny entered struck her as a far cry from brimstone and burning pitch. A fire burned in the room, but it was of the cozy, coal-burning variety, separated from the rest of the room by a mundane brass screen. There was an occasional orange glow when someone puffed a cigar. But for a hell, there was a distinct paucity of smoke and ashes. It wasn't even sulfurous.

There were neither imps nor devils. No demonic overlords; the denizens here were mere sinners, every one.

If this was hell, hell was red velvet upholstery. It was the acridity of rancid tobacco and the sharp scent of spilled gin. It was the clink of coins and the dull murmur—in voices accented with those distinctive lazy drawls that bespoke wealth and years of education—of gentlemen engaging in the damnably honorable task of losing fortunes and pretending not to care.

Despite the warmth of the room, Jenny shivered. She understood why sailors gambled, why clerks scraping together their pitiful quarterly incomes wagered. After all, when you had little to lose, a chance win could change a life.

But these men had everything—wealth, property and

family connections. A handful of the coins these men tossed around would solve all Jenny's problems.

Ned slouched in a corner, surrounded by men she supposed must call themselves his friends. The sullen slump of his shoulders told her everything she needed to know. After two years of his acquaintance, she knew the ups and downs of his moods rather well. There was that jocular, irrepressible Ned that she normally knew. And then there was the fellow she'd first met. Dour. Quiet. *Depressed.*

Ned picked up his cards from the green baize before him. He stared at them dolefully and blew out his breath. He seemed oblivious to the gentlemen on either side of him; he certainly didn't look across the room to see where Jenny and Gareth stood, framed in the doorway.

Gareth shifted uneasily. "He doesn't listen to me. He must know he's destroying his place in society. He will be ostracized for the rest of his life if he persists in this sort of callous behavior. And you haven't heard Ware speak of his daughter. Do you have any idea what a duke is willing to do on behalf of his only child?"

Jenny interrupted Gareth's explanation with an upraised hand. "I know Ned when he's like this. He's almost past despair. Of course he won't listen to you—he can't feel anything right now."

"Can you stop it?"

"I did once." But she hadn't. Madame Esmerelda had.

Gareth clenched his fists. Then he looked at her. "Do it again. *Please.*"

She could bring Madame Esmerelda back. She could earn a livelihood. She'd have her independence and Gareth, too. Madame Esmerelda had done the impossible before. She could beguile Ned out of this mood. A soft smile; a whisper of hope in his ear. A few spoken words, and Ned would be as ensnared by her as always. All she had to say was that the past week had been a test, that he'd been meant to endure this misery for some fateful reason.

But what path was there through Madame Esmerelda's fraudulent ways for Jenny Keeble? Jenny was a simple girl with complex wants. Independence. Love. Respect. Family. A few hundred pounds.

Who am I, that I deserve these things?

She was a fraud, a charlatan and a cheat.

"First," Gareth mused, "we'll have to get rid of his friends." He scuffed his boot against the floor. "I doubt I could manage that. They don't *listen*."

"That part," Jenny said, flipping her palm up, "is easy. Pen knife."

"Pardon?"

"Your penknife. I need it. Give it over."

He didn't ask questions. Gareth fished in his pocket and retrieved the slim, polished blade Ned had once used to eviscerate an orange. She snatched the weapon from his fingers and marched on the gaming table.

Ned was still unaware of his surroundings. He rested his forehead on one hand, elbow propped against the table. The fingers of his other hand listlessly grasped his cards. He didn't look up when Jenny stopped in front of the table, although all his friends did. He didn't even flick a glance in her direction when she put one hand on her hip.

But he jumped when she grabbed his cards from his loose grip. The look that painted his face was sheer, un-adulterated shock.

"You gentlemen must be blind." Jenny waved Ned's cards at them. "These cards are marked."

A soft murmur of surprise met this announcement.

The other youths at the table turned their cards over in speculation. Ned's mouth hung open. He was not yet able to form words. Jenny laid the cards faceup on the table for all to gawk at, and transferred Gareth's penknife to her right hand.

"I don't see it. How?" A voice to her left. The men surrounding her were lords and gentlemen, powerful, wealthy fellows who could have her thrown into the street with a single word. But she couldn't let her uneasiness show.

Jenny flicked the blade open. "Like this." She impaled Ned's cards, stabbing the blade deep into the table.

Ned stared at the cards she'd pinned to the table, his mouth gaping. "Mada— I mean, Miss Keeble. What the devil are you doing here?"

Jenny put one hand on the knife handle. "What do you think I'm doing here? I'm scaring away your so-called friends." She surveyed the other gamblers. They'd turned as white as gristle on a cut of meat. Doubtless the only time they'd seen a woman at the gambling table was when one was brought up as a form of entertainment. "Well? Scramble, unless you want to be next."

As one, the men beside Ned scrambled. They left the table in a giant rush, retreating to huddle in the far corner of the hell like the rats that they were.

Jenny turned her attention back to Ned. "Now I've told you why I'm here. What are *you* doing here?"

"I— You—"

"Oh, don't bother explaining. I already understand."

He raised his chin. "You said you owed me, right? I want you to go away."

Jenny sat on the table and pulled the knife from the surface. It took a bit of tugging to free the blade. The tool snapped shut with ease and Jenny dropped it in her pocket. "Unfortunately, Mr. Carhart, you don't get to tell me how I pay my debts."

She swiped a handful of cards off the table and shuffled through them. Good. There were enough. She flicked cards into a pile, facedown, and shoved it over to Ned. "Now you're playing with me. There. That's your hand."

"But you looked at them!"

She had not thought beyond getting Ned alone. But she realized suddenly why Ned had sought out this game, and played for these high stakes. He wanted to frighten himself, to put so much at risk that he would snap to his senses. He was trying to fight the darkness that engulfed him.

Well. If Ned wanted a scare, Jenny would deliver.

"Ah, yes. I had nearly forgotten." She rummaged through the remaining cards on the table until she found the right suit. She slapped the card on the table. "Diamond's trump. Now are you going to wager or not?"

"No! This is ridiculous. It isn't random. And you haven't even dealt your own hand."

"Ridiculous seems to be your style. Shall we set the pool at five thousand pounds, or is that too low?"

He slammed his fist on the table. His cards bounced. "I'm not in! I don't want to play."

"Suit yourself. I was only trying to be helpful."

"Helpful! By cheating me and taking my money?"

"Yes," Jenny said. "As you are no doubt aware, I *excel* at cheating and taking money. Besides, I owe you a debt. It seems you want to ruin your life in a melodramatic fit of pique. Why dribble the task out over weeks and weeks? I can help you accomplish your goal within the hour."

"I don't— I wasn't— I can't—"

"Oh, stop sputtering, Ned. It's silly to deny what everyone can see. If you're not trying to ruin your life to prove you're in control of it, I don't know what you're doing."

His lips pressed together.

"Five thousand pounds not enough for you, then? Blakely," Jenny asked, "how much is Mr. Carhart here worth?"

"*Blakely's* here?" Ned turned his head and saw his cousin standing behind him. He sighed and put his head in his hands.

Gareth's expression shuttered. "Some eighty or ninety thousand, I believe. Maybe less after these last few days."

Ninety thousand pounds? The figure was dizzying. With ninety thousand pounds, Jenny could shatter society's requirements of respectability. She could invent a past, a family. She might even marry. She cast a glance at Gareth, and shook her head.

Not that he would have her, especially not if she stole the money from his cousin under his nose. Still.

Jenny swallowed this foolishness. "Simple rules. Five cards. Whoever wins more tricks takes the entire pool. You put in everything you have—some ninety thousand pounds. I wager…"

Jenny pushed away her uncertainty and reached behind the waistband of her skirt. It took a few moments to pull the small pouch of coins into her hand. It had seemed so light when she'd sold the dress just that morning. Now the sack weighed heavily in her hand. She upended it, and small change rolled about the table with a clatter.

"I wager sixteen pounds, five shillings." And eight pence, although in the face of Ned's wealth, there was hardly any need to mention those sad coins. If she did, she might let the two men who watched her with open mouths realize that all her wealth in the world was laid out in specie before them.

Sixteen pounds was a number Jenny understood. It fit inside her head, a sum she could hold in her hand. It was all it took for a shrewd woman to survive a quarter while she looked for other work. It was bread and cheese and the occasional apple for months. It was a roof over her head. It was three months spent trading kisses with Gareth while she tried to find an honest alternative to her former career. Sixteen pounds was Jenny's last hope.

She glanced at Ned. *It need not be.*

"That's not equitable," Ned groused. "Ninety thousand against a few pounds?" He swept his hand across the table.

Jenny tried not to wince as her coins went flying. "That seems about right," she snapped. "Everything you own pitted against everything I own. You want to destroy your life? At least have the courage to do it all at once like a man."

"Very well." Ned drew himself up, anger hardening his features. "I accept. You've already ruined my life once. I might as well let you have a second go at it."

She could give most of it back, after Ned was well and truly shocked to his senses. What if she retained a mere four hundred pounds, as a fee of some kind? Maybe a thousand pounds, enough to keep her in independence for the remainder of her life. She could find the respect she'd wanted, no matter who her parents had been. After all, money spoke.

But temptation whispered.

Jenny's head buzzed with the possibilities. Her hands trembled.

Who am I? The question echoed in her head.

The hubbub of the hell seemed to cut off around her, as smoothly as driving rain turning to drizzle. Quiet blanketed her mind. For a bare moment, everyone else disappeared. There was nothing but Jenny and an immense stillness in the midst of a sea of temptation. Into that great silence, she repeated herself. *Who am I?*

She hadn't expected an answer. But it came anyway, from somewhere deep inside of her.

Who do you want to be?

It was all the answer Jenny needed. The world thawed. Noise returned, almost deafening after that slice of tranquility. But despite the frenetic worry that boiled around her, she carried that still center inside her. It did not waver. No mere fear of poverty could budge it.

Behind Ned, Gareth reached out toward his cousin's shoulder. He stopped, inches away. Ned huddled in his chair, and didn't glance behind him. Finally, Gareth drew his hand back and wiped it against his trouser leg.

Jenny smiled and picked her own cards from the leftovers and arranged them in order in her hand, from lowest to highest.

Ned gathered up his cards—a handful of carefully constructed threes and fours—and sighed. He let a card fall on the table. Jenny trumped it easily with the jack she'd dealt herself. She took the next trick, too, and yawned as she did.

She'd managed at least one thing. Ned clutched his cards, holding them as if they mattered. For the first time since she'd seen him that evening, he cared about losing.

Across the thin table, Ned's despair was as palpable and acrid as the smoky air Jenny breathed. Already, she'd managed to convince him he had something to lose. Jenny wanted to smile. Instead, she played her next card.

It was the two of clubs. Ned stared in disbelief. Every card in his hand could beat it. Tentatively, he selected one and placed it on the table. He won the next round, too. They were left with one card each in their hands, and an even score.

"You're cruel," Ned said bitterly. "Trying to show me how close I could come?"

He threw the four of diamonds on the table. Gareth set his hands on Ned's shoulders.

For one last time, Jenny was Madame Esmerelda again, smiling that mysterious smile at two men who had no idea what would happen next, but every expectation of a poor result.

She placed her card gently on the table.

Ned and Gareth stared, twin expressions of shock writ over their faces. Neither moved. Then Gareth reached out one finger to prod its edge—gently—as if somehow, he could not believe what he had seen.

Ned found his voice first. "You lost. You lost on purpose." He scratched his head in confusion. "You lost *ninety thousand pounds* on purpose."

Jenny hopped off the table and leaned down, picking up the coins Ned had scattered onto the floor. "No, Mr. Carhart. I lost sixteen pounds, five shillings on purpose." She stacked his winnings gently atop the final cards. "And eight pennies. You shouldn't forget the eight pennies."

Ned stared at the coins. "But *why?* I don't understand."

Jenny shrugged. "I told you I was a liar and a cheat. I didn't tell you who I planned to cheat."

Ned shook his head. "What kind of idiot cheats himself?"

There was no need to respond to that one, not even with a wry gesture at the culprit. Ned flushed pink.

"When you first came to me, Ned, I had a choice of lies. You wanted to know if there was anything in your future besides unhappiness and irresponsibility. I could have told you the truth. The truth is, people rarely change. The truth is, men who drink too much often lead foolish, irresponsible lives. The truth is, you had too much money and not enough sense to ever grow into the kind of man you yearned to be."

Ned flinched with every sentence.

"So I lied to you."

"You told me what I wanted to hear." His voice was small.

Jenny shook her head. "I told you what you *needed* to hear. I still see it, you know. When I look at you, I still see a boy growing into a man, honorable and tall. I see a man who will one day command respect."

Ned's hands shook and his eyes glistened. "Another lie?" His voice trembled. "You don't know what it is really like, what I have thought—"

"It is as much a lie today as it was then. And isn't it strange? Since I've known you, you've become intensely loyal, unwilling to let others look down on those who matter to you. I watched you grow into that falsehood I told. Not despite the lie, but because of it."

Jenny picked up the stack of coins on the table. Sixteen pounds. Every penny she owned in the world. She reached across the table and took Ned's right hand. The metal piled nicely into his palm.

"Just because I cheat," she said, "doesn't mean I cheated you. You see, there is nothing on this earth so powerful as a lie that can come true."

Ned let out his breath in a shudder. "Madame—"

"Jenny."

Ned shut his eyes. "Jenny. You don't understand. I've made a mess of my life. It wasn't much to start with. And—" His other hand closed on top of hers. "And you told me the darkness would not return, but it does. How can I fight it for the rest of my life?"

"What do you need to do today? Think of that. Don't let it out of your mind. And once you've taken that step, look to tomorrow. You don't need to figure out your whole life all at once. Just take one step at a time."

"You make it sound so easy," Ned mused.

"That's an illusion. It's very, very hard. But if you keep going, you'll get there." Jenny stood up and gently pulled her hands from Ned's grip. She leaned across the table and kissed him lightly on the cheek.

"Goodbye, Mr. Carhart," she whispered.

And then she turned. Her skirts tangled about her ankles as she hastened from the room.

GARETH TOOK ONE LAST LOOK at Ned. His cousin was staring at the coins collected on the table, a look of shock on his face. He looked up at Gareth. His eyes reflected Gareth's own dazed confusion. And for the first time since that dreadful evening when Gareth had walked in on that debacle with Lady Kathleen, Ned's eyes flared with hope.

"Well," Ned said, "What are you waiting for? Go after her."

Gareth turned and fled. He dashed downstairs, out of the too-hot hell into the chilled air. She was disappearing into the fog down the street.

He ran after her. "Jenny. Wait." She turned around. He caught up with her and grabbed her elbow. "You can't—"

The words choked him. If she'd just demonstrated

anything, it was that she *could*. After all, she *had*. It was he who hadn't been able to do what was needed.

"It's not safe," he finished idiotically, "for a woman to walk alone. Let me call you a hack."

She swallowed. "I haven't any money to pay one."

"I wasn't proposing to leave you with the fare." He stuck his hands in his pockets. "I wasn't proposing to let you walk out without a word, either."

Not that any number of words would ever encompass what he felt now.

She'd once accused him of seeing the worst in people. Perhaps that was because Jenny saw things outside the bounds of his comprehension. And not only did she see them, she spoke of them. And they became real on the strength of her hope.

Her gaze traveled down to the hand he'd clamped on her elbow.

"Very well," she said slowly.

He went through the motions of hailing a hackney driver and delivering her direction. Then he followed her into the hired conveyance.

A terrible lump built in his breast.

He wondered how much of Jenny's success as Madame Esmerelda had been built on the strength of that peculiar talent. Real hope, masked in mumbo jumbo and fraud. If he saw the worst in people, it was because he'd traded his own hope in years ago when he'd let Lord Blakely own the lion's share of Gareth's life.

Now he saw hope again and he didn't want to let it go. He didn't want to let *her* go.

Gareth had not believed in Ned. He hadn't really believed in his own sister. These days he scarcely believed in himself, either. He'd not believed he could find any measure of happiness in London. Before he'd met Jenny, his days had stretched in front of him, false and hollow, a line of dire backbreaking responsibility, untempered by any true joy.

He desperately longed for her benediction, for a measure of the grace she so easily bestowed on others.

"So." He kept his tone light. Jocular. He didn't dare betray how important the question was to him. "You look at my sister and see a powerful woman. You look at Ned and see an honorable man. I must seem a veritable giant of a fellow. Whatever do you see when you look at me?"

She responded to his tone with a casual smile. "Oh, all manner of wicked things."

Ah. So he was nothing but a bloody good shag. Gareth swallowed his leaden disappointment. *I was serious,* he protested internally. But maybe she had been, too. Maybe she uncovered by intuition what he had always known by logic: that there was no grace for him. She had told him he must be very lonely. She had been right—she'd seen through his pompous, arrogant mask, right to the bleak darkness inside of him that yearned for companionship and friendship.

Maybe that was all this meant to her. Sex and sympathy.

Gareth shut his eyes and fought for nonchalance. "Wicked things? What am I doing to you?"

She whispered in his ear. Her hand fell on his thigh. Despite the black roil in his gut, his body tensed, and he vowed to do every one of those things to her, and more. Tonight. Maybe, if he did them well enough she would see more than there was, in violation of all the laws of nature. Maybe he could fool her into believing there was more to him than a cold man with a deep-seated loneliness.

But her smile stretched too wide, her laugh pitched too high. She, too, was holding something back. It came to him. Those words she'd said—*everything you own, pitted against everything I own.*

She'd had no clients recently.

But she'd said—he'd been certain of it—that she had some money saved. He'd given the matter no more thought. Just as he'd thoughtlessly assumed she had a maid secreted away somewhere to assist her in putting on a gown.

"My God, Jenny," he interrupted, "you *really* mean you couldn't pay the fare."

She looked away. "It's none of your concern, Gareth."

"Not my concern! You told me you had money saved. What the devil did you mean by that?"

"I did," she said stiffly. "I had four hundred pounds. It's been…misplaced."

His head pounded. "First, four hundred pounds hardly signifies. I pay White more than that in a year. And second, why did you say nothing to me? What *am* I to you?"

"You aren't my banker, that's for certain."

His hand closed around her wrist. "What else can't you pay, Jenny?"

She sighed. "Everything. It's not a problem. I had a plan."

"Let's hear it."

She exhaled slowly. "I planned to sell everything I own and leave."

"Leave." His fingers convulsed on her wrist. "Leave me."

"Leave *London*," she clarified, as if that would ease the pain that spread like a net of fire, sharp pinpricks settling under his skin. Her pulse thumped through the wrist he clutched. It was steady and even. Staid. Her heart beat

in a normal tempo. Of course; it was only his that constricted into a cold, dark lump.

"Ah. And leaving me would just be an unintended
consequence. One you had not planned to inform me
about."

"I would have told you. Eventually. I didn't think I
meant that much—"

He kissed her, hard and fast, before she could finish
that horrendous lie.

"Humbug," he said when he let her go. "I know I never
know the right thing to say. I'm a damned nuisance. But
you're not stupid. You know I adore you."

She was silent. She should not have been silent. She
should have been throwing herself at him, professing her
own adoration. Jenny, the woman who saw strength and
courage everywhere else, had nothing to say about Gareth.

Well. He'd wanted to know how she saw him.

Now he knew.

CHAPTER NINETEEN

BY THE TIME THEY REACHED Jenny's home, separate factions in Gareth's head had broken out in a pitched battle. He could not help but respect what she'd done for Ned. He'd not known what to think, what to say. And when she'd laid that final card... He'd thought, in that second, that he was more than a little in love with her.

But she was leaving. She was leaving *him*—the Marquess of Blakely. There were no words for the fury that made him feel. Black rage boiled up. Without even trying, she'd walked into that gaming hell, her hair billowing around her like an aurora. She'd done with ten minutes and sixteen pounds what Gareth had not accomplished in two days. What he could not have done, if he was honest, in two years with sixteen thousand pounds. And she was leaving him, as if he were nothing to her.

She opened her door, unaware that Gareth was engaged in a fierce battle for his soul.

He reached for her before she could move. He caught her lips against his. Damn her, but she kissed him back without reservation, her hands roaming over his tense body. How well she knew him. How well she knew to touch him like *that,* running her hands down his abdomen, her fingers points of pressure against his skin.

Hot rage. Fierce love. Intense anguish. And above it

all, that damnable knowledge that she was *leaving* him. *She* was leaving *him.* God. He pushed her against the wall roughly, pressing his hips against hers.

She moaned against him, opening to his touch. If there were light, she would have seen the black marks that his coal-dark heart must be leaving against her skin. But there was nothing but murk inside. Murk and midnight. He unbuttoned the fall of his trousers and lifted her against the wall. He pulled her drawers down and pushed her petticoats up. And then, arms trembling, he thrust into her in one stroke.

She was wet and welcoming. She sank around him, and firm, tight bliss shot from his groin clear to the top of his head and then down again. The muscles of her passage gripped his member; she wrapped her legs around him. Pulling him against her. Welcoming him inside her.

He took what she offered. Every stroke sent longing spiraling through him. He didn't want to just flood her with his seed. He wanted to flood her with his entire being.

If he could bring her to climax before him, maybe he could make her forget that it had been he who'd been impotent to do anything about his cousin.

If he did it twice, maybe she'd forget she'd ever planned to leave.

Illusions all, but with her body clenched around his, illusions were what he needed.

And so he angled himself inside her. He circled his hips against hers while her moans grew sharper. Louder. Harder. Her hands raked along his back. And then she clamped down on him. Hot, hard waves crashed through her and into him. She screamed his name, her body tensing in his arms. Gareth rode those waves.

But in this thing, too, he was outside his skills. He'd

intended to calm down, to take her to pleasure once again. But he couldn't stop. Not with her body pulsing warmly around him. Instead, he let out a groan and pumped hard. Pleasure propagated down his stiff cock and out his groin. It filled him like dark, warm water. He grabbed her close and spent himself inside her with a wordless roar.

The fire passed gradually. And there was nothing around him but the dark of the night and the velvet warmth of her body.

He shivered inside her, pushing her against the wall. Not letting her go. His muscles trembled with the effort of holding her legs high on his hips, but he would be damned if he'd give up this closeness. Instead, he pressed into her. She sighed warm air against his neck.

She didn't say anything.

She didn't have to.

She was still planning to leave him, and the very thought choked all returning coherence from his mind.

The rage of lust had burnt from him. And now on this charred battleground, he realized that the war inside him had ended. Peace had broken out. But the surrender that had been negotiated was not a strict win for either party.

Gareth would not let Jenny wrap him up like a convenient package, brought to his knees. He'd make her need him as much as he needed her. More. She'd thought to let him go with no more than a sigh and a kiss goodbye? He would show her, once and for all, that she was wrong. She should have cared for him enough to not say goodbye.

His thoughts distilled until nothing was left but a single chant, repeated over and over.

"You're not leaving," he growled in her ear. "I'm going to keep you."

Her chest expanded against his in a shivering breath. She turned her head away in rebuttal.

He kissed her ear. "Are you planning to go any time before tomorrow at two?"

She shook her head. Her hair pressed against his lips.

"Good. I'll come 'round then and take you for a drive."

He couldn't let her go. He *wouldn't.*

NED HAD READ in travel diaries about northern climes where, when winter reigned, the sun disappeared for months. In summer, the sun would never set. That's how he'd classified his life. It fell into two parts: years of near-frenetic bliss, followed by months of darkness. Until last night, the two had never met.

But last night he'd won a portion of hope at five-card loo.

The Duke of Ware lived in a stone edifice in Mayfair. Solid blocks of stone, once white, now streaked with generations of London soot, stretched up four stories. The dark walls terminated in a slate roof, the steep line of which was interrupted by blackened chimneys and rectangular attic windows. The house was every bit as imposing as Ned had imagined it.

Ned took a deep breath and walked up the steps to the door. If Ned had asked, Blakely would have come with him.

But Ned hadn't wanted to delegate his life to another. Not again. Madame Esmerelda had lied to him; Blakely had shoved him around. In the end, none of it had made any difference. The darkness he'd feared had enveloped him anyway.

Still he stood, waiting to take one tiny step forward.

Last night, as he stared at the cards on the table, he'd realized one fundamental truth. Fate had not saved him from suicidal folly all those years ago. Madame Esmerelda had not intervened with the spirits on his behalf. There was only one conclusion: He must have unwittingly saved himself. What he had accomplished once by accident, he could do again by choice.

And so here he stood. Some rebellious part of him yearned to go lie down, to give in to the cloying despondency of the last few days. But he'd beaten it before with resolve, albeit a resolve bolstered by lies. He could win a second time with truth.

He knocked on the door. When the stiff butler answered, Ned handed over his card. "I'm here to see Lady Kathleen," he said.

The man glanced at the card. Ned hadn't thought the fellow could starch up any more, but the sudden rigidity in his joints made his previous posture seem downright malleable by comparison. The butler swiftly closed the door in Ned's face.

Resolve, Ned repeated to himself. Resolve and strength would unravel this tangle. Ned waited. And waited. And waited.

Fifteen minutes later, the door opened again. The butler nodded. "His Grace will see you now."

"But I don't wish to speak to His Grace," Ned said. His Grace had probably cleaned his pistols in preparation for this moment. "I wish to speak to His Grace's daughter."

The butler raised an eyebrow. "*His Grace* will see you now."

Ned sighed and followed the man. His Grace waited in the front parlor. He was in shirtsleeves, as if he couldn't bother to dress for Ned. A book was open on his lap. He didn't look up when Ned entered. Instead, he continued to pretend to read. And a pretense it obviously was. Aside from the carefully timed turning of the pages, the Duke of Ware stared at the pages blankly, his eyes unmoving, his hands strangling the spine of the book. It was precisely the sort of thing Blakely would do—ignore a man to put him in his place.

Ned balanced from foot to foot in indecision. He didn't want to antagonize the man. But then again, it wasn't as if the duke could hate him *more*. And he couldn't bear waiting for his life to happen to him. No; from this point onward, he would direct the course of his life.

He stepped forward and grabbed the book from His Grace's hands. "I apologize for the precipitate behavior," he said. "You see, you're either going to have to kill me or allow me to talk with your daughter. I'm very difficult to ignore."

Ware's face slowly mottled an unflattering orange as he looked up. "Blazing pitch and sulfur! *You've* ignored *me*. Twice, now, we've been scheduled to meet. Twice, now, Blakely convinced me not to hunt you down. I demand satisfaction."

"We all want satisfaction, Your Grace. Unfortunately, most of us are doomed to disappointment."

"Pistols or swords, you bounder!"

Ned shook his head. "I'm not going to fight you. If it comes down to it, I prefer pistols. Through the heart, please. I'd prefer not to linger from a gut wound."

"Confounded goat-lover! Puling rabbit!"

This was an easily recognizable pattern. Ned grasped at it.

"Ridiculous weasel?" he assayed.

Ware clenched his fists. "Impudent worm!"

"Five-toed chicken! Ravenous strawberry!"

That brought Ware up. "What? What did you call me?"

"Oh, were you calling *me* those names?" Ned replied innocently. "I thought we were playing a game. You know, irrelevant adjective applied to inexplicable noun. You know how it goes. First to string together a coherent sentence loses."

Ware stared in absolute befuddlement. Blakely, Ned had realized, had been *excellent* practice. Whether practice for getting himself killed or getting himself married remained to be seen.

"That," Ned added gently, "implies you lost. In case you hadn't noticed."

"My daughter is not a game."

It was time to test his resolve. "Then why are you toying with me instead of letting me speak with her?"

Ware's eyes drilled into Ned's sternum. His mouth set. Ned wanted to hide, but he made himself stand straight and return the look.

Finally, the duke stood and walked to the door, his legs stiff. He threw it open. On the other side leaned Lady Kathleen, her hand cupped where the door had been.

She stiffened into a guilty curtsy. "Papa. Mr. Carhart."

Ned bowed. "Lady Kathleen," he said. He shoved his hands in his pockets.

"Well, poppet," Ware said with a sigh. "Shall I slay him?"

The angelic Kathleen shook her head. The light caught her hair in a fine nimbus, almost like a halo. "No, Papa."

Ware deflated. "I was afraid you would say that."

"Not in the parlor," she added. "Blood stains so."

"So it does. So it does. I suppose you'll talk to him, then?"

"I'm afraid I'll have to."

Ware jerked with his thumb. "Call out if he annoys you. I'll come in and gut him with the poker."

Ned's gaze traveled to the fireplace where the implement rested. "But it's not even remotely sharp!"

Ware smiled broadly and rubbed big, hairy hands together. "I know."

Well. At least Ned could discard the worry that she'd turn him down because she feared he was mad. She was likely used to insanity. The door shut behind the duke, and Ned was left alone with Lady Kathleen. He knew what he needed to do. It should not have felt like such a hardship.

Right. He got down on one knee. She stepped back, her lips pressing together. Silence stretched.

"See here," he finally said. "We had better get married."

She winced and flattened herself against the wall. "A week ago, you sent me a letter, saying you wanted to speak with me alone. As a result of that letter, we were caught together in an improper situation, and you disappeared. It's been seven days since last I saw you. What the devil have you been doing?"

Ned grimaced wryly and glanced across the room at her. Explanations flitted through his mind. He finally settled on a variant of the truth. "I've been afflicted by madness. It was only temporary."

She shook her head. "This seems to be a common affliction in your family. Ought I be worried?" There was a hint of a smile on her lips; no doubt she thought he was joking again.

Ned thought of the darkness that came over him from time to time, robbing him of strength. And he thought of his own will. It seemed a slender reed to stand against that howling storm. "Yes," he said solemnly. "You should."

She shut her eyes. "Well. This is romantic. You don't really want to marry me, do you?"

A marriage, Ned thought, ought to be composed of a great many qualities. Affection. Infatuation. Friendship. But he had nothing to offer her except one last quality: Honesty.

"No," he said. "But then—do you really want to marry me, either?"

She was silent for a very long time. "I'm a duke's daughter. I never expected to marry for love. I always expected to marry the heir to some great title—and here you are." She looked at him through long lashes, and an uneasy roil built in his gut. "You make me laugh. You're not puffed up with your own importance." She glanced at the door. "You understand, I hope, that I'm my father's only child, and I'll be helping him with matters in the House of Lords. Will you interfere with that?"

"No." He swallowed uncomfortably and looked away. "Lady Kathleen," he finally said, "I don't want you to expect too much from me. I am, after all—"

She interrupted this speech by reaching for his hand. Instead of taking it in her own, however, she shook it firmly—as if she were embarking on a business deal, not a betrothal. "You'll do," she said.

And like that, Ned was engaged.

GARETH HAD ARRIVED precisely at the appointed hour. Jenny was aware of his eyes flicking toward her throughout the drive. The sun shone brightly; birds chirped merrily. It was a day pulled out of an idyllic romanticist's novel; a phaeton, a pair of smart-stepping horses and a handsome man. The world was sharp and crisp around the edges as their conveyance crossed Blackfriars Bridge.

But the handsome man wasn't speaking words of adoration, and besides, she was going to have to leave him.
What he did not say in words, he showed in gestures. She
read his unease in every movement—the tight clamp his
gloved hands kept on the reins, his monosyllabic re-
sponses. And always, always, the way he watched her.
Warily, as if she wielded some mighty weapon.

Jenny could have wept.

She put her hand over his. His jaw twitched and he
looked ahead. Stoic and somber.

Eventually, he turned onto a street labeled Half Moon
Lane, a quiet, respectable neighborhood. He pulled the
horses up outside an elegant row house. He tossed the reins
in one controlled flick to the boy who clambered down off
the back. The horses stamped and tossed their heads, but
stood. The afternoon silence, after the rattle of wheels over
cobblestone, pressed into her skin. Gareth removed one
black glove and held out his hand to her. She took it and
stepped down. He didn't retain her grip. Instead he turned,
jerkily, to the house and reached the door in a few strides.

Following behind him, Jenny noticed the knocker had
been removed from the glossy blue door. Gareth fumbled
in his pocket and pulled out a key. Seconds later, he
swung the door open, with the air of a sculptor unveiling
his masterpiece. The tense lines of his face set, and he
motioned her forward.

Jenny stepped into the hall. The soles of her shoes
clacked on black marble so polished she could have used
it as a mirror. Gold tracework climbed the walls. Her
vision followed the scrolling gilt up, up and still up. She
broke out in gooseflesh. That frightening sense of vertigo
assailed her, as if she were looking into a great chasm
built of money. Cherubs cavorted across the blue of the

ceiling. A lady of Gareth's acquaintance might have found their chubby smiles comforting. All Jenny could think was that some poor fellow had hung with his feet dangling all those yards above the ground for hours on end, all for the purpose of providing her with five seconds of pleasure should she happen to glance in the air.

"What do you think of it?" Gareth asked.

"It makes the bottoms of my feet tingle," Jenny said honestly.

He wrinkled his nose. "Well. That's ambiguous. You should see the rest of the house."

He took her arm and guided her through a doorway decorated with ornate molding. Black marble gave way to floors that gleamed like honey. The paper on the walls was a rich burgundy-and-gold. And the gold wasn't a mere yellow color; it shone with little flecks of gleaming metal. Traces of light seeped through drawn velvet curtains. Jenny turned around, her feet clopping noisily against the floor.

"It echoes," Jenny said experimentally. Her voice reverberated back to her.

"It's not furnished yet," Gareth said. "I wasn't sure if you wanted to do it yourself, or if I should hire someone for the task."

His words echoed, too. Jenny swallowed, a forbidding pit growing in her stomach.

"Gareth," she said quietly, "my furnishings would look rather ridiculous in here."

"Pshaw. As if I'd let you keep that rickety old table. Here, you haven't seen upstairs yet. You can see the back garden from the bedroom window."

Jenny planted her feet and shook her hand as he tried to lead her away. "What is this?"

"It's a house. A row house. I know it doesn't look like

much at the moment, but imagine it furnished. Paintings on the wall. A fire in the fireplace and a staff."

Jenny rolled her eyes. "I know what a house *is,* Gareth. And I have a perfectly functional imagination. I don't know why you're showing it to me."

"My solicitor's drawing up the deed. I'm giving it to you."

The world stood still. "What?"

"I'm. Giving. It. To. You. Oh, stop standing there with your mouth open. If you want to thank me, I can think of several ways for you to do so."

Suggestive words, but he delivered them so stiffly.

Her heart constricted. She'd told him not to send furniture or bring her jewels, so he gave her a *house?* Had he understood a word she'd told him?

"Well?" He reached for her hand. "Come along."

"It's a nice house. A very nice house. It's a little…" *Formal. Big.* None of that really seemed to match the shrieking horror inside her. "It's a little outside my means to maintain properly," she finally managed.

"Don't be obtuse, Jenny. It's a perfectly legitimate bargain. I have money. You don't. You have you. And in a matter of days, I won't. Well, trade and trade alike. I'm keeping you."

"I don't want to be kept."

His brows scrunched together in puzzlement.

"I don't want to feel obliged to you. And I certainly don't want you to pay me to do something I'd prefer to give freely."

Gareth switched the glove he carried to his other hand and slapped it rhythmically against his thigh. "Explain."

"I mean, that what you are proposing—it feels like a coffin to me."

The glove slapped once more and then stilled as black leather scrunched in his hand. "You, of all people, know I can never say things the right way. What I mean is—I can't let you leave me. I need you."

She wanted to take his hand and smooth out the tension in the muscles. She wanted to kiss his forehead and watch those furrowed lines sink back into comfort.

But.

There was always a but. And this one sank sharp needles deep in Jenny's chest.

"And what," she said slowly, "will I do with the other twenty-two hours of the day?"

"Pardon?"

"I assume you'll devote no more time to Jenny Keeble than Gareth receives. Gareth gets his two hours of scientific work in the morning. What do I get at night?"

"Jenny. You know I can't give more. It's my responsibility, and I cannot give it up—"

Jenny shut her eyes. Deep down inside her, that strong stillness she'd found waited. And no matter how much her heart cried out to go to him, that quiet center of strength did not recede.

"I want," she said, "my integrity. I don't want to be bought."

She stepped back. This marble tomb was just another form of abandonment—another way that a man could put her off in perpetuity. It reduced her longing for family and independence to a stark figure. The number of pounds it took to purchase a house in town. The number of minutes Gareth gave her. She would be nothing more than another column in his account books.

Account books could be closed, and entire columns could be set aside.

His mouth parted. He reached for her.

Jenny shut her eyes against stinging tears. "I don't want you to buy me. I want you to live. I don't want to be another one of your responsibilities. I want to be your—"

Your family.

She couldn't say the word. But he took her meaning instantly. "I *can't,*" he breathed.

Beneath wet lashes, she saw him turn away and grip the door frame.

"You want me to call you Gareth," Jenny said. "But Lord Blakely will always be between us. *His* responsibility. *His* estate. And now you're trying to make me *his* mistress. Do you really think—after all you've known of me—that you can buy me with money?"

"It's all I have to give."

Jenny opened her eyes fully. He was facing away from her, the muscles of his back taut.

"No." Her words sounded thin and metallic in her ears. As if she stood at a great distance from herself. "It is all you are *willing* to give. You hide behind money and responsibility."

He whipped around, his eyes flashing angrily. "I'm not hiding."

"You are. And you want to hide me, too. Well, I'm not having it. You can't purchase me with numbers or persuade me with logic."

He inhaled fiercely, his nostrils flaring. "Ask for anything else. And don't you tell me about hiding. You're the one who cringes when I talk of adoration and need. You won't even let yourself depend on me for this one little thing."

"No. If you want me," Jenny said desperately, "trade yourself."

"Damn you, Jenny," he snapped. "It's not a fair trade."

Jenny's world turned to crystal, all cold sharp edges. Brittle, and teetering on the brink of some high precipice. He needed her. He wouldn't give up his responsibility. But responsibility—that benevolent word encoded a malign sentiment.

Hire an estate manager, she'd suggested. He'd responded with, *Who would I trust? I was born to this.* He'd been taught all his life he was better than everyone else. That careless assumption of superiority left him unable to relinquish either duty or dominance.

"Not a fair trade." The words cut her lips as she repeated them.

He was angry. He felt betrayed. And he did never manage to say the right things. But only half of that could be attributed to underlying awkwardness. This time, he'd meant what he said.

"If I'm not a fair trade," she forced herself to say, "it's because you don't think I am worth as much as you."

And why would he? He'd been taught all his life she wasn't.

"Really, Jenny," he drawled. All emotion had washed from his voice—a sure sign, Jenny knew, that he was too caught up in hurt to dissemble. "Be rational. Who *would* think you my equal?"

"I can think of one person." Jenny squared her shoulders. Her throat ached. She met his eyes, dead-on, without flinching. "Me."

His eyes widened and he reached for her wrist, but he moved as if through honey. Jenny stepped back, evading his hand. His glove fell as he stretched for her. It hit the floor with a hollow thump.

"Don't go." His words resounded in the cavernous room. "I didn't—"

He caught himself, and Jenny knew that same implacable honor prevented him from finishing that lie. Because he really had meant it. And without once saying goodbye, he'd managed to abandon her in every way that mattered.

Jenny backed away. When she judged there to be enough distance between them, she turned and walked swiftly to the door. Her footsteps echoed all the way out the foyer, but his did not sound in pursuit.

CHAPTER TWENTY

GARETH FELT as if he had aged twenty-four years in the twenty-four hours since Jenny had left.

He stared listlessly out the window as White droned on. The man's voice was almost soothing. It was difficult to focus on the concepts—farming improvements. Agriculture. Portraits.

Instead, he nodded his head and shut his eyes. He'd nothing to hold on to but this responsibility. It would eventually expand to fill the void.

But perhaps it only seemed so empty because White had stopped talking.

Gareth opened his eyes. "Any other business?"

"Yes. A letter. It's from a ladies' school in Bristol."

Gareth paused. "Bristol? What the devil does a ladies' school in Bristol want from me? Contributions?"

"It's from a Mrs. Davenport, sir. It comes roundabout, by means of the inquiries you asked me to make about a Miss Jenny Keeble."

Gareth fished in his pocket for his knife. His pocket was as empty as his life.

It did no good to find the information when he'd lost the woman. She wouldn't take his money, wouldn't take him. "Never say that name to me again. Send her ten pounds and burn the letter."

White ignored this sally. "She writes a very sly letter, if you ask me. She says she knows of J—of the name I am not to mention. She was a pupil in her school, years ago."

Gareth inhaled. The odor of wood smoke was faintly comforting. Jenny. Just thinking of her made his ribs ache.

It was madness, what she asked of him. He'd lost everything—his mother, his sister, his wistful desire for love—because of the obligation the title of Blakely imposed on him. If he were not, in truth, superior, that sacrifice would be meaningless.

"White, can I ask you a question?"

"Naturally, sir."

"Do you consider me wealthy?"

White rubbed his head in puzzlement. "Yes."

"And I have an ancient and honorable title?"

"Yes, my lord."

"And my looks—am I incorrigibly ugly?"

White looked wildly about the room. But there was no escape; Gareth was his employer, and that gave him the right to ask impertinent questions. "I can't rightly say as how I've taken particular notice, but your features do seem put together in the proper order. If I may take the liberty of conjecturing as to your next question, my lord, your personal odor is inoffensive."

Gareth nodded in grim acknowledgment. "That's what I thought."

White crossed to the fire and pulled the screen away with an ungodly clatter.

"What are you doing now?" Gareth asked crossly.

"I'm burning the letter."

Gareth jumped to his feet. "No! Give it here. What are you thinking?"

"I'm not thinking at all, my lord." White smiled, privately. "I'm just following your express orders."

Gareth pointed a finger at his hapless man of business. "How the devil am I to find this woman in Bristol if you've burnt the address?"

"But you said—"

"Damn what I said." Gareth snapped his fingers. "Hand it over."

White smirked with satisfaction and placed that last precious connection to Jenny in Gareth's waiting hands.

ONCE IT BECAME OBVIOUS Jenny could not stay in London, her life simplified. With no need to consider whether to stay or go, the question of money resolved itself. She'd kept only a few articles of clothing and one last, vain memento of the previous weeks. The vast majority of her household effects, she hawked for nine pounds.

But she sold the ungainly bed Gareth had sent her for thirty-two pounds.

When the last pot had been carted away, Jenny turned around in her front room. It was empty of everything except a lonely valise, packed with serviceable clothing. Her footsteps rang against the hard floor.

Her forty pounds was spoken for already. She'd purchased passage in steerage on the regular packet to New York. It left in a handful of days; she'd have just funds enough to reach her final destination and see herself settled. Until then, there were beds in lodging houses. She had half an hour to say goodbye to this empty hole. Thirty minutes was too much time to fill with melancholy, and too little in which to make her heart release its grip.

Twelve years later, she had nothing left. Nothing, that is, except herself. It was still there inside of her, that warm, still center. It had not vanished, and neither bank cashiers nor Blakely could threaten it.

Jenny stood up and reached for her valise. But before she had adjusted to its weight dangling from her arm, a sharp rat-tat-tat sounded at the door. After two years, she knew that knock all too well. Her heart leapt. Jenny dropped her burden, dashed to the door and threw it open.

"Mr. Carhart!"

Ned peered into her room. His expression changed from solemn to bemused. "You're leaving?"

Jenny gave a nonchalant shrug. "There's nothing to keep me here any longer."

"Going back home?"

Jenny sighed wistfully. *Home.* She'd never had a home, or a family. She'd had lies and recriminations. Somewhere in the world, she hoped there still was a home for her. It just wasn't here.

"Cincinnati," she said.

Ned frowned.

"It's in America. I picked the name out of an emigration pamphlet. I had never heard of it, and so I suppose *it* will never have heard of me. Which is just as well. I need..."

She trailed off. She needed stability. She yearned for it. She wanted a place where she could earn the respect and trust of those around her. And she needed to get away from this cage, where bloodlines and belongings trumped accomplishment. Here in London, the temptation of seeing Gareth again—of taking that easy path, accepting his offer, knowing what it would mean—was too great.

"You need," Ned prompted.

"I need a fresh start," she finished quietly.

Ned nodded and shoved his hands in his pockets. He

walked around the room, and Jenny wondered if he, too, was seeing echoes of his former entrapment.

Finally, he looked up at her. "I'm to be married in a week."

"Congratulations, Mr. Carhart." She looked down. They'd talked once before, about his antipathy for the state of matrimony. Marriage could not have been a hastily made decision on his part. But she did not know if they could fall back into the easy state of conversation they'd once enjoyed. She bit her lip, holding in the questions that bombarded her.

But she no longer had the right to pry into his affairs. "Gareth is pleased, I'm sure. I hope you are, too."

Ned stepped back, a puzzled expression on his face. "So *Blakely* is Gareth and I am Mr. Carhart?"

There was no real way to respond to that. No way, except the truth. "Yes. I give you leave to call him by his Christian name, by the way. Someone must continue to do so once I am gone. He needs to be reminded, you see, that there's more to him than Lord Blakely. He'll forget otherwise. And he mustn't forget."

"Jenny," Ned interrupted, "I came here to ask you to come to my wedding. It's a small affair. Family only."

A lump formed in Jenny's throat. "I couldn't."

"Why not? I just asked you."

"No, I really mean that I *can't*. My packet leaves in five days."

"Can't you change to the week after?"

She could. But there was another reason. "G— I mean, Blakely will be there. And I'm not part of your family, Ned. I wouldn't want to intrude."

"You've faced my cousin before. Why can you not do so now?"

Because I cannot bear to see him again. Jenny let out a sigh. "Must I really spell it out?"

Ned searched her face and must have found the answer. "Really? *Blakely?*"

She blushed, and bent to rummage in her valise for her one last memento. "That," she said, straightening, prize in hand, "and he'll likely set the law on me once he realizes I absconded with his penknife that night in the gaming hell."

Ned stared at the elegant knife. The weapon was as much Jenny's connection to Ned—loyal, trusting Ned— as it was to Gareth. Her memories of the knife were bound up with Ned. Ned stabbing the orange. Jenny piercing the cards in front of him.

Ned speaking up, telling Gareth that Jenny was more his family than anyone else he knew.

Jenny sighed wistfully.

But Ned did not speak of the knife. Instead he said, "When I was very young, I told my mother I wanted an older sister. She laughed at me and told me that nature didn't work that way. But a younger sister was not forthcoming, either. There was always only me. I have had my problems—of my own devising, you understand. And at one point, I thought there was no hope for me. No encouragement. Then I met you."

"I *lied* to you, Ned."

He reached out and gently took the knife from her grasp.

"Sisters usually do." He opened the blade and switched it, awkwardly, to his other hand. And then he held out his right hand. The knife scored his flesh, cutting a thin red line down his palm. Blood welled up.

Ned held out the knife expectantly. "You told me to take this one step at a time. Well? Here I am."

Jenny hesitated. It was too much. He offered truth in exchange for lies. Loyalty, for fraud.

And then he bounced expectantly on his toes, and he was impatient Ned again. Ned, who offered, quite simply, love for love. If she couldn't believe she was worthy of it *now*, she might as well give up on the whole thought of finding any place on the face of the earth where she could command respect.

Jenny's fingers trembled as she took the knife in her left hand. The sharp blade slid into her flesh. At first, she didn't feel a thing—not the cut, nor any attendant pain. Then Ned reached out and clasped her hand in his. He squeezed, and the wound stung. Her eyes smarted. Her heart swelled, and suddenly, her echoing rooms seemed neither desolate nor empty.

She'd waited thirty long years for a little brother. It had taken him a while to appear, but he'd been worth the delay.

"I know you're leaving," Ned said softly. "Truth be told—I'm not sure I can do this, either. Be her husband. Live a normal life."

A thousand reassurances swam through Jenny's head. But he squeezed her hand. "I'll manage," he said. "At least now, I believe that."

"I'd rather see you happy," Jenny whispered. "But I suppose I won't see you at all."

"America. England. What does a little thing like a few thousand miles matter, among family?"

"Nothing," Jenny said. "It's nothing at all."

GARETH'S JOURNEY HAD BEEN long and jolting, but after two miserable days on the road, he arrived.

Three solid graystone buildings made up Elland School in Bristol. The trees on the grounds gathered naked, gray branches primly about their trunks, as if they were preparing for winter instead of participating in the spring that had arrived everywhere else. A few stray handbills were strewn about the streets, but not one dared mar the strict order of the yard. Even the cobblestones the carriage clattered over seemed laid in a geometric pattern. The formal grounds were in such contrast to everything Gareth knew about Jenny that it seemed impossible he would find any trace of her here.

He strode to the main entrance and gave his card to the hunchbacked gentleman who answered the door. He was shown into a dim, drab parlor, the striped paper on the walls faded but clean. A coal-fire smoked fitfully in the hearth.

A few books stood at attention on a shelf. Gareth peered at their spines. *A Brief History of Western Etiquette* stood next to *The Rules of Precedence*. The thin volume on the end was imprinted with the illuminating title of *Forks, Spoons, Knives and the Proper Use of a Serviette.*

Gareth would have been willing to bet that Jenny, his mischievous, exuberant Jenny, had never set foot in the room.

The door opened behind him. Of course, it did not do anything so uncouth as creak; instead, it sighed, a dim sound.

"Lord Blakely. How can I be of service? What can I tell you of our school? Would you like to sit?"

The voice was old. The words formed questions, but the tone was dry command. It was the voice of a woman who had ordered young girls for so long she knew no other way to communicate.

Gareth turned. The woman who stood there was as exact as every other aspect of the school. Not one strand of gray hair escaped her precise bun. Her colorless face blended into the tired, pressed gray of her dress. Her lips formed straight lines, as if any bend or kink would offend her orderly nature.

"You must be Mrs. Davenport," Gareth said. "You wrote me."

Her eyes narrowed in disbelief.

"In answer to the inquiry my man of business made," he continued. "I'm here about Jenny Keeble."

It would have been gauche for Mrs. Davenport to show emotion. But the emotion she very carefully didn't show—not even a hint of surprise that a strange man would ask after a pupil who attended her school more than a decade before—was all too telling. It was the decorous, hopeful blankness of a gossipy woman who had a scandalous story to tell, and who expected to receive a juicy tidbit in exchange.

"Is there some problem? Is Miss Keeble…" Mrs. Davenport paused delicately.

"Dead? Convicted? Wanted for fraud?"

Mrs. Davenport's eyes grew wider with every possibility Gareth listed. Satisfaction radiated from her.

Gareth drummed his fingers against the leg of his trousers. "No. She's not."

A subtle tension entered the woman's shoulders. "Well. That child gave me more trouble than any other girl in my twenty-nine years here. If you know her, you know she has a predilection for…" Another delicate pause.

"Lies," Gareth supplied helpfully.

"Mistruths," finished Mrs. Davenport. "And indirection. Often involving money. But you seem to have news of her. I dare not hope she has adopted an honest profession?"

Mrs. Davenport raised one perfectly formed eyebrow. Hidden behind the brittle cold of her censorious glare lay a spark of avaricious desire.

"My God," Gareth said. "You really *are* a vulture, aren't you?"

Her lips pursed. "If it would please you, my lord. Don't take the Lord's name in vain. There are young girls here, and they *will* repeat every last naughty word they hear."

"I'm here to find out more," he said. Once he'd imagined that if he could uncover her deepest secrets, he'd be able to put her behind him. He didn't fool himself that was still the case. Now, he just wanted to *know.* "What was she like? Who were her friends?"

"Friends?" Mrs. Davenport scoffed. "A girl of *her* like doesn't have friends among proper women. I made sure of that. I protested her admittance, I did. No good can come of girls with uncertain parentage. They come from shame, and can bring only shame upon themselves and those they associate with."

Gareth swallowed. "Do tell."

Mrs. Davenport looked off into the distance. "But she was a tricky little thing. She'd get the other girls talking to her, friendly like, every time she had half the chance. If I hadn't watched, she'd have wrapped them all 'round her finger. She had them fascinated, she did. I told them over and over, stay away from that Jenny Keeble. They listened, mostly. But…"

But Jenny had done her best to win them over anyway.

"She was four when she came here," Gareth observed mildly.

"You can't fight nature, my Lord Blakely. What's bred in the bone will bear fruit in the character. What do you suppose happens to a girl who never knows her parents?"

A girl who was lied to from the age of four and told she was formed for ill-behavior from birth? Gareth could only imagine. And yet…it hadn't happened to Jenny.

"I suppose," Gareth said quietly, "you did your duty by the girl and informed her what to expect from life."

"Oh, yes," Mrs. Davenport said with relish, leaving little doubt about precisely how she'd performed that responsibility. "And—just in case—" She crossed over to a desk, shuffled around in a drawer. And then she pulled out a yellowing sheaf, the edges of the papers crackling. "There. I recorded all her misdeeds. I saved these, in the event I was ever asked to testify as to her character, and the magistrate was inclined to foolish lenience."

Gareth held out a hand. "She was damnably silent about her childhood."

Mrs. Davenport's eyes narrowed, but she handed over the papers. "Language, Lord Blakely. Watch your language. Tell me, did she become a…"

"A whore?"

Mrs. Davenport sniffed. "Language! A soiled dove."

"She's spent the last twelve years pretending to be a mystic with the power to foretell the future."

Mrs. Davenport raised a hand to her mouth, the proper picture of horror. "Not exactly a life of virtue. How do you know her?"

"My cousin went to see her. I believe that over the course of their acquaintance, he paid her a good bit of money."

The woman's face grew gleefully gluttonous. She clutched at her handkerchief. "Fraud! A felony, to be sure. Will she hang? Be pilloried? Transported?"

Gareth glanced down at the paper in his hand.

14 August 1815. JK told two lies and shirked washing behind her ears.

He flipped through more pages, all filled with minor infractions. Some did not even count as that.

12 May 1820. JK, sick with fever, infected three other girls. Likely intentional.

Gareth had suffered his grandfather's cold and cutting comments. But underneath his grandfather's chill, there had always been high expectations. He'd always assumed that Gareth would, and could, perform his duties as capably and honorably as every Blakely before him. Money and rank had bought him every privilege.

But Jenny had grown up in this cold place. Instead of a mother, she'd had this frightening woman who whispered lies about her, ostracizing her from the only companions who could bring her comfort. How desperate for affection must she have been, when she ran away at eighteen?

And how devastated when she discovered that first lover, like the rest of the world, valued her at nothing? No wonder she'd turned to fraud.

"Lord Blakely?" Mrs. Davenport intruded on his reverie. "Will there be a prosecution?"

"Silence," he snapped. "I'm thinking." Gareth stood up and paced in front of the fire.

There was more to it than mere devastation. For all the coldness of her upbringing, it had been Jenny who'd seen the best in those around her. It had been Jenny who'd seen Ned's clever loyalty, Laura's quiet strength. She'd even seen something good in *Gareth,* for God's sake.

With no reason to hope ever given her, she'd hoped. And if she'd been unwilling to take that last step—if she'd been unwilling to need him, to love him, when he'd thought to relegate her to the cobwebbed corners of his life—how could he blame her? Nobody had ever valued her as she deserved. Least of all Gareth.

Gareth was a scientist. When the evidence came together, sometimes, it showed truth so clearly that no rationalization could deny it. Now, in this lifeless room, with a horrid harridan watching him think, bloodthirst shining in her oh-so-proper eyes, Gareth realized the truth.

Jenny wasn't his equal. She was his better.

And he was the world's most gigantic ass. An ass, and an idiot. Because Jenny had seen the best in herself, too, and he'd denigrated that, because he'd not wanted to admit that anyone could be his superior. Least of all the woman he needed.

Everything receded from him, like a tide traveling out to sea. He'd held on to his superiority as justification for every solitary year of his life. But what if he wasn't superior? The thought had once felt threatening. But now… If other people were better than him, he was not nearly so constrained by Lord Blakely as he'd thought. He was free. He could have everything he'd once wanted and shoved aside. Lord Blakely shrank in importance until he became a tool and a title, not an impenetrable barrier.

If any of this was going to work, it had to start with one person. Jenny. His Jenny.

Gareth's limbs stung, as if his blood had suddenly returned to circulation. He stopped pacing and fixed Mrs. Davenport in his sights.

She rubbed her hands greedily. "Will she hang? Have you decided what to *do?*"

"Yes, I know what to do." Gareth hefted the records in his hand. "I'm going to make sure you never speak of her again."

He crossed to the fire and tossed the papers on before she could protest. The dry paper ignited. Mrs. Davenport's faint cry made Gareth smile in satisfaction.

Jenny didn't need his money. But if there was one thing Gareth was good at, it was wresting respect from others. He could give Jenny that protection. He'd be damned if he ever let anyone denigrate his Jenny again.

"Listen to me." His voice dropped a register. "Whatever you think of Jenny Keeble, you will keep to yourself. If I hear you have breathed one word of the woman, I will destroy you. I will ruin this school and destroy the bank that holds your pension and bribe a magistrate to send you to Australia in a prison hulk. In the *men's* prison hulk. Do not doubt I can do it."

She shrunk away from him. "I thought you were going to give that Jenny Keeble what she deserves!"

Gareth thought this over. "As it happens, I will."

But first he had to get back to London. Now.

IT TOOK GARETH a frustrating forty-six hours to travel from Bristol to London. Despite his dust, he didn't stop by his home to change. Instead, he ordered his driver to go directly to Jenny's house. A thousand tremulous wings flapped in his chest as he jumped from the carriage. He banged on her door with his fist.

No answer.

"Jenny," he called. "Jenny, are you there? Jenny!"

No answer.

Perhaps she had gone shopping. Perhaps—he looked at the door more carefully—damn it. She hadn't removed the knocker from her door because she was out buying gloves. As if to underscore this point, the door above his head opened.

"You looking for Madame Esmerelda?"

Gareth whirled around and craned his neck upward. A woman stood behind another door. "Where is she?"

"She left. Took all her things, she did. Flat's empty—and I should know, 'cause I wanted to pick through what she'd left behind, and there were none of it."

"Well, where did she go?"

The woman shrugged. "She's a Gypsy, ain't she? Who knows where she went?"

A cold hand caressed Gareth's heart. "But she left a message for me, didn't she?"

The woman shrugged apathetically. "I can't say as she did. If you're wanting your fortune told, I imagine I could make shift. She told me how it were done the once."

A second roaring sounded in his ears. He'd realized Jenny was too good for him. He hadn't expected her to discover it, too. Foolishly, he'd hoped she would remain so deluded as to welcome his suit. But why should she sit at home? Jenny didn't mope. She *acted.*

What an idiot he was. She was the irreplaceable one. She could have any man she wanted. She wouldn't even have to lie to get a quarter of them.

"Did she leave a message for *anyone?*"

The woman peered down at him craftily. "Well, I suppose I could ask the spirits—"

"The spirits can go hang," Gareth muttered, and turned savagely on his heel.

CHAPTER TWENTY-ONE

GARETH HAD COME to his wits' end by the time he thought
to ask his cousin for Jenny's whereabouts. He burst into
the Carhart breakfast room at ten in the morning after a
sleepless night.

For once, Ned was properly dressed and shaved, sitting before a well-stocked china plate. Gareth was the one
out of place. He'd abandoned his cravat long before, and
his hair was disheveled and dusty. Nothing so trivial as
attire mattered; he had to find Jenny.

"Ned," Gareth said. "Have you any idea where Jenny
has gone?"

Ned carefully set down his fork. "Gareth. I see you've
returned to town for my wedding. Thank you for your
fine felicitations. Your manners, as always, are impec-
cable."

"Hang your wedding," Gareth said. "Hang Ware and
his daughter and your mother. And hang you, for not answering my question."

Ned shook his head. "You're not talking sense,
Gareth."

"And since when do you call me by my Christian name?
I've never given you leave. You've never done it before."

Ned opened his right hand and looked at it. Then he
smiled and clenched the hand into a fist.

"That," Ned said, "is a present from Jenny. She told me I could. In fact, she ordered me to do so. She said somebody had to keep you in line. I've been trying to work on my resolve, so I figured that someone had better be me."

Gareth scowled and scuffed his foot against the floor. Of course Jenny would do that. She'd thought of Gareth, of how he hated his title. He'd let her go; but she hadn't abandoned him.

Ned pushed his chair back and strode closer. "That, as I said, was a present from Jenny. This is a present from me."

He slammed his fist into Gareth's face. Stars burst across Gareth's vision, and he went flying. He crashed on the floor and skidded ignominiously into a wall. For a stunned moment, he lay there, too shocked to even catalog his hurts. But then his jaw started throbbing and a sharp network of needles lanced through his back where he'd struck the floor.

He opened his eyes to see Ned standing over him.

"What in blazes was that for?"

"You think just because you're a marquess you can take advantage of any woman you choose?"

"I didn't—"

"And leave her destitute? Alone?"

"I offered—"

Ned shook his head. "You offered her no real choice but to flee to another country."

The pain in Gareth's jaw was nothing to the impact of those words, slamming into his chest like a hatchet. He couldn't speak. He couldn't breathe. He doubled over on the ground. When he could finally catch his words, he pleaded. "Where? When? And *how do I get her back?*"

"You don't, you ass."

"I *know* I'm an ass. I'm an idiot. But I'll do anything to get her back."

Ned tapped his fingers against the leg of his trousers. "What are your intentions?"

"Exceedingly dishonorable," Gareth confessed. "If I have to trick her into marrying me, I will."

Ned's fingers stilled, his mouth falling open. "Marriage. You? Where's the advantage in that for her?" He looked off to the side, his lips moving.

Perhaps he was totting up the many times that Gareth had failed him. Gareth feared that balance sheet. "Don't you see," he broke in, "if you do the accounting, I'll never come out even. I can't do this—I can't make up for *anything* without her. Not with you. Not with Laura. I know you're counting all the ways you can pay me back—"

Ned looked at Gareth in mild surprise. "Actually," he said, "I was counting the hours until her ship sails. And trying to think of a reason I should let you have a single one. I'd like her last memories of England to be pleasant. Why should I let you ruin them?"

"Because I have to try again. I have to make it right—"

"Wrong answer." Ned turned away. "'Because I want to make her happy' might have worked."

"That, too."

"If you really cared for her," Ned scoffed, "you'd have dealt with that louse at her bank instead of gallivanting off who knows where."

And those words didn't make any sense at all. Maybe Gareth was entirely befuddled because he could sense Jenny slipping through his fingers. Still, he tried. "Louse? Bank? What are you talking about?"

Ned eyed him carefully. "I'll tell you," he finally said,

"but don't think it will change a thing. I'm still not letting you make her unhappy. Not again."

THE BANK NED POINTED HIM TO was smaller than the institutions Gareth typically did business with. It was also shabbier. The rosewood furniture was nicked and in dire need of a good polish. The green draperies were sun-faded, and Gareth was willing to wager that if he beat them, they would exhale huge clouds of dust.

As he and Ned entered, the clerks and managers snapped to attention. It was not just the sleek air of wealth Ned radiated. They were accompanied by the wily white-haired solicitor who helped manage the many Carhart interests. Even if the men occupying this place of business didn't recognize the Marquess of Blakely on sight, they recognized his solicitor, Martin Scorvil. The elderly gentleman was considered something of a genius in the administration of trusts and, as such, his clients typically held tremendous wealth.

Gareth found the response amusing. The bank manager hurried over to Ned almost on the instant, and shook his hand excessively. He was babbling almost incoherently. The rotund man bowed and bowed until he was out of breath. And as soon as he realized he had a marquess in the room—a marquess he'd ignored, because Gareth had not yet changed out of his traveling clothes or donned a cravat—he whipped out a handkerchief and wiped his forehead. But Gareth was not here to open an account for himself. He made the appropriate noises, and soon Ned and the solicitor had engaged in conversation over one of the trusts Ned planned to set up for his wife.

Gareth wandered about the room, exchanging a few

words with one of the cashiers. Seeking information. The clerk pointed back across the room at another man, huddled in conversation with Ned. The fellow was busily taking notes next to the bank manager. He had a sharp nose, like a weasel, dressing a too-handsome patrician profile. Gareth's lip curled. He had not come here to serve as mere window-dressing, a noble ornament designed to lend the financial proceedings appropriate *gravitas*. He had other responsibilities.

And, at this moment, the responsibility that weighed most heavily on his soul was the need to make things right with Jenny. He vibrated with frustration, knowing she was leaving. Gareth was more than willing to wreak his vengeance on any useful object.

Jenny and vengeance. Two words that were rarely coupled. And yet that was why he'd come here.

Ned caught Gareth's eye, and jerked his head in prearranged signal. Gareth walked back. The bank manager was handing Ned a pen, so that he could sign the first of many sheaves in an agreement.

Gareth covered the page with his hand. "I believe there is one condition we must discuss first."

"Yes, my lord. Of course, my lord." The manager wrung his hands attentively.

The cashier, next to him, echoed these officious sentiments with an unctuous wriggle.

Gareth pointed a finger at the man. "Is this individual Mr. Sevin?"

Mr. Sevin started and dropped his pen. Ink spattered over his shoes. "My lord? Have we been introduced?" He bent awkwardly and fumbled for the utensil. "I am most apologetic. *Most* apologetic. I do not recall—that is to say, perhaps I am remembering now. If perhaps your lordship would be so kind as to—was it at some sort of gathering? In June of last year? I did once attend—"

Gareth stemmed this unwelcome deluge with a raised hand. "It was a yes or no question, Mr. Sevin. Not an invitation to gabble away at me like a flock of outraged geese."

Mr. Sevin swallowed. "My lord?"

"Answer the question. Are you Mr. Sevin?"

"Yes, my lord."

"Excellent." Gareth turned to the bank manager. "Give him the sack. He's going to New South Wales on the next available ship."

"What?" Mr. Sevin squawked, his cheeks turning white. "Me? Why? My lord, please! I have a wife and a child. I cannot take them with me to that savage land."

"No," Gareth agreed. "you'll have to travel on your own. In your absence, you'll have to establish a trust for their support."

"A trust? I am a mere bank clerk. Trusts—such things are for the wealthy. I—"

"Ah," Gareth said. "But you are not a mere bank clerk. You have recently come into some four hundred pounds."

Mr. Sevin slowly straightened from his grovel, comprehension dawning across his face.

Gareth continued. "I will see you sent to New South Wales, one way or the other. You can leave your wife and child in comfort and travel in a cozy berth, or you can be dragged away in shackles for larceny. I leave the choice to you."

Ned met Gareth's eyes over Mr. Sevin's cringing, and grinned in vicious pleasure. Sharing this moment of victory with his cousin… He'd never imagined such a thing.

Jenny had been right. It was lonely being superior to everyone.

Gareth glanced at Mr. Sevin, who quivered in frustrated fury. And he amended the thought. It was lonely being superior to everyone, but there was real joy in being superior to *some* people.

And yet the moment was far from perfect. He turned to Ned, and suddenly he felt like begging. He swallowed dryness. "Any chance you'll relent?"

Ned's pleasure evaporated, and he shook his head slowly. "I have to do what's best for her. And I am sorry, but it is not you."

"Ned, where are we going?" Jenny asked for the third time.

It was her last day in England. London had been left behind nearly half an hour ago. The horses clopped lazily down a dirt road, spumes of dust trailing merrily in their wake. Light clouds obscured the direct sunlight, but let a hazy, insubstantial warmth shine all around.

"D'you remember my friend Ellison? The one from the hell who wanted to put his lions up as stake?"

Jenny shook her head.

"Well, he still has them. I figured it was time for a picnic by the menagerie."

"And you brought me? Why not take the woman you're marrying?"

Ned shrugged. "She's grown up with the Duke of Ware. Lions seem less ferocious. Today, it's just the two of us. As it should be."

He jiggled the reins and the horses turned off the main road. They trotted down a narrow path, no more than heavy wheel-ruts carved through the grass.

After a while, Jenny spoke again. "Don't the lions get miserable in the English clime?"

"I suppose. They're caged, too. Would they nab Ellison for poaching if we opened up the cage and they went after the King's deer?"

Jenny looked skeptically around the flattish meadow. "Deer? I think they'd pull down the horses. Or you."

Ned shook his head happily and pulled on the reins. The horses halted. They'd stopped outside a small cottage. In the distance, two large barns loomed. Jenny supposed a barn was as good a place as any to keep a lion's cage. But at the thought of those great beasts, the hairs on the back of her neck twitched. At any moment, she could be bowled over by some large, stalking cat.

"Here," Ned said, handing her a basket. "Go set up behind the cottage while I see to the horses."

"By myself?"

"Yes, by yourself."

"Near the lions?"

Ned grinned as he unhitched the horses. "Near the caged lions, yes. You're not afraid, are you? You'd better rethink your travel plans. I hear that lions roam the wilds of Cincinnati with surprising regularity."

Jenny took the basket and walked. She'd miss Ned. She was going to miss England—dreary, clouded England. It was all she'd ever known.

And she already missed Gareth.

But, she mused, what she missed in him wasn't just his presence. It was his potential. Those rare moments when he smiled. When he stopped using Lord Blakely as a tool to smite the mere mortals who incurred his wrath. If he'd been a farmer in Cincinnati or a tradesman in Brazil…

Jenny shook her head free of all foolish thoughts and set the basket down behind the small cottage.

A thick blanket covered the provisions in the basket. She was laying it on the ground when she heard the sound behind her. Quiet and careful; prowling. Her shoulder blades itched, as if it really were a lion she heard behind her, instead of a man's steps.

She turned, slowly, and swallowed.

She'd prefer the lion. She'd rather sharp claws rip into her than feel this pain slam inside her once again. Just looking at Gareth, she remembered what he'd said. *Who would think you my equal?* Those hurtful words were still embedded in her, like bits of shrapnel no surgeon could remove.

Well, he didn't look so superior now. What he looked was miserable.

And ridiculously handsome, his sandy brown hair tousled, his cravat askew. A blue bruise decorated his jaw. And there were his eyes—that startling golden brown. He could well have been a large predator, so intent was his gaze on her. She could have been his prey, so much did she want to give in to him.

"Ned," Jenny said. "Ned is responsible for this. I will shake him."

He winced. "I convinced Ned to give me one last chance. I know you won't give me one—you have every reason to despise me. But—listen—just—" He broke off and fumbled in his pockets. He pulled out a sheet of crinkled paper and handed it to her. "There."

Jenny smoothed out the crumpled wad. "What is this?"

"Title," he said, "to what's inside the barn."

"I already told you, you can't buy me."

His eyes raised to hers. "I know," he said softly. "There isn't enough money in all the world. But I'm begging you to let me—let me—" He scowled and scuffed his feet.

Jenny's stomach turned over very slowly. Her toes curled inside her slippers.

"Just go inside," he whispered.

She crossed the cropped grass and pulled open the heavy door. It creaked and sent a cloud of dust, woody with a hint of mold, whooshing around her. When she stepped inside, the temperature of the air dropped ten degrees. The familiar odor of clean hay met her. But there was a smell unlike anything she'd ever experienced. A whiff of acidity touched her nose, followed by a sweet, warm scent. Lions?

No.

There were no heavy iron cages. But nor was the barn divided into efficient cow-size rectangles. Instead, all the barn was open; one giant hayrick lay in the middle. And there, next to that golden pile, placidly munching hay, it stood.

Large and gray. Floppy ears wiggled in languid pleasure, as its trunk leisurely brought another bite of hay into its ivory-tusked mouth. It rolled its eyes when Jenny entered, but made no further movements.

Jenny was shocked into silence. Gareth came up behind her. Her heart was racing, a faint pitter-patter.

"What," Jenny asked steadily, "am I going to do with an *elephant?*"

"I don't know," said Gareth. "What are you planning to do with all my points?"

Points? It took Jenny a moment to remember what he was talking about. Points, when he smiled. She turned around slowly and put her hands on her hips.

"*Your* points? Those are *my* points. *I* earned them. You can't have them."

Gareth scowled and shoved his hands into his pockets. "Bollocks. I had to smile very hard for every single one of them. And if you don't take this elephant and marry me, I swear to God you'll never get another point again."

Jenny's world froze. Outside, she could hear the clear voice of a blackbird singing. It was overwhelmed by the ringing in her ears. She turned to Gareth slowly.

"What did you say?"

"I said, you'll never earn another point again. I haven't smiled since you left me, and I miss it." He kicked at the ground, his eyes tracing the dust. "I miss *you*."

"No, before that."

"Take this elephant—"

"After."

He looked up. That feral light shone in his eyes again, but this time the wild look was a plea. A lion yearning to be freed from its cage. "Take me." His voice was thick and husky. "Please. Jenny. I'm begging you."

She didn't know what to say in answer. He'd shocked the words right out of her skin. She could only stare, as some frozen expanse inside her tingled to life. It hurt to want.

"I can't take this elephant," she said, focusing on the one part of what he'd said that she could understand. "Do you know how miserable this poor beast will be in winter? This is cruel."

"She's African," Gareth said disjointedly. "From the bush. I was thinking maybe she could go back."

"Back? Back where? Back how?"

"Back to Southern Africa. Perhaps this winter. The trip might take six months." His voice took on a wistful quality. "I've always wanted to go. It's supposed to be a lovely place. Especially for someone with theories on bird migration…" He shook his head and cleared his throat. "But."

"But surely Lord Blakely could not abandon his estates for so long."

"No. Lord Blakely could not. Not unless he had someone he could trust to run his estates in his absence. And Lord Blakely… Well, Lord Blakely did not trust anyone."

"Lord Blakely is talking about himself in the third person, past tense," Jenny said. "It's disturbing."

"Then let me switch to the first person plural. What Lord Blakely could not do, *we* can. I would not trust anyone else to manage my estates, not for the shortest space of time, because I thought I was better than everyone else. I was wrong. You see, Jenny, I need *you.* I need someone who will see the strength buried deep in the hearts of men. Someone who can tap into that strength. I need someone who can look at a man and move him to become more. I can't do it alone."

Jenny looked at the elephant. No thinking man would ever have purchased an elephant as a wedding gift. And yet there it stood. It flicked an ear at the two of them— likely elephant language for, *go on, this dramatic performance is quite interesting.*

There was only one possible conclusion. Gareth had stopped thinking. For the first time in a week, Jenny allowed herself to hope. Really hope. She reached out and brushed his cheek. It was stubbly beneath her fingers. God knows when last he'd shaved. Probably before he'd obtained that bruise.

"Gareth."

"I haven't arrived at second person yet," he said

quietly. "You. You. Always you. I love you, Jenny. When you left me, all the warmth went out of my world. When I said those horrible things, I didn't realize then how much I needed you—how superior you were to me."

Jenny's heart gave a little flip.

"This entire country suffocated me, cold and dreary and monochromatic. Then I met you. And you spread color everywhere I looked—in every aspect of my life. You put texture in a flat world. Before I knew you, I despaired of ever seeing Brazil again. I can't think of a single reason why you should stay with me, but you're a great deal cleverer than I, and I'm hoping you can imagine something."

Gareth set his gloved hands on her shoulders. His golden-warm eyes were covered with a sheen that looked suspiciously like moisture. Inches from his face, she could see reddish veins throughout his cornea. The haphazard stubble on his cheeks stood out, darker brown than his hair.

"Gareth," Jenny asked, "when was the last time you slept?"

"I don't know. Does it matter?"

"And you call yourself a rational man."

He didn't argue. Instead, his fingers on her shoulders tightened their grasp just the smallest fraction.

"I can give you one thing," he said huskily. "One thing besides myself, that is. Nobody will ever look down on you again. Not with my title, nor with my protection. My grandfather taught me to fend off those sorts of attacks. Let me put them in your service now. Let me stand beside you."

It was in that moment that Jenny realized he would not abandon her. Not ever.

"Gareth," Jenny said imperiously, "give me your hand."

He froze, his head half-turned away. "What?"

She didn't bother to repeat the question. Instead, she took his wrist and stripped off the riding glove. His breath hissed in when her thumb traced the lines of his palm.

"You're a stubborn man," she said. "A rational man. You're excessively proud, damnably responsible and all too awkward."

He hunched miserably under her analysis. "I can change."

Jenny peered into his palm. "No." She dismissed this with a sad shake of her head. "You won't. Change is not what I'm seeing in the future."

"I can try."

"You won't change," Jenny said briskly, "because I love you the way you are."

Shock filtered through his features, but Jenny wasn't finished.

"Do you know what I see when I look at you, Gareth?"

He shook his head.

"I see a strong man. Honest, and good. Perhaps a little inflexible—but smart enough to know his limitations. Clever enough to pick a woman who will push him to be better. I see a man who makes mistakes, but is willing to admit them and work to better them. I see a man who was willing to put aside his own pride for his cousin's sake. And for mine, just now."

"What else do you see?"

She pulled his hand to her and set it on her waist. He leaned in, his fingers closing about her. Tugging her next to his heart.

"I see that I'll say yes."

"Yes?"

"Yes, I'll take you. If you'll take me."

When his lips met hers, she could taste the smile on his face. He pulled her against him. And when, after a long, leisurely time, he raised his head, he laughed. For one eternal instant, Jenny had no label for the swelling rightness that filled her chest, no words to describe how she felt. But then the thought came.

Ah. So this is what home feels like.

EPILOGUE

IF THERE WAS ONE CONSTANT in the highest echelons of London society, it was the Marquess of Blakely. For nearly two centuries, Blakelys had been a constant edifice. They stood as bulwarks against change; the old guard, reminding younger rabble of the obligation of nobility. Nine generations of cold, chilly men had been counted on to depress the pretensions of those who overreached their stations.

And so, when the ninth marquess purchased an elephant on one day and announced he was married on the next, gossip flurried. Because he had not married the expected peer's daughter. Nor had he married an heiress, which would have been titillating enough. So who *had* he married?

Nobody could quite figure out.

Oh, they knew what she looked like. She was a friendly woman with striking dark hair and a pleasant figure and an extremely bright smile. And they knew her married name—Jennifer Carhart, Marchioness of Blakely—but they knew nothing of her family or her fortune. It was a puzzle, because everyone knew that a Blakely simply could not have married anyone unsuitable.

Stories flew.

At first, some insisted that Blakely's bride was the woman who'd been called Mrs. Margaret Barnard. But that woman had been in society so little, and those who had been closest to the woman—Blakely himself, as well as his cousin, his cousin's wife, and his sister—insisted it was not so. And besides, Mrs. Barnard had been a distant connection of the Carharts, so distant that polite society hadn't even bothered to remember her. Blakely would never have stooped to marry her. And that put paid to that guess.

The new Marchioness of Blakely busied herself in the planning of the much larger wedding of Blakely's sister. High society, not wishing to be left out of the hubbub entirely, busied itself spinning theories.

Someone suggested she was a foreign princess from a tiny country south of the equator.

Someone else insisted she had the look of Gallic nobility, and was thus the last remaining scion of some family that had fled the Terror.

Yet another person claimed that the marchioness had once been a fortune-teller, capable of calling spirits from the ether and lightning from the skies.

By the day of his sister's wedding, society had divided into bitter camps on the question. When the marquess and his marchioness disembarked from their carriage, outside the church where Miss Edmonton was to marry, they were the object of intense scrutiny. His lordship was impeccably turned out in burgundy velvet. Her ladyship wore a diamond pendant and a dress of blue water-shot silk. They looked at one another a great deal, and touched an unfashionable amount.

After the ceremony, the Countess of Lockhaven pushed through the crowd of the wedding breakfast. She caught Lord Blakely's arm just as the man found his sister.

"Lord Blakely," she simpered. "And Lady Blakely."

Blakely looked down at the hand on his sleeve. His gaze traveled up her arm. That cold expression—for which Blakelys had so long been known—froze Lady Lockhaven.

"Well?"

Lady Lockhaven dropped her hand. "We were wondering if—well, if you could say something about..." In the hush that fell, everyone could hear her gulp. "About your lady's birth? And her people?"

If Lord Blakely's face had been cold before, it turned frigid now. He looked the countess disdainfully up and down. Everyone in the crowd suddenly remembered her mother had been a soap manufacturer's daughter, married for her thousands of pounds. They remembered her husband's first marriage had been to a country girl he eloped with, who'd had the good grace to die before she embarrassed the family by providing an heir.

"My wife's birth?" He drawled the words insolently, and the crowd shivered as one. "A damned sight better than your own."

That was the last time anyone asked the marquess about his wife's origins.

Not solely because society feared his response. Rather, his conduct directly thereafter settled the debate for once and all.

After Blakely delivered that infamous and much-repeated set down, he transferred his gaze to the new Marchioness of Blakely.

She shook her head, once. Firmly. "Gareth," she said dryly. "It is your sister's wedding day. Behave."

Silence. He'd lifted his chin, in typical Blakely arrogance. The crowd waited for the blast.

And then Lord Blakely shrugged and grinned helplessly.

Grinned. Helpless. A *Blakely.*

"Oh," said his sister, from where she stood near him. "Is *that* how it's done? I'll have to practice that."

Like that, everything society knew about nine generations of Blakelys went up in smoke.

Since that day, there had been no question. Lady Blakely had been granted otherworldly powers at birth. Every smile she coaxed from him, every laugh that she surprised from his lips, stood as testament to her arcane abilities.

And those that questioned her worth still had only to see the look in his eyes when he watched her to find all the proof they required.

* * * * *

Don't miss Ned's story,
TRIAL BY DESIRE,
coming later this year
from Courtney Milan